THE KITCHEN HOUSE

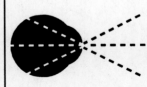

This Large Print Book carries the Seal of Approval of N.A.V.H.

THE KITCHEN HOUSE

KATHLEEN GRISSOM

KENNEBEC LARGE PRINT
A part of Gale, Cengage Learning

GALE
CENGAGE Learning·

Detroit • New York • San Francisco • New Haven, Conn • Waterville, Maine • London

GALE
CENGAGE Learning®

LIBRARY OF CONGRESS CATALOGING-IN-PUBLICATION DATA

Grissom, Kathleen.
  The kitchen house / by Kathleen Grissom.
    p. cm. — (Kennebec Large Print superior collection)
  ISBN-13: 978-1-4104-4462-2 (softcover)
  ISBN-10: 1-4104-4462-7 (softcover)
  1. Indentured servants—Fiction. 2. Slaves—Fiction. 3. Plantation
life—Southern States—Fiction. 4. Large type books. I. Title.
PS3607.R57K57 2012
813'.6—dc23   2011043981

Published in 2012 by arrangement with Simon & Schuster, Inc.

For my beloved parents,
Ted and Catherine Doepker,
and for my dear mentor,
Eleanor Drewry Dolan

PROLOGUE

1810
Lavinia

There was a strong smell of smoke, and new fear fueled me. Now on the familiar path, I raced ahead, unmindful of my daughter behind me, trying to keep up. My legs were numb, unused to this speed, and my lungs felt as though they were scorched. I forbade myself to think I was too late and focused all my strength on moving toward home.

Foolishly, I misjudged, and meaning to take a shortcut to the stream, I swerved from the path to dash through the trees. To my horror, I found myself trapped.

I pulled to free my long blue skirts from the blackberry brambles that ensnared me. As I ripped my way out, Elly caught up to me. She attached herself to my arm, sobbing and trying to hold me back. Though a seven-year-old is no match for a grown woman, she fought fiercely, with strength fostered by her own terror. In my frenzy, I pushed her to the ground. She stared at me with disbelieving eyes.

"Stay here," I begged, and raced back down the path until I reached the stream. I meant to cross over by stepping on the rocks in the shallow water, but I didn't remove my shoes, which was a mistake. Halfway over, I slipped on the river stones, and with a splash, I fell. The cold water shocked me, and for a moment I sat stunned, water bubbling by, until I looked up and recognized our smokehouse on the other side of the stream. The gray building reminded me that I was close to home. I rose, my skirts soaked and heavy, and scrambled my way across the water by clinging to the jutting rocks.

At the base of the hill, I leaned forward to breathe, gasping for air. Somehow Elly had reached my side again, and this time she clung like a kitten to my wet skirts. I was terrified of what she might see, but it was too late now, so I grasped her hand, and together we crested the bluff. There, I froze. Elly saw it, too, and whimpered; her hand slipped from mine as she sat on the ground. I moved forward slowly, as though in a dream.

Our massive oak tree stood at the top of the hill, its lush green leaves shading the thick branch that bore the weight of the hanging body. I refused to look up again after I caught sight of the green headscarf and the handmade shoes that pointed down.

CHAPTER ONE

1791
Lavinia

In that spring of 1791, I did not understand that the trauma of loss had taken my memory. I knew only that after I woke, wedged between crates and bags, I was terror-stricken to discover that I did not know where I was, nor could I recall my name. I was frail after months of rough travel, and when the man lifted me from the wagon, I clung to his broad shoulders. He was having none of that and easily pulled my arms loose to set me down. I began to cry and reached back up for him, but he pushed me instead toward the old Negro male who was hurrying toward us.

"Jacob, take her," the man said. "Give her to Belle. She's hers for the kitchen."

"Yes, Cap'n." The old man kept his eyes low.

"James! James, you're home!"

A woman's call! Hopeful, I stared up at the enormous house in front of me. It was made of clapboard and painted white, and a wide porch framed the full length of the front. Towering columns circled with vines of green and violet wisteria stood on either side of the broad front steps, and the air was thick with the fragrance this early April morning.

"James, why didn't you send word?" the woman sang out into the morning mist.

Hands on his hips, the man leaned back for a better view. "I warn you, wife. I've come home for you. Best come down before I come up."

Above, at a window that appeared open to the floor, she laughed, a figure of white froth capped by billowing auburn hair. "Oh no, James. You stay away until you've been washed."

"Mrs. Pyke. Prepare yourself," he shouted, and bounded over the threshold. Inside, he continued to shatter the peace. "Where is everyone?" I heard him call. "I'm home!"

At a run, I began to follow, but the dark old man caught my arm and held me. When I fought him, he lifted me up, and I screamed in terror. Swiftly, he carried me to the back of the house. We were high on a hill, and out farther, lesser hills surrounded us. A horn blasted, frightening me further, and I began to hit at my captor. He shook me firmly. "You stop this now!" I stared at him, at his foreign dark brown skin that contrasted so with his white hair, and his dialect so strange that I scarcely understood. "What you fightin' me for?" he asked. I was exhausted by it all and dropped my head on the man's thin shoulder. He continued on to the kitchen house.

"Belle?" the old man called. "Belle?"

"Uncle Jacob? Come in," a feminine voice called, and the wooden door creaked as he pushed it open with his foot.

Uncle Jacob slid me to my feet while a young woman came slowly down the stairs, then came forward, quickly tying a band of green calico around a thick braid of glossy black hair. Her large green eyes grew wide in disbelief as she took me in. I was comforted to see that she was not as foreign-looking as the man who had brought me to her, for though her light brown skin still differed from mine, her facial features more resembled my own.

Uncle Jacob spoke. "The cap'n send this chil' to you. He say she for the kitchen house."

"What's that man thinking? Can't he see she's white?" The woman sank in front of me and turned me around. "You been sick?" She wrinkled her nose. "I've got to burn these clothes. You nothing but bones. You wanting something to eat?" She pried my thumb from my mouth and asked if I could speak. I could find no voice and looked around, trying to place myself.

Belle went to the enormous fireplace that stretched the length of the room. There she poured steaming milk into a wooden mug. When she held it to my mouth, I choked on the milk, and my body began an involuntary tremor. I vomited, then I passed out.

I awoke on a pallet in an upstairs room, too frightened to move after realizing that I still had no memory. My head ached, but when I rubbed it, I withdrew my hands in shock. My long hair had been cut short.

I had been scrubbed pink, and my skin was tender under the coarse brown shirt that covered me. My stomach turned from the scent of unfamiliar food rising up the open stairway from the kitchen below. My thumb pacified me, and I soothed myself as I studied the room. Clothes hung from pegs on the wall, and a pole bed stood off to one side with a small plain chest next to it. Sun streamed through a window, open and undraped, and from the outdoors came the sudden peal of a child's laughter. It rang familiar, and forgetting all else, I sprang to the window. The brightness stung so that I needed both hands to shade my eyes. First all I saw was rolling green, but below the window, I saw a path. It cut past a large fenced-in garden and led to a log house where, on steps, sat two small dark brown girls. They were watching a scene up toward the big house. I leaned out farther and saw a towering oak. From a thick low branch, a little girl on a swing sang out to a boy behind her.

When he pushed the swing, the little girl, all blue and blond, squealed. The tall boy laughed. There it was again! A laugh I recognized. Driven by hope, I ran down the wooden stairs, out the open door of the kitchen, and up the hill to them. The boy pulled the swing to a stop, and the two gaped at me. Both had deep blue eyes, and both exuded vibrant health.

"Who are you? Where did you come from?" the boy asked, his yellow hair glinting in the bright light.

I could only stare back, dumb in my disappointment. I did not know him.

"I'm Marshall," the boy tried again, "and this is my sister, Sally."

"I'm four," said Sally, "how old are you?"

15

She tapped the air with her blue shoes and peeked out at me from under the flopping brim of a white bonnet.

I couldn't find a voice to answer, so I felt a rush of gratitude for Marshall when he pulled the attention away from me by jiggling the swing. "How old am I?" he asked his sister.

"You're two," said Sally, trying to poke at him with her foot.

"No, I'm not." Marshall laughed. "I'm eleven."

"No, you're two," teased Sally, enjoying a familiar game.

Suddenly, I was swooped up in Belle's arms. "Come back in," she said sharply, "you stay with me."

Inside the kitchen house, Belle set me on a corner pallet opposite a dark brown woman who was suckling a baby. I stared, hungry at the intimacy. The mother looked at me and although her face was young, she had deep lines around her eyes.

"What your name?" she asked. When I didn't answer, she continued, "This be my baby, Henry," she said, "and I his mama, Dory."

The baby suddenly pulled back from her breast and gave a high shrill cry. I jammed my thumb into my mouth and shrank back.

■ ■ ■ ■

Not knowing what was expected of me, I stayed put on a pallet in the kitchen. In those first days, I studied Belle's every move. I had no appetite, and when she insisted that I eat, my stomach emptied violently. Each time I was sick, it meant another cleaning. As Belle's frustration with me grew, so did my fear of upsetting her. At night I slept on a pallet in a corner of Belle's upstairs room. On the second night, unable to sleep, I went to stand at Belle's bedside, comforted by the sound of her soft night breathing.

I must have frightened her, for when she woke, she shouted at me to get back to my own bed. I scurried back, more afraid than ever.

The dark haunted me, and with each passing night I sank further into loss. My head throbbed with the struggle of trying to remember something of myself. Thankfully, relief from my sorrow came just before sunup, when the roosters and the horn called everyone to rise. Then another woman, Mama Mae, joined Belle in the kitchen. The two women worked easily together, but I soon sensed that, though

Belle was in charge of the kitchen, Mama Mae was in charge of Belle. Mama Mae was a woman of size, although nothing about her was soft. She was a sober woman who moved like a current, and her quickness made it plain that she did not suffer idleness. She gripped a corncob pipe between her tobacco-stained teeth. It was seldom lit, though she chewed the stem, and after time I decided that it served the same purpose to her that my thumb did to me. I might have been more frightened of her had she not given me an early benediction of her smile. Then her dark brown face, her flat features, and her black eyes wrinkled into kindness.

In the days that followed, I no longer tried to eat, and slept most of the time. On the morning Mama Mae examined me, Belle watched from across the room. "She's just being stubborn. When I get her to eat, she just brings it up, so now I'm only giving her water. She'll get hungry soon enough," Belle said.

Mama held my face in her strong hand. "Belle!" she said sharply. "This chil' not fightin' you. She too sick. You got to get her to eat, or you gonna lose her."

"I don't know why the cap'n give her to me. I got enough work."

"Belle, you ever think maybe when I first

18

find out they movin' you to the kitchen house, I think that way 'bout you?"

"Well, I sure wasn't making a mess, throwing up all over you."

"No, but you was 'bout the same age, maybe six, seven years at the time. And you was born and raised here, and you still carried on," Mama Mae scolded.

Belle was silent, but following that, she was less brusque with me.

Later that day, Mama Mae killed a chicken. She made a broth for me, and for the first time my stomach tolerated something other than water. After some days of this healing liquid, I began to eat and then to retain solid food. When I became more alert again, Belle began to quiz me. Finally, summoning all of my courage, I managed to convey that I had no memory. Whether it was my foreign accent or Belle's surprise at my information, I do not know, but she stared at me, disbelieving. To my enormous relief, she didn't question me further. Then, just as things began to settle, Belle and I were called to the big house.

Belle was nervous. She fussed at me with a comb until, in frustration, she finally wrapped my head in a scarf to cover the chopped mess that was my hair. I was dressed in a fresh brown shirt that fell below my knees, over which Belle tied a white apron that she had stitched hastily from a kitchen cloth.

"Don't suck your thumb." Belle pulled my swollen finger from my mouth. She stooped down to my level and forced me to meet her eyes. "When she ask you anything, you say, 'yes, ma'am.' That's all you say: 'yes, ma'am.' Do you understand?"

I understood little of what was expected, but I nodded, eager to still Belle's anxiety.

I followed closely behind Belle on the brick path that led us up to the back porch. Uncle Jacob nodded solemnly while holding open the door. "Clean those feet," he said.

I stopped to brush fine dirt and sand from my bare feet, then felt the smoothness of the highly polished wood as I stepped across the threshold. Far ahead, the front door was open, and a light breeze swept down the long hallway, past me, and out the open back door. That first morning I did not note the mahogany high-boy standing sentry in the hall; nor did I see the tall blue and white tulipier, displayed proudly as the latest expense from across the sea. I remember very clearly, though, the terror I felt as I was led to the dining room.

"Well! Here they are!" the captain's voice

boomed.

At the sight of me, little Sally squealed, "Look, Marshall! It's that girl from the kitchen. Can I play with her, Mama?"

"You stay away from her," the woman said, "she looks sick. James! Whatever . . ."

"Steady, Martha. I had no choice. The parents died, and they owed me passage. Either she came with me, or I had to indenture her out. She was sick. I would have got nothing for her."

"Was she alone?"

"No, she had a brother, but he was easy enough to place."

"Why'd you put her in the kitchen house?" Marshall asked.

"What else could I do?" his father replied. "She has to be trained for some use."

"But why with her!" Marshall nodded toward Belle.

"That's enough, son," the captain said, waving me forward. "Come here, come here." Though now clean-shaven and dressed as a gentleman, I recognized him as the one who had lifted me from the wagon. He was not a tall man, but his overall size and his loud voice put forth a large presence. His gray hair was tied in the back, and his deep blue eyes peered at us over spectacles.

The captain looked past me. "How are you, Belle?" he asked.

"Fine, Cap'n," she replied softly.

"You look fine," he said, and his eyes smiled at her.

"Of course she's fine, James, why wouldn't she be fine? Look at her. Such a beautiful girl. She wants for nothing, head of a kitchen at her young age, and practically owning her own fine house. You have your pick of beaus, don't you, Belle?" The woman spoke quickly in a high voice, leaning her elbow on the table as she pulled repeatedly at an escaped strand of her red hair. "Don't you, Belle? Don't they come and go?" she asked insistently.

"Yes, ma'am." Belle's voice was strained.

"Come, come," the captain interrupted, and again waved me forward. Closer to him, I focused on the deep lines that creased his weathered face when he smiled. "Are you helping in the kitchen?" he asked.

"Yes, ma'am," I croaked, anxious to follow Belle's instruction.

The room exploded in laughter, though I saw that the boy, Marshall, did not laugh.

"She said 'yes, ma'am' to you, Daddy." Sally giggled.

The captain chuckled. "Do I look like a 'ma'am' to you?"

Uncertain of my answer, for I did not understand this unfamiliar form of address, I anxiously nodded. Again there was laughter.

Suddenly, the captain turned, and his voice boomed. "Fanny! Beattie! Slow down, you'll blow us out of the room."

It was then I noticed the two small dark-skinned girls and remembered them from the first day when they had been seated on the steps of the cabin. Through kitchen conversation, I had learned that they were Mama Mae's six-year-old twins. Now they stood on the other side of the table, each pulling a cord. The cords were attached to a large fan suspended from the ceiling that, when pulled, flapped over the dining room table like the wing of a gigantic butterfly, thereby creating a draft. With the excitement of the laughter, their enthusiasm was overventilating the room, but after the shout from the captain, their dark eyes grew solemn and their pulling slowed.

The captain turned back. "Belle," he said, "you've done well. You've kept her alive." He glanced down at some papers before him and spoke directly to me after skimming a page. "Let's see. You'll soon be seven years old. Is that right?"

I didn't know.

In the silence, Sally chirped up, "I'm four years old."

"That will do, Sally," Martha said. She sighed, and the captain winked at his wife. When he removed his spectacles to better study me, I felt faint under his scrutiny. "Don't you know your age? Your father was a schoolteacher, didn't he teach you numbers?"

My father? I thought. I have a father?

"When you feel stronger, I want you to work in the kitchen," he said. "Can you do that?"

My chest ached, and I was finding it difficult to breathe, but I nodded.

"Good," he said, "then we'll keep you here until you've grown." He paused. "Do you have any questions?"

My need to know surpassed my terror. I leaned closer to him. "My name?" I managed to whisper.

"What? What do you mean, your name?" he asked.

Belle spoke quickly. "She don't know her name."

The captain looked at Belle as though for an explanation. When none was forthcoming, he looked down again at the papers before him. He coughed before he answered. "It says here your name is Lavinia.

Lavinia McCarten."

I clung to the information as though it were a life raft. I don't remember leaving the room, but I surfaced on a pallet in the kitchen to overhear Uncle and Belle discussing the captain. He was leaving again in the morning, Belle said, and she was expecting a visit from him that evening.

"You gonna ask for those papers?" Uncle Jacob questioned.

Belle didn't answer.

"You tell him that you needs them now. Miss Martha got her eye on you. The cap'n know she take the black drops, but he don't know that she drink the peach liquor with it. You gettin' more pretty by the day, and after all that drinkin', when Miss Martha pick up that mirror, she see that she lookin' more than her thirty years. She out to get you, and time goes on, it only get worse."

Belle's usual determined voice was subdued. "But Uncle, I don't want to go. This place my home. You all my family."

"Belle, you know you got to go," he said.

Their conversation ended when Uncle Jacob saw my open eyes. "Well, well, well. Lil Abinya wake up," he said.

Belle came over to me. "Lavinia," she said, pushing my hair from my forehead, "that name sounds like you."

25

I stared at her, then turned my face away. I was more lost than ever, for I felt no connection to that name.

The next evening I was sent home with Mama Mae. I didn't want to leave the kitchen house, but Belle insisted. Mama said that her twins, Fanny and Beattie, the two girls I had seen working the fan, would be there with me. On the walk over, Mama Mae held my hand and pointed out how the kitchen house was just a short distance from her own small cabin.

Fanny and Beattie were there to greet us. I hung back, wanting to stay next to Mama Mae, but the girls were eager for a new playmate. They drew me into a corner of the small cabin to a shelf that had been carved into one of the logs, where their treasures were kept.

The taller of the two, Fanny was the leader, with her mother's quick eyes and direct speech; her arms and legs were like those of a colt. Beattie was short and plump, pretty already, with a broad smile emphasized by two deep dimples.

"Look," Fanny instructed me as she withdrew toys from the shelf. She handed down a doll-size table with two chairs, constructed of small twigs held together with bits of

26

animal sinew. Beattie showed me her doll, then offered it to me to hold. I grabbed for it with such hunger that Beattie hesitated until her generous spirit won out and she released it. "Mama make her," she said with pride, looking back to Mama Mae.

I gripped Beattie's prize, my heart pierced with longing. The doll was made of rough brown cloth; her eyes were stitched in black thread, while black wool stood out in braids. I fingered the doll's shirt, styled like the one the twins and I wore. She wore a red apron, and I recognized it as the same fabric as Mama Mae's head scarf.

As dark descended, Dory and baby Henry joined us. They had frequently visited the kitchen house, where I had learned that Dory was Mama Mae's eldest daughter. I liked Dory well enough, for she left me alone, but I wasn't fond of the baby with his harsh cry.

Although distracted by the girls and their play, I kept a close eye on Mama's reassuring presence. When the door suddenly opened, a huge dark bear of a man stood framed against the even blacker night sky. I flew to Mama's side. Fanny and Beattie scrambled to their feet and ran to the man, who scooped them up. "Papa!" they cried. After he released them, they went back to their play, and with Mama's encouragement, I joined them.

"Evenin', Dory." The man's voice was so deep, he might have been underground, and when he paused by baby Henry's mama, his large hand covered the top of her head. "How your lil one doin'?"

"Not so good, Papa," Dory answered, not looking up from the bench where she sat nursing her infant. The child fussed when she gently pulled his swollen hands out to show her father. "When his hands get big like this, he cry all the time," she said.

Her father leaned down and, with a knuckle, gently stroked the baby's cheek. When he straightened, he sighed and then took a few giant strides across the floor to Mama Mae. The girls giggled and hid their eyes when their father reached for Mama, pulling her to him and playfully nuzzling her neck. "George!" Mama laughed, then shooed him off. When he stepped back, he caught my eye and nodded at me. I quickly turned away.

Belle was expecting a visitor, Mama Mae said to the man, as though to explain my presence, and the pair exchanged a look before Mama Mae turned back to the fireplace. She scooped out stew from a black pot that hung over the open fire, and Papa set the filled wooden bowls on the narrow table. Then she brushed the coals from the top lid of another black iron pot that was nestled in hot ash, and from it she removed a steaming round corn cake, browned to crispness around the edges.

The three adults pulled up small stools to the table, and Fanny and Beattie had me stand between them as they began to eat. But everything felt strange, and I wanted the familiarity of the kitchen house. With no appetite, I studied the food, and when Mama instructed me to eat, I began to cry.

"Come here, Abinia," she said, and after I went to her, she hoisted me onto her lap. "Chil', you got to eat. You need some meat on them bones. Here, I dip this into the gravy for you, and you eat so you get strong as Mama."

The twins laughed. "You treatin' her just like a baby, Mama," Fanny said.

"Well," Mama said, "maybe she my new baby, and I got to feed her. Now you open your mouth, lil baby." I so wanted her mothering that I ate the corn bread she dipped into the thick ham gravy. She continued to feed me as she spoke of the captain leaving and how Miss Martha's nerves were running over again.

Dory said she had to go back up to the

big house tonight, no telling what Miss Martha would do when the captain left in the morning. Mama Mae said how she wished she could go stay with Miss Martha so Dory could stay with baby Henry.

Dory answered with a deep sigh, "You know it's me she be wantin'," and Mama agreed.

We had almost finished the meal when we heard muffled voices from the outside. Papa George began to rise, and my stomach clenched when Mama quickly set me aside. "No, George!" she said standing. "Me and Dory go. Won't do nobody no good to throw another man in this stewpot."

I heard footsteps coming at a run, and when the door flew open, Belle came in gasping for air. Her green head rag was missing, and her usual night braid was undone. Mama Mae pulled Belle inside before she and Dory rushed out. Belle leaned against the wall, panting, then straightened herself before walking over to the table, where she sat across from Papa.

Belle said, "She comes down after him this time. She never do that before. And Marshall, he comes with her. When she sees the new comb and the book he gives me, she takes them up and throws them at me. That starts Marshall pushing and hitting on me.

The cap'n grabs him and sends him out the door, but then Miss Martha starts crying and hitting on him. He says, 'Martha, Martha, get ahold of yourself,' but she's so worked up, he tells me to go get Mama." Belle put her elbows on the table and rested her head in her hands.

Papa shook his head. "Did you ask for the free papers?" he asked.

Belle spoke through her fingers. "He says I'll get them next summer."

The air clicked with Papa's anger, and when he stood, he pushed back the table with such force that two of the wooden bowls flew to the floor. "Next year! Next year! Always the next time! Something's gonna happen here if he don't get you those papers!"

When the door closed behind him, I was more surprised than anyone that my supper came up without warning. With it, though, I felt some relief, as my involuntary action seemed to refocus Belle and steady her while she cleaned me.

The twins watched from their pallet, the sleeping baby Henry beside them. After Belle finished with me, she set me with them, then straightened the room. When everything was in order, Belle came to us, eased the sleeping baby into her arms, and nodded for me to join her. We were all startled to hear a loud thunking sound from outside, but as it continued, Fanny identified the source. "Papa choppin' his wood again," she whispered.

When we left for Belle's house, white moonlight offered only shadow on the far side of the cabin where Papa worked.

"Papa?" Belle called softly. "Papa?"

The pounding stopped.

"Papa, don't worry. I'll get the papers," she said into the silence.

CHAPTER TWO

Belle

Mama says, "One more time the cap'n home just long enough to get the place upside down."

And she's right, like always. What's he doing, giving me this sick child? During the day she can't keep her food down, and at night she scares me, sitting there in the dark, looking off.

'Course, the cap'n is known for this, coming and going, telling nobody nothing. That's the way he always is, says Mama. She is right, 'cause I know what she knows. When I was little, when I was living up at the big house, I'd wait at the front door for his carriage, and sure enough he comes riding up the back way, sitting on a horse. Next time I wait for the horse, he comes pulling a loaded-up cart.

I'd never know when he was coming, and I'd never know how he'd come. For sure,

33

though, always, one way or another, he shows up.

Back then my white grandma, Mrs. Pyke, was running this place. The cap'n's daddy died early on. He fell off a horse, Grandma said. The cap'n was just a little boy, nine years old, and he was hit hard, so the next year Mrs. Pyke sent him to school, to London, hoping he'd be a lawyer, but when he came home at nineteen, all he wanted was to get back on the water.

"Why don't he stay?" I asked her every time he left, and she'd say he has his business with his ship, so he's doing his part to keep this place going. When he did come home, she'd always tell him everything is fine here. She didn't say anything about him staying to help with the place.

Mrs. Pyke raised me in the big house and taught me everything, just like a white girl. She even shows me how to read and write. She says there's no reason to act like I don't know better, just because I'm half Negro. We sit at the table, her and me, with Mama Mae bringing in the food. Mrs. Pyke shows me how to use a napkin and to sit up straight. She takes me out riding with her to see that the fields got worked. Then one day just like every other, I go to wake her. There she is, passed on without saying good-bye. I screamed and cried until I can't no more. For seven years that woman was like my whole world.

After she's gone, the cap'n, old already and never been married, decides to bring home a young wife, twenty years to his forty. They move me out of the big house because the cap'n don't want Miss Martha to know about me.

Down in the kitchen house, Mama Mae don't care that the cap'n is my daddy. She tells me it won't do me no good and maybe even makes it harder if I hold it up for anybody to see. "You learn to cook," she says, "that way they don't get rid of you." Time passes and I do like Mama says, but that don't mean I think the cap'n is doing right by me.

This time Dory and Mama say it's going to take a long time before Miss Martha settles down. But then she always takes it hard when the cap'n leaves. Of course, almost every time he comes home, she gets caught with a baby. Trouble is, those babies don't live too long. She's buried two already. Each time another one comes and goes, she takes more of those drops. Once the cap'n is gone, Miss Martha just stays up in that house, wandering around from room to room. Then, too, soon as his daddy goes, Marshall gets back to pestering me, throwing rocks when I'm working in the garden. He's a sly one. He only acts up when nobody sees him. I know he's thinking that I'm the problem with his mama. Sometimes I wonder what would happen if I'd sit him down and say, "Hey, boy, do you know you are throwing rocks at your big sister?" But I guess that's the cap'n's business.

Against everything that's right, I've got to cook for Miss Martha and my brother and sister up in the big house, and sometimes, especially when the cap'n's home, I get to thinking how wrong this is. Then watch out! Pots go flying all over the place.

I'm eighteen now and old enough to know what I want. This kitchen house is my home, and no matter what, I'm not leaving here for nobody. I don't care what they say. I don't want no free papers. They're just a way for the cap'n to get me out of here.

CHAPTER THREE

Lavinia

When Belle found Beattie's stolen doll under my upstairs pallet, she was furious and insisted I take it down to the kitchen immediately.

"Why you take this?" Mama Mae asked when I handed it to her.

I cowered, my thumb in my mouth.

"I told you, she's a sly —" Belle began.

"Belle!" Mama checked her. "This be Beattie's best thing," she said sternly to me.

Unable to stand her anger, I ran out to the back of the kitchen house and hid myself behind the woodpile for the rest of the morning. Later, I crept back in, up the stairs, and fell asleep while I waited for Mama Mae to leave.

I wouldn't come down until the next morning, when Mama Mae called for me in a voice that wouldn't accept no. Slowly, I descended the stairs to where the twins waited beside their mother. Beattie stepped forward to hand me a package wrapped in a kitchen cloth. Inside was a doll that had red braids and a body made of white cloth; it wore a brown dress and an apron made from the same green calico as Belle's head rag.

"Mama make her for you," Fanny offered.

I held the doll, afraid to believe Fanny, and looked to Mama Mae. She nodded. "Now you got somethin' of your own," she said.

By July of that first year, my health was returning, though my memory was not. I was quiet but encouraged to speak, as everyone found my Irish dialect amusing. My appearance was often a topic of discussion. Fanny hoped that the freckles across my nose would fill in to give my pale skin more color. Beattie was always trying to fluff my red hair over my pointed ears, and even Belle commented on my oddly colored amber eyes. When Mama overheard their criticisms, she told me not to worry, assuring me that one day I would grow into myself. By this time I was devoted to Mama, and I lived for her notice of me. I kept a distance from Belle, sharing her rooms but watching her closely; she saw to my care, but she was no more at ease with me than I was with her.

During the day Mama encouraged me to go off with the girls. We often went down to the barns where Papa George worked, and there, I met their older brother, Ben. He was Belle's age, eighteen, and even larger in stature than his father. Because of his great size, I might easily have been frightened by him, but I became enamored.

Ben was an outgoing man with a hearty deep laugh, and I watched in envy as he gently teased his little sisters. He must have taken pity on me, for he soon included me, calling me a little bird. How could I fly with my thumb in my mouth? he wanted to know. After that comment, determined to please him, I made certain to keep my hand away from my face when in his presence. Following my first introduction, my one request to the twins every morning was to go down to see Ben. The girls teased me, and when Belle overheard, she asked, "You like Ben?" Though embarrassed, I nodded. She smiled at me, the first time ever. "At least you got good sense," she said.

I began to keep aside a bit of my evening meal, and in the morning I could hardly wait to give Ben my offering. He never failed to show surprise and always ate it with a great show of pleasure. One day, in return, Ben presented me with a bird nest he had found. All the riches in the world couldn't have bought it from me; it was to become the first in my collection of abandoned bird nests. I carefully placed it on the floor beside my pallet, next to my treasured doll.

The twins and I were playing by the stream the afternoon Jimmy, a young man from the quarters, stole the board. We didn't know how to swim, so we waded knee-high near the mossy bank, tossing white water into the air and twirling into it, finally exhausting ourselves. We were resting on the stream bank when Fanny's finger suddenly went to her lips to quiet us. We followed her as she crept into the thick bushes and parted the leaves to see a young dark Negro man a short distance downstream, crouched in the shade of the springhouse. That building, I knew, held cooled butter and cheese and often some puddings, and my first thought, when I noted his thin bare chest, was that he looked hungry.

He glanced back and forth and, seeing no one, sprinted up to the next building, the smokehouse, which held the year's supply of meat. A pungent scent of hickory smoke seeped from the building, where it permeated the heavily salted pork and beef cuts hanging from the beams inside. Fanny and Beattie both sucked in their breath when the man undid the latch and entered. Beattie whispered that it should have been locked and that Papa George carried the key.

We watched until we saw him again. He left, but not with meat. Instead, he had a board under his arm: It appeared to be a floorboard about three feet long. He ran back to the cover of the springhouse, then, after a short pause, turned and dashed through the woods, down the hill, in the direction of the quarters.

I ran after the girls when they went for Papa George. We found him with Mama Mae in the chicken pen, helping her catch a hen. As we rounded the corner, he caught one and held the squawking bird by its feet.

"Papa," Fanny called as we ran up to him. "Papa! Jimmy from the quarters take another board from the smokehouse."

Mama Mae took the chicken from Papa and walked to the back of the coop. The three of us followed as Papa and Mama Mae began to argue.

"This has got to stop," hissed Mama.

"They needs the salt," Papa said. He left

then, and Mama Mae furiously plunked the chicken on the wood block.

She turned to look at the three of us. "You saw nothin'," she said before she lifted a small ax and, with one blow, chopped off the chicken's head. She flung the chicken's body to the ground as blood pumped from its neck. The head lay severed while the body stayed on its feet, terrifying me with its morbid death dance. I turned and ran for the kitchen house, passing Papa George, who was headed for the smokehouse with a replacement board. Belle was in the kitchen yard, tending a large pot of boiling water over an outdoor fire. I surprised both her and myself when I ran and clung to the safety of her skirts.

When Mama Mae followed, I was relieved to see that the chicken, hanging upside down in Mama's grip, was now still. I stayed next to Belle and watched Mama dip the bird in the scalding water. When she pulled it out, she did not wait for it to cool before plucking the feathers. I thought she was angry, but after she'd eviscerated the chicken, she called me over to see how the insides held a perfectly formed egg. "See, no reason to get so scared," she said. "Mama just killin' a chicken." Then she gave me the egg to have for my supper. It was still warm.

A few weeks later, I went with the girls down to see the children in the quarters. The twins were forbidden to visit without their mother, but Fanny, already rebellious, convinced Beattie and me to go with her.

The quarters were set up far down the hill, alongside the stream. Coming from the woods, we approached the cabins from the backside, where attached lean-tos sheltered stacks of split wood. The cabins were built of rough-hewn logs and chinked with mud. Each had two doors with a wall in the center of the cabin that created two separate homes. When we peeked in one, the room looked small. Pallets were piled in the corner, and a large black iron pot stood alongside the fireplace. Wooden spoons hung from pegs on the wall, and worn rags were draped over a piece of rope strung across the room. Under a small open window, flies buzzed, searching unsuccessfully for crumbs on the homemade table and the wooden bowls stacked there.

Fanny said this was where Jimmy and his many brothers lived. With her fingers, she named each of them. "Ida his mama, and she have this many boys." She smiled, holding up six fingers.

We heard children and followed the sound. It led us past a number of double cabins and several small gardens. When we rounded the final cabin, we found ourselves in a large dirt yard. Down a distance was a clapboard house, and Beattie whispered that this was where the overseer lived, away from the others. "He white," she said in my ear.

From the center of the yard, an old woman called out a greeting. "Well, well! It de Fanny and de Beattie." She straightened up her thin rounded back as best she could and continued to stir the contents of a black kettle that bubbled over an open flame. "Yous here to eat?" she asked. A group of children stood back from her, watching carefully.

"No, Auntie. We got to go right back up," Fanny said.

"And who dis?" The old woman's dark eyes peered at me.

"This Abinia, Auntie. Belle her new mama," Fanny answered. I glanced at Fanny, wondering at the title she'd given Belle.

"Uh-huh," replied the old woman, looking me up and down before turning back to her work. She called over two of the boys to help her remove the pot from the fire and set it on the side to cool.

When she took a large wooden paddle to stir the cornmeal again, I caught a pleasant waft of the salty smell of pork, but I was surprised to see her stir up a piece of board from the bottom. She looked about carefully before removing it, then threw it quickly on the fire. I'm not sure how I knew, but I was aware that this was a piece of the board from Jimmy's smokehouse theft.

With the help of the boys, she poured the hot meal into a wooden trough not unlike the one Papa George used for his pigs. A tall girl emptied a small wooden bucketful of buttermilk over the stiffening corn mush, and the old woman used her cooking paddle to combine the two. When she nodded to the children, they rushed eagerly to their meal. A few of the babies clung to their older siblings and were settled on a lap or placed at the trough, where they all began to eat. Some of the children had thin pieces of wood to help scoop up the food, though most used nothing but unwashed hands, and the yellow mixture soon turned dark. When I saw their hunger, I was struck with a deep familiarity and turned away, my mind anxious to keep at bay memories it was not yet ready to recall.

We were back at the kitchen house in time

for our own afternoon meal. That day our wooden bowls contained a roasted sweet potato, a generous slice of boiled ham, and an ear of sweet corn. I felt guilt as I began to eat, remembering the children we had just left, but the cause of my guilt soon changed when I heard Fanny lie to Mama Mae about where we had spent the afternoon.

As cold weather approached, our responsibilities grew. The girls were taken up to the big house to learn from Mama, while I was kept down with Belle. When Fanny balked at the housework, Mama sat her down in the kitchen house and, within earshot of Beattie and me, lectured her daughter. "What you thinkin', Fanny? You forgettin' that you a slave? You don't know by now, anytime the cap'n want, he can sell you? Anytime Miss Martha say she want you gone, you gone."

"I'd just say no, I'm stayin'," Fanny sassed.

Mama's voice shook. "You listen, girl. I'm gonna tell you what happens when you say no to a white man. I watch my own daddy get shot when he saddle up and ride out on a mule to get help for my own sick mama. She havin' a baby, cryin' out for help. I stand-in' right there when that masta say to my daddy to get down from that mule. When my daddy say, 'No, I's going for help,' that old masta shoot him in the back. That night all I know to do is keep the flies away when I watch my mama die. When that old masta sell me, he say I'm good for nothin' but the fields. And that's where I grow up, workin' hard, right 'longside Ida, until old Mrs. Pyke call me up to the big house to feed Belle. It don't take long for me to see what I got to do to stay up there. I work for Mrs. Pyke like I don't know what tired mean. Nothin' that I won't do. 'Yes, Mrs. Pyke, you right, Mrs. Pyke,' that all I say. You girls watch me close. I act like I don't have no mind of my own, except how to make everybody in the big house happy. That because I mean to stay up there, and I tryin' hard to keep you girls with me.

"There's not a day go by that I don't say, 'Thank you, Lawd, for sendin' me up to the big house and for givin' me the cap'n for my masta. I know there nothin' right about being a slave, but who I gonna tell that story to?

"Now, Fanny, you still wantin' to get yourself sold, you ask Papa how he get here. Then you get yourself ready, because he gonna cry when he tell you, and by the time he finish, you be cryin', too."

Wide-eyed, the three of us had nothing to say when Mama finished.

Later that month, the twins told me of a new arrival, another adult, who had come to join the family. He was from England, a tutor, they said, sent by the captain to teach his children. When Fanny declared that she didn't like him, I don't remember asking her why.

I was certainly curious about the big house and the children in it, but the girls told me that they did not often see the inhabitants. If they should, they were instructed not to initiate conversation but to nod and go about their tasks. When Beattie supported Fanny in saying that their work, dusting and cleaning floors, was tedious and unexciting, I ceased to mind that I was kept back in the kitchen.

Belle was softening toward me, and as she did, I became even more eager to please her. It was already my responsibility to scatter the corn and wheat for the chickens, so I was doubly proud of myself the day she trusted me to go down to the chicken house to collect the eggs. When Papa George saw me leaving the hen yard, he came my way. Eager to shine at my new responsibility, I painstakingly placed my full basket on the ground before carefully closing the gate behind me. "You good with the hens, Abinia," he said. "You a good girl."

His smile radiated through to my lonely heart and suddenly opened it to a new possibility. "Papa," I asked, "is Dory your girl?"

"That she is," Papa said.

"Are Beattie and Fanny your girls?" I asked.

"They sure enough is," he said.

"Papa," I asked, "is Belle your girl?"

"Why you ask all this, chil'?" he said.

"I was wondering, Papa . . ." I said, then stopped and focused on my toe as it drew a line in the dirt.

"Go on, chil', what you wonderin' about?" he encouraged.

"Could I be your girl, too?" I asked quickly.

The large, broad-shouldered man looked away before he answered. "Well, now," he said, as though he had given it deep thought, "I sure do think I would like that."

"But," I said, concerned that he hadn't noticed, "I don't look like your other girls."

"You mean because you white?"

I nodded.

"Abinia," he said, pointing toward the chickens, "you look at those birds. Some of them be brown, some of them be white and

49

black. Do you think when they little chicks, those mamas and papas care about that?"

I smiled up at him, and he rested his huge hand on my head. "I think I just got me one more baby girl," he said, tousling my hair, "and I'm gonna call her Abinia. How about that! I say, 'Thank you, Lawd!' Ain't I just the luckiest man!"

I skipped all the way back up to the house. Belle scolded me when she found a broken egg, and I promised her that I would be more careful the next time, but my singing heart wasn't apologetic in the least.

A light snow was falling the early December night when Mama Mae brought the shrieking baby Henry to the warm kitchen. The twins followed her, and we three sat together and watched as Belle and Mama Mae applied warm soaks to the baby's swollen feet and hands. But he would not stop his agonized screams.

"Fanny, you go up to get Dory. Miss Martha takin' the black drops all day, and for sure she sleepin' by now. Uncle Jacob keep an eye on her till Dory get back."

Fanny turned to run, and Mama called after her, "Tell Dory to bring the black drops with her."

When Dory arrived, she tried to comfort

50

her baby by nursing him. In his pain, he refused the solace, tossing his head back and forth. Dory herself began to cry. "Mama, what can I do?"

"He not good, baby," Mama Mae said to her oldest daughter. "I see this before, down the quarters. We give the drops to ease him."

Mama held the little brown bottle. Dory had brought from the house and mixed some of the dark liquid with warm water. Dory held the suffering child while Belle opened his mouth and Mama carefully dripped the mixture in. Baby Henry coughed when he swallowed, but to our great relief, he soon fell into a deep sleep. Later, there was a light knock, and Uncle Jacob entered.

"Miss Martha callin' for you, Dory," he said. "She want you now."

Mama Mae took baby Henry from a reluctant Dory. "Go on," she said, "he gonna sleep now."

After Dory left, Mama showed Uncle Jacob the baby's swollen hands and feet. He shook his head. "He not gonna be here long," he said.

"This be hard on Dory," said Mama Mae.

"Hard on Jimmy, too," Belle added. "Don't forget, he's the daddy. Every day all he wants to see is his Dory and his baby boy, but he's got to stay away. The overseer warned Jimmy that if he finds him close to Dory again, he'll sell him. He says Jimmy's a field-worker, so he's got to go with a field woman, and he's not supposed to have nothing to do with a big-house girl."

"Don't nobody ask the cap'n if Dory can jump the broom with Jimmy?" Uncle Jacob asked.

"Rankin say he the overseer. That mean he the boss, and he say who marry who," answered Mama Mae. "That Rankin just wantin' to be ugly."

When Mama Mae took notice of the three of us, the twins were sent home, and I was sent upstairs to sleep. After Uncle left, Mama Mae stayed with the baby and sat beside the fire to talk with Belle. I fell asleep, comforted by their soft, low voices.

Baby Henry died that night. In the early morning Papa George came with a small board over which Mama and Belle fashioned a small pallet. Dory stood near the door, holding her now quiet baby. Mama went to her. "Give him to me," she said softly, reaching for baby Henry.

"Mama, no." Dory turned away with her bundle.

Papa George came over and put his arm

around the thin shoulders of his firstborn daughter. "Dory, he okay now, he with the Lawd. You give him to Mama."

Slowly, Dory held baby Henry out. "Mama, you fix him? You always so good with him, Mama," she pleaded.

Belle took Dory's arm and led her outside. I watched from the door as they walked down past the barn and into the woods. Snow was falling, draping a clean sheet of silent white. Mama Mae watched them leave before she came back to Papa George. She placed baby Henry on the pallet, and together, using a long brown cloth, they bound his small body to the wooden board. As they finished wrapping, Mama Mae looked up at Papa. Tears dripped down her round face. "It best for this chil' that he go, I knows this," she said, "but I afraid he take Dory's heart with him."

"Our girl gonna be all right," Papa said, and wiped Mama's face dry with his fingers.

The twins were there, and they were crying, too; I was not. I felt empty, and when they all left for the burial, I stayed back until, terrified of the isolation, I ran after them, down to the cemetery by the quarters.

I stood in the shelter of the trees to watch. Ben was standing beside a small grave he had dug next to other small graves that were marked by jutting stones. When they lowered baby Henry into the earth, Dory loosed a series of long, wrenching wails. My mind, caught in the rush of her grief, tunneled away. It was as though a veil had been torn back and I'd left this place of sorrow to enter a deeper one, one that held the other me, which had been lost until this day. I was back again on board ship, unable to stand its violent rocking and the desperate nausea of my own sickness.

The shrouded body had become my mother's. I watched again as they lowered it, deep and away, into the wild water. Days before, my father had led the way; he went in the water, too. I looked around me through the snow for my brother, Cardigan. Certain I heard him calling, I left to find him.

Jimmy, baby Henry's father, found me and brought me to the kitchen house. I had been missing all of that day. In the evening after dark, when Jimmy had gone alone to mourn his son, he had stumbled upon me in the woods.

They say I rocked silently for almost two days. Finally, Mama Mae came. She sat down next to me on my pallet, then she told Belle and the twins to leave. "Abinia," she said firmly, "why you rockin' like this?"

I rocked wildly as I clung to the memory of pain, to the memory of my mother. I couldn't release it; I would lose her again.

"Abinia," she said, trying to hold me still, "you tell Mama Mae why you rockin' like this." She held my face and forced my eyes to meet hers. "You talk to Mama. Abinia, you got to talk. Don't you go away like this. You talk to Mama. You tell her what the trouble is."

I tried to pull away, needing the force of motion to still the nausea, but Mama took my rocking self to her lap. Pressing me to her strong bosom, she slowed my rhythm to match her own. "Mama gonna take this pain from you," she said. Rocking back, she breathed deeply, pulling me in to herself, and as we rocked forward, she exhaled in deep guttural moans the sorrow I was holding.

Back and forth she rocked, bringing to the surface the festering poison of the nightmare I had been hiding. I tried to breathe with her, but my breath came in short rasps, and I felt as though I were drowning.

"Now," she said. "You tell Mama."

I whispered the horror. "Baby Henry is in the water."

"Baby Henry not in the water," she said,

"that baby is with the Lawd. He in a good place. He laughin' and playin' with other children of the Lawd. He not hurtin' no more! He in a good place."

"My ma is in the water," I whispered again.

"Abinia, your mama is with the Lawd, just like baby Henry. Matter of fact, she be holdin' baby Henry, and they playin' together right now. Listen, you can almost hear them laughin'. This world is not the only home. This world is for practice to get things right. Times, the Lawd say, 'Nope, that mama, that baby Henry, they too sweet to stay away from Me no more. I brings them home.' I knows this, Abinia," she said, her solid arms and words of conviction anchoring me. "Mama sayin' there are times we got to trust the Lawd."

Somehow I heard Mama Mae's truth, and my heart believed her. Having found my past, I clung to this mother who now gave me my future. "Ma!" I keened. "Ma!" and my cries finally released the tears I had stored since my arrival.

"Mama's here," I was reassured. "Mama's here."

CHAPTER FOUR

Belle

To tell the truth, when baby Henry passes, he's suffering so much, it's the best thing that he goes. Poor Dory's wanting to save him, but Mama says she sees this before in the quarters and it always ends bad. Now Dory's eyes look like Miss Martha's after she loses her babies.

When Lavinia sees baby Henry going in the ground, she goes off her head. When Jimmy brings her back, I can't do nothing with her, but Mama knows what to do. Then Lavinia remembers being on the ship and seeing her mama and papa dying and them being dropped in the water. What are those men thinking, letting a little one see that?

Now she knows where she comes from, Ireland, but she says that her mama and papa had nothing there and come here looking to work. She says she has a brother, Cardigan.

Funny name, Cardigan. I don't ask more because I see she still have a hard time talking about him.

Since her day of remembering, it's hard to believe the change in that chil', though she's still like a mouse, skittery and scared of the world. She makes a big thing of doing her chores, and when she's done, she always comes for me to look. When I say "good job," her little face has a smile to light up the kitchen house.

I got to say, when the twins tell me that she's bringing food to Ben, that little girl warms my heart. She don't know why I give her extra to take down, but I got to laugh when I think that we both got our eye on the same man.

CHAPTER FIVE

Lavinia

After I remembered the death of my parents, other memories began to surface. Of course, at that tender age, I had few years to draw from, but when a sound or a scent brought forth another image, it was often enough to leave me devastated. Overcome by loss, I could do nothing but grieve. I had kind parents, though both were under strain at the time we boarded the ship. My ma did not want to leave Castlebar, the city in Ireland where both of her parents still lived. But my da, with no relations that I could recall, was determined to provide a better life for his family. I had memories of the two often arguing, but I could not forget my ma's terrible grief when my da died. And then I lost her. For the rest of the voyage, I clung desperately to my brother. My last recall of Cardigan was his helplessness to respond to my imploring screams as the captain took me from him.

I eased the pain of these memories by making a promise to myself: One day I would find my brother.

My health was returning, and though I was now deeply attached to Mama, I also was beginning to look to Belle for comfort. Her attitude toward me had changed since baby Henry's death — so much so that one night, when she heard me crying, she brought me into her own bed. There she put her arms around me and stroked my back until I slept. From then on I was often granted permission to climb into her bed at night.

When the captain arrived home in time for Christmas, we in the kitchen were told how Miss Martha had once again come to life. These past months, while the captain had been away, the mistress had her meals served in the upper sitting room adjoining her bedroom. The children were there with her for dinner, but for other meals they ate with the tutor in the study. Since the captain's arrival, and with the approach of the holidays, meals had taken on a festive air and were served once again in the dining room.

With extra help needed in the kitchen, to

my delight, Beattie was brought down to the kitchen house, while Fanny stayed up to work alongside Dory. Everyone was kept busy baking for the holidays, and even Ben came up from the barns to help. He chopped the wood that kept the kitchen fires burning hot, as well as supplying fuel for the fireplaces in the big house. Beattie and I were thrilled when we were given the chore to help Ben carry wood. We ran outdoors to greet him, eager to please.

"You too little for work," he teased both of us.

"No, we're not," we assured him.

He gave each of us a small piece of kindling. "More," we begged, "more," until he packed our arms. We stumbled from the woodpile, determined to show our strength, but when we arrived in the kitchen, Mama Mae called out to him, "Ben! Ben, you come here!"

Ben stood so tall that he had to lean forward when he came through the kitchen door. He straightened and smiled. "You call me, Mama?" he asked.

Belle turned to look, and Ben acknowledged her with a nod. Belle, whose face had taken on a pink glow, returned the nod, then turned quickly back to measuring a pound of sugar. Belle was thin, but I noticed that when she leaned forward to cut from the sugar block, her waist curved up to show a generous bosom, giving her a graceful shape. Glancing at Ben, I saw that he was noticing, too.

"Ben," Mama said, "what you doin' with these girls, makin' them carry so much wood?"

He winked at us. "Mama, they my big strong helpers."

We ran proudly to his side, ready for more. "We're helping him, Mama," we said.

"Ben," Mama said, laughing, "you sure gots the way with the women."

He chuckled and looked directly at Belle. "You think so, Mama?"

Belle turned her back to him, but the vigor with which she put pestle to mortar, grinding the solid sugar, gave evidence of a response.

"So, Abinia. Belle take care of you like a good mama?" Ben asked me.

I looked to Belle, and when she met my eyes, she smiled. I turned back to Ben and nodded.

"That Belle got herself a baby pretty as her. You need yourself a daddy?" he asked.

"No," I said, confident in my answer. "I have Papa George."

The adults laughed.

"That my daddy, too," he teased.

"I know," I said proudly, "and Dory's and Fanny's and Beattie's and Belle's."

"Well," he said, "Belle, your mama. Papa, your daddy. Then who is Mama Mae?"

"She's the big mama," I said, surprised he didn't know.

I felt enclosed in the laughter that followed, and although I wasn't certain of my exact position in the family structure, I began to feel there was a place for me.

"Ben," Mama said, "you be easy with workin' those girls, they still babies."

"Come on, then, babies," he said, taking our hands, "we got plenty a wood to carry."

Belle turned to us. "Ben," she said, "you take good care of my baby."

A thrill went through me at her reference, and Ben, at a loss for words, scooped us up outside and swung us in turn until we shrieked with joy.

On Christmas morning, Fanny came from the big house to the kitchen house with her eyes aglow.

"Marshall got two new storybooks," she said, "and both those chillun, they get pots of colors and the brushes to paint with. Marshall gets the soldiers, and Sally, she gets a doll that looks like her, and dishes, and more and more things. The mistress gets this long string of shiny beads, they callin' them pearls!" She flung her arms open and spoke to the heavens. "It be like when I die," she said dramatically.

"You gonna die if you don't get in here to help," said Mama, but she smiled as she said it.

More excitement followed when guests arrived at noon that day. I had not seen such happy commotion since my arrival. Fanny, Beattie, and I watched from the corner of the big house as the horses charged up the drive. The captain stood at the doorway, but Miss Martha left his side and flew down the stairs. She ran toward the carriage, forcing the driver to sharply rein in the horses. The carriage door flew open, and with a cry, a woman flung herself out and into Miss Martha's arms. They clung to each other for a long time.

"They sistas," Fanny whispered.

The captain came down the steps to greet the short, balding man who exited the carriage next. With him came a young girl close to my age, dressed in a vibrant red coat and a hat that was trimmed in white. Marshall observed the welcoming from the doorway, while Sally ran to meet her cousin Meg.

The guests were ushered indoors and

shown to their rooms for a rest. We watched as Ben, Papa George, and Uncle Jacob helped the driver unload all the trunks. Finally, when the mud-encrusted carriage and lathered horses had been directed to the barn, we girls headed back to the kitchen. Belle and Mama Mae had worked for days in preparation for the feast that was to take place, and our help was needed.

Midafternoon, we began to carry food from the kitchen to the big house. We approached the dining room through a side door, avoiding the parlor where the captain and Miss Martha were entertaining. The large paneled sliding doors leading from the hallway to the dining room were closed, so we, too, had privacy from the big house's occupants.

This was only the second time I had seen the dining room, and I wondered at it. Dory, Uncle Jacob, and Fanny had decorated the room with greenery and mistletoe. Sprigs of holly adorned the windowpanes, their berries perfectly matching the lush red drapes. Centered on each deep windowsill, a low porcelain bowl held the sweet-smelling potpourri that I had helped Belle prepare in the fall by combining dried rose petals, lavender, rosemary, and apple slices and sprinkling them with grated cinnamon and nutmeg. The potpourri scent intermingled with the pleasing smell of the fresh-cut pine boughs decorating the mantel.

The table was set over two white damask tablecloths I had seen Mama iron a few days before. The top cloth looked rich and thick, like heavy cream. Silver cutlery and glassware shone beside dinnerware painted with bright-colored birds. Belle told me they were peacocks and that the captain used to have one on this plantation.

"Noisy old bird," Uncle Jacob muttered.

"Yes, Uncle, he was," Belle said, "but wasn't he pretty and proud?"

"Till that old fox get him." Uncle laughed as he placed another log on the crackling fire. Then he began to light the many candles.

We each carried prepared dishes up from the kitchen house while Mama Mae and Belle placed them strategically on the table, giving balance to the feast. A large smoked ham, wrapped in a napkin and garnished with pickled plums and brandied peaches, anchored one end. Belle surrounded the platter with deep green magnolia leaves, and next to the silver sugar shaker, she arranged a crystal condiment dish filled with a tangy mustard and honey sauce.

Mama and Belle together had to carry up

the large platter holding a succulent cut of beef. It had been roasting slowly for hours on a spit, and underneath, a pan of sizzling potatoes caught the drippings. Four side dishes, all painted with the peacock design, cornered the table and held the vegetables. Green peas were prepared in a heavy cream sauce, small red beets glistened with butter, sweet potatoes dripped with honey, and white parsnips looked festive, sprinkled with fresh green parsley. In front of the mistress's place setting, Mama set a steaming tureen of oyster soup, flavored and garnished with green sprigs of thyme.

Dessert, a rich plum pudding, was warming in the kitchen, but on the sideboard, awaiting their turn, was a tray of jellies and crèmes. Next to those treats stood four miniature silver carts drawn by tiny silver goats. Belle had given me the privilege of burdening them with sweetmeats and dark raisins.

Dory came to the door as we stood back to admire our work. She had been with the captain and the mistress, serving sherry in the parlor, and though I envied her for what she'd seen, she looked weary and uninterested. Suddenly, Sally pushed in past Dory.

"Fanny, Fanny!" she cried happily, and ran toward us, carrying her new porcelain doll. "Come here, Meg." She waved to her cousin, who waited at the door. As the twins examined Sally's doll, the girl, Meg, approached slowly. She walked with a slight limp, but what caught my attention most were the tiny spectacles that she wore. Her brown hair had been pulled back in a purple ribbon, but tight curls refused containment and frizzed out to soften her sharp features. In spite of her solemn demeanor, I felt an immediate liking for her.

"Do you have a doll?" Fanny asked Meg.

"I don't like dolls!" Meg answered.

"But you like birds, don't you, Meggy?" Sally asked.

"I like birds," Meg admitted.

"She has one that talks," Sally said, "but she had to leave it at home."

"One that talks?" Fanny asked.

Meg nodded, turning shy with our attention.

"I like birds," I said, helping her out.

She stared at me through her spectacles. "What kind?" she asked.

"Chickens," I said.

"Do you have one?"

I nodded. "A bunch. They live down at the barn. I feed them every day. And I get the eggs. When it gets warm, Papa said they'll have chicks."

"Ohhh . . ." she said longingly.

Dory interrupted us. "Miss Sally, you take your doll outta here before you come in to eat." As the girls left, Dory whispered loudly to Mama, "Miss Martha coming with Miss Sarah." When they entered, I stared in dumb surprise. The difference between the two women made it difficult for me to believe they were sisters. Miss Martha, willowy and tall, was dressed in a simple but beautifully cut blue brocade, while Miss Sarah, short and plump, contrasted sharply in a voluminous and vibrant red silk that was ruffled from waist to floor. Their deportment, too, was opposite. Miss Martha, quiet and subdued, brought with her an air of elegance, while Miss Sarah, enthusiastic and outgoing, gave the appearance of being fussy and easily excited.

Miss Sarah immediately began to exclaim about the holiday decorations, but then she caught sight of me standing with Mama Mae and the twins, and her eyes opened wide. Disliking her scrutiny, I stepped behind Mama.

"Why, Martha, dear! Who . . . what . . . ?"

"I know, I know. I haven't had time to . . . She was on board ship. James brought her home this past spring."

"But my dear! She must be given a

69

chance! To put her with —"

"Sarah! Might we speak of this later?"

"Yes, yes, of course. But you understand my surprise."

Miss Martha ended the conversation by turning to Mama and thanking her for her hard work. Then she sent us out, though Belle was told to remain. We listened from behind the door as Miss Martha sharply questioned Belle as to why her head wasn't covered. When Belle tried to explain that she had removed her head rag because of the heat in the kitchen, she was silenced.

"Must you always seek attention!" Miss Martha said sharply, then quickly dismissed Belle when the captain and the others began to enter.

It took a while before Belle joined the family at Mama and Papa's house for a Christmas meal. Belle's mood was subdued until Ben, on whose lap I sat, gently teased her into good humor.

After our meal, we were each given a few raisins and a fresh apple from the storage barrel. Papa cracked open some nuts, and Ben picked out the meat using the horseshoe nails he always carried in his pocket.

Uncle left again to work at the big house when a bottle of peach brandy, a gift from the captain, was produced. Mama poured a drink for each adult, including Ben, Dory, and Belle. Talk turned lively after the second round of drinks, and I was soon caught up in the fun when I learned we were going to a dance that night down in the quarters. Papa George and Ben left shortly after, eager to get the chores done.

When the dishes were clean, Belle took the twins and me back to the kitchen house. She went upstairs, and when she came down, I hardly recognized her. Under her winter shawl, she wore a white top I had never seen. Around the neckline, a small ruffle matched the one on the white petticoat peeking out from under her full skirt. Her long hair was combed down and curled around her face. The twins and I stared at her, and we all wanted a turn at touching her long soft curls. Belle smiled and told us to stop fussing with her, but her green eyes shone.

She handed Fanny and me her silver comb, her silver hand mirror, and some blue ribbon to carry back to Mama's house. She and Beattie each carried a large gingerbread cake that had been baked earlier. Before we left the house, I was told that I was not to eat the cakes at the party.

"Why?" I asked.

"Because we already ate our sweets," Belle answered.

When we returned, Mama was trying to convince Dory to come to the dance. "You come, baby, you gots to keep living," Mama said. "Besides, I know one man gonna be looking for you tonight."

Dory turned away from her. "I just can't, Mama," she said.

"All right, then," said Mama, taking off her apron and sitting down at the table. "I stay here with you."

"No, Mama," said Dory, "I don't want you missin' the fun."

"Then you come with us," Mama said. "You come and sit with me, and we watch the dancin'."

Belle pulled Dory over to sit on a stool. "Here," she said, "let me fix your hair." Belle removed Dory's head rag and wove a blue ribbon through Dory's braided hair. When she'd finished, she held up the mirror. Dory glanced at her reflection, then her face crumpled and she began to cry. Belle leaned down to hug her. "Baby Henry is happy where he is, and I know he'd want you to be happy," she said.

Mama was watching, and when we saw her use her apron to wipe tears from her own eyes, we three girls also began to sob.

And that was how Ben and Papa George found us when they opened the door.

"Well, well, well," said Papa, "this sure looks like these womans good and ready for the party, don't it, Ben?"

"Uh-huh, Papa," Ben said, "they sure singin' real good."

"Which one you gonna dance with, Ben?" Papa asked.

"I pick my mama," said Ben. "She cryin' the best. We hears her down at the barns."

Mama laughed while drying her eyes. "You mens stop with that," she said.

"Well, I think I pick Dory," Papa continued to tease. He went to her and placed his arm around her shoulders, then looked back at her face and said, "Her eyes so puffed up, everybody think I got me a new woman."

We all laughed, and even Dory smiled. Together, we all left for the party. It was dark outside and the evening cold. We hadn't seen snow since the day we had buried baby Henry, but the ground was frozen, and our feet crunched on dried leaves. It hurt to walk in the heavy shoes, which chafed my ankles, but it wasn't necessary to complain, as Fanny protested enough for both of us.

Mama scolded her. "Those peoples down

in the quarters would give anything to have those shoes," she said, and I was glad I had been silent.

From the top of the hill we could see the orange of a blazing fire. As we drew closer, I recognized the strain of a fiddle and could hear people laughing and singing. Secure between Belle and Ben, I held tight to each of their hands, a link to their happiness, as we moved through the dark woods toward the joyful music.

Our small party was greeted with shouts of recognition. Belle's cakes were gratefully received, and the women quickly brought a bench and invited Mama, Belle, and Dory to sit with them. A large area around the fire had been swept clean, and already some were dancing. On the far side, men were playing lively music with homemade instruments: Two played gourd fiddles, two others played reed flutes, and another drummed on pots and lids with sticks and bones.

I stayed close to Belle until Beattie and Fanny came for me. We approached a group of children, but they stood back, wary of us. Some were girls our age, but they didn't speak. Our clothing was different, certainly more substantial than theirs, and they studied our feet as though they had never seen shoes.

Soon the three of us found our way back to Mama, Belle, and Dory. Belle allowed us a sip of the peach brandy the women were drinking, a rare treat sent from the big house for this holiday celebration. Rough tables stood end to end, and off to the side, men eagerly shared two jugs of corn whiskey, another gift from the big house.

Everyone became alert as the women gathered and agreed that the chickens, roasting on a spit over a bed of red coals, were cooked through. In short order, a man speared two large hams from boiling water and placed them on wooden slabs set on either side of a large black caldron of steaming black-eyed peas. The women brought simmering pots of late-season garden greens and turned crisp hot corn bread out onto the table. Others used sharp sticks to draw roasted sweet potatoes from the ashes. Finally, supper was announced.

The women served the men first and then helped the children. They insisted that we from the big house eat with them, and I was surprised to see my family do so. They took small portions, but I saw the smiles from the women when Belle, Mama, and Dory told them how good the food tasted. When I set my bowl down, I had not finished a small piece of the ham.

Belle leaned down to me. "Eat it all," she said quietly, and I knew from her tone not to protest.

After the women had eaten, the children were called back and given the little remaining food. On seeing their excitement, I realized this was a rare happening and was embarrassed to think that Belle had to tell me to finish the meat.

When the fiddle started up with a lively tune, the other instruments soon joined in. With a whoop, a few young couples got up to dance. The older audience members began to clap, and soon the circle around the fire was filled with happy dancers. After a few rounds, the fiddler called out, "Who gonna show us how to set de flo'? George, Mae, come on, you show us. You show us," the older members called as they began a rhythmic clapping.

Papa George came for Mama. "Mae," he said, bowing down, "let's show the young ones that we still can dance." With a show of reluctance, she rose to her feet, and when he took her to the dance floor, everyone cheered them on. Papa bowed from the waist, and Mama curtsied to him as the lively music began. Papa George repeated each step Mama Mae set out, and I could see him having fun trying to anticipate what her next step would be.

Others danced after Papa and Mama, but none generated the same excitement until Ben and Belle took their turn. Belle looked shy when she did a deep curtsy, but as she raised her eyes to Ben, he winked. To this, she responded with a strong stomp, setting the pace for a wild dance.

I overheard some women talking behind me. "She his daughter, all right," I heard one say, "she sure the high cullah."

Dory, seated next to Mama Mae, heard, too. She turned back to face them. "Belle a good woman. She can't help who her daddy is," she said.

"We know Belle a good woman," the speaker replied, "we just sayin' that she could pass, that all we sayin'."

"What she pass to?" asked Dory, her voice hard. "This her family. Where she go? This her home. She born, raised here."

Hearing Dory's tone, Mama was about to join the conversation when a dark, thin figure standing back in the shadows caught her attention. It was Jimmy, baby Henry's father. He beckoned to Dory, and when she saw him, she almost tripped over Beattie in her haste to follow him into the dark woods. "You be careful," Mama whispered to Dory

77

as she left.

After the two slipped away, an exceptionally dark and reed-thin woman approached Mama. Her hands nervously rubbed her jutting round belly. Fanny identified her to me as Jimmy's mother, Ida.

"What we gonna do, Mae?" Ida asked, looking over her shoulder. "Rankin say he kill my Jimmy if he go by Dory again."

"I talk to the cap'n," said Mama. "I see him before he leave. I gonna ask that they jump the broom."

"You knows they don't want the mens from the quarters mixin' with the womens in the big house. You knows that, Mae," said Ida.

"Those two don't stay away from each other, that what I know," said Mama. "I tell the cap'n that Jimmy a good man for Dory. The cap'n always like Dory."

"If the cap'n say yes, Rankin don't like it," said Ida.

"That overseer don't like hisself, how he gonna like anything else?" asked Mama.

The talk stopped short when, as though summoned, the captain and his portly brother-in-law stepped into the light of the fire. Marshall and another tall man followed. The music ceased.

"Don't stop!" the captain called out. He

raised two more jugs of whiskey over his head. "Would any of you be wanting more of this?" A cheer went up, and the music began again.

"That Mista Waters, the tutor," Fanny whispered to me, pointing out the man standing behind Marshall.

The odd-looking man had my attention. He stood with his hand firmly on Marshall's shoulder and stared arrogantly at the people of the quarters and their surroundings. He leaned down occasionally to say something to Marshall, and it struck me how distressed Marshall looked, though he made no move to distance himself. I realize now that even as a young child, I guessed the vile nature of this man, and though I did not understand, I already sensed Marshall's entrapment.

"Go get Dory and Jimmy," Mama said to Ben, and he sprinted off into the dark woods.

The captain looked around the outside circle until his eyes rested on Belle. He did not pause, but came immediately over to her. "Belle," he greeted her, "you look lovely."

"Thank you," she said quietly, looking down.

The captain turned to Mama Mae, who

had been seated beside Belle but now stood.

"Mae," he said, "that was a fine feast you and your family provided for us today."

"Yes, Cap'n," Mama Mae answered.

"Does your family have everything they need for a good holiday?" he asked.

"Cap'n, we sure do have plenty," Mama said.

"Good, good," he said, and as though at a loss for words, he turned to look at the dancers.

"Cap'n?" I heard Mama speak again.

He turned back. "Yes, Mae?"

"Cap'n," she said, "I needs to talk to you. It about Dory."

"Mae," he said, "I know about the baby. I was sorry to hear it."

"That not the problem, Cap'n," she said. "Dory wantin' to marry Jimmy from down here in these quarters. He the daddy of her baby."

"Well, Mae," he said, "I don't know about that. Rankin was talking to me about getting Jimmy with another girl. He seems to think that Dory is trouble for Jimmy."

"I think he wrong about that," said Mama.

"Do you, Mae?" the captain asked.

"I think it be good that they jump the broom," Mama said. "George think so, too."

"Well, Mae, you and George are family to

80

me, and Dory means everything to Miss Martha. I suppose we could make an allowance here. But Jimmy would have to stay in the fields, and Dory would have to live up at the big house."

"That be fine," said Mama.

"When were they wanting to do this?" he asked.

"Quick as you say," Mama said.

He laughed. "Tell you what, Mae. If you think it a good idea, they could marry here tonight. Would that suit you?"

"That suit everybody just fine," said Mama, "but it maybe not good with Mr. Rankin?"

"He'll be back in a couple of days. I'll talk to him then. Don't worry, Mae; I'll take care of it. Now," he said, looking around, "where is the young couple?"

Fortunately, Ben had found them, and they stood together next to Papa George. Mama waved them forward, and they came, with Papa George taking the lead.

"Dory, your mama says that you want to marry this young fella here," the captain said.

Dory had been crying again. Her eyes were swollen almost shut, but she nodded.

"And Jimmy, you are wanting to jump the broom with Dory?" the captain asked.

81

"Yes, Cap'n," Jimmy said, "I sure do."

"Somebody get a broom," shouted the captain, "we're going to have a wedding."

The music stopped, and the crowd gathered around. There was a low murmur of voices, and someone produced a broom.

"Now the two of you hold hands," the captain instructed Dory and Jimmy, "and I'll perform the ceremony."

The broom was placed in front of the couple; the captain asked if they would be good to each other, not go with anyone else, and have lots of babies. They both answered yes, and then he told them to jump over the broom. They held hands and jumped together, but when Jimmy tripped, everyone laughed, including the captain.

"Well, Jimmy," he said, "we know who will be the boss of this family."

That was it. Belle told me they were married.

"Now we celebrate!" the captain called out, and he sent Ben up to find Uncle Jacob at the big house to get more liquor. The music began again, and I was surprised when the captain came to Belle, extending his hand. "Belle," he asked, "would you dance with me?"

Belle rose. When they approached the dance area, the other couples moved back, and as they dropped away, Belle and the captain were the only couple left dancing. It grew quiet as the two moved together, their feet pulled by the haunting strains of a lone fiddle. When Belle looked up at him, her beautiful face was flushed from the brandy. The captain gazed down at her with pride, and as he guided her around the circle of fire, his love for her was clear.

I looked for Ben, but I couldn't find him. Then I saw Marshall. The tutor had left, and Marshall stood alone, watching the dancing couple. A chill passed over me when I saw his look of hatred.

CHAPTER SIX

Belle

If Miss Martha keeps digging at me, one of these times I'm gonna hand her the truth. Trouble is, if I do that, for sure the cap'n will send me away.

Christmas is always the worst time for me. It's what I remember best, living up there in the big house. And now Marshall is sleeping in my old bedroom.

Uncle Jacob knows the story about my real mama. He says the cap'n, thirty-four years old and still not married, was down in Richmond, walking through the yard where they was selling Negroes. The cap'n sees them poking at this woman who's standing tall on the box, looking away, like she's the tree and they're the dirt. When the cap'n says, "I'll take her," everybody laughs, and they say, "You best watch out. She's the kind that kills you in your sleep."

When the cap'n brings her here, his own

mama, Mrs. Pyke, was real sick. My black mama knows how to work plants and gets Mrs. Pyke back on her feet. The cap'n stays here over that time, and don't you know, that's where I come in. But when I was born, my mama got the fever and died. They say the cap'n carried on like she was a white woman.

Ben was born that same year as me, 1773, so when Mrs. Pyke sees that Mama Mae is nursing, she brings her up from the quarters to feed me, too. Mama Mae is a hard worker, and before you know it, she's helping Uncle in the big house and then cooking in the kitchen house. Thing was, Papa George was already working up in the barns.

Uncle say I was like the light of day to Mrs. Pyke. My grandma showed me that there is always something to learn, that everybody got something to tell you. She got Uncle Jacob to show us how to write the Arabics, and we listened when he told us about his Foulah tribe and his Allah.

After Mrs. Pyke passed on, everything changed. When she was living, the big house was my home.

Dory always says how Miss Martha changes when the cap'n's home, but Dory says it surprises her beyond all else the way Miss

Martha's like another woman with her sister in the house. She's never seen her this happy.

Dory still misses baby Henry, but jumping the broom with Jimmy worked out good for her. Mama say, "Thank the Lawd. I always worryin' 'bout those two gettin' caught together." Surprising me, Mama asks me about Ben. "I watch the two of you dance," she say, "that tellin' me somethin."

"And you and Papa? You both in your forties and still dancing like that. That tells me something, too."

Mama don't smile. "That don't tell me what I'm askin', Belle."

I get up to start cooking. "Maybe Ben is the one for me," I say.

"Belle, you best be careful. You know the cap'n gonna give you the free papers and that he wantin' to take you away," Mama says.

I don't tell her that Ben and me already have a kiss. When we was little, Ben was my best friend, but this year he's more quiet and looking at me in a whole different way. It makes me smile, 'cause I'm looking back. One time, back of the henhouse, he catch me and pull me to him for a kiss. I say, "No, Ben." He looked hurt, like I don't want him. Then I take his sweet face in my hands and kiss him so good that he pushes me away. "Don't you know what you doin' to me?" he asks.

"You don't like the way I kiss?" I say, teasing.

"Belle," he says, "you know I'm wantin' you." He starts talking 'bout jumpin' the broom, but then I run back to the kitchen house. We both know that ever since I was little, the cap'n always says that one day he's taking me away to Philadelphia.

And now every time the cap'n's home, he's talking about making plans. But I always cry and say, "Wait, please don't make me leave my home." He don't know what to say when I cry, so he leaves and I get to stay. But he always makes me promise not to take up with any man, and I keep that promise. Until now.

CHAPTER SEVEN

Lavinia

Although the house guests stayed for two more weeks, Belle and I were kept busy down in the kitchen house and had no further contact with them. One evening before they left, I overheard a conversation between Uncle Jacob and Belle. They were speaking of Miss Martha. "I don't know what she gonna do when these holidays over," said Uncle Jacob. "Her sista goin' back, and the cap'n leave again. Miss Martha gonna take to her bed, that for sure. I don't know what that man thinkin', to leave that woman alone again." According to Uncle, the cap'n had done this ever since he had brought her here as a bride, believing that she would take over running the plantation in the same way his mother had.

"He have his business in Philadelphia and Williamsburg," Belle defended the captain.

"I knows this, Belle. But it long past time

for him to stay here. Miss Martha don't know nothin' 'bout runnin' this place. Every time he leave, Dory say she takin' more and more of the drops. And Miss Martha don't let that lil Sally outta her sight. The only one she trust that chil' with is Dory," Uncle said.

"She's so afraid she's gonna lose another one. Mama says Miss Martha's not acting right ever since she lost that last baby," Belle said.

"All I know is, it time for the cap'n to stay back and pay attention to what's goin on 'round here. That Rankin no good down at the quarters, and for sure that tutor no good."

"Is something wrong with the tutor?" Belle asked.

"There's somethin' not right with that man," said Uncle.

"What are you saying?" asked Belle.

"Why the man needin' to lock the door when he teachin' the young masta about the books? What happenin', I don't know, but I hears the boy cryin' more than once when I go past the door. I tell the cap'n, but he say to me that the young masta need to have some discipline, that it time for him to do book learnin' so he can run this place when he grow up."

Belle sighed.

"Time, too, for the cap'n to do somethin' about you," Uncle said.

"Well, I'm deciding I don't want to go," Belle said. "He's just gonna have to talk to Miss Martha. Why he's wanting to get me out of here now, I don't know!"

"Belle, you gettin' too old to stay. All along, Miss Martha thinkin' you Mae's girl," Uncle said. "Now, when the cap'n comin' down to the kitchen house, givin' you the combs and ribbons, she wonderin' what's goin on. It time for him to give you the free papers. He right, Belle. It time for him to get you outta here."

"Everybody's always saying I got to go. But you all forget, this is my home! I'm gonna tell the cap'n I'm staying here, maybe even marry Ben."

"Ben! You be careful." Uncle Jacob's voice was sharp. "Ever since you was lil you know the cap'n have other ideas for you."

"I best close up for the night," Belle replied, ending the conversation.

When Belle came up to bed, I crawled in beside her. She was turned away from me, but I knew she was crying, so I patted her back, as she often did mine. I was unsure, though, for it seemed that my efforts at comforting her only caused her to cry all the more.

When the houseguests left, the mistress surprised everyone with her continued good humor. The captain stayed home until mid-February, but this time, to everyone's surprise, Miss Martha remained in good spirits after his departure. Before the captain left, he gave permission for Papa to bring Jimmy up to work with him in the barns, and Dory began to smile again. Increasingly, Miss Martha began to accept Fanny as an alternate caretaker for Miss Sally, leaving Dory free to spend more time with the mistress.

We knew spring had begun when the hens laid eggs and baby chicks hatched. I couldn't have been more excited. Fanny, obliged to remain indoors with her charge, became impatient.

"That Sally just a spoiled lil number," Fanny told us, but she wasn't very convincing, because we knew how much she cared for the golden-haired child.

To our amazement, one warm spring morning, Fanny appeared at the kitchen door with Sally in hand. "Miss Martha say it all right we go see the baby chicks," she said.

Belle and Mama exchanged a look.

"Where Masta Marshall?" Mama asked.

"He's studying," the little girl said.

"What he studyin', Miss Sally?" Mama asked.

"Books," she said. "He has a tutor, Mr. Waters, but Marshall and me don't like him." She looked up at Fanny. "Do you like Mr. Waters, Fanny?"

Fanny looked at Mama, startled.

"Why don't we go see those baby chicks?" Mama Mae said quickly.

In her excitement, the little girl spurted ahead. Her white bonnet, so large only a few blond curls peeked out the back, flapped into her face, and she raised her chubby arms to hold it back when she ran. As she did so, white petticoats peeked out from under her pink dress while the gold buckles on her pink shoes sparkled as though ignited by the sun.

We soon caught up to her, and when we reached the chicken coop, Fanny took the little girl to a patch of grass and carefully sat her down. Then Fanny went into the pen and risked a peck from a mother hen as she snatched a chick away. Sally waited patiently until Fanny came to place the yellow bird in her outstretched hands.

"Don't hold it too tight," Fanny warned,

"you kill it easy that way."

The little girl seemed to stop breathing. "Oh, it's so soft, Fanny," she whispered.

"That 'cause it a baby," Fanny explained to her charge.

"Just like me," Sally said. "Mama said I'm still her baby. Even when the new baby comes, she said, I'll still be her baby."

"Is your mama goin' to have a new baby?" Beattie asked.

"Yes" — the little girl nodded — "a real one. And I can hold it, Mama said. You can, too, Fanny," she offered generously.

We stayed awhile longer, but Mama stood by and watched uneasily until Fanny safely escorted Sally back to the big house.

"I'll come back," the child called over her shoulder to those of us who waved from the kitchen yard.

She was true to her word. From that day on, weather permitting, Fanny brought her new charge down to us. The swing was Miss Sally's favorite joy, and we all took turns sending her into the air. Marshall was not around often. The few times we saw him were when his small sister could persuade him to push her on the swing. The little girl worshipped him, and it was clear that he was devoted to her as well.

93

During that spring and summer, we all fell in love with Miss Sally. She was a generous and fun-loving child, innocent of all pretense. She insisted on bringing along her dolls and china dishes from the big house and always delighted in sharing them. Only Belle kept her distance from the child.

"Don't you like me?" Sally asked her one day.

Belle looked down at her, and Sally met her gaze with wide questioning eyes. I thought for a minute that Belle would cry. Then she said, "Why, sure, I like you, Miss Sally."

"Oh, good," said the little girl, " 'cause sometimes you don't look like you do."

"That must be times when I have a headache," Belle said.

"Do you get headaches, too?" Sally asked. "My mama gets headaches all the time. They're very painful. When I grow up, I hope I never get headaches."

"I sure you won't," Belle said. Then she offered the little girl a small bunch of raisins. Belle watched Sally go to each of us with an open hand, sharing generously, and I saw then that Belle had been won over as well.

It was not often that summer that the twins

and I had leisure time, but there was such a day on a late-August afternoon. Shaded in the woods, the three of us lay on a bed of pine needles, discussing the exciting news that both Dory and Miss Martha were going to have babies.

"How did that happen?" I wondered out loud. Fanny felt free to share a theory that shocked me. After Beattie verified that knowledge, the three of us pondered it in silence. Suddenly, Fanny sat up and turned her head to better listen. Then Beattie and I heard it, too. We all recognized Marshall's pleading voice. As it became louder, we heard an adult telling him to be quiet.

"You want me to take your little sister next time instead of you?"

"No, no, leave her alone. I'll be good, I'll be good," Marshall said.

I don't know who was more startled when Marshall was pushed into our clearing. He looked both relieved and terrified to see us. The tutor's angry surprise at finding us glinted in his narrowed eyes.

"Well," he said, wiping the corners of his moist mouth, "it appears we have some company."

"Get out of here," Marshall hissed.

The girls ran, but something about Marshall's distress caused me to stay.

95

"Come with us," I said, pulling his arm, but he appeared rooted to the spot.

Mr. Waters advanced, smiling. "So, who do we have here?" He grabbed for my arm and latched on, but Marshall, in a burst of rage, pulled the tutor off and screamed for me to go. I was so frightened, I ran.

The girls had already found Papa George in the big barn. When they explained why they had come for him, he didn't wait for them to finish, but grabbed a pitchfork and set out for the woods. However, before he crossed the stream, the tutor and Marshall appeared. Marshall looked imploringly at Papa as he made his way toward them. What Papa said, I do not know, but it caused the tutor's face to turn a bright red. "This boy is my charge!" he shouted. "You're nothing but a barn nigra. If you aren't careful, I'll have you working the fields."

"Papa, you needin' help?" It was Ben, coming quickly from the barns. He had been working at the forge, a hot job on a sweltering day. A dark leather apron covered his front, protecting him from the sparks that flew when he hammered the white iron. Black coal streaks marked his dark wet face, and he carried the sledgehammer that was used to coax metal into shape. His wide shoulders back, Ben walked with the air of a warrior.

Papa turned. "We all right, Ben. I just tellin' this man that we lookin' out for Masta Marshall."

Mr. Waters saw Ben move closer and pulled Marshall with him when he turned quickly toward the house. Ben moved to follow, but Papa grasped his son's arm and whispered urgently, "Ben! Wait!"

I stared, unable to take my eyes off Ben as he watched the tutor disappear into the big house. Fury had changed the gentle man I knew. Ben's neck bulged. He spoke through clamped teeth and I did not recognize his voice. "Let me go, Daddy! I gon' set this right," said Ben.

"No, Ben. He waitin' for that. Next thing you know, he get Rankin up here. Rankin kill you or sell you, then tell some story to the cap'n. Miss Martha havin' that baby any day now, and the cap'n say he be here for that. Till then we wait and watch the best we can."

When Papa got Ben turned back toward the barns, I ran for the safety of the kitchen, where I found Belle. I flung myself around her waist and clung to her. Once again that night, everything terrified me. I lay awake in the dark next to Belle, trying to understand what had happened. I had no words to describe my fear, and I felt a terrible sense of foreboding.

I was happily distracted when, in late September, Dory delivered a baby girl. For the next few weeks, she was given the luxury of spending work time in the kitchen, and I was allowed to help care for her newborn.

She was named Sukey and was completely unlike the screaming baby Henry. This dark, round-faced child was like a doll to me, and I delighted in her. Mama took over for Dory in the big house and reported daily of dealing with the frustration of the bedridden Miss Martha.

"A couple more weeks and the baby will be here," Belle reminded Mama.

"And thank the Lawd the cap'n promise Miss Martha he home before that day," Mama said.

By now Fanny had almost exclusive responsibility for Miss Sally. Most afternoons she brought her to the kitchen area, where we three girls entertained her with play. The little girl had fallen in love with Dory's new baby and was thrilled when she was allowed to hold it. One morning she surprised all of us by appearing in the kitchen yard with Marshall in tow. As she pulled him forward, I saw her bracelet catch the sun. Fanny stood awkwardly behind them.

Ben, up from the barns, was behind the kitchen house, chopping wood for Belle's outdoor fire. Beattie and I were again his eager helpers, carrying the wood over for Belle's use as she stirred and cooked the first apple butter of the season.

"Can Marshall see the baby?" Sally asked Belle.

"You go ahead," Belle directed her. "Dory's in the kitchen house."

Marshall looked embarrassed but showed interest when Dory brought the baby to the door of the kitchen house for him to view. "It's nice," he said, sounding genuine.

"Thank you, Masta Marshall," Dory answered.

"Will our baby be like this?" Sally asked Marshall.

After a silence, Marshall shook his head. "No," he said.

"Why not?" asked Sally, surprised.

"It just won't," he mumbled as he turned pink.

"But I want a baby just like this one."

"Well, you can't have one," Marshall said, short with her now.

Sally began to wail. "I want a baby like this one."

Belle set aside the stirring paddle and

came to hunch down by Sally. "Where'd you get this pretty thing you have on your arm?" she asked in an effort to distract the child. It worked.

"My daddy gave it to me for Christmas. Look," Sally said, "it's a picture of him." She turned the painted miniature so Belle could have a better look. The charm was edged in gold and tied to her wrist with a pink velvet ribbon.

"This is so pretty," Belle said quietly.

"Come on, Sally, let's go." Marshall was impatient, tugging at her arm.

The little girl remembered the baby and pushed back at her brother. "Belle, can I have a baby like this one?" she said.

Belle reassured her, "Your mama's gonna have a pretty baby, nice as this one."

"Will she, Belle?" Sally asked.

Belle nodded. "Yes, she do."

"See," Sally said. "See. Belle said it will be just like this one."

Marshall glared at Belle, then walked away. His little sister, alert to her brother's unhappiness, ran after him. Fanny followed, but Beattie and I stayed back at the woodpile with Ben, watching them go up toward the big house. Sally reached the oak tree and scrambled onto her swing. "Marshall! Push me," she called, kicking out her feet.

Marshall ignored her and continued on toward the house.

Fanny went to her, but the child insisted that she wanted her brother. "Marshall! Come! Push me on the swing," she called to him.

He disregarded her appeals. Then the little girl caught sight of the tutor, standing at the back door of the big house, and she changed tactic.

"Mr. Waters, Mr. Waters," she called, "tell Marshall to push me on the swing."

Marshall stopped and looked up. He saw the tutor taking steps and quickly turned back toward Sally. When he reached the swing, Marshall grabbed hold of the seat and pushed fiercely, almost unseating the child.

"Marshall," the little girl called, "not so hard."

He pushed her again, harder still. Frightened, Sally kicked at him and called for him to stop, but he shoved again, as if fueled by his sister's cry. When Sally let out a shrill scream, Belle came running up the hill. Ben came, too, sprinting behind her. Belle called out for Marshall to stop, stop! Fanny ran at him and used the force of her body to throw him to the ground, but not before he was successful in a last hard shove. The swing flew and reached a pivotal height, then jerked before its descent.

No one was sure whether the child fell or jumped. When she landed, there was an audible snap; she lay still, her head pitched back from her body and her little arms stretched open as though to welcome the heavens.

Even the birds stopped singing.

CHAPTER EIGHT

Belle

The first time I see that little Sally, I don't like her just for being who she is. She's my sister, but I can't tell her that. And just because she's all white, she's never gonna be moved to the kitchen house like me. But this summer, after I come to know the child, I see she got the same ways as Beattie, smiling and happy to give what she has. After a time I come to like her and think, Maybe when she gets older, I'll tell her myself that we're sisters. But then, just like that, she's gone. After she dies, before the doctor gets here, Mama tells me to wash Sally and put on her best dress.

I say, "No, please, Mama, let Dory," but Mama Mae says, "Belle, you know how much Dory love that chil'. Besides, she nursin', and that maybe stop her milk." Then Mama looks at me real good before she says, "But you still want Dory to do it. I get her up here."

"No, Mama, you're right. I just don't like to touch something that don't have life in it."

"Nobody do," says Mama.

When I was washing that child, she feels soft like a baby bird. It don't seem right that she's going in the ground. When I clean her little arm, I take off the bracelet that has a likeness of the cap'n. I put it in my pocket, thinking it's mine now, but I start to cry and take it out again, because I know that thing was never mine, just like living in the big house is never gonna be mine. When Uncle comes, I'm crying so hard I jump when he touches my shoulder.

"Come, Belle," he says, "everybody die sometime or 'nother." But his own eyes was wet by the time we finish. "She a good lil girl," he says over and over. When we get done, I give him the bracelet. He looks at it, then he looks at me. He shakes his head real sad, like he knows everything I'm thinking, before he puts it in his pocket.

Chapter Nine

Lavinia

It was said that Miss Martha's screams for her daughter were heard by the workers all the way out in the fields. Immediately after Mama gave her the terrible news, Miss Martha went into labor.

Fanny, sure that she was the cause of Sally's death, couldn't stop shaking and wouldn't let go of Beattie. Mama had Dory take them down to the kitchen to give Fanny a drink of brandy, then to stay with her. Papa carried Miss Sally to the house, while the tutor took a stunned Marshall to his room. Uncle Jacob and Belle stayed with the child's lifeless body and waited while Ben rode out for the doctor. I was the only one left to help Mama when baby Campbell was born.

I stood back at the doorway, trembling, unsure if Miss Martha's agonized cries were for Sally or from the spasms that arched her swollen abdomen. Mama called me to her side, but when Miss Martha gave another ear-piercing scream, I froze, and my hands flew to my ears. Mama came to me and grabbed my arm. She whispered into my ear, "Miss Martha just lose one chil', you want her to lose this baby? You here to help, and you helpin' nobody when you actin' like this."

Mama's anger affected me more than the terror of Miss Martha's screams, so I accepted the damp cloth that Mama handed me. "Go dry her head, Abinia. Easy now, Miss Martha. Easy with the push, easy with the push, there we go."

From what I have since learned, it was a quick birth, but that afternoon Miss Martha's agony seemed to go on forever. Finally, the baby came.

"Abinia, give me the string, now take the scissor, cut here, don't worry, you not hurtin' him. All right, give me the blanket." My hands shook, but I was able to follow through.

The baby coughed and choked as Mama cleaned him, then he began to cry. Tears of relief and wonder rolled down my face, and helpless to stop them, I wiped them away with the back of my hand. Mama wrapped him in a blanket and took him to his mother.

"It a boy, Miss Martha," she said, "it a big strong boy."

"No!" Miss Martha pushed away Mama and the crying baby. She turned her face and closed her eyes.

"Here, Abinia, you hold him." Mama nodded me toward a chair. I sniffed loudly, and she whispered urgently, "Abinia. This no time for cryin'. You got to hold this baby tight. Come. I needin' you here."

Again I sobered. Determined to win Mama's approval, I reached for the baby. "I can hold him, Mama," I said. Instinctively, I began to rock him back and forth until he quieted. While Mama cared for Miss Martha, I looked at my charge. As his hands moved in the air, I noted his tiny fingernails and watched their purple color turn pink. I couldn't quite believe his miniature features, and when his eyes opened, they focused on me. His little mouth worked as though trying to speak, and from deep within me, love took hold.

Mama tried again and again to get Miss Martha to take her child; each time she rejected him, I couldn't wait to have him back in my arms. Mama's relief was evident when the doctor's carriage arrived. He stopped first at the nursery to see Miss Sally, then he came, white-faced, to see Miss

Martha. He examined her, though all the while she did not respond to his questions. After, the doctor took Mama aside. He pulled a brown bottle of dark liquid from his case and gave instructions. "You know how to use the drops, Mae," he said. "Give her enough to let her sleep until . . ." He nodded toward the nursery.

The baby began to fuss, and the doctor came over to where we sat. "You'll have to bring someone up from the quarters to feed him. Do you have anyone?" he asked Mama.

"My girl Dory got a new baby," said Mama quickly, "she feed this one, too."

The doctor examined the newborn; he rubbed the baby's fine blond hair, and I wondered if Miss Sally was going to think this baby was as pretty as Dory's. With a shock, I remembered that Miss Sally was dead.

"Masta Marshall needs lookin' at," Mama told the doctor. She led him across the hall and knocked until the tutor opened the door. Mr. Waters invited the doctor in but shut the door, leaving Mama Mae out. She returned, her face grim. A short while later, we heard both the doctor and tutor speaking as they went downstairs. When they closed the doors of the library behind them, Mama went across the hall to check on

Marshall but came back to say that he was sleeping. Then she took the baby from me and sent me to get Dory.

I don't know why I didn't go out the back door but went out through the front. Perhaps because it stood open; certainly, I was disoriented from the day's trauma. I stopped for a minute on the front porch, surprised at the normalcy of a golden sunset. I walked down the front steps past the side of the house, then hung back, frightened to turn the corner. I knew the oak tree with the hanging swing waited there, and I didn't want to see it. I paused under the open window of the library. The boxwoods had grown high, and although no one inside could see me, I was able to clearly distinguish the voice of Mr. Waters.

"It was that Ben fellow from the barns," he said. "He has no business with the children, but there is no one, it seems, who can control him. He has the run of the place, and more times than not, he is sitting behind that woodpile, sleeping. I don't know why he took it upon himself to put that little girl on the swing and push her like that. I don't suppose he meant to kill her, but the way he was pushing that swing, I don't know what he was trying to do."

I ran then to the kitchen, wanting to tell

Dory about the tutor's conversation with the doctor, but when I arrived, Dory, still in shock from Sally's death, was in such a state that she told me to shush. I remembered my original purpose. "Dory, Mama wants you," I said urgently. Dory was trying to prepare the evening meal while her own baby, Sukey, was fussing to be fed. "What!" she asked. "What she wantin'? She know I got enough to do, tryin' to keep up down here!"

I insisted that Mama needed her up in the big house to feed the new baby. Dory glared at me, slammed down a bowl, then picked up her own baby and left for the big house with me following close behind.

The cry of Miss Martha's newborn greeted us. Mama had him in her arms when she met us in the blue sitting room directly off the mistress's bedroom. There, at Mama's instruction, Dory reluctantly put Miss Martha's baby to her breast. I went over, anxious to see him fed. As he eagerly suckled, Sukey began to fuss in Mama's arms.

"Mama," Dory said, "how this can be? My Henry gone, lil Sally gone, and now this one." She looked over at her own child, crying in her mother's arms. Angrily, she looked down at the nursing infant. "He

110

nursin' like this his right." She began to sob. "I don't wanna do this, Mama."

Mama pulled her chair close. She spoke quietly but firmly. "Come on, chil'. Don't you forget, this all workin' for you. It keep them needin' you up in this house. Stop your cryin' now. He got a right to live, same as you and me. A baby don't need you cryin' when you feeds him. You don't want nobody sayin' that your milk no good. Next thing you know, they get somebody else in here. You sing to him. That make the milk settle good." Mama rocked Sukey until she quieted. "You feed this new baby first, he need the milk. Then you feed your own sweet chil'," she said, hugging Dory's baby. "You got plenty to give the two of them. All you got to do is eat more."

Dory sniffed hard. "I try, Mama," she said.

I could scarcely wait for Dory to finish so I could hold Miss Martha's baby again.

Mama Mae praised me for my help and said that I had done very well for my age. I reminded her that I was already eight years old. She shook her head and wondered out loud how she could have forgotten that. She said I was so good with the new baby that she thought maybe I could stay with him the next day. Eagerly, I reassured her that I

111

could, and I held the baby in my arms with great care as she set up a nursery in the blue room.

The overseer wrote Ben a pass, and he left on horseback to take word of Sally's death to the captain. Early the next morning a minister arrived, and a few neighbors came in carriages and in wagons. They brought food, and Mama was kept busy running back and forth to the kitchen, then back up to check on Miss Martha. Finally, Mama asked if I thought I could give the mistress her medicine when she awoke. Although apprehensive about this new request, I was eager to continue winning praise from Mama, so I agreed. Mama measured the dose and left it with careful instruction, assuring me that I would not be alone for long, as Dory was coming soon to feed the baby.

The baby was sleeping in his crib, so I looked into the bedroom. When I saw Miss Martha stir, then open her eyes, I did not hesitate and carried the drink to her. She seemed to know what I offered and drank eagerly.

Then she rested her head back on the pillows and, with a sigh, dropped her arms on either side of her thin body. Her wrists lay exposed, and blue veins pulsed under her white skin. At that moment she looked as fragile as her newborn. She did not wear a nightcap, and her thick red hair framed her delicate face. Her eyes, green as grass, settled on me.

"Isabelle?" she asked. She reached for my hand, and I let her touch me. When her eyes closed and I moved to leave, she called me back. "Isabelle."

"I'm Lavinia," I said.

"Don't go," she said.

Recognizing her helplessness, I was no longer afraid and stayed to hold her hot dry hand. She did not address me again but stared past me until her eyes closed and she fell into a deep sleep.

I was not a part of the services they had for Miss Sally, and I did not witness the burial, though sometime later, Belle took me to the small cemetery. It was located a short distance from the house, on the other side of the orchard. We passed through a black iron gate set in a stone wall and sat together on a wooden bench inside the enclosure. I was surprised at how peaceful it was. "Why didn't they put baby Henry here?" I wanted to know, finding comfort in the idea of the two innocents resting together.

"This place is only for the people of the

big house," Belle explained. "My grandma's here." She went over to a very large headstone. She rubbed her hand along the side of it.

"Where is your mama?" I asked.

"She's down same place as baby Henry," she said.

"Will you go here when you die?" I asked Belle.

"No," she said sharply, "I told you, only the people from the big house go here." She added, as though to soften her words, "I don't know what they'll do with me, Lavinia. Maybe just put me under the kitchen house." She leaned down to look at Miss Sally's headstone.

"What does it say?" I asked, confused and eager to change the subject.

" 'Sally Pyke,' " Belle began, and as she traced the letters with her fingers, tears rolled down her face. " 'Sally Pyke, Beloved Daughter of James and Martha Pyke.' "

Over the next days, the doctor visited Miss Martha again and gave instructions for the opium to be continued until the captain's return. "Let her sleep," the doctor advised Mama Mae.

"This drink mix her up in the head," Mama told him.

"That will sort out," the doctor reassured her. "Continue to give it to her."

After Miss Martha drank the mixture, it often took a while before she slept again. When awake, she regressed to childhood, and for her, I took on the persona of her young sister Isabelle. As the medication took effect, it wasn't unusual for Miss Martha to have me sit beside her on the edge of her bed. She would undo my braids and nervously untangle my hair, smoothing it until she soothed herself to sleep.

Dory fed the baby and kept him clean, but I was the one who loved him. I held him at every opportunity, and when alone with him, I hugged him and nuzzled my nose in his soft neck to breathe in his sweet fragrance.

The day after the funeral, I was sitting alone in the blue room, holding him. He was awake and gazing at me when, with a sudden sharp memory, I remembered a baby brother of mine, one born in Ireland. One who had died.

"I'm going to call you Campbell," I whispered as memories washed over me. "Campbell," I repeated. He grasped my finger and clung to it. "You are my pretty boy," I cooed. I jumped when a voice interrupted.

"I need to see my mother." Marshall stood

at the open door.

"She's sleeping," I said. I hadn't seen Marshall since Sally fell off the swing. His pale face showed his deep misery, and I felt pity for him. "Come see the baby," I said. To my surprise, he came. "See how fat he is?" I pushed back the covers to show his healthy arms and legs.

In spite of his reticence, Marshall knelt beside the chair. "What's his name?" he asked.

"Campbell," I said, trying it out. I held up one of the baby's feet. "Look at his little toes."

Marshall took the baby's foot gently in his hand.

"You can kiss it," I said.

"No!" As though touched by a hot poker, he pulled his hand back. His head dropped, and I thought he was about to cry.

"Marshall, you didn't mean to hurt Sally," I said, wanting to comfort him.

His shoulders slumped, and he looked up at me helplessly. He was about to speak when his mother called from her bedroom. "Isabelle. Isabelle."

Marshall leaped up. "Who is she calling for?" he asked.

"For me," I said.

"Is that your name?"

"No," I said, "I'm Lavinia, but your mother believes I'm Isabelle. Mama Mae thinks that's her sister."

Although I wouldn't have thought it possible, his face lost even more color. "It is," he said, but added with disgust, "She's dead!" He left and slammed the door behind him.

The captain arrived the next afternoon. Dory was in the blue room, feeding the baby, and I was sitting on the edge of the bed next to Miss Martha. She was near sleep, and I sat with her hand in my lap.

"Martha," the captain said, standing in the doorway.

His powerful presence frightened me, and I felt I could not leave fast enough, but Miss Martha gripped my hand.

"Martha," he said again, his voice catching, and I pulled away as he strode toward us. He smelled strongly of grime and horses, but when he sat and gathered her to him, she burrowed her face into his neck.

"James," she whispered, and the anguish seemed fresh when she began to call out her daughter's name. My own throat stinging with tears, I left as he tried to soothe her.

■ ■ ■ ■

The next evening Marshall joined his parents in the bedroom for a light supper. Miss Martha remained in bed but was propped up to eat. Mama served the meal while Dory and I cared for the baby in the adjoining room. Uncle Jacob was setting a fire in the fireplace when Belle burst into the blue room.

"Mama," she called, "Mama, they have Ben! Get the cap'n!"

Mama came running with the captain and Marshall following behind.

"Belle," the captain said. "Quiet! Please! Martha's been —"

"They have Ben!" she said.

"What?" The captain looked back protectively toward his wife's bedroom.

"They took Ben," Belle cried. "Rankin and the patrollers are with him. They're all drinking. They're saying that Ben killed Sally."

Stunned, Mama sat down on the blue silk chair.

"They tied him up to take him," Belle said. "You got to go get him! They're gonna kill him!"

"Calm down, Belle," the captain said.

"What are you saying? Why would they think that Ben —"

Marshall stepped back when the tutor appeared in the doorway. Belle swung toward Mr. Waters. "You!" she said. "They're saying you told them that Ben killed Sally."

The tutor frowned disbelievingly.

"What's this about? Someone tell me what this is about!" the captain shouted.

The tutor addressed Belle. "I spoke to no one about your lover. I was not even witness to the accident. I can only repeat what Master Marshall has told me, and he informed me that Ben pushed Miss Sally off the swing."

We all looked to Marshall. They were going to hurt Ben! I knew the tutor was lying. Why didn't Marshall speak up?

"Marshall?" his father roared.

Marshall's panicked stare went from his father to the tutor.

"Just tell the truth, Marshall," Mr. Waters said.

Marshall's eyes remained fixed on the tutor.

"They'll kill Ben!" Belle was frantic. "Marshall, please. Tell the cap'n! Tell him you pushed Sally."

Belle's terror for Ben became my own.

"Who was pushing the swing?" the captain

119

bellowed.

"Marshall was," I blurted out. "We all saw him. But he wasn't trying to hurt her." I ran to Mama.

"Belle?" the captain asked her. "Belle?"

"It was Marshall!" she said. "Please! Go! They'll kill him."

Her words propelled the captain into action. We watched as he swung from the room and ran downstairs to the library, where he unlocked the gun case. After he handed Papa George one of the rifles, they galloped off, the night lit blue from another full moon.

It was almost dawn when the captain returned to his sleeping wife. He woke me as he passed through the blue room, where I slept alongside Campbell's crib. I wanted to follow him and ask about Ben, but I dared not. Instead, I watched as he went to the head of the tall post bed, its blue and white curtains pulled back. He leaned to kiss Miss Martha, then gently shook her arm, but she slept an opium sleep. When she didn't respond, he straightened up. He gazed down at her for a long time before he went to the dressing table. There he lifted up the glass bottle, shook it, then sighed deeply and sat on the small chair beside the dressing table.

He set the bottle down, but when I heard his sharp intake of breath, I guessed at what he next saw. On the day of Sally's funeral, while the mistress slept, Uncle had carefully placed the piece the captain now reached for. It was the porcelain miniature of her father that someone had untied from the little girl's wrist.

The captain drew the bracelet to his chest. As though the pink ribbon pierced his heart, he moaned and leaned over. When he straightened again, he brought the piece to his lips.

Campbell stirred and began to cry. I picked him up and walked with him until he quieted. When I looked up, the captain was standing in the doorway.

"Is Ben all right?" I couldn't hold back the question any longer.

The captain looked at me as though surprised at my interest. "He'll recover," he said. He came forward and awkwardly took the baby from me. "Who's feeding him?" he asked.

"Dory," I answered. "She's coming right away."

"Good," he said. "What's his name?"

"Campbell," I answered.

"Campbell. Campbell?" he repeated.

Before I could explain, before I could tell

him that I had named the baby, Dory appeared.

"How's Ben?" the captain asked. "Did they stop the bleeding?"

"Yes," Dory said, "but he cryin' out from it hurtin' so bad." Her hands trembled as she took the baby from the captain.

The captain went back into his wife's bedroom and returned with the bottle of opium. "Take this to Mae," he instructed me. "Tell her to give some of this to Ben."

I took the bottle and ran, anxious to see Ben myself. Day was breaking, and Uncle Jacob was returning from Mama's house. He nodded at me when he met me on the porch landing. A brilliant sunrise in a cloudless sky threw gold on our small world. Smoke curled reassuringly from Belle's kitchen chimney, and I sighed with relief to see that another day's routine had begun. "Is Ben all right, Uncle?" I asked.

Uncle Jacob looked off into the distance. "That up to Ben," he said. "Now he have the fear. If he put that fear into hisself, nothin' make him happy. If he put the fear back into the world, everythin' be a reason to fight." He breathed in deeply as he raised his arms. "You and me, we give this to Allah," he said. "We say, 'Allah, take this fear from Ben.' " He bowed his head and raised it again. His arms remained outstretched as he looked around. "We see the sun, we see the trees, we see the new day. We say, 'Thank you, Allah. Thank you for helpin' our boy.' " Tears rolled down his face, and he bowed once again. Then he lowered his arms and dried his eyes.

Wanting to please Uncle, I, too, leaned toward the sun. "Thank you, Allah," I said, "and make sure you listen to Uncle Jacob."

"You a blessin', Abinia," Uncle said, gifting me with a smile before I ran off to Mama's house.

When I got to Mama's cabin, I heard Ben calling out in pain. I was so frightened that I could scarcely knock at the door and was relieved when Mama came and refused me entry. I handed her the drops, then ran quickly to the safety of the kitchen house. Belle's eyes were swollen from crying, but she gave me some milk and corn bread, then rebraided my hair and had me wash up. While she did this, I asked about Ben, but she dismissed my questions by telling me that he would soon be all right. Certain of Ben's safety, I was exuberant in my relief. I chattered away, telling her about my conversation with Uncle Jacob, which led me to ask her who Allah was. She told me that Allah was Uncle's god, like the Lawd was Mama's god.

"Who is yours?" I wanted to know.

"Both," she said. She looked at me in puzzlement. "You don't talk this much since you get here."

I smiled but had no answer. I could not explain to her my happiness. I knew only that Ben was back, and up in the big house, I had a baby to love. One who needed me.

Chapter Ten

Belle

Just one bad thing happening after another. First little Sally, then they get Ben.

Last night out of nowhere, they come for Ben. Who's leading the pack but that overseer, that dirty Rankin. Four men jump Ben when he comes out of the pig barn. They tie him and ride off before Papa or Jimmy get there to stop them. I don't wait. I run for the cap'n. He takes Papa and they ride out. They get to Ben after the men had him down to nothing, after they took all his clothes, just for ugly.

"Nigga, you confess or we gonna kill you," they say, but Ben says he knows they're gonna kill him, don't matter what he say.

He asks, "What I do? What I do?"

"You kill that little white gal," they say.

"I don't know what you talkin' about," Ben says, but they get him down, kicking at him, telling him to say he done it.

"Here," one of them says, "here, use this." He takes one of Ben's horse nails he carries in his pocket. "Take his ear off. That'll get him to talk."

Everybody knows, over at the courthouse, when a Negro done wrong, they nail the ear to the tree before they cut it off. So that's what they do to Ben. They get his one ear off, and they're getting set to do the other one, but the cap'n get there and shoots the top of the tree.

"Loose that man!" says the cap'n. "He's my property."

They're all drinking and don't want to stop, but Papa George lifts his gun and gets ready to fire. The cap'n says, "Easy, George, just keep that gun steady for them to see. Let me try to work this out." The cap'n gets down from his horse and goes over to the men. He knows them good enough to say their names.

Rankin steps out. "Cap'n, I'm just doing my job, taking this boy in."

"Rankin. Gentlemen," the cap'n say, "I'm afraid there's been a misunderstanding. My man here did nothing wrong."

They don't want to give Ben up, but they know he's the cap'n's property. Rankin's smart enough to know to stand with the cap'n, so he tells the men to go on. He says

126

he'll help the cap'n settle this at home.

Blood is pumping from where Ben's ear is off, and Papa tears his shirt to wrap it tight. "Ben not hisself," Papa says. "He just walkin' in circles, sayin', 'Papa, where my clothes, where my clothes?' "

In all that mess, Ben won't get up on the horse until his clothes was back on. The cap'n took Rankin's horse for Ben and told that overseer to walk. Everybody knows that Rankin's gonna take this out on somebody down the road.

My Ben don't want me to see him, but I go over anyway. He won't look at me and keeps his eyes closed. I helped Mama to get the bleeding stopped, but back in my kitchen house, all I can do is cry for what he looks like. He's still my Benny, but not his pretty self. Why did they do this to him?

Next day, when I'm getting dinner on, the cap'n comes down here, banging open the door. "What did Waters mean when he said that you had a lover?"

"I don't know," I say, scared. I never did see the cap'n mad at me like this before.

"Is it Mae's boy he's talking about? Is it Ben?"

I shake my head. "I don't know what that tutor's talking about."

"I'd sell him if I thought he touched you!"

"Ben don't do nothing to me," I say.

"Belle, this has been put off too long. I'm getting your papers in order. In summer you'll go up north. I'll find the right husband for you. I won't have you ruining your life here."

"But I want to stay! This is my home! I have Mama and Papa here. Dory and the girls, they're like sisters to me."

"They are my slaves!"

I get mad. "Are you forgetting about my mama? She was your slave, too. You bring slaves on your ship! You sell them!"

"No! Never on my ship. I never brought them over."

"But you bought them! They're yours. Except for Rankin, everybody down in the quarters is a slave."

"My father bought all of them," the cap'n says. "He needed them to get this place started. And you know I need them now to keep it going."

I breathe in a couple times, trying to slow my mouth. "First you say that I can't stay in your big house. Now you say I can't stay in my kitchen house. Why do you always got to keep me moving?"

"Belle," he say, his voice going soft, "I

want a good life for you. You are my daughter."

Hoh! He calls me his daughter, and all the time he's got me working down here in the kitchen house! "So if I die, do I go in the ground next to Miss Sally, or do you put me in the ground down by the quarters?"

"You go too far! By next summer I'll have you out of here. In the meantime, you stay away from that man."

"Ben a good man, Cap'n," I try again.

"Listen, Belle. I've instructed Rankin to watch out for him. He'll take action if need be. I warn you, Belle, the consequences will be harsh."

"Please," I say.

"Belle! Enough! I just lost . . . I have to leave in the morning, and I need to know that this matter is settled."

First time ever, I see he's looking older than his fifty-some years. "Are you leaving again? This quick?" I say.

"I have no choice, Belle. But I know it's time for me to come back here to run this place. Martha can't keep going like this, and Marshall —"

"That tutor's not right with Marshall," I say.

The cap'n hold up his hand. "I don't want

129

to hear anything more about Marshall. If nothing else, he needs dicipline."

"But —"

"Belle," he stops me, "no more! Now give me your word that you will not allow that man around you."

And so I do.

CHAPTER ELEVEN

Lavinia

The afternoon following Ben's return, I was
sent up again to the big house to sit with
Campbell. The house was quiet, and I was
dozing alongside the baby until I was
awakened by the captain's voice on the
upstairs landing. "Where are you going?"

"Under the circumstances, I felt it best if
I sought employment elsewhere." I recognized the tutor's voice.

"Listen, Waters," said the captain, "this is
a difficult time. I can't afford any further
disruption in my household. I have to leave
again tomorrow; I have a crew to settle with,
a cargo to unload, repairs to see to. I'll be
back in less than two months, certainly by
Christmas. I would appreciate it if you
would consider staying at least until then.
My son clearly needs a firm hand. Martha
can't deal with him right now. Besides, I
believe her indulgence is a great part of the

problem."

"I do feel responsible for my part in his misrepresentation in the death of —" the tutor started.

"That rests with my son," the captain interrupted. "He must learn to be accountable."

"Yes," said Waters. "I feel it my obligation to tell you that since my arrival, I have been aware of Master Marshall's need for strong guidance. Your house servants and those at the barn favor the boy, and I am reluctant to say they have tried on occasion to interfere."

"I will speak to them. How is he doing with his studies?" the captain asked.

"Poorly, I'm afraid," the tutor replied. "He is not used to discipline, and his attention is easily distracted."

"If you are willing to stay, I give you full authority to use whatever measures you feel necessary to guide him."

There was a pause before the tutor replied. "Captain, under the circumstances, I feel duty-bound to continue on here with my services. I will do my utmost to help Master Marshall."

"Good. Good," the captain replied. "It's time the boy was taken in hand." He called for Jacob then, and when Uncle Jacob came, the captain asked him to take the tutor's bags back to his room and unpack for him.

"Yes, Cap'n," I heard Uncle Jacob's quiet reply.

On the morning of his departure, the captain came to talk to Dory and Mama in the blue room. "I don't want Miss Martha to have the laudanum anymore," he said. "She'll never get well if she keeps sleeping like this."

"The doctor say she needin' those drops," Mama replied.

"I don't care what the doctor said. I say she is not to have them any longer!"

"Yes, Cap'n," Mama said.

"Mae," he said, "I'm counting on you. Mr. Waters will take Marshall in hand. I leave you to watch over Miss Martha and Campbell." He nodded toward the cradle.

"Cap'n," Mama Mae said, looking back toward the door, "I got to talk to you about Marshall and Mr. Wat—"

The captain cut her off. "Waters has agreed to stay on. He is in charge of Marshall. I need you and the others to let Waters do his job."

"But Cap'n —" Mama tried, but again he interrupted.

"Mae! Not now. He has told me there has

been interference, and I won't have it! Everything stands as it is until I am home again at Christmas." He walked quickly to the bedroom door and looked in at his sleeping wife before he left.

After he was gone, Mama asked Dory, "What the cap'n call that baby?"

Dory shrugged.

"Campbell," I said.

Mama Mae puckered her face. "Where he get that name?"

Dory grimaced in reply.

I was silent.

A routine was soon established. First thing in the morning, I was sent to help Dory care for the babies in the blue room. When Miss Martha rose and sat in a chair for her breakfast, Mama changed the bed linen, and I was given the chore of assisting Miss Martha with her morning toilette. Though I was proud of my new responsibilities, I was often unsure what to do, and I constantly looked to Mama Mae for direction. In those first weeks, Miss Martha was dreadfully unhappy. She continually demanded more drops, but though Mama maintained a pretense of giving a large dosage, I had no doubt that she was keeping her resolve to follow the captain's orders. Gradually, as the tonics lessened in strength, a new, more stable Miss Martha began to emerge. When she walked about the room, she often stopped to stare out the window. The first time I saw her standing there, I sensed rather than heard her sob. Thinking that she was missing Sally, I went, uncoached, to stand quietly at her side. She looked down at me and stroked my head. "Dear Isabelle," she said.

Daily, my compassion for the woman grew, but as it did, I felt disloyal to Belle. I did not fully understand Belle's reasons for her anger toward Miss Martha and one day questioned her about it.

"You'll see everything when you're old enough," Belle instructed. "When you're up in the big house, just do like Mama say." Those words served me well, for in the end, the woman I most wanted to please was Mama Mae.

Miss Martha still showed little interest in Campbell, though he was brought to her at least twice a day. When pressed, she held him, but the moment he fussed, she handed him back and asked that he be taken from the room.

She made no mention of Marshall until one morning in November, when he appeared in the doorway of her bedroom. I was removing pins from Miss Martha's hair, and Mama was straightening the bed.

"Hello, Marshall," his mother greeted him, sounding genuinely happy to see him. "Goodness," she added more soberly, "you've . . . grown so tall."

At thirteen, he was lanky, and his arms hung much longer than his sleeves. But dark circles shadowed his intense blue eyes; and his hair was chopped close to his head unevenly, as though he might have done the deed himself without benefit of a mirror. He closed the door quickly. "Mother," he said, approaching her swiftly, "I want to stop."

"Stop what, dear?" she asked.

"My studies." He glanced back at the door.

"Oh, Marshall," she said, "you know you must study. Your father has hired the ahh . . . Mr. . . . Ahhh . . ."

"Waters!" Marshall whispered fiercely. "His name is Waters!"

"Of course," Miss Martha said.

"Please, Mother," Marshall began to plead, "send me away to school."

"Why do you want to do that, Marshall? Where is Mr. Waters?" Miss Martha asked. "Would you like me to speak to him? Is he too demanding?"

"No," Marshall said, looking back to the door. "Don't tell him I came to you."

"Where he now?" Mama Mae asked, shaking out the white bedcover.

"He's out," Marshall said.

"He out with Rankin?" Mama Mae asked Marshall, but her eyes were on Miss Martha.

"That's none of your business!" Marshall was suddenly furious.

"Marshall!" his mother said sharply. "You apologize."

"Why? What can she do anyway? She's just a nigra!" His face went bright pink, and without warning, he picked up his mother's drinking glass and threw it at Mama. She dodged, and it flew past her to hit the wall. Miss Martha rose swiftly to clutch Marshall's arm. In a rage, he swung her away, throwing her against the dressing table. She tried to catch herself as her hand slid the length of the table, toppling a silver mirror and sending her porcelain and glass treasures crashing to the floor. Somehow she grasped hold and kept herself upright. Marshall stilled in the silence that followed. When his mother uttered his name in disbelief, he looked about as though lost. Then, like one defeated, he left the room.

■ ■ ■ ■

That night, after the mistress was settled, Mama and I came to the kitchen to pick up the stew Belle had prepared for supper.

"You come eat with us tonight," Mama invited Belle.

"Thank you, Mama, but I think I'll stay here tonight," Belle said.

"You feelin' all right?" Mama asked.

"Uh-huh," Belle said, rubbing at a stain on her apron. "Uncle Jacob's coming here later."

Mama studied Belle. "It be all right with you, Abinia come eat with us?"

"Of course it's all right, Mama."

"I send her back with Ben after we eat."

"She's big enough to run back by herself." Belle would not meet Mama's questioning eyes.

"That be fine, Belle," Mama finally said, motioning for me to come with her.

The twins were waiting on the steps of their cabin as Mama and I approached. This family seemed a world apart from the big house, and I left the worries of that day behind when I joined them. Papa George was coming up from the barns, and the twins and I ran down to greet him. He leaned down for Beattie to climb onto his back, then he reached both arms out for Fanny and me to pull him up the hill. Once there, he shrugged us off and straightened up.

"You're nothin' but a big old chil' yourself," Mama scolded. "Now go wash up."

"First I get a kiss from my womans," he said, reaching for Mama. She brushed him away but laughed with us when he squeezed her in a hug.

Inside, I happily helped the girls pull their playthings from the shelf. Papa sat at the table and talked to Mama as she prepared corn bread for our meal. "Marshall say the Waters man with that Rankin again today," Mama said.

"They takin' the food those poor niggas supposed to get, and they sellin' it," Papa said.

"How you know?" asked Mama.

"I talk with the mens," said Papa. "They ain't gettin' what the cap'n say they supposed to get. Those two even startin' to go after the womans down —"

Mama looked over at us and shook her head at Papa just as Ben opened the door. I had not seen him since his abduction, and I was unprepared for the shock of his mutilation.

A dark angry wound had replaced his ear, but worse, that side of his face and neck was so badly swollen that I scarcely knew it was him. I stared in horror.

"Abinia!" he said in happy surprise, until he saw my distress. He walked to the bench by the table and sat, then called me over. I stuffed my thumb into my mouth and shook my head, refusing him. "Come here, Birdie," he said, reaching out for my hand. Reluctantly, I walked to him. He gently pulled me around and angled his injured side away from me. "See," he said, "I still Ben."

I recognized him then. When I burst into tears, he lifted me onto his lap, and I hid against his great chest. He covered my head with his large hand and gave me shelter while I grieved for what had been done to him.

"I gonna look better in time," he soothed, and he had me settled by the time Mama served our meal. Everyone ate quietly until Ben asked for Belle.

"She stay back," Mama answered. "She say Jacob comin' by."

"When I done, I take Abinia back," Ben said, looking at Mama.

"I don't know, Ben," said Mama, "somethin' not sittin' right with Belle since the cap'n leave."

■ ■ ■ ■

There was no moon, and it was a dark night, but I felt safe when Ben held my hand and walked me across the yard after supper.

"Does your head hurt, Ben?" I asked.

"Yup, it do, but it gettin' better," he said.

"Do you want me to get you some more drops?" I asked.

He laughed. "How you gonna do that?"

"I'll ask Miss Martha," I said.

"Why, I sure do thank you, Birdie, for lookin' out for me, but I think I gonna be all right." He squeezed my hand.

When we got to the kitchen door, Belle came and, avoiding Ben, abruptly took me in.

"So. Now I too ugly-lookin' to you?" he asked, then turned and left before she could answer. Stricken, Belle called out after him, but he did not turn back. She sent me up to bed, but later, when I heard her sobbing, I crept down.

"What's wrong, Belle?" I asked.

"Go back upstairs," she cried, "go to sleep."

I hesitated, then used what I knew would get her attention. "Today Marshall pushed Miss Martha, and she fell."

141

It worked. Belle stopped crying. "What?" she asked.

I repeated myself. Belle blew her nose, then patted the seat beside her. "Come here," she said. "Now what're you saying?"

I was relieved to tell all. Belle was silent when she took my hand and entwined my fingers with her own. "It's good you're telling me this," she said, looking me over. "You're getting to be a big help."

"I'm eight already," I reminded her.

"You too big to sit in my lap?" she asked. I shook my head, pleased. "Come," she said. I had grown since my arrival, but I was still thin as a twig, and she lifted me easily. I rested my head on her shoulder, and we stayed nestled that way in front of the embers for a long time.

Dory and I were sitting together in the blue room, and while Dory fed Campbell, I held Sukey. It was an early week in December, the first hog-killing day. I asked Dory why there was such excitement about the event.

It was a break for those in the quarters, she explained, and they looked forward to a feast when they finished. Also, during this week, they were given extra meat with their rations of cornmeal.

"Otherwise, do they only eat cornmeal?" I asked.

No, she said, they were also given a weekly ration of salt pork. Most everyone in the quarters had small gardens where they grew greens, sweet potatoes, field peas, and beans, and some, she said, even had a few chickens.

"Why don't they get food from the big house?" I asked. I had gone with Belle often enough to the storage rooms in the basement of the big house, and I knew of the abundance there.

"They jus' don't." She sighed. "Belle right. You sure askin' a lot of questions these days." That ended our conversation. I was beginning to see that questions about the quarters were discouraged, and if an adult's answer was forthcoming, it was clear that the subject made them uncomfortable.

As the babies settled for their nap, Dory suggested that I go down to help Mama and Belle in the kitchen house, where the work had already started. I was eager to go but first had the chore of emptying the chamber pot from under Miss Martha's bed. Carrying the lidded porcelain pot, I headed down the back stairs and outdoors toward the nearest privy. There were two outdoor toilets. The one for the house servants was at the back of Mama's house. The one I now went to, the one used by people from the big house, was located in a more secluded area back by the orchard.

The early-morning air smelled clean and crisp, and I was happy to be outdoors. I walked slowly, swishing through the fallen leaves. By the time I was within sight of the privy, the chamber pot had grown heavy, and I set it down for a rest. Under a nearby tree, I noticed an overlooked red apple nestled in the brown leaves. My mouth watered for it, but I decided to pick it up on my return and share the treat with the twins. All at once I heard unfamiliar sounds coming from the privy.

I thought I recognized Marshall's voice, but the sounds were oddly disturbing. Instinctively, I ran behind the protection of the garden fence. I hunched down and peered through a gap between the boards. When the privy door swung open, the tutor stood in the doorway. Then he turned back, kicked at something on the floor, and said for it to get up. Somehow I knew it was Marshall. I pulled back when the man scanned the area, and I didn't dare look again until he was up at the big house. I waited until he was inside before I cautiously ran to the privy. When I peeked in, I found Marshall, partially clothed, sitting in the corner on the floor. He looked dazed, and when I called his name, he didn't seem to hear me. For some reason, I ran out for the apple, and when I returned, I offered it to him.

"Here, Marshall, you can have this," I said. He didn't appear to notice. I picked up his hand and tried to place the apple in it, but his fingers refused to close. "Here, Marshall," I said, "you eat this, and I'll get Papa." When he still didn't respond, I took a small bite and placed the piece in his mouth.

"Chew it," I instructed, and when he slowly began to do so, I again placed the apple in his hand. This time his fingers closed around it. "I'll come back with Papa," I said, and I left him then.

I flew through the orchard, past the gardens and the far side of the kitchen house. When I rounded the corncrib, I stopped. Horrified, I couldn't move forward. I had arrived in the barnyard where the men were butchering pigs. My eyes fixed on a barrow, already dead, hanging from one leg and suspended over a steaming pit of hot water. Beyond it was one hanging from a pole, its belly splayed open. When I saw a third, its neck dripping blood into a pan underneath,

I felt myself begin to sway.

"Abinia! What you doin' here?" Ben's angry voice brought me back. He shook my shoulders until I centered on him. "You get back to the house, this no place for you," he said.

"Papa?" I said.

"What's wrong, Abinia?"

"Papa?" I said. "Where's Papa?"

"He with Rankin." Ben pulled me back behind the corncrib. He scrunched down to meet my eyes. "What goin' on, Abinia?" he asked. "Why you wantin' Papa?"

"It's Marshall," I said. "He's sick. He's in the privy and can't get up. He won't talk."

"What?" Ben asked.

"The tutor," I said. "He was kicking him out in the privy."

Ben's look frightened me, and I was reminded of the day he had carried his sledgehammer up from the barns. He looked around. "Don't go to Papa, he with Rankin. I see to Marshall. You get Mama, she in the kitchen. Send her to me."

When Ben sprinted off, I headed back for the kitchen house. When I arrived in the yard, I saw more of the pig slaughter, but this sight was less disturbing. Here the women from the quarters worked on long planks that served as worktables, cutting up

146

portions of fresh meat to prepare for the smokehouse. I saw Mama Mae at one of the tables, working and laughing with the others. She turned impatiently when I pulled at her arm, but when she saw my face, she leaned down.

"Ben wants you," I whispered loudly.

"Ben?" She looked puzzled, then alarmed.

"He's with Marshall in the privy," I said. "The tutor hurt him."

Mama Mae dropped the small handsaw she had been working with, went to Belle, whispered something to her, then hurried off.

It was midmorning before Mama came back, and when she did, she had lost her earlier good cheer. She took Belle aside before she hurriedly went back to working outdoors with the other women, but after that, Belle, too, became serious.

"Is Marshall all right?" I asked.

"Ben's staying up there with him," she said.

I was relieved to know that Marshall was safe with Ben, though I felt that something still was very wrong. Soon, though, Fanny distracted me. She was back to her old self, making Beattie and me laugh at her antics. First she pulled a pig's tongue from a bucket and stole up behind us, relishing our squeals of disgust. Then, from outdoors, she found two pigs' ears and hooked them between her braids. It took a minute before we noticed her standing in the doorway, the pigs' ears flopping over her own.

"Fanny, you're something else," Belle said, shaking her head but smiling in spite of herself.

"Well, now, isn't it nice to see everybody having fun." Rankin, the overseer, watched from the doorway, but his hard eyes glinted with something other than amusement. Grayish strands of hair clumped and hung to his shoulders, and his brown clothes were bloodied from the slaughter. He hooked his thumbs into the waist of his pants, and I noticed the caked dirt under his long fingernails. He eyed Belle from head to toe before he paced off the kitchen, making a point to carefully look in all the corners. "I'm looking for that Ben boy. Good to see he's not hiding in this kitchen," he said.

"Mr. Rankin, can I get you something?" Belle asked.

"Where'd a little nigra like you learn to speak so nice?" he said. "You almost sound like a white woman. Hell, you almost look like a white woman. I can see why the captain wants to keep you for himself."

Belle looked him over as she might a bug. When she walked past him toward the door, he caught her arm. "Now, I didn't mean to scare you off none," he said.

Belle stared down at his hand on her arm until he released it. "There's plenty of work to be doing," she said.

"I was hoping you'd have a little drink with me tonight. Maybe after the dance?" He winked at her.

She walked out.

"Well now," he said, "that's one high-thinkin' nigra. I'm guessing I just might have to bring her down a notch or two. Don't you think so?" He slammed his fist on the table and shouted again, "Don't you think so?" We jumped, and he laughed. "Now, that's the way I like my women. They need to know who's boss."

When Mama Mae walked in, she looked surprised to see him, though all along I had seen her shadow outside the door.

"Why, Mr. Rankin," Mama said, "it good to see you here in the kitchen."

"I'm looking for that boy of yours. Where's Ben? I ain't seen hide nor hair of him for some time now," he said.

"Mr. Rankin, I sure not surprised you don't find the peoples that you wants. You so busy, I don't know how you do everythin' you do. It a mighty long day for you."

"It's a busy day, all right," he acknowl-edged.

"You a mighty good overseer," said Mama. "That cap'n sure do the right thing when he brings you to this place. George sayin' all the time, 'Cap'n, that Mr. Rankin sure get the work done.' "

"Well now, I'm happy to hear that, Mae."

Mama went to the brandy jugs that Uncle had brought earlier for the evening's feast. She uncorked one, poured some of the amber liquid in a cup, and handed it to Rankin. "You workin' so hard, I thinkin' you might like to get started on some of this," she said.

He smiled as he accepted the drink, tossed it down, and held the cup out for more. "Now, you, Mae, you know how to make a man happy," he said. After he finished the second drink, he straightened himself and sighed. "Well, I've got to get back out there," he said. "You know those nigras. Leave 'em alone for a minute, and they'll do nothing but sit."

"Mr. Rankin, you sure right 'bout that," said Mama. She waited until she was sure he had gone, then posted Fanny at the door, found a bench, and sat down with purpose. "I don't have time for this," she said to no one in particular, "but I gonna sit for everybody out there. I sure do hope the good Lawd don't do to me what I thinkin' that I wanna do to that ugly lil rooster."

Late in the afternoon, Belle brought us a treat. It was a small bowl of cracklin', crunchy bits of pork fat she had scooped out of the rendering lard. We ate them with zeal. There would be more, she said, with tonight's meal, when she would make cracklin' bread for all the people from the quarters.

"Cracklin' bread?" I liked the sound.

"It the best," said Beattie.

"She mix the cracklin' in the corn bread," Fanny finished for Beattie.

"Mmmmm," they said in unison.

In the early evening, as darkness fell and the outdoor work was finishing up, Beattie and I were sent up to the big house to help Dory. Fresh pork had been roasting over an open pit through much of the late afternoon. Sweet potatoes baked in the pit coals, and Belle, with Ida's help, was making huge amounts of the cracklin' bread in the large kitchen fireplace.

Mama came to us before we left. "Uncle Jacob stayin' with Masta Marshall. Ben keepin' hisself around the house in case Dory or Uncle be needin' him. After I get done here, I comes to stay with the babies and Miss Martha, then you girls come back with Dory for your supper and the dancin'." So Beattie and I left, hand in hand, happy to know that we would be back soon.

The big house stood in shadow against the darkening light, and when we entered, the downstairs was eerily silent. Uncle Jacob had lit one of the lamps in the long hallway, but it flickered and cast dark shadows; we hesitated, our hands still tightly clasped. "Let's run," I whispered.

"Mama say no runnin' in the big house," Beattie whispered back, so we set out together at a walk, though we quickly picked up speed as we passed the dark cavernous rooms that stood open to the stairway. We were on the first landing when we heard Uncle Jacob's firm voice. "I say I stayin' here with the boy," he said.

We continued up, though more slowly.

"He is my charge, and you will leave him to me!" It was Mr. Waters. At the sound of his fury, I would have turned back in fear, but Beattie pulled me on. We arrived at the top landing just as the tutor tried to push past Uncle, but with that, Ben stepped out of Marshall's room and placed himself squarely in the doorway. "Just like Jacob say, we stayin' here with Masta Marshall till the cap'n get home."

"Nigras running the house? Have you all gone mad?" the tutor said, backing away.

Ben didn't answer, but even in the dim light, I could see his eyes flash.

"You just don't learn your lesson, do you?" Mr. Waters spat out. "I wonder what Mr. Rankin will have to say about this."

He swung around, and no sooner had he hurried down the stairway than Ben directed us in a loud whisper, "Get Dory! Tell her to go get Mama!"

When we opened the door to the blue room, it felt as though we were in another world. The room was quiet, but not silent, like the rest of the house. Though lamps were lit here, too, their light was steady and soft. The blue and ivory colors shimmered in the glow from the fireplace, and the room smelled of babies and lavender. The infants both slept, Campbell in his crib and Sukey on a floor pallet. Faint music seeped in from the outdoor celebration, and through the large closed window, I saw a bonfire blazing like a beacon from the kitchen yard.

"She finally sleepin'," Dory whispered to us as she came from Miss Martha's room. "This a bad day for her. She hear those pigs squealin' all day and —"

"Dory, Dory." Beattie ran to her.

"Shh! You wake her. What you wantin'?" Before Beattie finished her explanation, Dory was at the door. "I come right back," she said. "Pick up the babies if they cry." She slipped out just as Campbell began to fuss. Beattie and I both hurried over to the crib, and when I felt his damp bottom, I knew he needed changing. I confidently undid his bed gown and proudly showed off my newly acquired skills as I untied the first layer of wool cloth, then untied and removed the underlying clout. I hoisted his bottom up by grabbing hold of his ankles with one hand, then slid the fresh fabric under him with the other. Although the room was cool, he seemed to enjoy the freedom and churned his little legs in the fresh air. Beattie and I laughed as we watched and studied together the obvious difference between boys and girls.

"I wouldn't want that thing," Beattie said solemnly.

"Me, either," I said, making a face.

"It sure funny-looking," she said, and I agreed.

We peered closely.

As though waiting for this moment, his male difference straightened and shot a fountainlike stream into the air, spraying our faces. We gasped and jumped back. When we caught each other's eyes, we began to snort and then tried desperately to contain the peals of laughter that followed. Each time we gained control, one of us would gesture a reenactment that started another round of helpless laughter. We were brought back to good sense when we heard Miss Martha's alarmed call.

"You go in there," Beattie said. "I put the clout on Campbell."

"Isabelle!" Miss Martha greeted me as she sat up in bed. "Listen," she said, cupping her ear toward the window, "someone is calling."

I parroted Mama's usual words. "Everything is all right," I said, "there's a party in the kitchen yard."

"Oh," she said, then directed me to pour a tall glass of sherry from the decanter that stood on her dressing table. She drank the glass empty, then began to sip on another. "Listen!" she said again. "Don't you hear that? Someone is calling."

My heart thumped when I, too, heard the call of distress. Immediately, I guessed it was Dory. I didn't explain myself as I ran from the room, past Beattie holding Campbell, and out across the hall to rap loudly

155

on Marshall's door.

"Ben! Ben!" I called out, and at once the door flew open. "Dory is outside, and she's calling for you."

Ben did not hesitate but grabbed a small sledgehammer before he rushed toward the stairs. "Go back to the babies," he ordered, "and stay in that room."

When I returned to Miss Martha's bedroom, she was calling for Mama Mae. "Where has she gone?" she asked irritably. Hoping fervently that it was true, I assured her that Mama was on her way. Miss Martha set down her empty sherry tumbler, then threw back the bedcovers and announced that she had to relieve herself. I pulled the chamber pot from under the bed, helped her up, then turned my back while she made use of it. After she finished, I covered the pot and slid it back under the bed, wondering who had retrieved it from the orchard, where I had left it that morning. Miss Martha was unsteady on her feet as I helped her into bed. She settled back against her pillows and gazed about the room. "Would you have Jacob put another log on the fire?"

"I can do that," I said quickly, and went to the fireplace.

"Thank you, Isabelle. Come sit here," she invited, patting the bed beside her. "Are the children all right?" She was beginning to sound tired.

"Yes."

"Is James home yet?"

"Not yet."

"Don't leave me," she murmured. Her eyes closed as her words ran together.

I stayed until I was certain she had fallen asleep, then I went out to the blue room again. I surprised Beattie, who was gently bouncing up and down in the blue silk chair. She looked at me guiltily. "It so soft," she said, smoothing it with her hand.

I didn't have a chance to respond before Dory burst into the room. Her eyes were wild, and she was gasping for breath. Blood dripped from her nose, staining the front of the torn shirt she held closed over her chest. "Go get Mama," she said in a high urgent whisper. "Go get Papa. Go! Go!"

We ran down the stairs and through the house. In the dark, we almost fell over Ben sitting on the steps of the back porch. Seeing him I thought for a moment all was well, but from the quiet way he urged us to find Papa, I knew there was trouble.

People were still eating, but the musicians

had already begun to play, and some of the children, including Fanny, were dancing. Papa was at the end of a long food table, pouring drinks from the brandy jugs. We headed for him until we saw Rankin seated on a bench next to him. We changed course and ran to the kitchen, where we found Mama Mae, Belle, and Ida preparing to carry out gingerbread cakes.

Beattie stumbled over her words, but Mama understood enough to act immediately. "You two stay here," she directed us, then went to the corner under the stairs where all the tools from the day's slaughter were stored. As she grabbed a pointed knife and slipped it under her apron, Ida spoke up. "Mae! You best send George!"

Mama shook her head. "Rankin out there with him." Then she left, moving at a casual stroll through the kitchen yard. Belle instructed us to stay in the kitchen house, then she and Ida quickly set out the cakes.

Belle was back in the kitchen with Beattie and me when Mama Mae returned. Mama's breathing was labored, but she took swift action. First she sent Beattie over to the door and told her to start singing loud if anyone came. Then Mama waved Belle into the corner to whisper in her ear. Belle gasped and pulled back to look Mama in

158

the face, but Mama didn't waste time with further explanations. Instead, she pulled a bottle of the captain's house whiskey from under her apron and set it on the side table, then reached into her deep skirt pocket and withdrew Miss Martha's brown bottle.

Belle's eyes grew wide as Mama uncorked the bottle and poured a generous dose of the laudanum into the liquor. Mama corked the bottle, shook it, and handed it to Belle. "You got to get this into him. Enough to keep him sleepin' through the night. Soon as he down, send Papa up to the big house." She went again to the pile of tools. Quickly sorting through them, she pulled out a small meat saw and hitched it up under her skirts.

Suddenly, Beattie began to sing. She clapped and stomped while singing about a river at the top of her lungs. Mama headed toward the door, and Belle went to the fireplace and busied herself.

"Stop that screeching," Rankin said to Beattie as he passed her in the doorway. When he saw Mama, he looked at her disapprovingly. "Mae," he said, "I thought you'd be out helping with the food."

"Mr. Rankin, I sure sorry I can't stay, but I got to get up to the big house. Miss Martha not doin' so good," Mama said, again moving toward the door.

Rankin stopped her. "Say, where is your boy? I haven't seen much of him all day."

"You just miss him again." Mama's voice was at an odd pitch. "He down at the barns doin' the chores."

When Rankin looked hard at Mama, Belle came forward from the fireplace. Her face was flushed from the heat, and she had never looked more beautiful. "Mama," she said, "I'm sure it'd be all right with Mr. Rankin if you go ahead. He know Miss Martha's waiting on you. Mr. Rankin," she asked, coming closer to him, "did you have a piece of my gingerbread cake?"

"Why, yes," he said, looking at her with surprise, "and I sure did enjoy it. Right now I'm having to do some business with Mr. Waters, but later, I was wondering if you would have a dance with me? I hear you sure can dance."

Mama slipped out the door.

"Mr. Rankin," Belle replied, "it'd be my pleasure." She went to the side table and picked up the whiskey bottle. "Before you go, I was wondering if you might want some of this. The cap'n brings this for me special from his boat."

"Why, thank you," he said, holding up a mug, "but I have a drink right here." He eyed the whiskey bottle. "I will have a drink of that later, though, if the offer is still good."

Belle laughed softly. "Surely a man like you can finish that little bit you have left in your cup so I can pour you another drink?"

Rankin preened. "Looks to me like a hard day's work agrees with you."

"That and a little bit a this," she said, holding the bottle to her, smiling.

He emptied his mug, wiped his mouth with the back of his hand, and held the cup out for Belle. "I think maybe I will try some of that," he said, watching her carefully as she tipped the bottle and poured him a generous amount.

"Won't you sit?" Belle asked. "Girls," she said, addressing Beattie and me, "it's time for you to go out and dance."

I hesitated, but Belle gave me a look that was not to be disobeyed. We went to join Fanny, but I kept one eye on the kitchen house, hoping to catch sight of Belle. When I saw Rankin close the door, shutting Belle in with him, I had all I could do to keep myself from running back to her.

I watched, and it seemed like forever before the door opened again. When it did, Belle came out, leading Rankin by one of his dirty hands. "Come back in the house," he whined. He swayed as Belle enticed him to dance.

"Just one dance, then we'll go back in," she promised. When he protested, Belle lifted her skirts and began to sway. The other dancers stepped back as Rankin unsteadily reached for her. Belle whirled away. Spittle drooled from his mouth as he stumbled after her, but again and again she moved out of his reach. He took a final drink before his cup dropped and he fell forward. Papa immediately headed for the big house.

The music had ceased, but Belle couldn't seem to stop herself from twirling. Round and round she went, until Ida went to her and caught her in her arms. Ida was a tall woman, and Belle looked like a child when she pressed her face against Ida's thin chest. Belle's back was heaving as Ida spoke low in her ear, "He down, honey. He down. He ain't gonna get you."

CHAPTER TWELVE

Belle

In one night I see trouble like I never did see before. I no sooner get out of Rankin's clutches than Mama's needing me up at the big house. Here's what happened: Waters goes after Dory and now he's a dead man. Ben sees to that. And now the privy behind Mama's house got something in there that nobody's gonna talk about. We work fast, Mama, Uncle Jacob, and me, to clean out that tutor's room. I don't know who's more scared. Anybody finds out what happened here, we're all good as dead. We work all night, then just before morning, before I go back to the kitchen house, Mama tells me to write a letter to the cap'n. I have to make it look like it come from Waters, saying that he got to go. I use my dictionary, and before I'm done, I write down his name just like it is on the paper we find in his room.

Then I tell her we got to make a seal, like

the cap'n do. I show Mama how to put the burning candle under the wax that I'm holding over the paper, but she's so tired and scared and shaking so hard that she gets my finger.

"Ouch!" I say. "You getting too close with that fire."

"You movin'," Mama says.

"I don't move, you're moving," I say.

"Hold still," Mama says, but when I see her coming again with the candle and her hand's still shaking, I know she's gonna burn me again, and I start to laugh.

"Don't start laughin' now," Mama says, then we both get started. Mama got to put the candle down, she's laughing so hard, and I'm doing just like her.

That's when Uncle Jacob came into the room. "Jimmy back," he says. "Jimmy say that horse crazy like Waters. He say he don't need no whip to send that horse off runnin'. He say it a long time before they find that tutor's horse."

"Dory pick a good man," Mama says, trying not to laugh, 'cause Uncle's looking at us funny. Mama gets up and gives the candle to Uncle Jacob. "You best help Belle finish up here," she say. "I gonna look over that room one last time to see that it cleaned out. Then I see that Papa and Ben get that fire cleaned up. Papa say anything left, he push it down the privy."

"How he gonna make it stay down?" I ask, then I snort like a horse, and Mama has to sit again, she's laughing so hard. The more Uncle look at us, the more we carry on.

"Womens," he say, shaking his head.

CHAPTER THIRTEEN

Lavinia

Belle was so edgy and distracted the morning after the hog killing that had I not reminded her, she would have forgotten to give me something to eat before she sent me up to the big house. Dory, too, jumped when I opened the door to the blue room, but in turn, I gasped when I saw her. Her right eye was puffed and circled in purple, and her top lip was swollen and bruised. She turned her face from my inspection and sharply directed me into Miss Martha's bedroom.

The minute I came in, Mama excused herself, saying she would be back within the hour. Miss Martha sat propped up in bed, her morning care already completed. Alone with her, I felt shy. I remained back a distance from the bed while she studied me. "Hello, Isabelle," she said. Unexpectedly, she added, "Would you bring Sally to me?"

I looked back for Mama, though I knew she had already left. My legs went weak with apprehension, but seeing no alternative, I moved closer to the bed. I met Miss Martha's eyes, took a deep breath, and said in a loud whisper, "No, I can't. She fell off the swing."

The pale woman inhaled deeply and covered her face with her hands. I was about to run for Mama when Miss Martha looked at me again, her green eyes dark with suffering. "I keep hoping it's a dream," she said, "a terrible dream."

"My name isn't Isabelle," I said, hoping to distract her.

When she looked away from me, I feared I had said the wrong thing, but when she faced me again, she smiled. "I know, dear, but please indulge me. You remind me of my sister, and it gives me such comfort to use her name."

Certainly I understood, having named Campbell for that very reason. "It's all right if you call me Isabelle," I said.

She reached for my hand. "I know I must get strong again, I must get out of this room, but it all seems so pointless." She looked at me, searching my eyes. "I don't know what to do."

I remembered Uncle Jacob's wisdom.

"You can give it to Allah," I said.

"Allah?" she asked. "Who is Allah?"

"That's another name for the Lawd." I said. "Mama says Miss Sally is playing with my ma and that the good Lawd is watching over both of them."

Miss Martha looked at me curiously, then patted the bed. "Come sit by me," she invited, and I did so. "How did you become so wise?"

I shrugged.

She fingered my braids for a minute. "How is the baby?" she asked.

"Do you want me to get him?" I asked hopefully.

She shook her head. "Not right now," she said. Sensing my disappointment, she added, "Maybe later."

I nodded, and we sat together in silence.

"Could you read to me?" she finally asked.

"I can't read," I said.

She looked taken aback. "Then I shall have to teach you."

She had just opened a book when we heard Mama's loud voice from the blue room. "I go to her first! She a lady and don't want no man in her room 'less she say so!"

"You make sure she knows I'm out here to see her on business." My neck went prickly at the sound of Rankin's voice.

Mama came into the bedroom and closed the door behind her. She came over to Miss Martha, leaned close to her, and whispered that the overseer was here. "He think he the masta, the way he goin' through this house. He say you just a pitiful sick woman and that he the boss of this place till the cap'n get home."

Miss Martha raised her eyebrows, and her cheeks colored. "Going through my house? He called me pitiful? How dare he!"

"That man out there thinkin' he runnin' your house. You gonna see him?"

"Yes, I most certainly will!"

Mama went toward the blue room, but Miss Martha called her back. "Mae. We're not in a rush. Could you give me my hand mirror?"

Mama came back to do as she was asked.

Miss Martha removed her bed cap and handed it to Mama. "Now give me my brush," she said, and had me hold the mirror for her while she arranged red curls around her shoulders. She pinched her cheeks and blinked in wide exaggeration, then looked up to see me staring at her transformation. I flushed when she smiled at me.

Mama glanced nervously back toward the door.

169

"Mae," Miss Martha said, "you sit in the chair. Isabelle, would you please open the door for Mr. Rankin?"

I went to the door, but as I opened it, Mama called for me to wait. She went over to the chamber pot and pushed it under the bed, then pulled an undergarment off another chair and quickly put it away. Meanwhile, through the slightly opened door, I observed Rankin standing next to Dory in the blue room. "Who hit you in the face?" he asked.

"Nobody. I fell," Dory said quickly.

"You fell?" he said, looking her over carefully. "You sure you fell?" When Dory, clearly petrified, didn't respond, he continued, "You sure a purty little thing." He laughed. "It looks to me like you have plenty of milk for those two babies." He paused. "What do they call you again?"

"Miss Dory," Dory said with defiance.

"Miss Dory! My, my, my! We sure have some uppity folks in this big house, don't we?"

At Mama's wave, I pushed open the door and nodded to Rankin that he was to enter. He leaned down to Dory's ear before he left her. "You know Mr. Rankin always looking out for the pretty gals." He strode confidently into the bedroom. His appearance hadn't improved any, and an unclean smell trailed him. He carried a document.

"Mr. Rankin?" The tone of the mistress's voice stopped him from a closer approach. He looked surprised to see Mama Mae sitting in a chair.

"Well, now, Miss Martha," he addressed her after a slight hesitation, "it sure is nice to see you looking so good."

"Yes," she replied. "As you can see, I'm feeling very well."

His dirty hands fidgeted with the paper he held.

"How can I help you?" the mistress asked.

"This says that Waters has left." He approached her and handed over the document.

She took it and examined the broken seal. "This is addressed to the captain," she said.

"Yes, well, with things being . . . with you being . . ."

She held up her hand to quiet him while she read the document. "So. Mr. Waters has left?" she asked, refolding the paper.

"Yes. Yes. His belongings are gone, and it seems he took his horse, but I'm not sure . . ."

"Not sure of what, Mr. Rankin?" Miss Martha asked.

"Well now, he didn't tell me that he was

going to leave," said Rankin.

"And why would he do that?" she asked.

He seemed at a loss for words.

"As I see it, Mr. Rankin, this is a matter for my husband. He is due back any day now. I shall let this matter rest until his return. I do thank you for your concern, but as you can see, I am quite capable of handling the house and its affairs."

"Well, I am only trying to do my job," Rankin said. "When he left, the cap'n asked me to look after the place. He didn't tell me I'd be answering to his wife, but I suppose —"

Miss Martha's tone turned frigid. "Mr. Rankin, do not let me keep you from your other duties."

The man bowed foolishly before he headed toward the door. As he left the blue room, he stopped beside Dory, who had finished with Campbell and was now feeding Sukey. On his approach, she quickly covered her breast. He stood over her for a minute, then he reached down and pinched the baby's face. Sukey cried out, and when Dory pushed away his hand, he grabbed her wrist and held it viselike while staring into her eyes. Finally, with a coarse laugh, he released her, then left, leaving Dory to soothe herself and her baby.

From behind me I heard Miss Martha tell Mama that, as of today, Miss Martha would begin to take more exercise.

Later, after the midday meal, Miss Martha rested, and I sat with Campbell while Dory went for her dinner. The baby was awake, so I picked him up and cuddled him while humming one of Mama's songs. Marshall poked his head in the doorway. His eyes were lidded, and he appeared half asleep from the opium Mama had dosed him with the night before. "Why is Waters's room cleaned out? Do you know where he is?" he whispered to me.

"He's gone," I said.

"Waters? Gone where?" he asked.

"I don't know. Mr. Rankin was here today, and he told your mother that Mr. Waters left."

"I don't believe it," Marshall said angrily, looking out into the hallway again.

"It's true," I said. "Mama said he's gone to see the debil."

"Where?"

"To see the debil," I repeated.

"The devil?" he corrected.

"I guess so," I said.

"Don't start talking like that," he said. "You're not one of them."

"What do you mean?"

"They're not like us," he said. "They're stupid."

"Who is stupid?"

"The nigras!"

"Not Belle," I said, ready to inform him of her reading skills.

"Belle!" He spat out her name. "She's nothing but a yella whore."

I was silent, not knowing the meaning of this.

"Don't trust any of them," he said. "They'll turn on you the minute you turn your back."

"Do you mean Ben and Papa, too?" I asked.

"They're the worst kind," he said, "the ones closest to you. They'll kill you when you sleep."

"Who said that?" I asked.

"Waters and Rankin," he said. "It happens all the time. They told me about plenty of slaves killing their masters. You've got to learn to control them before they kill all of us."

I stared at him. Marshall spoke with such conviction that in spite of myself, I wondered if there was cause for fear.

"Don't worry, though," he said, "I'll look out for you."

Campbell began to fuss, so I loosened his blanket. When I looked back up, Marshall had left. I was troubled by what he had said, and later that night I asked Belle what he could have meant. She told me it was foolishness and that it sounded as though Marshall had spent too much time with Rankin.

Miss Martha's mental and physical health strengthened as her laudanum doses diminished. Now, in the late mornings, she kept me with her. She had writing slates brought to her and began to teach me to read and to write. I was an eager student and relished her attention, though I wondered that she did not care more for her own children. She never asked after Marshall, and when she began to visit the downstairs rooms again, she was content to view Campbell in Dory's care but never requested to hold him. I noted, too, as we made our way through the upstairs hallway, past Sally's room, that she kept her eyes averted.

Downstairs, there were four very large rooms for us to visit. The hallway, painted a vibrant blue, ran the center of the house and was large enough to accommodate furniture of its own, but the wide stairway was its focal point. On the east side, to the back, the dining room had walls covered in murals that displayed panoramic views of blue water with ships and green hills with horses. This splendid room was fronted by a formal drawing room.

Across the hall on the west side of the house was a large parlor, and behind that, the library, also known as the study. The parlor was the least formal of the rooms, and it was here that Miss Martha seemed to find something of herself.

As in all the downstairs rooms, the parlor had twelve-foot ceilings. Its three large windows had wooden shutters that folded neatly back into wall pockets when daylight was desired. The walls were painted bright green, and the pine floors were covered in different-size rugs, each of intricate pattern and of varying color. Gold-framed portraits graced the walls, and although I intended to ask their origin, the opportunity never presented itself in those years.

In a corner opposite the marble fireplace, where Uncle Jacob never failed to have a blazing fire, was a harpsichord; in the companion corner stood a tall clock, its casing made of rich black walnut. Between the two, a handsome library table held two large books; resting beside them were spectacles that I assumed belonged to the captain. In the center of the room was a tea table and, circling it, a settee and three comfortable chairs. While I sat with her there, Miss Martha told me stories about herself and her childhood, and over the course of those days, she spoke freely of her early history, obviously glad to recall a time when she felt safe and loved.

She had two sisters. The older sister, Sarah, had been the visitor from Williamsburg. The younger one, Isabelle, "died when she was twelve. It was a great loss," Miss Martha said, then quickly began to speak of her mother. She was from England, stern and exacting and intent on raising proper English daughters. Her father was the opposite. As a young man, he had come from Ireland. With opportunity and dedication to hard work, he had become a wealthy merchant. A loud and boisterous man, he was forever embarrassing his wife, but she tolerated it, as he was a force to be dealt with in Philadelphia society. Most important to Miss Martha, her father loved his daughters with a pride that knew no limits. "He spoiled us so," she said. "If we asked for a gown, we were given two; if we asked for a bonnet, we were given three."

"Did they ever come here to see you?" I asked.

"Only once," Miss Martha said. "The trip was so long, and my mother's health was already failing by then. I sometimes wonder if the trip here hastened her . . . passing."

During one of these story times, Miss Martha took me into the study. She went to a large desk and paused to run her hand along the polished edge. "This was my father's desk," she said. She opened the drawer and removed a packet of letters bound with a grosgrain ribbon. "These are from my mother."

"That's a pretty ribbon," I said.

She invited me to sit on a chair next to her. "Yes," she said, untying the bow, "blue was always my favorite color. What is yours?"

"Green," I said, thinking of Belle's head rag and my doll's clothing.

"Ah," she said, smiling at me, "the green of Ireland."

She read aloud passages from at least a dozen letters. I could almost see Miss Martha's mother — an imposing woman, I imagined — writing from her own desk back in Philadelphia. She wrote of social events and of how Miss Martha's girlhood friends had married and were now taking part in glamorous affairs. Her mother voiced a parent's concern for her daughter and advised her to care for her health. She sympathized with Miss Martha in her loneliness yet reminded her that she had made the choice to leave. Miss Martha stopped reading and gazed out the window.

"Why did you want to come here?" I asked.

She laughed a little, as though at a private joke. She reached into the desk to withdraw a small book. From inside the book she pulled out a yellowed newspaper clipping. She read it as much to herself as to me. It told of a beautiful young woman, Miss Martha Blake, marrying Captain James Pyke, forty years of age, a successful merchant and owner of a ship. They were to reside at Tall Oaks, a tobacco-growing plantation in southern Virginia. The article stated that Miss Martha, being herself of vibrant nature, was certain to be the perfect mate for this illustrious and adventuresome man.

"Was that about you?" I asked. It was difficult for me to believe that the glowing article, referencing a vibrant woman, was about her.

"Yes. I was young and foolish," she said. "I was not yet twenty. I thought that this would be an adventure. I had no idea what awaited me here. I had images of myself as a country gentlewoman, one who would have large numbers of servants to assist me when I gave my country balls. I imagined I would be busy planning these events while waiting for my husband to return from his trips. I thought that if I became lonely, I had only to travel back to Philadelphia or make an exciting trip to Williamsburg to visit my sister. But that was not to be." She was silent again.

"What happened?" I could not contain the question.

"When I arrived and saw this house, how isolated we were, I wanted only to return to Philadelphia. I thought that I had made the wrong choice, even perhaps that I had married the wrong man. But James was so charming, so reassuring, and he promised that soon he would sell his ship and settle his business affairs to be here with me. But the years have passed . . ." She stopped herself.

"Don't you have any friends here?" I asked, wanting to interject some hope.

"The nearest neighbor is a bachelor of many years, and he lives in a most unsuitable manner with . . . one of his servants." She shook her head as though to clear it of the thought. "I cannot travel without a male escort, and I cannot travel with a man" — she hesitated, then looked at me — "who is

180

not of our color. It is simply not permitted for a woman to do so. That leaves me to travel with our Mr. Rankin, and I am sure you are old enough to know why that speaks for itself."

"You have Mama Mae and Belle and Dory," I said. "They are your friends."

She checked the door, then looked back at me. She spoke quietly. "They are not my friends," she said. "They are my servants. They look out for themselves. Mae knows that her eldest daughter consorts with my husband, although she denies it. You are young, but surely you understand. Almost from the beginning, I suspected their secrets."

Though I was unclear of her meaning, I began to offer reassurance of Belle's loyalty to her, but she quickly interrupted. "Don't speak to me of her!" Immediately, she saw the effect of her sharp words and patted my hand. "You will understand one day, my dear. I know I am foolish to speak to a child of these matters, but I am so lonely that some days I feel I shall die of it."

"Can't you go to see your sister?" I asked.

She shook her head and sighed. "I haven't been strong enough. Marshall was born a year after we married. In the following years I had other babies who . . . didn't survive. I couldn't seem to recover my health, although I was getting so much stronger just before Sally . . ." She paled as the memory hit, then closed her eyes as though to ward off the grief.

"Should I get Mama?" I asked.

She shook her head, then opened her eyes.

"What did you do when you were a little girl?" I asked quickly, incorporating another of Mama's techniques to lead the conversation away from a dangerous subject.

Miss Martha remained quiet as she carefully folded the newspaper article and returned it to the book before replacing it in the desk drawer. She folded the letters and began to retie them, and I wondered if she had heard my question. "Can you hold your finger here?" she asked, indicating the fold in the ribbon.

I carefully placed my thumb in position as she tied a beautiful bow. She held the packet in her lap and lightly fingered the ribbon as she spoke. "When I was a young girl in Philadelphia, one of my greatest pleasures was to accompany my sisters to the city market. Sarah, Isabelle, and I often went out. Of course, we had our maids following us, but what adventures we had. City life was wonderful, Isabelle. There were restaurants!" She looked at me with shining eyes.

"Every Sunday afternoon after church service, our father would take our family to a restaurant. What a fuss they made over us, although we sisters already knew that we were quite pretty." She stopped to remember. "How I miss those Sundays."

"Why?" I asked, afraid her storytelling would end.

"There was a church, Isabelle, its steeple so high I do believe that it was the most prominent feature in Philadelphia at that time. On Sunday mornings we would dress in our finest and walk to that Anglican Christ church. We always walked together as a family. How I long to attend a church service again."

"Don't they have churches here?" I asked, sure I had heard Mama speak of one.

"It's Presbyterian," she said, as though that were an answer she needn't explain.

I could see she was tired so I didn't ask her to relieve my confusion.

One gray afternoon after it had been raining for two days, Miss Martha sat at the harpsichord, which she then began to play. When she finished, she turned to smile apologetically. "I'm afraid I don't play very well."

I'd been captivated and assured her that

183

the music was beautiful.

She grew sober with her next words. "I don't play often because it makes me feel too lonely."

I understood, for when she began another melody, I felt the loneliness as each note pulsed and echoed throughout the beautifully furnished but empty room.

CHAPTER FOURTEEN

Belle

We're all working on a story for the cap'n. We go over and over the way it happened, then we go over and over the way we're gonna say it happened. Papa's wanting to tell the cap'n the truth, but Mama says he's forgetting that Waters was a white man, and if we tell the truth, for sure they'll hang Ben. First time ever, I see Mama Mae and Papa George not standing together.

Everybody's scared of Rankin. Ever since he went up to the big house and Miss Martha talk smart to him, Ida says he's hitting on them like never before. He knows something's up about Waters, but nobody's talking, and that's making him mad. Then, too, he got it in for me since that night when I give him the whiskey and he don't get to me. Now every morning he comes here to the kitchen house.

When I tell him that I don't think the

cap'n means for him to bother me, fire like to shoot outta his eyes. He says he's running the place for the cap'n and that he's watching out for Ben and me, just like the cap'n tell him to. Then he stands there smiling, just watching me. All the time I'm wondering how much room there's left in that privy.

And Ben, instead of being scared from doing Waters in, now it's like he's thinking he's a man that can do anything. He's taking too many chances. Last night Ben finds me when I'm working at the storage room in the basement up at the big house. I was pouring brandy on the cakes for Christmas when he slips in and closes the door. I say, "Benny, you best get out of here!," but he says, "Rankin sleepin' from the liquor." Then he asks, real quiet, "Belle, you don't care about me no more?"

My feet, by their own self, want to run to him, but I stay put. "No, I still like you, Benny, but in summer the cap'n's gonna take me away to Philadelphia."

Ben comes over to me. His eyes take me in, and I know I can't stop myself if he touches me. "Belle," he says, then goes to kiss me, but Uncle Jacob come in the door just in time. Uncle gives me the eye, but I say, "Benny's here, just making sure that everything's all right." After Benny leaves, Uncle says, "You wantin' that boy dead?" "No!" I say, but Uncle says, "This whole thing on you, Belle. Somethin' happen to Ben, Mae and George, they gonna blame you."

I know I got to keep Ben away, but I'd just as soon cut off my hand.

CHAPTER FIFTEEN

Lavinia

In the last weeks before Christmas, Miss Martha went repeatedly to the windows and looked out expectantly for the captain's wagon. Each day Mama reassured her, "He comin' soon. You put on the good dress today so you look like that pretty girl he marry."

One morning when Dory was upstairs with the babies and Beattie and I were downstairs helping Miss Martha put holly and cedar greens over the parlor mantel, Mama burst through the doors. "The patrollers here, and they takin' Jimmy!" she said, gasping for breath.

"Mae, for heaven's sake!" Miss Martha exclaimed. "You frightened me."

"The patrollers!" Mama repeated. "They here, down at the barns, and now they goin' to the kitchen house. They say they lookin' for that man Waters. They beatin' on Jimmy!

They say he know somethin' and they takin' him." Mama was frantic. "Rankin say next they takin' Ben!"

Miss Martha tossed down the greens, then called out for Uncle Jacob as she went for the gun case that stood in the library. "Here, take this," she said, handing a pistol to Uncle Jacob, then taking another from the case. Her hands shook as she loaded it, but it was evident that she was familiar with the workings of a gun. She stepped out the back door into the bright cold day with Mama and Uncle on either side. No one noticed that Beattie and I followed. Horses were saddled and tied beside the kitchen house, where our small party headed. Papa was in back of the kitchen house, loosing an ax from a wood stump.

"You won't need that, George. Come, take this and stand with me," Miss Martha said, handing him the pistol that Uncle carried. They rounded the house together. Jimmy's hands were tied to the saddle of a bay; his head leaned against the horse's flank, and I looked away when I saw his bleeding back.

Papa spoke low as he passed him. "You hold on, son."

Shouts and laughter came from inside the kitchen, and it didn't take long for us to see why. Four men, one of them Rankin, stood in a circle. They were tossing Belle, sending her spinning, one to the other. In a corner of the kitchen, Ben thrashed about on his stomach, his hands and feet tied together and his mouth gagged. Fanny, crying and trembling, crouched next to him.

"Who's gonna talk first?" one of the patrollers asked.

Rankin laughed roughly, catching Belle and holding her to him. "What are we gonna have to do to this little gal to make that boy on the floor talk?" Marshall watched, his eyes excited. Another man, standing opposite the room from Ben, was not part of the circle. Younger than the others, he looked unsettled by the game.

The blast from Miss Martha's pistol stopped everything.

"Gentlemen," she said to no one in particular. "Now that I have your attention, I want to assure you I can use a pistol more precisely than I have just done." She paused to look up at the splintered ceiling. "Goodness, I've blown a hole into my own kitchen!" Turning to Papa, she said, "George, I'm afraid that I've added to your work." She looked back at her stunned audience, then asked, "Would someone be kind enough to tell me the meaning of this?"

Rankin swaggered toward her. "Well now,

Miss Martha, these law-abidin' citizens have come to inform us that the horse Mr. Waters rode out on was found over in Buckingham County. Since Mr. Waters has yet to be found, they were thinking that someone here might have information that they haven't seen fit to tell."

Miss Martha stared coldly at Rankin, then turned her gaze to the other men in the room. "I'm afraid that you gentlemen have been misinformed. The matter of Mr. Waters's departure is waiting to be settled until my husband's return. Mr. Rankin has no business up here. He is employed to keep order in the fields, where utilizing some of this treatment" — she looked down at Ben, then up again — "might be necessary. It is, however, unnecessary to do so with my house servants." She looked at Belle. "You are aware that you are toying with one of the captain's most prized possessions?" Frost hung from her words.

"She's just a whore, Mother," Marshall called out.

If Miss Martha was surprised at his outburst, she did not show it. "Yes, Marshall, that she is," Miss Martha said, "but she's your daddy's whore, and heaven help the man who forgets that."

The men stared at her, their startled eyes

reminding me of the peacock dinner plates.

"Gentlemen," she addressed them, "I appreciate the fact that you are all such law-abiding citizens. However, now I'm asking you to leave my property. I expect you to untie the boy outside and leave him to me."

The young man from the corner stepped forward, removed his hat, and ran his hand through his straight dark brown hair. "We do apologize for disrupting your day, Mrs. Pyke. It appears that we've been misinformed."

The others glared at him. "This is a matter for the law," one of them mumbled.

"And what is your name, sir?" Miss Martha addressed the young man who had apologized to her.

"It's, ah . . . Stephens," he stammered. "Will Stephens."

"Stephens?" she said. "That is a familiar name. Does the captain know your daddy?"

"Yes, ma'am," he replied, fingering his hat. "We rent the property from the captain down the east side."

"Don't tell me you're the little boy who helped us out here at the barns the year that Marshall was born?" she asked, her voice taking on a lilt.

His face flushed. "Yes, ma'am. One and the same."

"My goodness! You've grown up," she said. "It makes me feel so much better knowing that I have you watching out for us up on the hill. And you tell your daddy I said that, won't you?"

He assured her that he would.

When Rankin made his exit, the others quickly left with him. Papa remained at Miss Martha's side when she followed. As the others rode off, Rankin headed toward the quarters.

Miss Martha's voice caught him. "Mr. Rankin."

He turned back.

"I don't want you to worry about a thing up here," she said. "My house servants will be armed." She indicated Papa standing to her side with the pistol. "I expect they'll be nervous from this excitement. I do hope that my sleep will not be interrupted by the sound of gunfire, but they shall be encouraged to use the firearms should they suspect an intruder on the grounds of the big house."

Rankin's face darkened, but he said nothing as he turned back toward the quarters. To my surprise, Marshall ran to follow Rankin, but his mother called him back. For a moment it looked as though he was going to disobey, but when she called again,

Marshall kicked the dirt and ran up toward the big house.

"I need to sit." Miss Martha had suddenly lost all her color. Mama reached for her and supported her into the kitchen, where Uncle was helping Ben to his feet. Once free, Ben rushed out the door. Belle, leaning on the table, struck it over and over again with the flat of her hand. From outside, Papa called for Mama to come help with Jimmy. Uncle Jacob seated Miss Martha before he went to Belle.

"Belle," he said, placing a hand on her arm and speaking firmly, "Jimmy out there needin' help. Come now."

"It's fortunate that no one was hurt," Miss Martha said.

Belle swung toward her, eyes blazing. Uncle stepped between them. "Miss Martha, we best get you back up to the big house. Mae and George take care of everythin' down here. If the cap'n come home, he want you up there waitin' for him. Come, I take you back." He extended his elbow, and Miss Martha rose to take his arm. Uncle signaled with his eyes for me to follow. I didn't want to go; I was scared and I wanted to stay with Belle. I wondered where Ben was and if he was all right. I could not erase the look I had seen on his face when he lay bound, unable to help Belle.

In spite of my reluctance, I was obedient, but when our small party had almost reached the big house, we heard muffled crashes coming from behind us. It sounded as though pots were being hurtled against the kitchen house wall.

Chapter Sixteen

Belle

Everybody's full of nerves. Every day now we're all waiting on the cap'n to get home. Since Rankin and the men showed up here in the kitchen house, Ben don't come to see me no more. It's better this way, but I think he stays away because he shamed hisself. The day Rankin was throwing me around, Ben run out of here stinking like a privy. It's not his fault. After they take his ear, I know how scared he's got to be. That day here in the kitchen house, there was nothing Ben could do, I know that. But he's a man, and maybe he don't see it that way.

Everybody's stepping real careful. Rankin's just looking for something to get ahold of.

CHAPTER SEVENTEEN

Lavinia

A wagon pulled up the day before Christmas, and the mistress joyfully ran to the front door. Piles of gifts and a letter arrived, but the captain did not. Miss Martha went pale when she learned that he had not come, and Uncle Jacob quickly led her to a sofa in the parlor, where she sat in disbelief, clutching an unopened letter.

"He isn't coming," she said to herself. "Dear God, he isn't coming."

Mama rushed in.

"He isn't coming, Mae." Miss Martha looked at Mama as though she might say otherwise.

Mama looked as upset as Miss Martha. Finally, she said, "You best read that letter."

"Yes." Miss Martha looked down at it in her hands. "The letter." She seemed to have forgotten that she was holding it.

Marshall appeared at the door. "Where's

Father?" He looked around the room expectantly.

"Give me a minute, Marshall," his mother answered. "I'm reading his letter." Her eyes skimmed the beginning paragraph. "He has sold the ship!" she cried. "But he cannot finish the business of it yet. He begs our forgiveness, but he won't be home until spring." She set the letter down in her lap.

Mama Mae lowered herself onto the nearest chair.

Marshall snatched the letter from his mother's lap. There was a hollow silence while he scanned the paper. "He's taking you to Philadelphia. I'm to go to Williamsburg."

Miss Martha looked up at her son's face. "What? What did you say?"

"Read the rest." Marshall handed back the letter and pointed to the information. As she read, Miss Martha's face began to show color again.

"Marshall!" she said excitedly. "You're right! He has found a school for you — in Williamsburg! And he's made arrangements for me to visit my father in Philadelphia. I am to see Father again! We shall stay the whole summer!" Tears began to slide down her face, and I watched them drip onto the bodice of her blue brocade dress.

Marshall abruptly left the room, but the strain on Mama's face remained.

Christmas came and went with little celebration, although there was a dance down at the quarters. Ben was the only one to attend, and when he returned, drunk, he woke us by knocking on Belle's kitchen door and calling out for her. He made such a noise that Papa came to get him. Papa spoke urgently to his son, and I thought I heard Ben crying when they walked away. Belle was crying, too, so I climbed into her bed and tried to comfort her as Mama might have done, but I fell asleep before she stopped weeping.

The mistress waited two long days before deciding that she was in the mood to open her Christmas gifts.

"Can Beattie and Fanny watch with me?" I asked.

"I suppose that would be all right," she agreed reluctantly. When I ran to find them she called after me, "See if Marshall will come, too."

The girls and I went to find Marshall, but Papa, cleaning out a stall in the barn, told us that he was out riding with Rankin. The twins and I ran back to the big house, filled with excitement at the prospect of watching Miss Martha open her gifts. I told Miss Martha of Marshall's whereabouts, and she frowned. "What does he do with that man?" she asked. I didn't have an answer, though I don't suppose she expected one. "Oh well, he'll soon be away from here," she answered herself. "We'll go ahead, then. He has already opened his gifts."

Beattie, Fanny, and I watched, awestruck, as Miss Martha lined up her packages after a note instructed her to open the gifts in sequence. From the first parcel, Miss Martha withdrew two dolls. She read aloud, " 'I have been assured that these moppets are wearing the very latest in London fashion. I am having both of these copied for you by an excellent dressmaker here in Williamsburg, and I will bring the finished product to you in the spring. It is my heart's desire to see you wear them in Philadelphia. I am hopeful that you approve of the fabric and color selection. Yours, as ever, James.' "

We girls had never seen such delightful beauty. The moppets were wooden dolls with painted faces, and their human hair was done up in elaborate curls. Their dresses were of a gossamer fabric: one was an empire style in blue, the body and train trimmed in elegant silver embroidery; the other, similar in style, was a pale cream trimmed with white embroidery and ivory ribbons.

The next two packages each held a pair of shoes. One pair of delicate slippers was made of blue silk satin trimmed in silver embroidery, the low heels covered in ivory satin. The other pair was of ivory silk trimmed with pink ribbon rosettes and had heels covered in pink satin. I simply couldn't imagine something that beautiful was to be worn on a foot, and I told Miss Martha so. She laughed and pulled off the brown leather shoe she was wearing, then slipped her slender foot into the blue satin slipper and held it up for us to see. She turned her ankle in a circle and pointed her toe, then laughed again when we all exclaimed at the perfect fit.

Furthur packages included elbow-length silk gloves and two pairs of embroidered stockings. Miss Martha explained that these accessories were to complement the dresses.

Finally, from the bottom of the last box, Miss Martha removed a flat brown envelope and studied it. My reading had advanced enough for me to recognize Belle's name printed boldly across the top. Miss Martha frowned, turned it over a few times, then rose. Telling us to stay seated, she carried the package to the study. I thought I heard the desk drawer open, and when she returned without the envelope, I guessed that she had placed it with her letters, those wrapped in blue ribbon.

"Was that for Belle?" I asked.

She looked startled for a minute. "No," she said, "that is for me to open later."

I knew from her tone that the subject was finished, and I thought then that I must have misread Belle's name. Dory called for me soon after, needing me to care for Campbell, and I forgot all else but the beauty of the gifts that I had seen unwrapped that day.

CHAPTER EIGHTEEN

Belle

Never before do I see Mama Mae worked up like this. Rankin is nosing around, talking about how he's gonna find out what happened to Waters before the cap'n gets home. Then, too, Rankin's bragging all over the place that he got orders from the cap'n that if he finds Ben fooling with me, he's to sell him off. Mama Mae tells me over and over again to make sure I don't have nothing to do with Ben, that if he comes to see me, I got to send him away. Mama says to keep praying that the cap'n gets home quick.

Then, don't you know, the cap'n sends a letter saying he's not coming back until the spring, when he'll take Miss Martha to Philadelphia. That night when Mama comes to give me the news, I ask Mama what's gonna happen to me when the cap'n comes home. Is he gonna take me along back to Philadelphia? Is he thinking that he can put

Miss Martha and me in the same carriage all that way?

Mama says she don't know when the cap'n's taking me, but it's best I get away from here soon as I can. When she says that, I jump up, yelling, "Well! It's easy to see that you don't care about me and that Ben is the one you're looking out for!"

Mama gives me a look like I hit her in the face. She stands up. "That what you think, Belle? You think I don't want you here?" Her mouth is moving like she's gonna cry. "You think I don't want you to stay? You don't know that when you go, it like I'm losin' my own chil'?" Then Mama starts to cry.

I go to her, put my arm around her, and sit her down beside me. "I'm sorry, Mama," I say. "I know you care about me like you do your own family. Mama, please stop crying."

She pulls out a rag, blows her nose, and looks at me, her dark eyes scared. "Belle, you got to get outta here. That Rankin's gettin' more worked up every day. He can't stand it that he don't find out what happens to that tutor. My nerves can't hardly take it when I see him nosin' around. He won't stop till he gets Ben. That I know."

"Mama," I say, and this time I know I got

to stand by it, "you don't worry about Ben and me. I don't have nothing to do with him no more."

After Mama goes, it takes me a while to settle down. This is the first time I see how this is all getting to her. I see that even Mama got limits of what she can take.

One more thing. Papa's saying how Marshall's spending all his time with Rankin. He's letting that boy drink liquor, and young as he is, Papa says, Marshall's already got a taste for it. Papa says Rankin got it in for Miss Martha and he doing everything he can to turn her boy against her.

I don't see nothing but trouble coming every way I look.

CHAPTER NINETEEN

Lavinia

The spring of 1793 came early. One afternoon at the beginning of May, the twins and I, celebrating our ninth birthday, sat outside the kitchen house fashioning honeysuckle wreaths. The white and yellow heady-scented blooms permeated the air as our nimble fingers worked quickly to see who could finish first.

"Mama say one day you live in a big house, maybe even that you have the house servants workin' for you," Fanny said, placing her completed wreath on her head.

"No," I said, quite happy with the arrangements as they were. "I want to stay with Belle."

"No." Fanny shook her head. "Mama say that Miss Martha teachin' you to be the white girl."

"I don't want to be the white girl," I said, fear rising in me. "I want to live with Belle, and then I'm going to marry Ben!"

Fanny, who had been resting back on her elbows, sat up straight to look at me. "You best get over that idea right now," she said. "You never gonna be cullad like us, and that mean you a white girl and you goin' to live in a big house. Anyway, you can't marry Ben. He cullad."

"Fanny right about that," Beattie agreed.

I began to cry. "I can marry Ben if I want to. You can't make me be a white girl." I tossed my wreath aside. "And you can't make me live in the big house."

Mama came to the door. "Abinia, that you cryin'? You nine years old and still cryin' like a baby?"

"She wantin' to marry Ben," Fanny explained. "She not wantin' to live in the big house, she not wantin' to be a white girl."

As Fanny spoke my truth, I began to howl.

"If that don't beat all!" said Mama. "This the first time I hear a somethin' like this. Come here, chil'."

I went to her, hiccuping between sobs. She sat on a bench, took her pipe from her mouth, and lightly tapped my chest with it. "So you think that you wanna be cullad?"

I nodded.

"Why that be?"

"I don't want to live in the big house. I

207

want to stay here with you and Belle and Papa."

Mama's voice was tender. "Chil', there things in this world you don't know about yet. We your family, that never change. Even when you find a white boy and gets married, we still your family. Mama always your mama, Belle always your Belle."

I stopped crying. "What about Papa and Ben?" I asked hopefully.

"They watch out for you just like now. Abinia" — Mama looked into my eyes — "you on the winnin' side. One day might be you lookin' out for us."

Her words calmed me, but that day I was awakened to a new realization and made aware of a line drawn in black and white, though the depth of it still had little meaning to me.

Throughout that spring, Marshall spent most of his time with Rankin. The mistress had lost control over her eldest son; he was as removed from her as she was from Campbell.

Miss Martha continued to include me in many of her routine activities. She read daily from the Bible and stopped occasionally to give me her interpretation of certain passages. She continued to teach me to read and write and, to my great delight, to play the harpsichord. Some days, at my request, she allowed Beattie and Fanny to observe, but she was always hesitant to include them. One afternoon, after watching the three of us laugh together, the mistress took me aside. "You must not become too friendly with them," she said. "They are not the same as us."

"How?" I asked. "How are they not the same?"

"You will learn." She sighed deeply. "When I come back from Philadelphia, I will teach you your proper place."

Campbell was my love. In the mornings following his feeding, Dory bundled him and sent him in with me to Miss Martha. Compared to Sukey, Campbell was still a sober little fellow, but I knew how to make him smile. The mistress watched his happy response to my games, but she seldom joined in.

"Why doesn't she want him?" I asked Dory one day when I brought him back.

Dory's reasoning was that the mistress was afraid to love another baby the way she loved little Sally.

"Doesn't she love Marshall anymore?" I asked.

"I think she blamin' Marshall for pushin' Sally off the swing."

"But Marshall didn't mean to hurt Sally." I was sure of that.

"I know, but it seem like his mama don't know," she said. "And now Marshall goin' wild, sassin' her and spendin' his time with Rankin."

"Where do they go?"

"To do bad things."

"What bad things?" I asked.

"You learn about that soon enough," she said, ending the conversation.

The second week of May, I was waiting at the front door with Miss Martha when the captain finally arrived. The reunited couple held each other for a long while before they went to the front parlor and closed the door behind them. The house pulsed with life as we all scurried to set the table for a late-afternoon dinner in the dining room.

When the captain and his wife emerged, Miss Martha's face had a pink glow that set off her sparkling green eyes. Her mouth was red and full, and her hair, which had been pinned up, now was tousled down around her shoulders.

"Mae," the Captain said to Mama, "you have given me back my girl."

"She sure back to her old self," Mama said, smiling.

The captain gazed down at his wife. "That she is." Miss Martha blushed and leaned her face against his arm. "My bride is still shy," the captain teased. He looked around. "And where are my sons? Where is Marshall? Where is Campbell?"

So connected was I to Campbell that when Dory handed him over to his father, I felt pride when the captain commented on his son's healthy appearance. "Martha," he said proudly, "you have given me another wonderful son."

"Yes, yes." Miss Martha motioned for Dory to take the baby away. "Come now, we must go in to eat while the food is hot."

I disliked that Miss Martha wanted the captain's attention for herself. I held Campbell for a long while that afternoon, trying to understand how she could care so little for this child whom I adored.

The following week Marshall was dispatched to Williamsburg: The captain sent him to stay with Miss Martha's sister and her husband while he attended school. Marshall left alone in the carriage, and he did not turn back to wave.

At the finish of that green and shining

May, another carriage arrived. This one was large and glossy black, a surprise for Miss Martha and purchased new for this very trip. When it left for Philadelphia, it carried away Miss Martha, the captain, Dory, and my darling baby Campbell. Sukey, eight months old, was left behind in our care. When Dory handed her baby over to Mama Mae, she cried so hard that I feared her heart would break. Belle hugged Dory. "You're gonna be back in a few months," she said. "We'll all take care of Sukey, you know that."

"Abinia." Dory pulled away from Belle and took my shoulders. "You know what she like, what she want. You watch her for me."

I nodded, but my throat hurt too much to speak.

"Tell Ida that she like to nurse before she play," Dory instructed me, "then after, you hold her. She know you. You play with her."

I nodded again, wanting only to turn away from the pain on Dory's face. As we watched them drive away, this time it was Dory, holding Campbell, who did not turn back to wave. Belle had her arm around my shoulders, and I hid my head against her as I began to wail at my loss.

■ ■ ■ ■

Ida, nursing a child of her own, came up from the quarters to feed her grandchild, Sukey. Screaming for most of the first day, Sukey wouldn't nurse. Finally, to everyone's great relief, she accepted Ida's nourishment that evening. She nursed, stopped to cry, then suckled again. Later, Mama took her home but returned soon after with the crying child. I must have seemed the most familiar to the baby, for when Sukey saw me, she reached out her dimpled arms and clung to me.

It was decided that she would sleep next to me on my pallet, with Belle watching over us. When Sukey woke during the night, Belle lit a lamp and made her way through the darkness down to the springhouse. On her return, she warmed some of the milk she had fetched. We dipped a corner of a clean cloth into it, and although the baby fussed, she swallowed the warm liquid that dripped into her throat.

It took a full week before Sukey settled into a routine, accepting Ida's breast morning and evening. Belle and I supplemented those feedings with cow's milk. That first week I felt alternately flattered by the baby's preference for me, then overwhelmed by the responsibility of it. I longed to be holding Campbell and could only hope that Dory was caring for him as I was caring for Sukey.

Before the captain's departure, he made a decision that affected everyone for the better. He employed Will Stephens, the young man who had stood back from the patrollers in Belle's kitchen. I knew that Papa George and Mama Mae had met with the captain about hiring him.

A few nights before the departure, Belle, too, had a meeting with the captain. I was not there, but the encounter had an unhappy effect on Belle. Even with the frantic preparations to send off the travelers, it was easy to see that Belle was upset.

After they left, she withdrew into herself until, after a few days of isolation, Mama came for an evening visit. Sukey and I were already in bed, but I was wide awake as I listened to the conversation.

Belle steered questions away from herself. She asked Mama, "So why did the cap'n hire Will Stephens?"

"He gonna work with Rankin, but he mostly here if we needin' him up at the big house. He gonna write to the cap'n and tell him what happenin' while the cap'n and

Miss Martha away." Mama forged ahead. "Belle, I'm wonderin' what the cap'n say to you 'bout you leavin'?"

"Mama, he got a man for me to marry!" Belle began to cry. I felt better when her sobs became muffled because I knew then that Mama's arms were around her.

"What he tell you 'bout him?" Mama said.

"He's a free black man living in Philadelphia. He has his own business making shoes, and the cap'n says he's gonna buy us a good house. He's coming for me when the cap'n comes back."

"We always know this day comin', Belle," Mama said.

Belle blew her nose. "Make sure Ben stays away, Mama. The cap'n said again that Rankin got the right to sell him off."

"Papa makin' sure to keep Ben away."

"I don't want to go, Mama," she wailed.

"You got to do this, Belle. You gonna be free," Mama said.

"The cap'n said that he sent my free papers at Christmas."

"He send them?" Mama said. "Where they at?"

"I don't know. He say he send them with Miss Martha's packages."

"Did you tell him that you don't get them from her?"

"No, but they got to be up at the house."

"Belle, you got to find those papers!"

"I know, Mama, but there's somethin' else."

"What's that?"

"I asked to take Fanny or Beattie, thinking they'd get their free papers, but he said no. I got to take Lavinia," Belle said.

"He gonna let her go free?" Mama asked.

"That's what he said," Belle said.

"Well, then, that be that."

I sat up, my heart pounding with this news. I didn't want to leave. This was my home! When Sukey fussed, I lay back down and stroked her dimpled hand for comfort until I finally drifted off to sleep. But I woke again in the night, nauseated with fear. I had dreamed that I was riding away from the plantation in a large black carriage and that I was all alone, like Marshall.

The next morning I asked Belle if I was going away with her. "I think so," she said, "but we're here now, so there's no need to worry." When I pressed for more information, she answered me sharply. "Look, Lavinia, I don't want to talk about this no more. We'll see what happens when the cap'n comes home." I knew from her tone that Belle would not discuss it further, so I told her about the package that I had forgotten about — the one addressed to her, the one I had seen at Christmas. She and Mama had me show her the desk drawer that I thought Miss Martha had put it in, but it was not there. Together they searched the house for the papers, but they were nowhere to be found. The two finally gave up, knowing that on the captain's return, the matter would be resolved.

With Will Stephens in place, life for us that summer was easy. If it hadn't been for the knowledge that Belle and I were being sent away, it might have been the happiest of times.

Mama took the opportunity to teach the twins and me how to clean the big house. She showed us how to sprinkle fine sand on the yellow pine floors, then to sweep them clean with water. She instructed us on how to polish the furniture using linseed oil or beeswax, depending on the wood. Then came the day that Mama took us to clean out the nursery. Before he left, the captain had asked Mama to move Sally's things to the attic and have the room ready for Campbell on their return. After Mama opened the door to the children's room, the twins and I entered, mouths agape. There were two beds, two chests of drawers, and more playthings than I ever could have imagined. A child's table was draped with a small linen cloth and set with a miniature pink and white china tea set. A gray and white rocking horse stood at the ready, his black mane swept to one side, his dark eyes inviting us to ride. On one of the two child-size chairs, I recognized Sally's porcelain doll. The room was filled with the little girl's presence.

Mama nodded, giving us permission to examine the toys. We did not hesitate and soon were caught up in the excitement of touching so many treasures. I picked up a picture book and was delighted to find that I could read it. Fanny tried on a wide-brimmed straw hat that had been on one of the beds. Then she went to peer at herself in a small mirror that hung on the wall over a low dresser. Beattie reverently picked up the doll and held it in her lap while stroking its blond curls. We shared our finds until Mama, looking uneasy all the while, told us it was time to pack Sally's things away. After Uncle Jacob carried the boxes away to store them on the third floor, there was an odd, empty feel to the room, and we were happy to leave.

In the following days, Mama had us help her clean out the blue room, too. I was not prepared for the feelings of melancholy when I was surrounded by Campbell's things. I wondered how I could bear to be without him if I were to leave for Philadelphia.

We carried Campbell's cradle and supplies to the nursery, but now that room seemed dark and overlarge for a baby. I couldn't help feeling we should have left the room as it was, for with the removal of Miss Sally's belongings, we seemed to have taken away what had been left of her pink light.

Ben surprised everyone in early June when he announced that he had jumped the broom with a girl from down in the quarters. She was a field worker, and her name was Lucy. Mama seemed hesitant to tell Belle of the union, and when she did, though Belle said not a word, she could not keep the look of betrayal and hurt from her eyes.

The newly married couple spent the following nights in Ben's sleeping quarters down by the barn, but the bride left early every morning at the sound of the horn to join the others from the quarters as they headed out for the fields. Rankin had agreed to the wedding, providing that Lucy remain a worker under him.

■ ■ ■ ■

At the end of June, Will Stephens brought Belle the first letter from Philadelphia. He was a striking man with deep-set brown eyes, a firm jaw, and an easygoing smile. Of average height, he was strongly built and carried himself with assurance. He always took off his hat when he came indoors and had a habit of pushing back his thick brown hair before he spoke. Will's directness was his greatest charm. He looked into your eyes, and when you looked back, you knew he was incapable of deceit. When Will brought that first letter, I heard him apologize to Belle for the episode in the spring when Rankin had ahold of her. Will said he had shamed himself by not stepping forward to help her, and he asked her forgiveness. Belle was shy with him but accepted his apology. He then asked if he should read the letter to her, though he did not seem surprised when Belle declined and instead presented her open hand. After he left, she sent me to the big house to get Mama. On our return, I held Sukey while we listened to Belle read the letter aloud.

It told of the travelers' safe arrival and it carried alarming news as well. Miss Martha's father was ill, but worse, it was feared that Philadelphia was in the midst of a yellow fever epidemic. The captain stated his desire to return home, but Miss Martha refused to leave her sick father. Another letter was promised within two weeks.

True to his word, two weeks later, we received further correspondence from the captain. Will Stephens came again to deliver the letter, and this time Belle invited him in. Ben happened to be replacing the iron crane in the kitchen fireplace, and when he walked in and heard Belle cheerfully conversing with Will Stephens, he quickly rushed back out. I wondered why he looked so angry.

Again Belle waited to read the letter until Will Stephens left, then sent me in search of Mama. This time the news was grim. Miss Martha's father had died. The captain was now ill, and although he was still able to dictate the letter, he was unable to travel. Miss Martha, Campbell, and Dory were all well — Mama gave a sigh of relief — but they were not likely to return in August, as scheduled.

At the end of July, Will Stephens came to the kitchen house, holding open a letter that had been addressed to him. Mama, seeing his solemn approach, ran up from the chicken coop.

"I have bad news," he said, looking first to Belle, then to Mama. "I'm sorry to tell you . . . Dory has died from yellow fever."

Mama sank to a chair, and Belle rushed to her side.

"I'll get George," Will Stephens said. After he left, the silence was so deep that I held my breath, fearing the least sound would catapult us into pain. My arms felt weak, and I slowly set Sukey on the floor. Used to attention, she pulled my skirt to her eyes and played peekaboo, breaking the silence with her laughter. Mama gave a low moan and pulled her apron up to her face, trying to hide her anguish. Sukey, thinking this part of a game, crawled over and pulled herself up to stand beside her grandmother's knee. "Boo. Boo," she said with an expectant smile.

When Mama lifted up her grandchild, Sukey laughed and threw her arms around her grandmother's neck. When Mama Mae began to cry, we all began to cry.

CHAPTER TWENTY

Belle

For a couple a days after we hear Dory's gone, Mama don't act like herself. She walks up to the big house, then she comes down again to the kitchen, forgetting why she's going up there. She says, "Maybe Dory comin' home . . . maybe they got it wrong . . . maybe when that carriage come back, Dory come runnin' down to get her Sukey."

Papa says Mama just needs some time. It's hard on her, he says, not to see for herself, not to have Dory here to put down next to baby Henry. I know Dory's gone. I feel it when I hold Sukey. Dory's like my own sister. But I don't show my feelings. I try to stay strong for Mama.

Sukey's hanging on to Lavinia, who's good with her, but I know that Lavinia's waiting on Campbell. I don't know why she cares for that baby like she do. I wonder

223

what happens when we go to Philadelphia and she got to leave him behind.

Papa don't look me in the eye when he sees me. I know he got Ben to jump the broom with Lucy. When I think of Benny's lips on her, I want to stomp that girl's head. She's just some ugly thing up from the quarters! One night I go down to Ben's place, just to know for sure. I hear them together, and they're sounding like animals, but I stay to listen 'cause I can't move, my feet won't take me. My heart's banging so hard I sit right down in the high grass, never mind the snakes. I stay till Benny's snoring, then I go back to my house. I can't see for crying. Next day Ben's working here in my kitchen when Will Stephens comes with a letter. I talk to Will like he's one fine man. Ben's eyes are spittin' fire when he runs out of here! Makes me feel good.

Everybody's thinking that when I go to Philadelphia and get with the cap'n's shoe man, then I'm gonna be happy. But I don't want no ugly shoe man. I want my Benny. If they just put Lucy back in the quarters and give Benny to me, I won't say a thing about it. I don't sleep at night, thinking how to do Lucy.

CHAPTER TWENTY-ONE

Lavinia

The last of the leaves were falling the mid-November afternoon of 1793 when the black carriage rolled up the drive. The captain and his party had finally come home. Fanny and Beattie were in the big house with Mama and Uncle Jacob, preparing for the travelers' arrival. While Sukey napped, I worked alongside Belle in the kitchen, where we were about to put the finishing touches on plum cakes. To make them, we had added currants and raisins to a pound cake recipe, then poured the batter into small tins. The little cakes were still warm from baking, and before Belle gave me one as a treat, she drizzled a white-sugar coating over the crusty top. When I heard the carriage roll up, I gulped down the cake in a few large bites as I ran for the big house. I was beside myself with excitement. Campbell was home!

Uncle Jacob and Mama were already at the carriage; Fanny and Beattie stood to their side, prepared to help. Miss Martha was the first to emerge. It was hard to believe the toll that the past difficult months had taken on her. Before, I had seen her ill, but this was different. Now her face was drawn and deeply lined, and she squinted into the light as she stepped heavily down from the carriage. Nothing, though, prepared me for the appearance of the emaciated, aged-looking man Uncle Jacob helped from the carriage. The captain had survived yellow fever but looked to have lost his very person. After the captain and the mistress were taken into the house, I waited alone with eager anticipation for Campbell and his nurse to appear. Finally, I could wait no longer and approached the carriage.

"Campbell," I called softly, certain he would recognize my voice.

The interior of the carriage was surprisingly small and smelled horribly of sickness. After my eyes adjusted to the dark, I saw it was empty. I raced in through the front door and caught the small party as they headed upstairs.

"Where's Campbell?" I called after them.

Mama turned back and shook her head to silence me. "He with Dory," she said.

I stood for a long moment, trying to take in the meaning of Mama's words. Then I ran out again to look once more in the carriage. Stunned, I made my way down to the kitchen house. Belle had Sukey in her arms when she found me out beside the woodpile, where I was vomiting up the plum cake.

Belle's eyes filled with compassion when I recovered enough to tell her about Campbell. Sukey put her arms out for me, and to my own shock, I hit at her. She was startled, for she had never been struck. Confused, she began to scream for me, wanting me to hold her. I couldn't bear her tears and reached for her through my despair. "I'm sorry, I'm sorry," I cried, taking her in my arms. "I'm sorry, I'm sorry."

Belle held my chin and turned my face to hers. "Don't you go blaming yourself," she said. "You had nothing to do with that baby dying."

With Sukey's arms clinging tight round my neck, I wept. Through the next weeks, it was her need for me that brought me back.

Fanny, as it turned out, became the captain's favorite nurse. He was drawn to her quick ways, and when she expressed her observations coupled with her wit, she frequently coaxed from him a smile and even, on occasion, a chuckle. The doctor came often to bleed his patient, but after he left, the captain appeared more lethargic than before. Mama observed this for a few weeks until she finally convinced the captain to refuse the doctor his bloodletting treatments. After the captain agreed, she worked hard to stimulate his appetite. In the morning before the sun rose, Mama went out with one of the twins, and while they held the lantern, she killed a chicken. Then she brought it to the kitchen, cleaned the bird, and simmered it with a large handful of fresh green parsley from the garden, cloves of garlic, onion, and a generous amount of salt. Throughout the day Fanny spoon-fed him the broth. Chamomile tea was another of the liquids that Mama had the captain drink, and in the evenings she gave him a glass of sweetened and watered-down wine to help him rest. After a few days he was asking for bits of chicken, but Mama refused him. Instead, she mashed and stirred cooked carrots into the broth and promised that soon he could have the chicken. When that day came, Fanny carried back his empty bowl, as proud as if she had eaten it herself, and Mama breathed a deep sigh of relief. "He comin' back," she said.

Uncle Jacob did not leave the captain's

side but slept on a floor pallet at night. It was through his intervention that Belle was able to visit with her father when the mistress was asleep in her own bedroom.

On her first visit, the captain told Belle that her young man from Philadelphia would not be coming for her after all. He told her how, on their arrival, yellow fever was just beginning to take hold, and when the disease was later determined to be contagious, thousands of terrified citizens fled. Over that summer, even the president, George Washington, left the city, and the government was shut down. The captain spoke of Miss Martha's struggle, how she nursed first her father, then Dory, and finally, himself. He failed to mention Campbell, and when Belle asked about him, the captain hesitated but then seemed relieved to confide in someone.

"After Dory died," he said, "Martha was overcome with fear, certain I would die, too. I was too ill to help, but I knew that Martha wasn't herself. The baby cried for days. One morning when I no longer heard his cry, I insisted that she bring him to me. But he was already gone." He took a deep breath. "Thank God, help arrived. Your young man was one in a community of free black people who helped us. At first it was thought that

Negroes couldn't contract yellow fever, but after Dory died, we knew otherwise. There was little food, and farmers wouldn't come into the city markets, but when your young man came, he brought us food and took away . . . He proved again and again to be the man I thought he was. He would have been a good husband, Belle. I would have been proud to have you marry him. But he, too, died of the disease . . ." The captain's voice shook. "We visited hell, and now I fear for Martha."

As did everyone. Her behavior had no meaning. She wandered from room to room, moving furniture and household articles from place to place. Mama took me to her, thinking I might bring her what I once had, but the vacant look in her eyes frightened me, and she did not react to me as Mama had hoped. Once again the doctor made his appearance and prescribed doses of laudanum. If the truth be told, we were all relieved to see her take the medication that helped her to sleep.

In the following days, Belle, believing that she might now remain here, was almost giddy with relief. Taking her lead, I, too, began to hope again that my future here was secure. I did, however, intend to go to

Philadelphia when I was older. My child's heart would not accept the loss of Campbell; I convinced myself that a mistake had been made. Certain that he was alive and being cared for by loving people, I resolved one day to find him. I had never forgotten my brother and now decided that when I was old enough, I would be reunited with both Cardigan and Campbell.

Sukey's need no doubt saved me. She continued to share my pallet; hers was the first face I saw in the morning and the last I saw before I slept. She relied on me more than ever, and her first spoken word was Binny, her version of my name. I slept at night with Sukey clutched next to me, determined never to lose her.

Mama sent Beattie for me the cold December morning of hog-killing day. The squeal of the dying pigs had affected Miss Martha in a way that had her asking for Isabelle. Beattie and Sukey came with me and stayed behind in the blue room while I went in to see the mistress. When I entered the bedroom, Miss Martha appeared more lucid than before but, on seeing me, insisted that I bring the baby to her. I was at a loss until I heard Sukey's giggle from the blue room. I had a sudden thought and looked to

Mama. She read my intention and nodded, so I left and returned with Sukey. Miss Martha reached for the baby as though she were the very babe she'd asked for. Sukey, an outgoing child, was unafraid and readily went into the arms of the lost woman. The child sat back on the bed to study the surroundings, and when Miss Martha tickled her tummy, she giggled and clasped her fat little hands over Miss Martha's. When Sukey caught sight of the Williamsburg moppet poised on the dresser next to the bed, Miss Martha had me get it for her. Sukey took the doll and inspected it carefully, gingerly fingering its finery. That day Miss Martha watched the baby play with the doll until they both fell asleep.

Following that visit, Miss Martha asked for the baby almost daily. When Sukey came, anticipating play with the beloved moppet, Miss Martha held open her arms and was always satisfied when Sukey willingly obliged her.

There was increasing discord down in the quarters. With the captain home, Will Stephens had returned to his father's farm. Rankin, puffed up with power, was back in control. According to Ida, Rankin used her son to vent his frustrations, and Jimmy, fueled by his loss of Dory, threatened to fight back. Ida feared for his life, and in desperation, she asked Papa George to appeal to the captain.

Beattie and I were polishing the furniture on the upstairs landing when Papa George entered the captain's bedroom. He left the door ajar, so when Rankin followed soon after, we saw him listen, unnoticed, outside the bedroom door. When Papa made his case for Jimmy, the captain refused him. Rankin, Papa was reminded, had been on the plantation for the past five years, and although the captain knew that he was a tough taskmaster, the plantation was doing well. The captain said that until he was in better health, he must support Rankin in his decisions.

When Papa emerged, he looked startled to find Rankin in the hallway. Rankin, unseen by the captain, stretched his foot across the doorway, forcing Papa to step over it. I wondered why Papa didn't pick up the smaller man and heave him to the side; instead, Papa nodded to him. I noted, though, Papa's stiff gait and how he clenched his fists as he walked away.

At Christmas the captain, still not strong enough to go down to the quarters for the celebration, sent Papa and Ben with a barrel of apples, three large hams, and four jugs of brandy. We learned later through Ida that Rankin had sold two of the hams and kept two of the jugs of brandy for himself. There was growing discontent among the workers, as Rankin was again taking half the daily food rations and trading the corn and fatback for liquor for himself. The people were hungry, she said.

Ben confirmed the grim conditions in the quarters. Although he was able to provide food for Lucy, he wasn't able to keep her from the hard labor in the fields.

New sections of land were being cleared for tobacco growing, and the women as well as the men took part in the demanding physical labor. Rankin was becoming increasingly bold and dangerous, and no one dared speak up.

Ben had distanced himself from his family and most especially from Belle. At night he took his food from Mama's house and ate alone, or he waited in his shed for Lucy to come back up from the quarters.

Mama tried without much success to befriend Ben's wife. I knew even then how foreign and privileged our lives must have been in contrast to her own. On Christmas Day Lucy came to Mama's house with Ben, but she stood shyly at the door, refusing a seat. Ben grew frustrated and spoke angrily to her, and with that, she ran back to their shed. Ben silently ate his meal before he went back with Christmas dinner Mama sent for his wife.

Mama Mae said Lucy had always been shy. Mama knew Lucy's background and told us how, at Sukey's tender age, Lucy had been taken from her mother and brought to this plantation. She was given to the old woman who cared for the many children of the quarters. The old woman was not unkind, Mama said, but she had too many children to properly care for them.

"Lucy get took from her mama too soon," Mama Mae said. "You don't take animals away that young."

"Give her time," Papa said, "she come 'round."

For the rest of that winter, the captain's health remained unstable. As soon as he made progress, he pushed himself to exhaustion that sent him back to bed. Then, in spite of Mama's protests, the doctor came again to bleed and purge his patient. During those bouts, the captain was irritable and demanding, but Belle, with her nightly visits, and Fanny, with her cheerful wit, were the two who settled him.

For the most part, Miss Martha remained in her bedroom. Once, though, Uncle Jacob found her wandering at night, trying to unlock the gun case. She told Uncle Jacob that she was going to shoot the whore, but Uncle convinced her to return to her bed. From then on, Beattie slept in the blue room.

The spring of 1794 was cold and wet. Some of the workers from the quarters were ill with cough and fever, but Rankin insisted they were well enough to set out tobacco plants. Papa George said they were sick because they were close to starving. When our family sat down to the evening meal, it was difficult to enjoy the simple but plentiful food, knowing of the hunger such a short distance away.

There was a cold steady drizzle the morning Ida ran up from the quarters to pound on the kitchen door. She stayed outside, shaking, unable to speak until Belle pulled her in from the rain and threw a blanket around her trembling shoulders. When Ida finally spoke, it was difficult to understand her through her chattering teeth.

During a storm the night before, her oldest boy, Jimmy, and his younger brother,

Eddy, had broken into the smokehouse for food. "Just a scrap," she said, "for the lil ones." They waited for a flash of lightning to see the nails, then pried off the boards while thunder buffered the noise. After taking only one small piece of fatback, they reversed their entry and worked again with nature to replace the smokehouse boards.

They thought that Rankin was sleeping, but he smelled the boiling meat. When he burst into their cabin, he pulled Jimmy out and tied him to a stake in the yard. Rankin beat him until Jimmy finally admitted that he had taken the meat. Rankin was jubilant, certain that Ben was also involved in the theft, but Jimmy insisted that he had acted alone. Rankin, in an effort to have Jimmy name Ben, continued to hit him. Ida said, "I go to stop him, but he say he start with the lil ones if I don't stay back. Even though they his babies, he say they just lil nigras and they nothin' to him." In her terrible impotence, Ida pounded at her own legs. "He beatin' my Jimmy now!"

Belle moved fast. "I'm going up to the big house, Ida. You stay here," she instructed, but Ida left again for the quarters as soon as Belle left. I don't know what Belle said, but I do know that the captain dressed and had Ben and Papa George accompany him down to the quarters.

Jimmy, still tied to the stake, was dead. Ida sat next to him, holding his head out of the mud and talking to her son as though he were still alive. Men and women from the quarters circled the mother, afraid to untie the young man's body.

Rankin, drunk, was in his cabin. The captain, enraged, had him removed and thrown onto his horse. He was told that he would be jailed should he return. Then the captain sent Ben to fetch Will Stephens.

The captain offered Will Stephens a proposal. To the best of Fanny's understanding (she was the only one of us present at the meeting), Will Stephens was to act as the sole overseer for a period of five years. Each year he would earn fifty acres, and at the end of the agreed-upon time, he would be given his choice of four Negroes, two female, two male, to begin his own tobacco farm. Will Stephens accepted the offer, and because of it, we lived peacefully for the next two years.

Chapter Twenty-Two

1796
Belle

Every time we think the cap'n's getting better, he gets sick all over again. He goes up and down like this for almost two years. When the cap'n first tells me that the shoe man's gone from yellow fever, I want to jump up and dance, but I say real nice, "Do I still have to go to Philadelphia?"

"Yes. When I am well," the cap'n says. But in all this time, in the two years of him sick, he don't bring it up, and for sure I don't say nothing about it.

When Campbell don't come back, Lavinia takes over with Sukey like she's her own. You never see one without the other. One day Lavinia tells me to ask the cap'n about her brother, Cardigan, so I do. The cap'n don't know what happened to the boy after he sold him away, but he's thinking that maybe Cardigan got took up north.

He did remember that when Cardigan went off with the man, Lavinia screamed so bad that she hurt his ears. When I tell this to Lavinia, she starts to cry, so I tell her not to worry, that I'm always gonna take care of her. I say I know what it's like to be on your own.

The only problem I got is Ben's woman, Lucy, who don't like me. She's a big girl, shy with everybody, but always giving me the up and down. She knows that Ben still has his eye on me, and she knows that I got my eye on him. Truth is, I'm still wanting him like nobody else, but he jumped the broom with Lucy, and that be that. Least most days that's what I tell myself.

Will Stephens is running this place real good, and everybody's happy the way things are going. When Will Stephens looks at me, I know he likes what he sees. Me, too. He's a good-looking man. Not like Benny, oh no, but he's all man just the same. We talk, laugh, and sometimes with Mama and Papa, we sit out at night. When I'm talking and laughing with Will, it makes Ben real mad. One day Ben shows up when I'm feeding the chickens. "What you doin' with that man?" he asks.

"What you doing with Lucy?" I say. Ben's

eyes get so hot I laugh, then walk away, moving slow so he can see what he's missing.

Two years we go on this way. The thing is, the more time goes on, the better it is for me. I'm already twenty-three years old, and soon I'll be getting too old for the captain to find me a husband.

CHAPTER TWENTY-THREE

1796
Lavinia

In May 1796 the twins and I celebrated our twelfth birthday. We were given an afternoon free of chores and skipped away with glee, carrying between us the picnic basket that Belle had prepared. We chattered nonstop along the way until we reached the woods, where Fanny determined we would eat. She was the tallest of us and always famished. Quick-witted, Fanny was as plain-looking as she was plain-speaking, and she often needed reminding to attend to her appearance. Of a sharp nature, she observed out loud what most dared not think, and there were times her unsolicited remarks caused shocked silence, only to be followed by uproarious laughter.

Unlike her twin, Beattie seemed destined to be a beauty. She was soft-spoken and kind, and when she smiled, her deep facial dimples appeared as though to punctuate her easy disposition. Beattie was clean and careful in her dress, and she loved pretty things. Sewing and embroidery were her passions, and her clothes always had adornment. Nothing excited Beattie more than taking the scraps of discarded fabric Mama brought from the big house and fashioning the colorful cloth onto her clothing as collars and pockets.

I stood between the twins in size. I was slight and thin but not as tall as Fanny. I suspected I was rather plain, although no one told me so. My fire-red hair was darkening to auburn, and I wore it in long braids. Fanny teased me about the freckles spattered across my nose until Mama put a stop to that.

With the security of the past two years, I had become more sure of myself and was certainly more outgoing. Yet an underlying anxiety always stayed with me. As a result, I was careful to please and quick to obey.

Our days were filled with chores. Fanny helped out with the captain, while Beattie and I either worked with Belle in the kitchen or helped Mama up in the big house.

My chores in the early morning included helping Mama with Miss Martha's personal care. Since Philadelphia, Miss Martha did not live in reality, but doses of laudanam kept her subdued, and I no longer feared her as I had on her return. In fact, I welcomed the times I sat with her to read aloud or card wool as she rested. In the late afternoon, if Miss Martha's mood suited, I brought Sukey for a visit, for she elicited a vivid response. Miss Martha always brightened when she saw the child. As Sukey cuddled close, the woman would read to her from a child's picture book. In an odd singsong voice, she repeated the verses over and over until they both slept.

One afternoon Mama Mae glanced in to see them both asleep. "That the only good rest that woman get," Mama whispered to me, "but you never leave them alone together."

The captain couldn't seem to recover his health. In earlier days he had been able to walk outdoors, but those excursions ceased as an increasing lethargy overtook him. Fanny and Uncle Jacob continued to care for him, but Fanny was his bright spot. The captain taught her to play card games, and on her winning days, she was rewarded with coins that she proudly gave to her mother for safekeeping.

I can only imagine how Belle's nightly visits cheered her father. She took books from the big-house library and read to him, often late into the night. I awoke one such night to hear Belle's voice coming up from the kitchen. Careful not to disturb Sukey, I crept downstairs to find Belle at the table, studying opened books in the dim lamplight. She explained how she was going over the following night's reading. Unfamiliar with some of the words, she found them in a two-volume dictionary, then sounded them out to herself as her grandmother had taught her to do. After that, on my request, she included me, and together we furthered our reading skills.

That day in May, during our twelfth birthday picnic, Fanny's and Beattie's and my talk turned to the church event on the upcoming weekend. A sacrament service was planned, which meant a whole day away from home, where attention would be given not only to prayer and sermon but to food and socializing. The three of us spoke glowingly of Will Stephens, whom we had to thank for all this.

By making some humane changes, Will Stephens had won the goodwill of the people in the quarters. Under his supervision, the plantation not only thrived but had exceeded production of past years. Food allowances were increased, and salt was added as a staple. Saturday afternoons and Sundays became free time: a time for people in the quarters to work in their gardens, hunt or fish, wash clothes, and visit. They also were given the choice of going to church on Sunday.

Will Stephens had been raised to go to church, and every Sunday he hitched up a wagon inviting as many to ride as could, while others walked the hour's distance. I was beyond envy the first Sunday when I discovered that Beattie and Fanny, accompanied by Ben and Lucy, had been given permission to go with the group from the quarters.

"But why," I cried to Belle, "why can't I go?"

"You don't belong with them," Belle tried to explain.

I still wonder at the fuss I must have raised that caused Will to intervene and speak to Belle on my behalf. But he did, and I couldn't believe my ears when I heard him say that if I could go, he would look out for me. "Why don't you come, too?" he asked Belle. "You could ride in the wagon."

"Thank you," she said, "but I got to stay here to do the cooking."

And so we rode off, the twins and I, that

246

first Sunday morning. I was so happy to go that I did not question why I sat up front next to Will Stephens while the girls rode in the back of the wagon.

The church was rustic, a large log building with rough-hewn benches. It was in that house of worship that I first was made aware of the clear distinction that was made between the races. The white members were seated at the front, while in the back of the building, standing room was reserved for the black servants.

I looked back for the twins when Will tucked my hand in the fold of his arm and led me to a pew. Beattie saw me first and hid a shy smile, but when Fanny saw me, she waved openly, causing Ben to pull her arm down. I paused, wanting to return to them, but Ben gave a nod for me to continue on with Will. Throughout the service, I felt the separation and wondered if Belle had come, would she have been able to sit with Will and me. After the service, although other families stayed to socialize, our group left, excited to return home to share the experience with the others who had not come.

Sunday services became routine. I was given permission to go with the twins and Will each time they went. I stopped wanting Belle to join us when I began to develop a liking for Will Stephens that soon, on my part, developed into young love. Will, likely aware of my infatuation, was teasing and playful with me. He called me solemn and seemed to take delight when he was able to make me smile. As time went on, our Sunday rides to and from church gave us room for more intimate conversation, and eventually, he gained my trust. Then I became more talkative, and one day I asked him his age. Without hesitation, he informed me that he would be twenty-three years old this October.

"Do you have a girl?" I asked, and his smile was so warm I wanted to touch his arm, though of course I didn't.

"Why, no," he said. "Do you have anyone in mind?"

"How about Belle?" I asked anxiously.

He became serious. "She could never be my sweetheart," he said. Before I could ask why, he added, "We could never marry. You know that. It would be against the law."

I hadn't known that and didn't understand but didn't want to appear young and ignorant, so I said nothing.

"Do you have a beau?" he asked after a time.

"Ben used to be my beau, but he got married," I said.

"Oh." A smile curved his lips. "I could see why you would like Ben. He's a good man."

Suddenly, I felt bold. "You might want to wait for me," I said, "until I grow up. I could be your girl."

"Well!" he said. "Now there's an idea."

"I'm quite smart." I forged ahead. "And I know how to cook and read, and Sukey is wild about me."

"And who is Sukey?" he asked.

"She was Dory's baby, but when Dory died, Sukey wanted me to be her mother." I gave a sigh and crossed my hands in my lap.

"Aren't you a little young for that?" he asked.

"I'm twelve," I answered indignantly.

"Well, then, of course," he said.

"Belle says that I'll be a beauty one day." I looked to him for a reaction.

"I believe you already are," he said, and winked at me.

My face flamed, but I continued on, "Oh, and I know about raising chickens. I haven't killed one yet, but Mama says that day is coming soon." I shuddered, thinking of it.

Will squared his shoulders before speaking. "Let's see here," he said. "A beauty who can read and kill chickens. I think I might have to consider this proposal seriously."

"Are you teasing me?" I asked.

He flicked the reins and looked over at me with a beautiful smile. "Do I ever tease you?"

"All the time!" I said, and we laughed.

I suspected he thought of me as a child, but I didn't care. I was sure if I had anything to say on the matter, he would be my future husband.

"Abinia, Abinia," Fanny called me back to our picnic, "what you thinkin' of?"

"Nothing," I said.

Beattie smiled at me. "You thinkin' about Will?"

"Maybe," I said, returning her smile.

"You know Marshall comin' home this week," Fanny offered.

I rolled over on my stomach, recalling the forlorn image of the lost boy riding out in the carriage. "I wonder what he's like now."

"He only comin' for two weeks. Then he goin' back to study. The cap'n wantin' to see how he doin'," Fanny said.

During our picnic that day, Marshall did indeed arrive.

"He so growed up, it hard to believe it the same boy," Mama told us. How right she was. Late in the afternoon, I was sent up to the big house to sit with Miss Martha while she slept. There, I was startled to find Marshall seated at a window in the mistress's room. Although forewarned, I scarcely recognized him. He rose when he saw me. Shy, I stood back. In his sixteenth year, he was already the height of a grown man.

"Hello, Lavinia," he said. His childhood monotone voice had been replaced with a confident baritone.

"Hello," I said quietly.

"You've grown," he said, looking me up and down, and for the first time ever, I was aware of my drab homespun clothes. In contrast, he wore navy knee breeches and a waistcoat made of ivory satin. On it was stitched a pictorial scene of vivid colors, and I immediately thought of Beattie and how she would be captivated at the detail of the embroidery.

"Join me," he invited, setting a chair next to his at the window. Uncertain what to do, but seeing his mother asleep, I did as he asked. He positioned himself with assurance, and I seated myself as I had been taught by Miss Martha, with my feet together and my hands folded in my lap.

Marshall had grown into a strikingly attractive young man. His short blond hair curled loosely at his neck, and his blue eyes, which in my memory had been dull, now shone when he smiled.

"I often remember you," he said, then drained a glass of wine. "You were the one who cared so for my baby brother." He gazed out the window. The sun was setting, and the light cast his face in gold. I could hardly believe that he was speaking to me in this way, and I could not take my eyes from him. "I understand that you are a great help to my mother," he said.

"I read to her," I said, proud of the achievement.

"Do you like to read?" he asked.

"It's my favorite thing."

"I must speak to Father about you," he said. "I wonder what plans have been made."

I was spared an answer when Mama abruptly came into the room. She studied us for a moment before addressing Marshall. "You know the cap'n wantin' to see you."

Marshall flushed. He stood and, with a look of defiance, went to the blue room. There he stopped at the side table that held a wine decanter. From it he poured himself another glass of wine. He drank it in short order, then left the room.

Mama shook her head. "That boy drinkin' too much," she said.

I saw Marshall only in passing over the next few days, but each time he saw me, he nodded, smiled, and greeted me by name. I was flattered by the attention from this sophisticated young man.

"Marshall drinkin' all the time," Mama said at supper that evening.

"I tell him not to ride out when he drinkin' like that," Papa agreed, "but he go just the same, every day."

"Where he go?" Mama asked.

"Folks over at the other place say he find Rankin again . . . maybe Rankin find him, I don't know," Papa said. "It good that boy leavin' again in a few days."

"What gonna happen when the cap'n gone?" Fanny asked. "Will Marshall come back here to run this place? He be the masta then?"

Belle answered quickly. "The cap'n's gonna be just fine, Fanny! Every day he's getting stronger."

"Belle, you know he sick. You best talk to him about gettin' those free papers of yours," Papa George said to Belle.

"I will, Papa," Belle said. "I'll get the papers, but I don't want him to get started up again about sending me off."

"You tell him you need those papers," Papa said firmly.

"I will. I will," Belle answered, her irritation clear.

The Sunday of the anticipated sacrament service finally came, and the twins and I could barely contain our excitement. I had worked with Belle to prepare the feast we took with us for the communal picnic at the church grounds. We packed baskets of fresh biscuits and corn bread, pickled cucumbers and peach preserves, and my favorite, a pound cake with thick strawberry jam for topping.

Beside myself with excitement, I begged Belle to come along and bring Sukey. "Ben and Lucy are coming," I said as encouragement.

"Mama needs me to do the cooking for the big house," Belle said, "and I don't think I'm wanting to pray all day anyway."

She waved good-bye in the early-morning light. She had rushed to help us get underway and hadn't taken the time to attend to her hair. Her thick braid hung down, and when she raised her arm to wave us off, her shift dropped to expose a corner of her smooth tanned shoulder. She pulled it back quickly and blushed with embarrassment. I did not miss the admiring look Will Stephens gave her, and because of it, I was happy that she could not come.

I waved good-bye to her but felt a strange sense of foreboding when I looked up toward the big house to see Marshall at a bedroom window, watching as our wagon rumbled away.

Chapter Twenty-Four

Belle

I was in the kitchen by myself, sweeping, and I don't hear nothing until I got a knife at my neck and Rankin in my ear, telling me if I make a noise, that knife's going in. Then Marshall, drunk like Rankin, comes at me. I start kicking, but Rankin twists my arm and punches my stomach. I start screaming, but Rankin takes off my head rag and stuffs it in my mouth. It's hard to breathe and I'm choking on blood, but when I see what Marshall's gonna do next, I go wild. Then Rankin hits me and I go down. All the time Marshall's working on me, he's talking, but I don't hear what he's saying. Rankin is talking, too, but all I know is, I'm gonna die, I'm gonna die. When it's all over, when Marshall's buttonin' up, Rankin moves that knife real slow across my chest, watching my face. "You want me to cut these off," he says, "keep 'em for myself?" My head flies back and forth, back and forth. I can't stop it.

He says I tell anybody about this, he'll come back and cut 'em off, then he's gonna kill anybody I talk to. "Just like this," he says. He puts that knife up over me, then brings it down fast, right into the floor. Everything in me goes soft.

They go, and I pull myself to a corner and stay put, just trying to breathe. I keep choking. I don't even know to take my head rag out of my mouth. When Uncle Jacob finds me, he tells me to hang on, he's going for Mama.

"Who do this?" Mama asks, but I don't say nothing. Mama cleans me up and gives me some peach liquor. Then she asks me again, "Belle, who do this?" I'm sure those two are listening, so I don't say nothing. I know Rankin will do what he says. "Papa say Rankin and Marshall drinkin' and up to no good. Was they here?" Mama asks. I put my hand over her mouth, quick, to stop her. Mama pulls back, looks at me. Then she says that she's gonna go up and tell the cap'n, and that's when I start crying, "No, Mama, no." I hang on to her like she's gonna leave me. "No, Mama, no. Don't tell nobody!"

"Hush, chil', I don't do nothin' you don't

want me to do." She gives me another drink to stop my shaking.

I say, "Don't tell nobody about this, Mama, please don't tell nobody!"

Mama say, "That's all right. I do just like you say, Belle."

I drink some more, and the last thing I know is Mama's taking me up to bed.

CHAPTER TWENTY-FIVE

Lavinia

It had been a wonderfully long and enriching day. Driving home, we continued to sing hymns, repeating the songs sung earlier at the service. Lucy had surprised us all. She was a large dark woman, not given to talk, but God had blessed her with a singing voice that caused others to stop and listen. We pleaded on the ride back until we convinced her to sing a solo. Splendor radiated as she sang, and it touched everyone in the wagon.

At our first stop in the quarters, Ida and the other women climbed down from the wagon, and Ben hopped up to sit proudly next to Lucy. Will flicked the reins, and the horses walked on, stopping next at the kitchen house before their final stop at the barns. When the twins and I jumped off, we were surprised to see Papa seated on the rough pine bench outside the kitchen. He rose at our arrival and came to meet us. My eyes were accustomed to the night light, and I saw the worry on his face.

"Everythin' all right," he tried to reassure us, "everythin' all right."

"Papa?" Ben leaped from the wagon.

"Belle have some problems, but she gonna be all right," Papa said.

Will came down to join the men. "What happened here, George?"

Papa led the men a short distance away from the wagon before he spoke to them in a low voice. Their response to his quiet information was mutual; they gasped and turned their heads away from Papa. Ben faced the big house, and from the profile of the unscarred side of his face, I had never seen him look so angry. When he began to walk toward the kitchen door, Papa held him back.

"You take Lucy home," Papa said. "She don't need trouble, with her baby comin'."

As if on cue, Lucy came to stand beside Ben and tried to take his hand. He shook her off. "Get back on that wagon!" he said, then turned away, angrier still.

Lucy didn't get back on the wagon. Instead, she walked off alone in the dark, heading toward her home down by the barns. Papa gave Ben a strong look until

Ben followed after his wife. After Will left with the horses and wagon, Papa sent Beattie and Fanny up to the big house, where they were told they would spend the night together in the blue room. Mama was up there with Sukey, waiting for them. They left together, walking hand in hand in the dark, and I was left alone with Papa. He looked down at me as though uncertain what to say.

"Papa, where's Belle?" I could scarcely speak from fear.

"Mama comin' soon," he answered.

"Papa," I said, hardly daring to ask, "is Belle dead?"

"No, chil'," Papa said. He led me to sit on a bench and seated himself next to me. "Belle gonna be all right." He looked off when he spoke. "Belle have a bad day, that's all."

"What happened, Papa?"

"Some men show up. They drinkin' and they hit on Belle."

"Where was Mama?" I asked in alarm.

Papa breathed in deeply. "She and Sukey was up with Miss Martha."

"Who were the men?"

"Belle don't want nobody talking 'bout this," Papa said.

"But I want to know what happened," I said.

"She don't even want the cap'n to know," Papa said.

"Why, Papa?" I asked angrily. "Why won't she tell the captain?"

"Belle afraid that she get sent away," Papa said flatly.

When Mama came, she took Sukey and me up to bed, cautioning us to be quiet. Belle was already asleep in our dark room, and soon after Mama left, Sukey fell asleep. I stared into the night for a long while, too afraid to go to Belle, too afraid to go to sleep.

The sun was already up when I woke the next morning to feel Sukey's fingers gently outlining my face. I pretended sleep while she touched my eyes, then traced my eyebrows, tickling me. I smiled in spite of myself, then startled her by grabbing her hand. She fell against me laughing, and I hugged her to me, breathing in her delicious baby scent.

When I heard the kitchen sounds of pots and pans, I remembered the night before and quickly lifted up on my elbow to check on Belle. Her bed was empty and I was relieved to know she was downstairs preparing a morning meal. I stopped my play with Sukey and rose to pull my long brown skirt over my night shift, then told Sukey to wait until I came back.

"Belle," I called, leaning down, midway on the stairs. Unbeknownst to me, Sukey had followed and grabbed my skirt in play. Belle was working at the fireplace, and when I called, I startled her and she swung around. I cried out her name again when I saw her battered face. On seeing my horror, she tried a smile in an effort to soften the shock. It must have hurt her, for she grimaced and held her hand to her swollen mouth. I don't know when I first noticed her skirts in the embers, but when I saw they were smoldering, such was my alarm that I could not speak. Instead, I ran down the stairs, intending to pull her away from the fireplace. Unwittingly, as I ran, I pulled Sukey, who, with a cry, tumbled down the stairs. When Sukey began to scream, I froze, unsure which beloved to help first. I turned back to Sukey for a moment, then saw Belle rush past me to the child, unaware that the back of her skirt had begun to flame.

In shock, I was unable to move. To our good fortune, Will Stephens appeared. Within moments he pulled Sukey from Belle's arms and thrust the screaming child at me. He pushed Belle to the floor, stomped on her skirts, and called for me to bring the water bucket. I sat the shrieking Sukey on a chair and ran for the bucket of drinking water. Will pulled it from me and threw the water on Belle to douse her skirts. She gasped when the cold water hit her legs.

"No more," she cried, "no more." She rocked her head back and forth, and although her eyes were wide open, she wasn't seeing us.

Will sat beside her on the dirt floor and placed her head against his shoulder. "It's all right, Belle," he said, "it's over. Your skirts were on fire, and we put it out. It's all right."

Sukey continued to screech as I ran with her to get Mama.

By the time Ben and Lucy's baby, Junior, was born, Belle, though appearing to have recovered from her physical trauma, remained moody and withdrawn. Curiously, there was no explanation. From adult whisperings, Fanny, Beattie, and I tried to piece together what little information we could, but later that fall, when Belle's stomach began to swell, we did not associate the event with Belle's pregnancy.

When we were told she was to have a

baby, all three of us guessed Will was the father, as he had become a frequent visitor to the kitchen. I watched jealously at the concern he showed for Belle. I saw no physical contact between them, but in my young heart, I was convinced they were lovers.

One day, unable to hold back, I asked Belle to name the father of her child.

"You know we don't talk about this," she said coldly.

I didn't respond, but after her refusal, I became increasingly petulant. When, later that month, my body made the transition to womanhood, I went to Mama Mae to have her teach me self-care during my monthly time. After the instructions, Mama sat me down in her small house. "Why you so mad with Belle?" she asked.

I shrugged.

"I hear you talkin' to her in ways that not right," she continued.

I hung my head.

"Womans gets the bad feelin's sometimes, and they don't know why. It all right if you don't know why you so mad with Belle, but I thinkin' it have somethin' to do with Belle havin' a baby."

I stayed silent.

"Belle have no say about this baby. It for us to help her now. She needin' you, just

265

like Sukey needin' you." Mama pulled me to her and stroked my back. "I know you a good girl, Abinia. That day you come here be a good day for us. Now you like Belle's own chil'. That never change. But you growin' up and this be a time she needin' you." She reached down for my face and held it up. "Belle needin' every one of us," she said, looking into my eyes. "We her family, and we gonna help her. You part of this family?"

I yanked away and turned my back to her.

"Abinia?" she said with disappointment. "You not with this family?"

"I don't know!" I said, stomping my foot. "I don't know! Mostly it seems like I'm part of this family, but in church I have to go up front and sit with the white people. I want to sit with the twins, and they can't come up with me, and I can't go back by them. You aren't my real mama, and Belle isn't, either. Where will I go when I grow up? And I don't want to live in a big house, either!" I began to cry, and Mama waited awhile before she spoke.

"Abinia," she said, "if you and Beattie and Fanny was playin' in the stream and it got deep like after the big rain and you all needin' help, don't you think I there to help you out, just like I do the twins?"

I thought about that for a moment. "But which one of us would you pull out first?" I asked, turning to face her.

"Whoever go by me first," Mama said quickly. We stared at each other, then laughed aloud at her honest answer. "Abinia," she said, "this I know. What the color is, who the daddy be, who the mama is don't mean nothin'. We a family, carin' for each other. Family make us strong in times of trouble. We all stick together, help each other out. That the real meanin' of family. When you grow up, you take that family feelin' with you."

"But I don't want to go away —" I started.

Mama interrupted. "Why you thinkin' about leavin' now? That some long time away. You look at today, chil'. You say, 'Thank you, Lawd, for everythin' you gives me today.' Then you worries about the next day when the next day come."

I sighed in relief.

"So, Abinia," Mama asked again, "you part of this family?"

I nodded.

She smiled at me. "Good. Then we best get back to work, 'cause we a workin' family." She rose to her feet, and I, feeling like a woman, followed her out the door and into the bright sunlight.

■ ■ ■ ■

Through that fall and winter Belle grew heavy and awkward. Remembering Mama's words, I tried to help her whenever she would allow. She remained temperamental, but we were close again, although neither of us spoke of the baby she was carrying. Fanny told Beattie and me that when the captain finally noticed Belle's condition, he became furious and demanded to know who the father was. Belle refused to discuss the subject and told him that she would not visit him if he were to ask again. He became enraged and told her to stay away. And so she did.

I was in the kitchen house with Belle and Mama on a cold February night when Belle's baby was born. The twins were up at the big house, and Papa came for Sukey when Belle's labor pains began in earnest. I wanted to go with Papa, but Belle clung to my hand and asked me not to leave. I looked at Mama, hoping she might send me off with Sukey.

"Abinia gonna stay." Mama set me with her eyes. "Abinia can almost do this by herself," she reassured Belle. "You remember how she help me when Campbell come."

This time I was older and more prepared for childbirth, but I felt sick with relief when Belle finally delivered herself of the child. Mama had me cut the purple cord, and after she cleaned and wrapped the child, she handed the baby to me. "Give him to Belle," she instructed.

I stared at the baby.

"Go on." Mama pushed me toward Belle.

"Belle!' I cried in delight. "Belle! He looks just like Campbell!"

Belle gave a sharp cry and turned her head away. Her reaction reminded me of Miss Martha's rejection of Campbell, and I felt afraid for Belle's baby. I looked to Mama for guidance and was surprised to see her drying her own tears. I waited, unsure, until the baby began to fuss.

Mama came. "Belle," she said, taking the baby from me, "come now. He your baby. This chil' come from the Lawd. He got the right to have a mama, and that mama is you. Now you take him, Belle, and you give him your milk. He a good baby. He gonna be a sweet chil'."

Belle lay with her head turned away, but Mama pulled back Belle's nightshirt to expose a full breast. Mama settled the baby next to Belle. As he hungrily sought a nipple and began to suckle, Belle gave a low moan when her body yielded to the need of her child. Her anguished eyes sought out Mama, but they softened the moment she looked down at her nursing baby. She cradled him, and made soft cooing sounds as she stroked his tiny white face.

I shed tears of relief and joy. Belle reached for my hand and pulled me toward her and the baby. "Lavinia," she whispered, "what are we gonna call him?"

Chapter Twenty-Six

Belle

At the end of May 1797, the cap'n calls for me to bring my baby, Jamie Pyke, up to the big house. First I say no, but Mama says, "Belle, you got to go. That man's gettin' sicker by the day. He can't hardly walk no more, and his color look like a dry old peach. You got to get the free papers for you and Jamie. If the cap'n die, what you gonna do? Stay here if Marshall take the cap'n's place? You want that?" First time ever, I know I got to get the papers. So I go to the big house and take my four-month-old baby with me.

Mama's right. When I see the cap'n, I see he's not gonna make it. My legs don't want to move, but I take Jamie over to show the cap'n. He just stares down. He asks me one more time who's the daddy, but my mouth won't work. Uncle Jacob, looking like he can't take no more, steps up. "It plain to see who the daddy be!" Uncle says. "And Belle don't have no say in the matter. And this a fact!"

The cap'n looks like he's having trouble getting air. When he talks again, he says he'll give the free papers to Jamie, but then I got to go to Philadelphia. I say all right, I'll go, but I tell him I'm still needing my own papers, too. He's thinking I have them, but I say no, I never do get them. "Come back in the morning," he says, "I'll have the lawyer here and the papers drawn up."

Then last night Mama comes running for Ben to get the doctor, but the cap'n's gone before they get back.

I don't have time for crying, only time for wondering what's gonna happen now. Mama's right. Now Marshall's gonna be the master. I got to get me and Jamie outta here. I don't know where I'm going, I just know that I got to get out before Marshall's heading back.

When everybody's working up at the big house, getting ready to bury the cap'n, I take the best knife in my kitchen house, wrap it good, then get busy and tie up everything I can carry. Tonight I'm gonna take Jamie and run. First I'm thinking to take Lavinia, but I know that she won't go without Sukey.

I wait until nobody's around, then I run down to hide my pack behind the springhouse. I don't see Ben following me. When he comes around the corner, he scares me so bad I start hitting him. He holds me back, but that makes me hit him more.

"Don't, baby, don't hit me," he says, and I say, "Don't you call me no baby," but he says, "Belle, you always my baby, don't you know that? I take care of you like you my own."

Then I get mad! My mouth won't stop. "You take care of me! When do you do that? That time Rankin and his men was throwing me around in the kitchen? Or I guess you was taking care of me when Rankin was holding me down and Marshall was on me? Or . . . no . . . no! That's right! You was taking care of me every night when you was on your Lucy!"

Ben lets go of me. He looks at me, and his big eyes tell me the words I use are cutting in. He backs away from me, holding up his hands to stop my talking. "You right," he says, "you right." When he starts to cry, all the fight goes out of me.

"Oh, Benny," I say, "I'm just saying words. They're not the truth."

But he keeps shaking his head, saying, "No. No. You right, Belle. I don't help you.

273

I never do help you."

I go to Ben, take my skirt, and clean away
the water coming from his eyes, but he can't
stop crying. "I'm sorry, Benny," I say, "I'm
sorry for saying all that." I touch his mouth
with my finger. "Shhh," I say. "Shhh." He
moans deep and loud, and he pulls me to
him. When we start to kiss, we both don't
care to stop no more.

That night I get with Ben again. He tells
me to stay until we see what Will Stephens
has to say. Ben says he's gonna run with me
if Marshall's coming back.

CHAPTER TWENTY-SEVEN

Lavinia

The captain was buried before Miss Martha's sister and her husband arrived from Williamsburg. In view of Miss Martha's condition, the doctor took it upon himself to decide on a fast and simple burial service. Only a few carriages arrived from other places, but all of us from the plantation were there. All, that is, but Miss Martha and Marshall, who, for reasons unknown to me, remained in Williamsburg.

After Mr. and Mrs. Madden arrived, there followed a busy week. When Miss Sarah came to her sister's room, she often found me attending to Miss Martha. I remembered her from her Christmas visit, and my first opinion was not much changed. It continued to astound me to see how different she was from her sister. Though under these circumstances she was solemn, her eyes were lively and quick. Miss Sarah's face was plump, as was her body, but I was to learn that her soft appearance belied her determination. As she took charge, she left no doubt that she was indeed capable of overseeing a household. In the first few days, she said little as she observed us in our daily care of Miss Martha. Then one day she addressed me. "Marshall told me how good you are to his mother. Now I see for myself how she relies on you."

"She likes me to read to her," I said.

"And who taught you to read?" she asked.

I intuitively knew not to include Belle. "Miss Martha," I said, "before she got so sick."

"And would you like to continue to learn?" she asked kindly.

"Oh yes," I said innocently.

Later in the week, she asked for my help as she sorted through her sister's clothes. I indicated Miss Martha's favorite dresses and also the shoes she preferred, pointing out those that pinched her toes. Somehow I did not guess that we were packing for an upcoming departure.

Mr. Madden, a lawyer, was executor of his brother-in-law's will. Papa George and Will Stephens met frequently with Mr. Madden, and finally, on Friday, all of the big-house people were called to the library.

Mr. Madden spoke first. Master Marshall, he said, had inherited the plantation and all that went with it. However, it was the captain's wish that Mr. Madden maintain control until Marshall's twenty-second birthday. That, he informed us, would be five years hence. Meanwhile, Master Marshall was to continue his studies in Williamsburg, where he planned to attend the College of William and Mary to study law. The house and farm staff would maintain the property until Master Marshall's return. Will Stephens, now the farm manager, would be in charge.

When Miss Sarah spoke next, she told us that Miss Martha was returning with them to Williamsburg. There she would be admitted to a noted hospital where patients with disorders such as Miss Martha's were often treated successfully. Miss Sarah felt certain they could help her sister. Also, Miss Martha would benefit from being near her son in Williamsburg.

I was surprised, then alarmed, when I was asked to stay after the meeting ended. I nervously looked back at Mama and Belle as they left. Belle looked as though she was about to cry, but Mama gave me a reassuring nod.

Mr. Madden, as rotund as his wife, sat at

the desk and peered through his eyeglasses at the papers before him. After the room had cleared, Miss Sarah coughed to get her husband's attention. He looked up. "Oh," he said, as though surprised to see me. "So you're Lavinia? I've been looking at your papers. Apparently, you'll be coming with us."

I must have shown my shock, for Miss Sarah took my hand and sat me in a chair. Then I connected Mr. Madden's words to the conversation I had overheard some nights before. That evening I woke to the sound of Belle's voice from downstairs. I glanced over to check on baby James, who was sleeping soundly in the sturdy cradle Papa George had made for him. Sukey was asleep beside me, and I leaned over to kiss her round face as I got up. Before I reached the bottom step, I saw the kitchen door standing open. For some reason, I stopped when I heard Mama's voice coming from the outdoors. It was the end of May, and the evening was warm; I thought how pleasant it must be for her and Belle to sit and enjoy the night air.

"But what if she don't want to go?" Belle said.

"This a good chance for her," Mama said.

It was Will's voice I heard next. "It's quite

an opportunity, Belle. They are good people, and they will give her an education."

In a flood of anger on hearing Will's voice, I rushed back up the stairs. It remained my belief that Will was the father of Belle's baby, and I could hardly keep my jealousy contained. But this was the first time I had heard them together at night, and my anger burned so fiercely that I lost interest in their conversation.

Now, in the library with the Maddens, I understood that they had been speaking of me.

"Lavinia." Miss Sarah took the paper from her husband. "You are already thirteen years of age, and in light of the fact that you have only a few years left to serve this household, we've decided to take you with us."

I nodded, although I knew little of my indentureship. Nothing specific had ever been laid out for me, and the truth was, I hadn't thought to ask for a better definition.

"I have watched you with Miss Martha, and I see how she cares for you."

I nodded again, numbed by my fear.

"We want you to come with us to Williamsburg. When Miss Martha is well again, you will serve her. Until then you will live with us. We have agreed," she said, glancing back for her husband's approval, "that you can study with the tutor who comes to teach our daughter."

I was silent.

"We are prepared to bring you to our home, to give you every advantage for your future."

The roaring in my ears prevented me from hearing further, and eventually, Miss Sarah sent me upstairs to resume my duties.

Beattie waited there, and from the way she observed me, I guessed she already knew of my upcoming departure. My feelings of betrayal were so acute that I refused to speak to her or to anyone else for the rest of that day. I planned to avoid everyone until I had to leave.

I became angrier still the following day when Mama had me sit with Miss Martha for much of the morning, then late into the afternoon. Fanny was caring for the needs of Mr. Madden and Miss Sarah, while Beattie and Mama were curiously absent from the big house. Uncle Jacob came to see me while Miss Martha slept, but I refused to speak to him. "Allah be with you," he said after I shrugged his comforting hand off of my shoulder. When he left, I kicked out at the air, furious with him and his Allah.

After Miss Martha finished an early supper, Miss Sarah came and gave me a small leather trunk, instructing me to take it to the kitchen house and pack my belongings.

I knew that I had little to pack, and when I told her that I would not need a trunk of this size, she smiled and told me to take it anyway.

The kitchen house was empty. Belle had not set out my usual supper, and that was almost more than I could bear. I believed then she had already forgotten me. Desolate, I went upstairs to pack, thumping the small trunk behind me.

There, to my amazement, I saw two of Miss Martha's dresses draped across Belle's bed. As I approached to look more carefully, Fanny and Beattie jumped up. "We help Mama get them ready for you!" they shouted. Together they ran at me and began to undress me, insisting that I try on the new dresses. As they did so, they told me how Miss Sarah had given Mama two of Miss Martha's day dresses, with instructions to cut them down for me. Fanny, closest to my size, had filled in for me so I would have a surprise. After I stepped into the pale blue calico, Fanny fastened the front buttons while Beattie pulled a folded blue ribbon from her pocket. She unfastened my braids and brushed free my long hair, then pulled some strands back from my face to tie them with the ribbon. They took my hands and, giggling, refused to tell me why they were leading me down to the quarters.

A bonfire was roaring. Food was lined up on makeshift tables; a feast had been prepared. There was clapping when I appeared with the girls, and it was then I understood that the party was for me. Belle came first to hug me, then Mama and Papa, followed by Ben and Lucy. Finally, Ida, along with all the adults and children who had been my church companions, came over to wish me well. I looked around in wonder to think that so many cared for me. How could I bear to leave them?

When the food was served, I was afraid to eat for fear of soiling my new dress. Ida recognized my dilemma, went to her cabin, and returned with a clean cloth that she carefully draped over my lap before handing me back my bowl. My eyes filled at her concern, and I longed for her to hold me, to tell me that a mistake had been made and I did not have to go away. All evening I fought tears. When the music began, Papa took me as his partner for the opening dance. As we circled, I looked out at the smiling faces and could not believe that I was leaving everyone in the morning. Then

Will came to me for a dance. His thick straight hair fell forward when he nodded, and he pushed it back before he reached for my hand. Beattie giggled, and Fanny poked me in the back as I rose to dance with him. While we danced, I refused his gaze, but he began to tease me, and it wasn't long before I laughingly sassed back. When the dance ended, Will returned me to Belle and the twins. "Don't forget, Lavinia," he said, "you said you'd be my girl. I'll be waiting for you."

I turned away, angry at him for daring to joke like that in front of Belle. I was happy when Mama said it was time to leave.

My family further surprised me when they all gathered at the kitchen house and each presented me with a gift. Ben gave me a small forged trivet in the shape of a bird. Mama had woven a basket; inside was Beattie's contribution of three wild turkey quills. They had been boiled, their membranes stripped, the nibs pointed, and were ready for writing. Some black walnuts were included, and Belle gave me instructions on how to boil them down for ink. Fanny presented a small pouch that held two coins.

"Fanny get those from the cap'n." Beattie said proudly of her sister.

Belle gave me her prized silver hand mirror, and when I attempted to give it back, she insisted I take it and asked me to think of her whenever I used it. Papa handed me a small wooden chick he had carved. "You know what this mean," he said, and I choked back tears, remembering our long-ago conversation when he had told me that he would be my papa.

Uncle Jacob gave me a whistle. It was a miniature, made from a small reed, and when he had me blow it, it sang a high wild note. "That the call for me," he said. "If you gots the trouble, you take that out and blow that. I listen good for that sound."

I don't know if it was the pitch of that whistle or his gentle words that touched me, but I could not stop the tears and leaned in to Belle as I began to cry. She hugged me while Papa began good-natured teasing to bring me back. Everyone laughed when he told me that I'd better use the whistle carefully, because Uncle Jacob couldn't ride a horse very well. Papa drew mind pictures for us of Uncle riding to Williamsburg, desperately hanging on to a horse while calling out that he was coming to save the day.

It worked. I was laughing through my tears when everyone said good night.

Belle helped me pack my trunk. There was

room for everything but my collection of bird nests, so Belle suggested that I take only two and that she safeguard the rest. I reluctantly agreed, but I had little choice, as my trunk was full the next morning when Ben carried it up to the big house and strapped it to the coach.

Everyone came to see us off. At the last minute, Miss Martha decided she did not want to leave. After futile attempts at gentle persuasion, Mr. Madden commanded Ben to lift her up and deposit her into the carriage.

I was the last to enter. The horses were eager to leave, and I was grateful for Ben's help when he assisted me up the carriage steps. He gave my hand a tight squeeze, but I dared not meet his eye. As the door closed, I saw Sukey running up the hill from the kitchen house. I had talked to her early that morning and had explained that I was leaving for a while. She had listened carefully and appeared unperturbed as she went about her morning business. She must have been forgotten in the excitement, and now she came carrying her heavy winter shoes and her moppet doll. "Wait, Binny, I comin' with you," she called, "I comin' with you!" Before she could reach the carriage, Papa George scooped her up in his arms.

We were off, but I couldn't keep myself from looking back out the window as the carriage pulled away. Sukey was frantic, and Papa was having a hard time holding her as she kicked and hit, trying to break free.

Inside the carriage, Miss Martha's screams spoke for me.

CHAPTER TWENTY-EIGHT

Belle

I sure do miss Lavinia. After she goes, I find out how much I don't like being by myself. Nights are the worst. Even though Marshall is still up in Williamsburg and Will Stephens says Rankin is long gone, just the same, I got a bolt put on my door and sleep with a knife next to me. One of them shows up, this time he's a dead man.

During the day I don't have time to think about this too long. Even though everybody in the big house is gone, I got my hands full with the gardens and Jamie and Sukey.

I wonder how Lavinia's doing without her Sukey. At night Sukey was crying, keeping me and Jamie awake, until Mama finally takes her and puts her with Beattie. That helps her some, but now she's not wanting to eat. Mama says it's like that little girl lost two mamas. First Dory, now Lavinia.

Truth is, when Mama took Sukey at night,

it made it easier for Ben to come see me. He can't stay away, and I don't want him to. First, though, I go to Ida to get something so I don't get caught with no baby. She said it only works for some, never did work for her, but so far it's working good for me. My Jamie's everything to me, but I don't want no more babies. Come a day I got to run, one child's enough for me and Ben to carry.

Then there's Lucy. Me, I don't like her. Just thinking about her living there with Ben makes me mad, but Ben don't want her knowing about us. He says if she finds out we're getting together, it's gonna hurt her, and Ben says she already got hurt enough in this life.

Then, too, we don't want Mama or Papa to know about us. But I know Mama. She'll find out soon enough, and then look out! Last night we got to laugh when I say to Ben that something's not right that at twenty-four years old, we're still watching out for Mama.

CHAPTER TWENTY-NINE

Lavinia

In 1797 Williamsburg was no longer the capital, but the town was noted for three remaining institutions. One, the focus of the town and the local gathering place was the courthouse. It was an impressive brick building, centrally situated, and appeared much as an anchor for the main thorough-fare, the Duke of Gloucester Street. A man of law, Mr. Madden was intimately familiar with this workplace.

The second, also central, was the College of William and Mary. Established in 1693, it had maintained an excellent reputation as a school for higher learning, particularly for law. It was at this institution that Marshall would further his education.

The third, the one that eventually took on most significance for me, was the public hospital. It, too, was a fine brick building. This one, built in 1773, sat on the edge of town and was more commonly known as the Hospital for the Insane. Its reputation was growing, and it was to this hospital that Miss Martha was admitted. The hospital accepted only those who were dangerous or curable. I was never told under which of these two categories Miss Martha was signed in.

The Maddens had an inviting home. Within easy walking distance of the courthouse, it was a rambling clapboard house, and though certainly impressive in size, it was not as large as the big house I had left behind. There were many rooms in this home, but the ceilings were low, and the rooms were more compact, more intimate, than those in Tall Oaks. Many of the windows held cushioned window seats, while on other wide windowsills, indoor plants flowered, often perfuming the room. Although there was a library, books were casually set about in other rooms, and I guessed rightly that reading in this household was routine. The furnishings here were not as extravagant as at Tall Oaks, but they were substantial enough for one to know that this home belonged to a family of means. At first glance I was taken aback by the colors of the rooms, painted in rich and vibrant hues, although in a short time I adjusted to that particular style of decoration.

To my great astonishment, I was given my own small upstairs room. Later, I was to learn that I was placed here, as this room was attached to the larger bedroom next door that was intended for Miss Martha's use on her return from the hospital. Nonetheless, I was astounded to be sheltered in the main house and to have it decorated so prettily. My room's lively green contrasted pleasingly with a white coverlet on the footed bed. A circular braided rug covered much of the pine floor, and on the edge of it set a small oak desk in front of a gabled window.

I looked out at the broad and busy street below, outlined by large elm and locust trees, and through them I saw other homes similar in character. Some appeared in need of repair, but almost all were surrounded by lush gardens filled with flowers, herbs, and shrubs.

My hosts had only one child: a much loved daughter named Meg. On my arrival in Williamsburg, she greeted me enthusiastically. She was twelve to my thirteen years, and though we had both grown since our first meeting years ago, now she was significantly shorter than I. She was slim, and her limp was more pronounced than I remembered, but her frizzed brown hair floated out as before, and I must say that on first approach, she struck me as an odd creature. She wore round eyeglasses, but while listening to you speak she removed them and peered directly at you, her large brown eyes never leaving your face, almost as though she were trying to study what generated your thoughts.

For the first few weeks, I was so shaken by my abrupt change in circumstances that I am not certain how I would have made it through had it not been for Meg. I found it especially difficult to reconcile living within the confines of a town. The constant activity unsettled me, and I found the sudden shrieks of neighboring children or the unexpected rattle of carriages going by unnerving. During the day, with so many around, the atmosphere of town living felt constricted, and I longed for the open fields and forest paths I had left behind.

But in Meg's bedroom, I found solace. In it was the world of birds and botany, the natural world that I thought I had left behind. I was delighted to see that she collected nests, too, and had them lined up across the windowsills amid rocks and leaves of all kinds. Framed fern species covered most of one wall, while prints of birds covered another. All of them, she told me, were indigenous to the region.

As I studied the prints more closely, I was startled to hear a gravelly voice call out from a far corner. "Hello!" I swung around.

"Sinsin," Meg said, going over to a large wicker cage, "you must be nice." She opened the door of the cage and held out her hand. A large black bird stepped out, hopped to her shoulder, then, cooing, nuzzled her ear.

"This," said Meg proudly, "is Sin."

"Sin?"

"Yes, I called him Sin. Mother named him. He is not her favorite. 'Black as sin,' she said the day I got him."

"Would he come to me?"

Meg beamed. "Of course." The bird came willingly and gave me giggles while he searched my hair with his beak.

"What does he eat?" I asked.

"Mice, frogs, peanuts, fruit . . ."

"What kind of bird is he?" I stroked his iridescent black feathers.

"He is of the genus Corvus. A black crow." She spoke formally, as a schoolmistress might. "I found him when he was very small, and he imprinted on me. He is quite intelligent, and I've taught him to speak." While she put him through his paces, I looked about the room.

A small plant, roots and all, was propped on her desk, and I saw on an open drawing pad the beginnings of a sketch. Seeing my interest, Meg brought out another prized possession: a long oval-shaped tin box painted a light blue. She explained that it was used to collect plant and animal specimens from the outdoors. It was attached to a leather strap, and she slung it over her shoulder to demonstrate how she could open the attached lid with one hand. The lid itself was delicately hand-painted with white and pink wildflowers, though some of the decoration had been worn away from use. It was a vasculum, she said, rolling her tongue around the word as though it were candy.

I was awestruck when she pointed out her shelf of books. They were all gifts from her father, she said, meant to assist her in her studies. After Sin flapped to a perch above the desk, I sat in a small chair to recover myself and stared about in fascination. Meg was thrilled at my interest in her world, and within days we were bonded.

At the beginning I was scheduled to take only reading and writing lessons with Meg. I was given some household duties, and

Miss Sarah had her Negro servant, Nancy, instruct me in those chores. Desperately lonely for the family I had left behind, I tried to establish a friendship with Nancy and her daughter, Bess.

Nancy and her husband, along with Bess, lived on the Maddens' property in a small home out back of the kitchen house. The two women cooked and cleaned and kept up the home under the supervision of Miss Sarah, while Nancy's husband maintained the property and the substantial gardens.

While working at my chores, I made overtures to Nancy and her daughter, but they, knowing nothing of me, kept their distance. One afternoon, finding myself with free time and thinking to pursue their friendship, I went out to the kitchen and there asked if I could be of help with the cooking. They looked at me, stone-faced. No, I was told, everything was just fine. They didn't need my help.

Later that day Miss Sarah came to me and asked that I not disturb the servants. They were very private, she said, and did not like others in their workplace. In my naïveté, I was confused by their rejection of me but made no further attempts to win them over.

At first I thought Miss Sarah overbearing, but in time I came to understand that her intentions were well meaning. Miss Sarah took her household seriously, and though her family was her first priority, her social obligations were also of great concern. Since her childhood, she had been afforded a place in society that carried with it luxury and privilege. Her mother had stressed the obligation of station, and Miss Sarah was determined to carry out her duty. I often heard her state how she felt obliged to help the less fortunate, and there was no doubt that my welfare was included under that dictum.

For Miss Sarah, appearance and propriety were of utmost importance, though she herself was stout, and her taste in clothing did not lend itself to flattery. She had a weakness for sweets, and as a result, her brightly colored dresses were often more fitted than the seamstress intended. Like Meg, Miss Sarah had an odd inclination to stare at one while he or she spoke, but what set her apart from her daughter was that Miss Sarah silently mouthed along with the speaker as though to better digest the words.

Mr. Madden was away a good deal of the time, but when not lawyering, he was taken up with gardening. He indulged Meg at every turn, which left Miss Sarah to draw a more solid line with her daughter. It was over dinner that I first witnessed the closeness between father and daughter. Both loved the world of botany, but while Mr. Madden kept his interest largely to his garden, Meg sought to understand what lay outside their domesticated backyard.

I was amazed to learn that Mr. Madden was the one who provided much of the live food for Sinsin. To Miss Sarah's dismay, it was often a topic discussed during our meal. There were days when I forgot to eat, so intrigued was I with the unusual dinner conversation. In due course, Mr. Madden tried to include me, but I was so stricken by shyness that I was almost unable to respond. It must have taken the better part of a year before I could look him in the eye to answer his questions.

I must add how surprised I was on the first day when I was told that I would dine with the family; heretofore, I had not sat at a formal table such as theirs. Guessing my need, Miss Sarah jumped at the task of guiding me through. I was eager to prove myself and immediately patterned myself after her example.

In the weeks that followed, Meg insisted that her mother release me from my household duties so that I might take part in all of her lessons. Our tutor was an older widow, Mrs. Ames, bright enough, though often sidetracked and much given to gossip. Daily, but for Saturday and Sunday, we had morning lessons in reading and penmanship. Art and music were reserved for two afternoons a week, while dance classes were given on alternating days. The rest of the time we had the freedom to wander out on excursions. Initially, I would have liked to go to the downtown shops, to see for myself what I heard existed there. But Meg was uninterested, so in our free time, I assisted Meg as she gathered new plant specimens for botanical study, or I helped her devise new ways to catch a fresh dinner for Sinsin.

With each passing month, I was introduced to other aspects of a new and pleasant world. Yet, though most of my days were spent in happy pursuit, always, underlying, was the tenuous feeling of an uncertain future. I was told on more than one occasion that my education here was to enhance my opportunities, but I was never informed as to what those opportunities were. Fearful, I kept the questions to myself. I was not ungrateful for the fortunate circumstances I found myself in, but through all my time in Williamsburg, my deep longing to return home did not abate. Early on, when writing a letter to Belle, I considered entering a plea for her assurance that I might one day return. But after reflection, I knew the futility of asking for her intercession and decided otherwise. That decision, though, left me feeling more alone than ever.

I dreaded bedtime, as that was when homesickness overtook me. At night my lovely bedroom felt empty and lonely. In the dark, I felt sick for the scent or touch of Sukey, and I longed for the late-night kitchen sounds or the familiar voices of Belle or Mama. Before sleep, I could not stop the memories. I replayed Sukey's run for the carriage over and over, and when the pain was too great, I took my blankets from my bed and arranged them on the floor to resemble my old pallet. From there I pulled Mama's basket from under the bed. I removed each treasure, then gave myself over to the impotent sorrow that engulfed me. When I finally slept, I often dreamed that I was on a ship. I would wake, my heart pounding from fear of the next wave, the one that would wash away all that was familiar.

The daytime was easier, as I had constant distraction. I was interested in all of the classes, but dance instruction provided the most amusement. Dance was taught by Mr.

Degat, and accompanying him with a fiddle was his longtime friend Mr. Alessi. The two shared a home but often did not see eye to eye, and each thought nothing of correcting the other's work. There were days when our class was suspended because one or the other stomped out, leaving only half a team to continue alone. Considering their interdependence, the one-man attempt was usually unsuccessful.

After one such episode, Meg informed the table at supper that evening of their latest unhappy drama. The two men were already tense when the class began. When a misstep happened between Meg and Mr. Degat, Mr. Alessi stopped his music and voiced the opinion that if Mr. Degat had moved to the left instead of to the right, all would have come off as intended. Mr. Degat expressed the view that if the fiddle playing had been more even, he would not have been so distracted. Mr. Alessi declared that his fiddle playing was above reproach and perhaps Mr. Degat would like to apologize for such a slur. Mr. Degat assured him that he would not, and with that Mr. Alessi put down his instrument and left the room for "some clean air." Furious, Mr. Degat walked over to the resting fiddle, picked up the bow, and snapped it in two across his knee. He then carefully replaced it beside the fiddle. Having spent his rage, he came back to us, nervously glanced at the door, then clapped us to order. Class would go on, he informed us. He would hum the accompaniment to our dance. And hum he did, after partnering me with Meg. We had scarcely begun to dance when Mr. Alessi strode in. A scream of outrage followed the discovery of his split bow. As he made his exit, he announced that Mr. Degat was a vile and wicked man. In response, Mr. Degat only hummed louder as he waved us on. Mr. Alessi had been gone under a half hour before Mr. Degat developed one of his debilitating headaches and had to cut our class short.

At the story's end, Mr. Madden, not one to voice an opinion on such matters, questioned Miss Sarah if she might want to consider hiring another fiddle player. Miss Sarah reacted with surprise. They came as a team, she said. And did he not realize that Mr. Degat was the very best instructor of the very difficult minuet? Besides, she said, the two of them always worked out their differences. I glanced at Meg and could see that she was as relieved as I when Mr. Madden did not voice any further disagreement. We both enjoyed our dance class as it was.

There was a Latin class taught on Saturday morning, and I was surprised to learn that it was taught by no other than Marshall. This was a free day for him from his own school, and by special arrangement made with his uncle Madden, he agreed to teach Meg the language he studied there. Although I had little interest in the subject, I was suffering from homesickness and looked forward to seeing Marshall. Upon our first meeting, he greeted me kindly and did not seem surprised at my new position in this household. I'd had only a little to do with him the previous year when he had come home to visit his father, but I did recall the attention he had shown me. And now, simply by seeing him, I felt a happy connection to the family I had left behind.

It was routine on Saturdays, following the lesson, for Marshall to stay on for the afternoon dinner. Mr. Madden and Miss Sarah showed a genuine interest and affection for Marshall, and because of my own similar needs, I recognized how he thrived on their attention and approval.

Marshall was a handsome young man; everyone said so. His blond hair had darkened to a sandy color, and if a facial feature had to be named as most prominent, I would reference his firm jaw and strong cleft chin. He had a full mouth, straight white teeth, and eyes of the bluest blue. Always well groomed, he stood over six feet in height and was broad-shouldered and of excellent physique.

Marshall was a good teacher, and although he confessed he did not have a deep passion for botany, it appeared to give him satisfaction to help Meg decipher the Latin terminology that held for her so many of nature's secrets. So, given my shared enjoyment of botany with Meg and the appeal of Marshall as a teacher, I began to look forward to the Saturday class.

One night after a terrible bout of homesickness, I formulated a plan. I decided that Miss Martha must recover, and when she did, I would return home with her to serve as her companion. That was when I first began my plot to see her.

In the first months when I asked to visit Miss Martha, Miss Sarah left no doubt with her adamant refusal that the hospital was not a place for someone of my age. I noted that Miss Sarah herself made fewer visits each month until, finally, late one Thursday afternoon on her return, I overheard her speaking to Mr. Madden. I unabashedly stopped outside the library door to listen.

"It is simply too horrible to speak of! I convinced him to come, and now to have this happen!" she said.

"He is her son," Mr. Madden replied. "You were right. It was time he went to visit."

"But you don't know . . ." She began to sob.

"Begin, then, my dear."

"I don't know if I can speak of this," she said.

"You must. Tell it to me straight."

Once Miss Sarah began, she told the story in a rush. "I said, 'Marshall, she is your mother. You are her only hope. Seeing you, she is certain to respond.' He didn't want to come. I could see how pale he was even as we approached the hospital. In the lobby, he had to sit, but I, thinking he might inspire a breakthrough, all but forced him to go through with the visit. She was sleeping when they unlocked her cell to let us in, and I suppose because of that, the attendant didn't stay. Marshall took his seat on a stool in the corner, and immediately, across the way, another . . . pitiful woman . . . reached her arm through the bars and screamed for his help. When I saw how this affected him, how he trembled, I took pity and was about to suggest we leave, but that was when Martha woke up. She was calm — until she saw Marshall. Before either of us had a chance to guess at what her actions might be, she rose from her pallet and flung herself upon him. When he tried to free himself, she caught his face and kissed him in a fashion that . . . surely she thought him her husband. When she began to . . . God help me . . . to touch him, he was in such a stupor that he could not protect himself. It took me calling for the attendants before he was able to free himself." Miss Sarah choked back sobs.

"Oh, my dear," Mr. Madden said.

"But that is not all," she murmured, and I leaned in closer to better hear.

"What, then? Say it once, and we shall never speak of it again."

"Before we could leave, before we could make our exit, she lifted her skirts and . . . urinated." When his wife began to sob, I imagined Mr. Madden holding her to him while he soothed her. After she quieted, he asked again about Marshall.

"He would not speak to me in the carriage. When I took his trembling hand, he pulled away. I tried to apologize for my part, but he would not look my way. How could I have failed him so dreadfully?"

"You did not fail him, my dear. You were right to include him. Of course you would presume his presence to have helped."

"But I might have guessed. Remember last Christmas dinner . . . when he had too much drink . . . how he claimed that Martha hated him, that she blamed him for Sally's death? And do you remember his anger when he spoke of her extreme laudanum use throughout his childhood?"

"But isn't laudanum one of her treatments now?" Mr. Madden asked.

"No, they've stopped it." There was a silence before she continued. "As it stands, I can't see how she will ever be released. They've tried everything. They bleed her every week, they purge her, they've tried intimidation and then the restraining chair. Many times they've used the cold baths, but nothing, nothing is working."

"My dear," Mr. Madden said, "why do you continue to visit? What possible purpose can it serve?"

"I cannot abandon her," Miss Sarah said. "It is my responsibility. She is alone all day in that terrible cell. She sleeps on a pallet, without even the dignity of a bed. They won't give her cutlery. She is forced to eat with her hands, like an animal!"

"Does she know it is you when you visit?" Mr. Madden asked.

"There are times after she's taken exercise in the yard — the mad yard, they call it — when she appears to have some recognition. But then she pleads for the baby, or for our sister Isabelle. I feel I must be honest, yet she grieves so when I tell her they are both dead."

I could take no more and, victim of my own indiscretion, ran to my room with this news that further troubled my already sleepless nights.

The following Saturday, after the visit to his mother, Marshall did not come to teach our Latin class, nor was he present for our afternoon dinner. On Miss Sarah's insistence, Mr. Madden went out to find him. The search ended in the late evening when Marshall was found drunk in a tavern some miles from town. Meg was already asleep, and I was with Miss Sarah in the front parlor when Mr. Madden returned with his nephew. Marshall was so inebriated that it took the three of us to get him to a bedroom.

As we settled him on the bed, Miss Sarah and I saw his right hand was badly bruised and cut. Together we cleaned it, and though our nursing must have pained him, he communicated only through incoherent mumbling. When he began to retch, we turned him to his side, but from the state of his clothes, it was clear that his stomach had already given up everything but the blood-stained gall that he now spat out. When he slept, we all retired for the night, only to be woken later by shouts from Marshall's room. By the time the Maddens reached him, he was crashing about the room.

Meg stood with me in the hallway, and we comforted each other until Miss Sarah came and sent us back to our rooms. There was activity the night long. Unable to sleep, I dressed at dawn and went out to ask Miss Sarah if I might be of service. Her eyes were red with fatigue. "If you could just sit with him, I might sleep for an hour," she said. "Mr. Madden is preparing to leave. He must see to . . . to take care of . . . the consequences."

I took the chair alongside the bed, assuring Miss Sarah that I would call if I should need her. After she left, I shyly looked over at Marshall, who slept. Where during the night, I had been frightened of his state, now he lay pale and vulnerable. I was reminded of his worst days as a child, of his haunted face after the death of Sally, of his beaten appearance when I found him in the privy, and my heart opened to him. How like his mother he looked, I thought, and I plummeted into sad longing for everyone at Tall Oaks. I could not help my tears and was drying my eyes when I became aware that Marshall was awake and looking at me.

"Don't cry," he said, reaching his bandaged hand toward mine. I stared in horror at his swollen purple fingers. At my reaction, he took note of his hand and rose on his elbow to take better stock. With that movement, he began to retch again, so I held the basin and comforted him as Mama Mae might have done. His face was damp from the strain, and when he rested back, I placed a wet cloth across his forehead. His blue eyes met mine, and when he tried a smile, I felt a rush of tenderness toward him that I had known only with Sukey and Campbell. I wanted to comfort him then, to hold him as a child in my arms, but I knew it was inappropriate and I held myself back. Confused by my feelings, I was happy to leave the room when Miss Sarah came to relieve me.

I did not see Marshall again until the next day. He was still too sick to eat and could retain only sips of water. Miss Sarah stayed at his bedside but eventually joined the family downstairs for breakfast.

"He says the only thing that appeals to him is Mae's soup," Miss Sarah told us.

"I don't believe coddling will help the matter," Mr. Madden said, helping himself to another waffle. "Perhaps a few days with an empty stomach will teach him."

"He must eat!" I spoke so passionately that everyone at the table stared at me, and I felt my face grow hot. "I'm sorry."

While Mr. Madden concentrated on his food, Miss Sarah spoke. "Of course Marshall will be given food, my dear."

In silence, I choked down the rest of my breakfast, then asked to be excused. As I made my way up the stairs, I overheard Mr. Madden's remark: "Loyal little thing. One can't fault her for that."

I waited until later in the day, when I found Miss Sarah alone, before I told her that I knew how to make Mama Mae's soup. Could I make it for Marshall? I asked, and she gave her permission.

Nancy and Bess did not welcome me into their kitchen, but neither did they hinder my work. They watched as I caught, killed, and cleaned the chicken, then chopped the parsley, onions, and thyme. I simmered the soup exactly as Mama Mae had taught me, and it was finished by evening. Miss Sarah was leaving Marshall's room as I brought a small cup of the steaming broth upstairs. Her concern for him was clear.

"I don't know," she said, looking at the cup I carried. "I doubt he can tolerate even that."

"Could I try?" I asked.

"Go ahead. Can you manage if I go for some supper?" she asked, and I assured her that I could.

By lantern light, I saw how little Marshall had improved; he looked at me listlessly as I perched on the edge of the bed. "I made you some soup," I said.

He looked at me. "I can't eat, Lavinia."

"This is broth. I made it just like Mama Mae showed me," I said as I placed a napkin across his chest. When I offered him a spoonful, he shook his head, but I persisted until he opened his mouth and swallowed the warm liquid. "Good," I said. I waited before offering more. Marshall did not take his eyes from me. Concerned only that he keep the liquid down, I did not rush, and in between spoonfuls, disregarding his gaze, I watched the flickering shadows in the darkening room.

"This is good," he said.

"I know," I said. "I had some in the

kitchen."

He gave a small laugh.

"Do you feel better?" I asked.

"I will if I can keep this down." He took a deep breath. "I heard that you took a stand for me?"

"What do you mean?"

"At breakfast."

"I only said that you needed to eat."

"Is Uncle angry with me?"

"I think so." I waited awhile.

He turned his head to the wall. "Well, it isn't the first time."

"What do you mean?"

"He has charge of me until I am twenty-two, and he is always trying to control me. 'Laying boundaries and setting standards,' he calls it."

I had no answer to that and settled the spoon in the empty cup. I rose to leave.

"Will you stay?" he asked.

"Would you like me to read? I can turn up the light."

"No. Just sit over there. Talk to me."

I wondered how I would entertain him, but no sooner had I taken my seat than his eyes closed, and soon he slept.

In the night Miss Sarah gave him another cup of the broth, and in the morning he was asking for more.

During the next few days of Marshall's recovery, I helped Miss Sarah care for him. Meg wanted nothing to do with the nursing, though she did take a critical look at his wound when we changed the dressing. She declared there was no infection, then instructed her mother and me to carry on. Miss Sarah lifted her eyes to the heavens and shook her head when Meg made her exit. When Meg later returned, it was with Sinsin perched on her shoulder and playing cards in her hand. That afternoon, and in the afternoons following, we played some lively games of loo.

In all, it was almost a week before Marshall left again. During that time, Mr. Madden arranged for Marshall to board at the home of one of the professors from the College of William and Mary. The professor and his wife ran a tight ship, and there were curfews that would be enforced. At Marshall's discharge, Mr. Madden extracted a pledge from him to stay clear of alcohol and, in the future, to have wine only with dinner.

Once I had learned of Miss Martha's sorry circumstances, after I knew that she had asked for me, for Isabelle, I felt compelled to see her and to have her see me. I grew convinced that if she saw me, she would become well again. A few weeks following Marshall's illness, I suggested to Meg that our botany excursions take us in the direction of the public hospital. The place was well known. Commonly called the madhouse, it was situated alone on a four-acre plot in a relatively undeveloped part of Williamsburg. It was within walking distance, and I shamelessly used the untamed woods behind it as a temptation for Meg to discover some new plant specimens. Although the two of us were given an unusual amount of freedom, I knew this was forbidden territory, as it was understood that our botany excursions were limited to the town park and to neighboring gardens. Meg, as I had hoped, was not bound by restriction and saw the excursion as an adventure.

I believe that initial visit was toward the end of October, my first year in Williamsburg, for I recall how Meg and I remarked on the red and yellow of the autumn leaves. We kept to the periphery of the woods that sheltered the hospital, and while Meg foraged, I found a space to peer between the tall boards of the wall surrounding the mad yard. An occasional shriek or shout came from this outdoor space where the patients took their exercise, and though fearful, I was eager to see what I might.

The day was cool, but the sun bore down into the enclosed area. My nervous eyes settled on a slight figure seated on a bench across from my makeshift window. As I watched, she pushed a heavy blanket back from her thin shoulders. At first I didn't recognize her, but there was something in the way she angled her head when she shrugged back the gray blanket that helped me identify her. I saw no attendants and called out to her. "Miss Martha." My voice broke, but I called again. "Miss Martha."

She heard me and looked up, much like a startled bird. I pulled my handkerchief from my pocket and waved it through the broken slats, then called again. She saw the white flash of my cloth, and her blanket dropped when she stood. Then she walked toward me as one who slept, sliding her feet one after the other.

I saw she was cared for, although her clothes were plain and cut loosely from a heavy brown homespun. Her beautiful long silky red curls had been cut short and, not anchored by pins or combs, stood away from her head in clumps. Dark blue half-moons emphasized her sunken eyes, and on either side of her forehead, angry red circles marked her pale skin. I later learned that this was where hot dry cups were placed during treatments by the physician in his attempt to draw the madness from her brain.

Frightened at what I had begun, I watched her slow approach but refused myself the temptation to run. As she peered out, her hot eyes met mine. I could scarcely breathe. "Miss Martha," I said, "it's me, Isabelle."

She gripped the fence with one hand to steady herself, then closed her eyes slowly and opened them again. When she reached through, her fingers brushed the side of my face. "Isabelle?" she whispered.

"Yes."

She pulled her frail hand back, then reached out again and softly placed the palm of her hand to the side of my neck. I was at a loss until I heard myself spontaneously recite a favorite passage from Sukey's bedtime story. As I finished the recitation with "and declares that she shall ride in her own coach," Miss Martha's hand began to tremble. "Baby?" she asked.

"Baby is at home," I said. "She is waiting for you."

Miss Martha stared at me, then her shrill screams pierced the air, setting off others as they joined her cries. I ran then, first to collect Meg, then to head for home.

As upset as I was after seeing Miss Martha that day, I still, in my naïveté, believed in her recovery.

Alone, I returned to the mad yard whenever I could summon the courage, but I did not see Miss Martha out until the following spring. Again I called to her, but this time she did not respond.

Distressed, I went to Miss Sarah and, without telling her the reason, asked that I be allowed a visit to the hospital. However, my request disturbed her to such a degree that I did not pursue it. I did, though, through the next years, continue to observe Miss Martha at the yard whenever I was able.

CHAPTER THIRTY

Belle

The first time I get a letter from Lavinia, I know being there is hard on her. Not by what she says but by what she don't say. She don't ask about Sukey, about Mama, about the twins. Lavinia's letter says she's got a tutor and she's living in the big house. I can see that her lessons are going good, because Lavinia's already writing good as the cap'n. First I'm thinking that I won't write back. I'm afraid that my writing don't look good as hers, but Mama says, "You write her, she don't care 'bout nothin' but that we all missin' her." So, I get out my dictionary and I write to Lavinia. I say that Jamie is just the best baby and that he's growing like something in my garden. I don't tell her that he looks just like the white boy and that I'm worried about his one eye clouding over.

I tell Lavinia that the twins and Mama say

hi, but I don't say that Mama's getting over a hard time, losing another baby herself. She says at her age she's too old to carry one, and I'm thinking she's right. By my figuring, she's got to be getting close to fifty.

I tell Lavinia that this place is running real good — that Will Stephens is doing a fine job. Ida says everybody's happy down at the quarters. But we all know it don't stay like this when Marshall comes back.

'Course I don't tell Lavinia that Ben and me get together every chance we got. And for sure I don't tell her about the time that Mama Mae gives me the eye when she says, "I guess you know that Lucy's gettin' big with another baby?"

"No. You sure about that?" I ask.

"You look at her, you sure, too," Mama says.

Next time I see Ben, I push him away. "All this time you're with me, you're still getting on Lucy?" I ask.

"Belle," he says, "you know you the one for me. But Lucy with me, too. You know this."

"You send her back to the quarters where she belongs!" I say.

But then Ben gets mad. "That girl know 'bout you, but she don't say nothin'. She already got it hard, workin' the fields. And she a good mama to my boy. I don't send her back down like she some dirt. She stayin' and that be that." He turns to go.

I'm still mad about Lucy's baby, but I know I got to take Benny like he is. "Come here," I say. Then I kiss him good and make him want me like he's a starving man.

CHAPTER THIRTY-ONE

Lavinia

As Meg and I grew older, Miss Sarah used our close relationship to teach the two of us the social skills required of young ladies in Williamsburg. Miss Sarah counted on my influence, as Meg often opposed these lessons, objecting to the time they took away from her beloved bird and nature study. I, on the other hand, knew it was in my best interest to please Miss Sarah, so I paid close attention. These were the polite accomplishments, she said, and was determined that we would not fall short in achieving them. Initially Miss Sarah's schooling attended to instructions as mundane as how to curtsy or how to correctly enter and exit a room. Gradually, though, these lessons became more sophisticated and included tasks such as how to act as hostess when presiding over a meal.

Although having tea was not the ritual that

it became in later years, the serving of it followed a certain pattern, and according to Miss Sarah, it was an important social skill that every young lady was required to know. Meg thought the whole subject a bore, but I was genuinely intrigued and encouraged her participation. As tea was very dear, Miss Sarah had her own tea caddy, a small box made of rosewood in which the precious commodity was kept under lock and key. Her beautiful tea set, imported red and white porcelain from China, had cups with no handles and a low squat teapot that differed so from a tall coffeepot. For the tea ceremony, Miss Sarah carefully directed us in all the necessary equipment. I was keen to learn this task, so Miss Sarah employed my eagerness as example: "You must be more careful, Meg. Watch Lavinia, see how she pours."

Despairing of Meg's lack of interest, Miss Sarah tried another approach. Using my fifteenth birthday as a means for exercise, she drew on Meg's fondness for her cousin and sent word to Marshall that Meg would host a tea in my honor the following Saturday afternoon. Could he attend, and would he bring a gentleman friend?

Meg was irritable from the start. Not fifteen minutes into it, the young man accompanying Marshall lost favor when he, with supercilious abandon, announced his disfavor of women studying Latin. Meg quickly replied that immature men with strong opinions were, by her estimation, very dull indeed. There was a long silence while Miss Sarah stared at Meg. Remembering my obligation, I fought unsuccessfully to recall a favorable subject to engage our stunned guests. Then (and I believe it was a true accident), in the passing of a full cup, Meg spilled some of the hot liquid in her guest's lap.

That ended poorly when the young man made an unkind comment, and as he departed abruptly, Meg ran from the room in tears. Miss Sarah, red-faced, did not stop to make apologies before she left the room to set things straight with Meg. Mr. Madden, not yet home from business, was not witness to Marshall and me laughing together at the debacle.

As the lone hostess, I decided there was only one thing left to do: I poured the rest of the tea and offered Marshall the last of the crumpets. When there was a conversational lull, I remembered my duty and asked my guest about himself. I listened for quite some time as Marshall went on, noting with an inward smile how right Miss Sarah had been when she said that no man could resist talking about himself. Marshall finished by saying that though he enjoyed the study of law, he was only marking time.

"For what?" I asked.

He looked surprised at my question. "To go home."

"Of course," I said. I was so taken aback at his announcement that I lost the ability to call forth another question. I looked down and began to smooth the embroidered pink edging on the sleeve of my new birthday dress.

"And you?" he asked. "What do you want in your future?"

When I looked up, his blue eyes observed me so intently and his smile was so genuine that I quickly looked down again, this time to straighten my skirt. "I am not certain," I said.

I was saved when the hallway clock struck. I quickly remarked at the hour. Taking my cue, as a gentleman would, Marshall rose and announced it was time to leave. As he prepared to depart, he asked if Meg was planning other social events.

"I have no idea," I said.

"Well," he said in a most serious tone, "could you please send me word, before I make a commitment to attend, whether or not the event involves hot liquid?"

We laughed again. Before Marshall left, he picked up my hand, bowed formally, and with merry eyes said how very much he had enjoyed my company.

"And I yours," I replied, and produced a curtsy.

I sat for a long while after his departure and pondered my confused state. Since Marshall's unfortunate bout with drink, he had been on his best behavior. Something about the episode appeared to have freed him, and once again he was making every effort to please the Maddens. Marshall intrigued me. He was older and, in my eyes, worldly and sophisticated. Although he was always reserved with others, he put on another face when alone with Meg and me. Never did he make me feel less than his equal. Yet — although no one spoke of this — I wondered if I was not still considered his family's servant.

I set those thoughts aside when Mr. Madden appeared. He took a seat and asked how the afternoon had gone. Before I had time to answer, Meg, red-eyed, joined us to sit on a stool at her father's knee. Taking his hand, she pleaded that he intercede with Miss Sarah on her behalf. She could not bear a lifetime of this! When Miss Sarah entered, Meg's words ripe in the air, I decided it was time to go to my room.

Meg continued to object to her mother's tutoring. What was the point? she questioned.

She further horrified her mother when she announced that she did not plan to marry, nor did she plan to take part in a social life, as it only took time away from her studies. I was sensitive both to Miss Sarah and to Meg, and because of that, I was able to intervene. Meg had a sense of fun, and as long as I approached the instruction with levity, Meg made an honest attempt to learn the basics. Then, too, when Miss Sarah tired of Meg's frequent opposition, I drew attention to myself. I asked questions and took pride in executing what I learned. Miss Sarah did not miss my contribution and praised me often for my good influence. Her focus on me did not trouble Meg in the least. On the contrary, Meg spoke to me of her gratitude.

Of course there were days when I, too, grew tired of Miss Sarah's scrutiny, but I quickly brought myself to order when I reminded myself how fortunate I was to have this opportunity. I was becoming more and more concerned about my future. It was never spoken of, but I knew my time here was limited. Miss Sarah had hinted that one day I might marry, but where a husband could be found, I did not know. We did little socializing, since Meg opposed most outside invitations, and as she matured, her stand only grew more firm.

I did not know where to turn with my concerns. I no longer communicated regularly with Belle; painfully, I was coming to realize that I would not be returning to Tall Oaks. Through sporadic visits to Miss Martha, I saw that her condition only appeared to be worsening, and I doubted that she would ever go home.

In my fifteenth year, I began to entertain thoughts of locating my brother. I had always dreamed of finding him. Now, along with my longing to be reunited with him as family, I reasoned that he was of an age where he might be in a position to be of assistance to me. Given my good fortune with the Maddens and their extreme generosity, I was reluctant to approach them with a request for their help. I did not want them to think that I was ungrateful, nor that I wished to leave their home. Thus I was silent about Cardigan until an unexpected opportunity presented itself.

Sunday mornings were always taken up

with church services, followed by socializing, wherein invitations were extended or
accepted for the afternoon dinner. Mr.
Madden preferred the company of steady
friends, so it had recently become routine
to have Mr. Boran and his young daughter
at the Sunday dinner table. Mr. B., as Meg
called him, was a partner in her father's
business. In the previous year, the unfortunate man had lost his wife — the mother of
his six-year-old daughter — to complica-
tions following the birth of a stillborn child.
In recent months, Miss Sarah had taken it
upon herself to help Mr. B. find a second
wife. To date, Miss Sarah had been unsuccessful, as she had rather rapidly run
through all of her possible candidates. It
was quite clear to me why this was so.

To begin, Mr. B. made a poor presenta-
tion of himself, though it was uncanny how
physically alike he was to Mr. Madden. Of
similar age, possibly around forty-five, Mr.
B. was also short and plump, balding and
bespectacled. But that was where the likeness ended. Mr. Madden was well dressed,
neat and tidy in appearance, and was the
social equal to his wife. Under all circumstances, he knew the etiquette required, and
although he was a private man who preferred solitary pursuits, when obligation

demanded, Mr. Madden rose to the occasion with outstanding form.

Mr. B., on the other hand, was disheveled and unkempt. His true failing was a shyness that so affected him he was unable to converse without stammering and stumbling for words. To observe him attempt conversation was painful, and I often found myself jumping to his rescue. Apparently, he was grateful for my help, and after the third or fourth Sunday dinner, he sought me out to express the same.

I must mention how taken I was with Mr. B.'s delightful daughter, Molly. She was around the same age that I had been when orphaned, and for this reason I felt a kinship toward her. She was well mannered and of a curious nature, and following the Sunday meals, I usually spent time next to her on the settee. There we played at games while she plied me with questions about my childhood.

It was snowing outside the winter afternoon that Mr. B. approached me. Molly and I were playing a game of dominoes, and while I waited on her next move, I glanced up. This day, particularly, there was an intimate feel in the room, helped out by the crackling fire. As I gazed about the room, I saw Mr. Boran's advance. So clear was his discomfort, I immediately urged him to take a seat. It was his disability that gave me courage, for he was a gentleman of an age that otherwise would have intimidated me. Miss Sarah, always observing my manners, gave a nod of approval, but as the man sat, I caught Meg's look of reproach. I flashed her a smile before I turned my attention to Mr. Boran. He situated himself, and then, as Molly and I conversed, he edged into the conversation. He appeared to be as eager as his daughter to learn more of my past. Molly had already told him that I was an orphan, he informed me. Had I no other family? Only a brother, lost to me, I said. How was this so? father and daughter both questioned.

When I looked over and saw the Maddens in discussion and Meg distracted by a book, I decided to tell my tale. At the finish, after a short silence, Mr. B. astonished me when he suggested that he might be able to assist in finding my brother. I hesitated only briefly, but he guessed the reason and assured me that he would first seek the approval of the Maddens. Grateful beyond measure, I wasted no time in telling him so. The man grew red while Molly took my hand in hers and rested her head against my shoulder.

After supper, the Maddens asked me to stay with them when Meg retired early to her room. They informed me that Mr. B. had asked for their permission to look for my brother. They voiced disappointment. Why had I not come to them? If only I had asked, they would have carried out the search themselves.

After I explained, they offered me their full support, but they hastened to warn me that the search could take many months. They added that oftentimes such a quest ended in vain, and I was to keep in mind that my brother might never be found. Their concern, coupled with my excitement, threatened to move me to tears, but as Miss Sarah often lectured Meg on emotional outbursts, I held myself together.

Miss Sarah concluded by saying that Mr. Boran was a good man and she was very pleased with the way I had put the poor man at ease. I left the room ready to burst from happiness, but I waited until I reached the stairs before I gave way to my excitement. Then I bounded up the steps two at a time and squealed as I flew into Meg's room.

She did not share my happiness. Instead, she was filled with forewarning. "He is using this as an opportunity," she said.

I sank into a chair. "An opportunity for what?"

"You know that Mr. Boring is looking for a wife?" she asked, sitting opposite me on the edge of her bed.

"It's Mr. Boran, Meg."

"It's Mr. Boring!" she said, and threw herself back on her bed with a great sigh, then flung her arm over her eyes.

I laughed.

"This isn't funny, Vinny," she said, peeking out from under her elbow. "Next he'll be proposing to you."

"Please, Meg!" I was astonished that she could even think along those lines. "I'm only fifteen years old. He is as old as your father!"

"That wouldn't hinder him; nor would it stop Mother if she thought there was opportunity for you," Meg replied.

As I prepared for bed that evening, I thought of Meg's words, but I soon dismissed her concern. Certain I would be reunited with my brother, I would let nothing cloud my happiness. That very night I sat at my desk and, for the first time in a long while, wrote a letter to Belle. I told her of the search for Cardigan and how I knew that within him lay the answer to my future. I then set before her my plan. Once I was settled with him, I would send for her and Jamie.

I always looked forward to Saturdays, when Marshall came to teach and then to spend the day. As we matured, our friendship grew and at times took on a flirtatious note. Increasingly, I found him attractive and often saw him studying me. Occasionally, he would tease me, and I felt quite pleased with myself when he laughed aloud at my returning quips. When Marshall periodically experienced his "dark moods," as Meg labeled them, I was flattered to see that I was the one who could best pull him out.

Then something of a more serious nature occurred, which might have given me pause but did not. During a class, Marshall and I began bantering, and Meg, attempting to dampen our sport, silently peered at us over the top of her spectacles. Her serious demeanor only encouraged us, and together we teased her to join our fun. Marshall playfully snatched her spectacles and perched them on the edge of his own nose. After Meg failed to retrieve them, she left the room in a huff. I saw her return, although Marshall, with his back to her, did not. I stayed quiet when she tiptoed up behind him, then pinned his arms while she called for me to take her spectacles from him. Meg was small but strong and determined. She had the advantage of surprise, and for a brief moment Marshall must have felt overpowered. His face whitened as he fought free. The stool he perched on flew over, and when he swung to face Meg, for one terrible moment, I was afraid that he might strike her. He stood over her, shouting, "Don't do that! Don't you ever do that again!" He was silent as he gathered his things and left the room, and he did not stay for dinner.

That outburst was never mentioned again. And there was a second.

It was a Saturday-afternoon dinner, and we were celebrating Marshall's nineteenth birthday. Because we had guests, Mr. Madden made available more than the usual amount of wine. This day Marshall partook liberally, and when his speech began to slur, I saw a look pass between the Maddens. Immediately, Miss Sarah declared the meal ended and quickly ushered us into the front parlor while Mr. Madden made an exit to his study.

Our guests, a young couple well known to the Maddens, accompanied us. The young lady, Miss Carrie Crater, and her twin brother, Mr. Henry Crater, had joined us for this celebratory dinner. Following, we were to have a lesson in dance, to be taught by Mr. Degat and chaperoned by Miss Sarah. Miss Crater, seventeen, clearly found Marshall attractive. During the meal, as a means of gaining attention, she wondered aloud at my good fortune to be at this table. This comment appeared to set Marshall's teeth on edge. As Miss Crater was a quick study, she noted how her statement had affected Marshall, and by the time we were set to dance she had wisely changed course.

Mr. Crater — Henry, as he insisted he be called — was an easygoing and likable character. Mr. Degat, who was to instruct us that day, was also to act as my dance partner. At the last minute he was unable to attend, although Mr. Alessi had come, ready to fiddle. I, without a partner, encouraged the others to take to the floor. Henry — I'm certain eager to impress Miss Sarah — insisted that I be his partner while his sister wait. Miss Crater, in an attempt to win favor in Marshall's eye, quickly agreed to his plan. I objected, but Henry would have none of it. He came to convince me otherwise, taking my hand and playfully kissing it, pleading dramatically for my participation. In spite of the fact that I knew he was teasing,

I became embarrassed, and my face went hot.

To everyone's great surprise, Marshall leaped at Henry, picked him up by the collar, and thrust him against a wall. He did this with such force that poor Henry had the air knocked from him. The worst of it was, Marshall did not stop there. He leaned over Henry, now sprawled on the floor, and shouted, "Leave her alone! Do you hear? You do not touch her!"

By the time Miss Sarah reached Henry, Marshall had already exited the room. Mr. Alessi, a veteran of drama, began to fiddle. Over the music, brave Henry attempted good humor. "Mrs. Madden," he asked, still slumped on the floor, "could you advise me on the correct protocol?"

For once, it seemed, Miss Sarah was without a ready reply. Though she quickly recovered and attempted to make light of the situation, I saw through her thin disguise at how shaken she was by her nephew's outburst.

I did not know what to make of the event, but if it was ever discussed, I was not a party to the conversation. As it happened, my life took a sharp turn, and this incident quickly faded.

■ ■ ■ ■

On a Tuesday evening in the spring of 1800, two weeks before my sixteenth birthday, Mr. B. came for supper. I wondered if it was possible that he brought news of Cardigan. It was out of the ordinary for guests to join us during the week, never mind the evening meal, and the fact that little Molly was not at her father's side further suggested something peculiar. Both of the Maddens were strangely subdued during the meal, and I, apprehensive, was quiet as well. Mr. B.'s behavior could not be judged, as he, at his best, said little.

That left Meg, but as this day she had finally received a long-awaited book, her goal was to complete the meal of cold ham and biscuits as quickly as possible so she might hurry off to her room. As the meal wore on, my stomach reacted, and by the time everyone had finished, I was afraid I would be sick. I was about to make my excuses when Miss Sarah suggested that I accompany Mr. B. to the front parlor. She would send coffee, she said. I forced back the nausea as I led the way. Once there, I sat on the green settee while the nervous man chose the wingback chair opposite me.

He fidgeted with his coattails until I could stand it no longer. "Please . . ." I began, but he interrupted.

"I have found him," he said, "but he is not alive."

Had a sword been plunged into me, I would not have felt such pain. I cannot describe the depth of those words, nor how deeply they cut. I closed my eyes and forced myself to breathe as I was made aware of the details. Cardigan had been indentured to a blacksmith not five miles from Williamsburg. Three years into service, while shoeing a horse, he had suffered an injury to the head and died shortly after.

My body grew damp with the effort of fighting to keep my supper down. My whole future had rested on our reunion. Cardigan had been the last of my true family; he had been my only hope. Now I was completely alone. As my time in Williamsburg had passed, maturity had shown me the impossibility of returning to Tall Oaks. I had been forced to accept that I would not be reunited with my adopted family. Now my deep desire to reunite with my brother was gone as well.

How it was that Mr. B. came to hold me, I could not say, but I found myself in his arms as I gave way to despair. When my tears subsided, I rested my head back, and the man, in a kindly gesture, pushed my damp hair back from my face.

"What will I do?" I whispered.

Mr. B. was on his knee before I could understand the purpose.

"Marry me," he implored.

CHAPTER THIRTY-TWO

Belle

In the winter I get a letter from Lavinia saying that she looking to find her brother, Cardigan. He's gonna come for her, and then she'll send for me and Jamie. I take the letter and run to go find Benny down at the horse barn, cleaning out stalls.

"Hey, baby!" he says when he sees me. He looks around, but he knows we're alone because Papa's working at the big house with Uncle Jacob. He puts the rake down, walks over real slow, looks me up and down, takes my arm, and pulls me to hisself. He's still wanting me like the first time, and he knows I feel the same way.

This time I say, "No, Ben. Wait." I wave the letter at him. "Lavinia says she has a brother, and they're gonna send for me."

Benny stops smiling and sits down. I see this is hard for him.

"But I'm gonna write her and tell her you

got to come with me."

Ben don't say nothing.

"Benny, do you hear me? I'll tell Lavinia you're coming with me."

He looks away.

"Ben?"

"Belle," he says, "how you gonna make that happen? She gonna buy me? And what about Lucy and the babies?"

"You're wanting to stay here? You're picking Lucy over me?"

"Baby," he says, "we both know this day comin'. We know you got to go before Marshall get back here."

I don't believe he's saying this. I start crying and can't stop myself. "Baby . . ." he says, and when he comes over to me, I start yelling, "Don't you call me baby! You're staying here? You're picking Lucy over me? Well! I guess you're happy that I'm finally going! I see now you're waiting for me to go all this time!"

His big old eyes fill up and run over until it looks like there's a bucket of water coming down his face. I don't care. I go running back to the kitchen house. When he comes, I don't let him in. I tell him to go, get away from me. Then Mama comes.

"You know you got to go, Belle," she says. I start to say something smart to Mama,

341

but she stops me. "Belle, you scared, I knows this, but don't get mad with me. You know you got to get out of here. This good for you and Jamie, going with Lavinia."

"But I want Ben with me!" I say.

"I know this, Belle," say Mama, "but Ben got to stay. He have no say. Where he gonna get his free papers? It gonna be hard enough on Lavinia, buyin' you and Jamie. And what about Lucy and her boys?"

After Mama goes, I just sit and cry. I know I got to get me and Jamie out of here. It's a blessing that Lavinia wants me, I know this, so in the end I write to her and tell her me and Jamie want to come. But I don't send the letter just yet. I put it in my writing box under my bed. There's still time.

Before supper, Will Stephens comes to talk. He stands outside the door. Like always when I'm alone, he don't come in the house. "What're you needing, Will?" I say. He asks me to come sit on the bench outside the kitchen, so I do. Finally, he speaks up. "I hear that you've had an offer from Lavinia?"

I nod, 'cause if I talk, I'm afraid I'll start to cry.

"Do you want to go?"

I know he see that my eyes are all puffed and red. I shake my head.

"Well," he say, "I've been thinking about this for a while now. I might have another offer for you."

I look at him, wondering what he's talking about.

He tells me, come spring, he got to go to Williamsburg to ask some questions to Mr. Madden and Marshall and to get some papers signed. What he says next almost knocks me off the bench. He wants to know it's all right by me if he gets me for his own farm. He got a contract, and it says he gets to take some people from here. He likes the way I'm always working, and he's wanting me to come work for him. "Of course," he says, "this means that I also want Jamie."

Will knows I go no place unless Jamie's with me. Mama's always saying I keep my Jamie too close to me, that it's not good for him. But he's a funny child. He'd rather stay with me than go play. He's a nice-looking boy, but he got one eye that's clouded up, and he can't see nothing from it. Mama says maybe it'll get better when he gets older, but it seems to be getting worse, more white. But he can still see good with the other eye.

I look back at Will Stephens and can't find no words.

"I'm also planning to negotiate for Ben

and Lucy and their two boys," Will Stephens says. He don't look at me when he says this, because by now he knows about Ben and me. For sure everybody else knows. Nobody fusses no more about it. Even Lucy and me don't fight no more.

"When's this all going to happen?" is all I say to Will Stephens.

"I'm not certain," he says, "but Marshall turns twenty-two next year. Then he will have control of this place. I don't know if he plans to come back. If he does, I suspect that he will want changes, and though I'm sure that Marshall has matured, I would like to get the papers in order before that happens. I'm guessing that Mr. Madden will be easier to deal with."

My heart's pounding and I don't know what to say, so I settle on "Thank you, Mr. Stephens."

He laughs. "Since when do you call me Mr. Stephens?"

I look down because I can't take the smile off my face.

"I know you as Belle, you know me as Will," he says. "That doesn't have to change — unless you want me to call you Miss Pyke?"

First time ever, somebody calls me that. I sit up, proud. "No, sir," I say. "Belle suits

344

me just fine."

"Well, then, Belle and Will it is," he says, and we laugh. "I do have one more question," he says.

"What's that?" I ask.

He takes his hat off, pushes his hair back, then goes to put the hat back on. I know something's up when he takes all that time working his hat.

"Well, I'm wondering about Lavinia . . . do you think she's grown up?"

"She was all grown up when she little," I say, and laugh to remember.

He smiles. "She was that. She's about sixteen now, am I right?"

"This May," I say.

"Then you think that she'd be old enough to court?"

"Well, Mr. Will Stephens!" I say, but then I try not to laugh. His face looks like it's burning up, so I say, "There's not a time she don't write about coming back here."

"So you've said," he says.

After he leaves, the first thing I do is tear up the old letter to Lavinia and write a new one. I write that me and Jamie will stay here and that Will Stephens has some good news. I'm gonna give this letter to Will when he goes. By the time she reads it, maybe she already says yes to coming back with him.

345

Ben's going to have to do some fancy talking to get back in my door. Trouble is, we both know it's just a matter of time.

CHAPTER THIRTY-THREE

Lavinia

My engagement to Mr. Boran was announced on my sixteenth birthday. Stunned by his sudden proposal, I could not respond that evening and told him so. "I can wait," he said, and offered me time to consider. I had no thoughts of marrying the man, but when I asked Miss Sarah for advice, her apparent relief had me reconsider.

"Oh!" she exclaimed, her hands clasped to her bosom. "I was hoping for this." She caught herself when my face gave away my feelings. "Of course, only you can make this decision, my dear," she added.

"I hadn't truly considered it," I said, and waited for her reply. "I mean . . . he is so old. I mean . . . for me . . ."

"Yes, I suppose you might see it that way," she said, "but there is also the fact that because of his age, he is well established. And you do get on so well with Molly.

"And think, my dear: I doubt you would want for anything. He was known to have been most generous with poor Mrs. Boran. And think of the changes you might bring to him! His clothes, his . . . I can scarcely imagine the improvement. Then there is the advantage that you would stay here in Williamsburg. You would not have to say good-bye to Meg, nor to us. Just think of it! Your own home, a place in this society — you would be readily accepted. I think this is most exciting, most fortunate. But the decision must be yours."

When I told Meg of his proposal, she was appalled. "How can you consider it?" she asked. "He is a boring old man!"

"I don't know, Meg. This might be my only chance."

"What can you possibly mean?"

"What else am I to do?"

"For heaven's sake, Vinny! Surely you can see beyond this!"

Fear underlay my angry response. "It's easy for you, Meg. You have this home, you have a family. Every day you make choices that suit you. I don't have that luxury!"

Meg misunderstood my anger. "Are you saying that my parents haven't offered you every chance?"

"I'm saying that I am considering mar-

348

riage to Mr. Boran, and I had hoped for your support!"

"That you'll never have!"

I swung from Meg's room and ran to my own. There, I shut the door and, too angry for tears, decided to write a letter to Belle. I sat at my desk and imagined her with me. I would tell her of my dilemma, of Cardigan's death, and of Mr. Boran's marriage proposal.

Then I thought of Mama Mae and of what she might say. I thought of Papa and the twins, and of how I longed to see them. Before I could stop it, my most distressing memory returned. It was of Sukey and her run to follow my carriage. Losing her remained so painful that I seldom allowed myself to think of it. Now, knowing I had lost them all forever, I was unable to write one word. I leaned over the paper, placed my head in my hands, and gave way to tears.

The following day I approached Miss Sarah once again and told her that I had decided to accept Mr. Boran's proposal. Delighted, she suggested that we announce the engagement on my sixteenth birthday. When Mr. Madden was informed of this development, though less enthusiastic than his wife, he agreed to the wedding provided that I not marry until my seventeenth birthday. I was relieved to hear of this stipulation.

The next month, on the morning of June 5, I was called to the front parlor. I was curious, for this was not a common occurrence. Having already completed my morning preparations, I wouldn't have bothered to stop and check myself in the long mirror, but I suspected Miss Sarah had a friend visiting and would prefer that I look presentable. My dress, made of fine muslin, was simple enough and of a pale green that Meg said complemented my eyes. It hung straight and soft, the line broken by a wide dark green ribbon meant to emphasize the fashionable empire cut. I turned to the side and smiled, pleased to see that my trim figure had rounded to womanhood. I leaned in to check more closely and wondered again if my odd-colored amber eyes were inherited from my mother or my father.

I had no complaint with the oval shape of my face nor with my high cheekbones, and I wrinkled my nose at myself, happy that I had grown into it. The freckles continued to vex me, and I thought my lips too full, but I was pleased that my teeth were white and straight. My hair hung down in a schoolgirl fashion, and I tossed it, noting with some pride the deep auburn that caught the sun's rays. The style of the day was to wear the hair in a knot with tendrils softening any severity, but Meg and I preferred our hair loose, using only combs to pull it back. Miss Sarah agreed to this provided we gave our promise that when convention demanded, we would dress it.

Ready to go, I looked out and was surprised to see Meg's door still closed. Not wanting to keep Miss Sarah waiting, I went ahead without her.

I recognized the voice before I reached the front parlor, and my heart began to race. When I saw Will Stephens, when my eyes met his, all of my good training was forgotten. "Will!" I cried, rushing toward him, "Will!" I stopped myself short when I saw Miss Sarah's frown. I remembered then to stand and wait for Will's approach. When he reached me, I offered him my hand.

"And who is this?" he asked, but I could see that he was teasing.

"Will!" I could only say. "Will!"

"Lavinia," Miss Sarah reminded me, "why don't you invite our guest to sit?"

"Oh, please do," I offered. Will smiled broadly as I led the way to the settee. After we were seated, Miss Sarah excused herself, saying that Nancy required her assistance.

"Will! Why are you here? When did you come? How is everyone? How long are you staying? Did anyone else come with you?" A hundred questions surfaced and tumbled forth.

Will laughed, and my heart was lost. My childhood infatuation came rushing back and my acquired years gave it additional weight. How beautiful he was: his smile, his sunbrowned face, his dark and happy eyes. I stared at him as he spoke, delighting in his every word.

All was well. He was here on business, he said, to renegotiate his contract as farm manager. He had some changes to make and wanted the approval of both Mr. Madden and Marshall before implementing them. He was proud to say the plantation was doing well, and as he told me about everyone, he remembered a packet from Belle. I held it, unopened, as I continued to quiz him about home.

Ben and Lucy had another baby. Uncle Jacob and Mama and Papa kept everything ready for the return of Miss Martha and Marshall.

I looked directly at him. "How is Belle?"

"She is as hardworking as ever," he said. "She still misses you."

"And Jamie?" I continued my hard stare.

Will noted me studying him, but his eyes held no embarrassment, nor did he waver when he answered, "He is well. How old was he when you left?"

"Nine months. He is at least three now."

"Ah, yes, now you would see he is a sober little man, much as you were a sober little woman."

I blushed with this tender intimacy. "And the twins?" I asked. "How are they?"

He laughed. He said that Fanny was proving to be a handful. Mama was keeping a tight rein on her since she and Eddy, Ida's son, had developed an interest in each other. Fanny alone, he said, was a handful, but Fanny in love was a force to be reckoned with. Beattie, he assured me, was the same gentle girl she had always been, and she had taken over the care of Sukey.

"And Sukey —" My question was interrupted by Mr. Madden's sudden appearance. He came forward to greet Will, then informed me that Meg and the tutor were waiting for me.

"Mr. Stephens will be here for two days," he said kindly when he saw my reluctance to leave. "You will have time for other visits, my dear."

I knew to excuse myself as Mr. Madden waited to settle himself in a chair.

It was a Thursday, so I was surprised when Marshall joined us for dinner that afternoon. Marshall had not responded to the announcement of my engagement any better than had Meg, though Meg was over her upset as long as I did not discuss Mr. Boran. I was on my way to her room the night I overheard a terrific row between Marshall and Mr. Madden. Their voices from the study were so loud that I could plainly hear them from the top of the stairs.

"I said, I refuse to release her! You know I still have rights to her."

"True, Marshall, the estate does. But her indentureship was not well defined, and surely you see why she must be given this opportunity."

"Opportunity! He has little to offer! He is nothing but a lecherous old man!"

"Take care, Marshall. This man is a colleague of mine."

"Uncle! You cannot presume that she will be happy!"

"Your aunt seems to think otherwise. She believes that this will be a good fit for Lavinia. And Lavinia is not opposed."

"Lavinia? Opposed? I've known her all of my life. She is the gentlest creature I've ever seen. When has she ever opposed anything?"

"I'm sorry, Marshall, but this marriage is

Mrs. Madden's wish. I'm afraid that I must overrule you on this matter."

"I refuse to go along with this! You cannot —"

"You know that I can, Marshall, and I will!"

The study door slammed, and after I slipped back to my room, I sat at my little desk, too despondent to cross the hall to visit Meg. I did not want to go through with the marriage, but I saw no way out. What alternative was available? Besides, I had made the commitment.

Little had changed after the announcement of our engagement. The Sunday dinners continued as before, though Meg refused to take part in the social gathering that always followed, where Molly clung to my side and Mr. Boran's eyes never left me. Mr. Boran and I had met privately only one time, the evening of our formal announcement, when he presented me with an emerald brooch. He did so while he made a stammering remark that emeralds could not enhance my beauty, but as they were the finest, they might hold up to my loveliness. I thanked him, pinned the gift to my dress, and found myself at a complete loss for conversation. Before I could stop him, he was on his knees. He reached for my ungloved hand and began to cover it with such ardent, damp kisses that I could only observe his growing passion with alarm.

Imagining Meg witnessing her Mr. Boring at work, I had a fleeting impulse to laugh, but when his lips moved up to my wrist, I claimed back my hand, rose quickly, and suggested that we join the others. Mr. Boran's eyes were glazed with desire, and I wanted to strike him when he jumped to his feet at my command. Yet as I wiped the remnants of his love kisses from my hand, for the first time ever, I felt the exuberant power of my womanhood. With horrid premonition, I saw in the future the likelihood of this man becoming a victim of my own unhappiness. Appalled at the thought, I was kinder than ever to the besotted Mr. B. for the rest of the evening, while Miss Sarah made much of my new jewelry.

Marshall had distanced himself from me following his argument with Mr. Madden. During our Saturday class, I often caught him observing me, and when I met his eye, he would turn away as though angry. Over the following weeks, without excuse, he often cut short our class and asked Meg to tell Miss Sarah that he could not stay for dinner.

■ ■ ■ ■

This day, with Will as a dinner guest, Marshall was pleasant enough at the start of the meal, although, with each glass of wine, he challenged Will in increasingly cool undertones.

I could scarcely contain my excitement with Will's presence. I proudly observed his grace and good manners, though it was true that had I not caught his eye, he might have used his dessert spoon for his soup. But he saw my signal and winked his thanks, then followed my example.

Miss Sarah kept the conversation flowing. Meg encouraged Will to speak of the farm and of my earlier years there. He told some stories of my childhood that he claimed exhibited my precocious nature. After one such tale, with everyone laughing, he ended by saying how very much I was missed at Tall Oaks. I couldn't help but smile broadly when his eyes rested on me.

We were all startled when Marshall stood to raise his wineglass. With flushed face, he spoke louder than was necessary. "Let us toast Lavinia," he said. "I have high hopes that soon she will be returning to Tall Oaks with me. But this time it will be under improved circumstances."

There was silence. Meg kicked me under the table. Will choked and began to cough. Finally, Mr. Madden responded. "Yes . . . well . . . one never knows, Marshall, ah . . . what the future might hold. But," he continued, "perhaps it more appropriate that we toast Lavinia's upcoming marriage to Mr. Boran."

Although my head was down, I could feel Will's astounded eyes on me. I was grateful when the toast was over and Miss Sarah rang the bell for dessert.

That first evening of Will's visit, after a light supper, he asked permission to escort me on a walk. Miss Sarah agreed but suggested that Meg accompany us. After a short distance, Meg pointedly began to lag behind. As Will and I walked ahead, he broke the silence.

"Belle was right, you know."

"About what?"

"Years ago, on a wagon ride to church, you told me that Belle said you would grow up to be a beauty."

I blushed to remember. "Thank you, Will."

"Is it true, Lavinia? Are you to be married?" he asked.

"It was sudden —" I said.

"Is it what you want?"

"I don't —" I began slowly.

Again he interrupted. "And what did Marshall mean at the dinner table when he spoke of you returning with him?"

"I don't know," I said. I began to walk quickly; without reason, tears were threatening.

Will reached for my arm and pulled me to a stop. He turned me to face him. "Lavinia, I might be foolish for saying this, but I've always thought of you as my girl."

My chest ached. His words sounded genuine, but before I could respond, before I could bring up Belle and question his relationship with her, Meg caught up to us. "Mother says that I am to stay with you," she said, rolling her eyes.

Will graciously offered his other arm to Meg. As he did so, he leaned over and spoke in my ear, his nearness so affecting that I felt weak. "We will talk later," he said, but to my frustration and regret, we did not have the opportunity to meet in private again that evening.

I read Belle's letter that night. Her sentences were short and puzzled me.

To Lavinia —
Everybody here is doing good. I don't write

to say I'm coming to stay with you and Mr. Cardigan because things change here. Will is going to tell you about it. I don't say no more. I hope you remember that Will Stephens is a good man. That's all I have to say. Everybody here is thinking of you every day.

Belle Pyke

At the bottom of her letter was my first note from Sukey, now a grown-up seven-year-old. It read: *Binny. I remember you. Do you remember me. Sukey*

I puzzled over Belle's letter yet realized she knew nothing of Cardigan's death, nor of my engagement. I thought of the letter I should have written to her. I had stalled, not wanting to put on paper the loss of my brother and that it meant I had to retract my offer to have her join me. Then, too, neither was my engagement to Mr. Boran a fact that I had been eager to share. Sukey's note touched me deeply, and I might have suffered from it had I not the knowledge that Will Stephens was asleep in the house and I would see him again the following day.

Marshall was back in the morning. The three men had a meal together in the library, and despite my growing impatience, their meeting continued on through the day. In the late afternoon, I put up my hair and changed into my best dress, a soft yellow muslin. I took a book and went outdoors to sit in the back garden under an arbor shaded by grapevines.

The garden was enclosed by a picket fence and prettily edged with green thyme and scented with pink roses. I hoped that Will might find me there when the meeting was over. Instead, it was Marshall who appeared. He thrust open the back door, slammed it behind him, then began to pace back and forth on the brick walk. I called out to him, and when he did not hear me, I called again. He strode over. "What is it?" he asked, his eyes dark with fury. When I sensed that I might become a casualty of his anger, I was uncertain how to answer.

"What is it?" he repeated.

"Marshall." I kept my voice calm and soft. "Come, sit with me. What is the trouble?"

"That bastard!" he said, sitting down and looking back at the house.

I touched his arm lightly. "Marshall," I said, "please. Tell me. What is the trouble?"

He stood. "We've just wasted the greater part of the day, all because of that whore!" When he saw me flinch at the word, he sat again. "I'm sorry, Lavinia, but you did ask."

He leaned down and rubbed hard at his eyes. "It's that woman Belle! She has been nothing but trouble all of my life, and still it continues."

I forced myself to silence.

"She was my father's whore ever since I can remember. My mother tried all of her life to get rid of her, and Father would not even discuss it. My God! Will it never end!"

"But she is not —" I could no longer restrain myself.

"I will not hear a word in her defense!" he shouted furiously. "It was she who drove my mother to madness. And now! Now she's Stephens's whore. He wants her for himself. His sole purpose of this visit was to acquire her so he could set up house with her. The only way he will continue on in my absence is if I agree to sell her and their bastard child to him on my return."

I could scarcely breathe from the shock. "And will you agree?"

"I have no choice. It's the only way he'll stay on, and besides, my uncle can agree to it without my approval, which he has told me he will do."

"And that is all he asks?" I said.

"Hardly," Marshall sneered. "He also wants Ben and his woman and their two brats."

"But where will he take them?" I asked.

"My father gave him land that borders mine. He will set up his farm there."

I knew that I was going to be sick and could take no more. Without apology, I abruptly fled to my room, leaving Marshall alone on the garden bench.

That evening, when I pleaded a headache, Meg brought me my supper. She asked no questions. Miss Sarah came the next morning to tell me to hurry, that Will was waiting to see me before he left. I refused. I had always suspected Will's relationship with Belle, but to have it confirmed was almost more than I could endure. I shed no tears when Miss Sarah closed the door and went down to tell him my headache continued but that I wished him well on his journey home.

It was after Will's visit that a melancholy wrapped itself around me, affecting me so deeply that Miss Sarah came to me and expressed her concern.

I did not tell her of my reawakened love for Will, nor of my sadness in learning of his intent to take Belle into his own home. I dared not tell Miss Sarah of how the very thought of marriage to Mr. Boran repulsed me, of how I saw no way out. Instead, I explained away my gloom by telling her only part of my truth, of my great longing for Tall Oaks and all the people there. Miss Sarah asked if I might care to accompany her to the hospital to see Miss Martha. She had recently had word that Miss Martha's condition had improved somewhat.

"Would it help you to overcome these low feelings if you were to see Miss Martha again?" she asked.

"Yes," I said, "yes, it would."

"You are older now," she rationalized her decision. "Why, by next year you will be a married woman."

My visits to the hospital had ended in the spring. Now, eager to see her, I asked if we could visit the following day. Miss Sarah agreed, but only after she extracted a promise that I would resume my daily good cheer.

We left for the hospital in the late afternoon. We were both tense when we were admitted through the front door. Echoing clangs and shouts greeted us from the interior, and I was relieved that we did not have to wait but were taken immediately to Miss Martha's cell. She lay sleeping amid the din. The golden afternoon sun shone through the high window, but the iron bars cast gray shadows on the whitewashed brick walls and across Miss Martha, curled on her straw pallet.

The attendant informed us that she had just been given a large dose of laudanum and would likely sleep through our visit. When he left, he locked the door behind himself. Miss Sarah, her face as white as the walls, perched in a corner on a low stool that was chained to the floor.

I went directly to Miss Martha, crouched at her side, and softly called her name. She woke much like a child, rubbing her eyes and murmuring to herself.

"It's me, Miss Martha," I whispered. "It's Isabelle."

Behind me, Miss Sarah gasped. "Isabelle?"

Miss Martha pulled her hands back from her face, and through heavy-lidded eyes, she peered at me. "Baby?" she asked.

"Sukey?" I said. "You want Sukey?"

She nodded.

"Who is Sukey?" Miss Sarah asked, but I did not answer. Miss Martha had reached for my hand and began to recite a line from Sukey's storybook: " 'Make her a present of a fine gold watch. Make her a present of a fine gold watch.' "

"Yes, yes," I soothed, and joined in to recite the line with her over and over until her eyes, drug-heavy, closed again. When I turned to Miss Sarah, her eyes were wet.

"I knew nothing of . . . if only I had known what comfort you give her," she said.

Once settled in our carriage, I told Miss Sarah of the fondness I felt for her sister and I explained about Sukey and her book and the part they played in soothing Miss Martha.

"If only I had known, if only I had known," Miss Sarah repeated. Finally, in an effort to ease her, I confessed to my earlier visits. I had expected her ire, but instead, Miss Sarah blessed me for my actions.

I asked for permission to visit regularly, and following that day, a carriage was readily provided for my use. Miss Martha almost always recognized me, and it quickly became known to the attendants that my visits were a comfort to their patient. The first tool they allowed me was Belle's hairbrush, and I used it as Mama had taught. As I gently groomed her tender head, Miss Martha relaxed under my familiar touch. In the weeks following, a grateful matron gave me permission to bring books and to read to Miss Martha. Though everyone praised me for the comfort I brought, no one knew that I received as much from these visits as did Miss Martha.

CHAPTER THIRTY-FOUR

Belle

Mama was working here with me, pickling beans, when Will Stephens gets back from Williamsburg. I know something's not right when I see him coming up to the kitchen house with his shoulders leaning down.

I say, "Come in, Will, sit down," then Mama asks him if he wants something to drink.

"That sounds good, Mae," he says. "I'd appreciate some water."

"How'd it go?" I ask, soon as he drinks the water. Mama gives me a look to stop rushing him, but I can't take it no more.

He smiles at Mama, gives the cup back to her, and says, "Thank you, Mae." Then he breathes in deep before he starts talking. "Everything is in order, Belle. You, Jamie, Ben, Lucy, and their boys will come with me when I finish my contract out here."

I sit down and Mama sits down. When

nobody's saying nothing, I say, "How is Lavinia?"

Will looks at his feet. "She was already engaged to be married."

"What!" I say.

"Who she marryin'?" Mama asks.

Will fingers his hat, trying to look like he don't care. "I understand he is a colleague of Mr. Madden's. I didn't meet him."

"What happen to her brother?" Mama asks.

"He died a number of years ago."

"Did she send us a letter?" I ask.

"No," he says, and I know there's a whole lot of talking he's not doing.

"How's our girl lookin'?" Mama says. "She all growed up?"

"She is that." Will Stephens can't help but smile. "She's awfully pretty. Her hair is darker now, not as red, but her eyes . . . well, she looks right at you, same as before."

"Is she more like Beattie, or tall like Fanny?" I say.

"She's tall as Fanny, but she isn't skinny." He gets red when he hears hisself.

"She happy to be marryin' this man?" Mama asks.

He shrugged and shook his head. "Ah, Mae, I don't know much about women."

Mama makes us laugh: "Will Stephens,

you men all the same. The whole bunch of you don't know much about women." Will looks like he getting ready to leave when Mama asks, "You see Marshall?"

"I did," he says. "He has grown up as well."

We look at him, and he knows we're asking for more, so he says, "I'm afraid I have nothing good to say about him."

The way Will says that, I get cold all over.

"And Miss Martha?" Mama ask.

"She is still in the hospital. Mr. Madden doubts that she will ever return home."

After Will goes, Mama and me talk. We both know something's not right. We wonder about Lavinia, why we don't get no letter. Why don't she write about the man she's marrying?

Mama's worried. What happens when Marshall comes home to run this place? She'd like to get her girls out of here, but Will Stephens already tells her he don't have the money. And I know what Mama worries most about. Does the same thing happen to them that happens to me?

Mama says it good that Ben and me are going to Will's farm. She's afraid that Benny will get hisself killed if Marshall ever goes after me again. But I think, If Marshall ever comes at me again, I don't need Benny to finish him off.

Chapter Thirty-Five

Lavinia

Although Mr. Boran wanted to marry immediately, Mr. Madden stood firm on our wedding date, set for the following June, a month after my seventeenth birthday. As time passed, I had a growing concern with Mr. Boran. With others, he continued as a meek, mild-mannered individual, but away from their eyes, he was another man. When the two of us were isolated, he quickly became amorous and exhibited what to me was frightening behavior. His actions were no longer the innocent, albeit passionate kissing of my hands; he had begun to touch me inappropriately, in ways that I would have thought were meant for husband and wife. Yet I wondered if, as his intended, I was meant to tolerate this.

I did not know where to turn for help. Meg was as inexperienced as I, but more to the point, she had made it clear from the beginning that she did not wish to discuss anything about my relationship with Mr. Boran. I attempted a conversation with Miss Sarah, but I believe she thought I was seeking information about the wedding night and, embarrassed, she cut short the subject. The next day she came to my room and gave me a pamphlet to read. Information in it implied that the union between married couples was, while performed by men, to be endured by women.

Meanwhile, Mr. Boran was becoming more and more adept at finding ways to get me alone. His excuses were varied: a letter that he wanted me to hear in private, a small gift he wished me to have. The Maddens always agreed to his requests and often, of an evening, retired early to give us our privacy. I discouraged his advances as best I could and tried to redirect him with conversation, but he was becoming more bold and demanding. During his lewd advances, I fought to control my outright disgust, and after, alone in my room, I promised myself to find a way out of this agreement. One night, in a moment of inspiration, I thought of our tutor, Mrs. Ames. I would ask her advice. Could I work as a governess? Did I have enough education to teach?

Her response was immediate. "My dear!

Why would you want to do that?" In the one-way conversation that followed, she explained that teaching was an acceptable fate only if there was no alternative. She listed her reasons. First there was the issue of finding an amenable situation. Then there was always the fear of losing the position. "It happens all the time, and where does that leave a young woman? To be thrown out on the street? No, no, no! A girl such as yourself wants marriage."

Much discouraged, I decided that door was closed.

Then came the invitation to an evening ball at the Raleigh Tavern. Offered by Mr. Boran, it included Meg. By now Mr. Boran had sensed Meg's opposition to our engagement, and I believe this invitation was his effort to gain her goodwill. At first I did not know why she agreed so readily, as it was customary for her to refuse these social excursions. She surprised me further when she appealed to her mother to provide each of us with a new dress for the occasion. Delighted at the prospect of her daughter's interest in a social outing, Miss Sarah had the dressmaker in the very next day.

Meg had grown over the past year, though at fifteen, she remained short and slight. She had developed few feminine curves but was really quite pretty when she removed her eyeglasses to accentuate her pert nose and large brown eyes. Her hair remained difficult to control, for it frizzed rather than curled, and only braids or tight combs could hold it in place. Pins gave her a headache, she said, so often as not, her hair did as it would.

Meg was as devoted to her study of biology as ever, but of late she appeared to have taken an interest in one young man. He was Henry Crater, the twin whom Marshall had pummeled a few years back. Meg claimed her interest in Henry was related strictly to nature study, for Henry, now at college, also studied botany. But recently, when he came by to exchange books on the subject, I noticed Meg's hair done up in combs.

The night of the ball, before we dressed, I piled up my hair and dressed it prettily with white ribbon. On seeing it done, Meg handed me some yellow ribbon and asked that I do the same for her. She chatted away while I did so and, to my amusement, let it slip that she hoped to see Henry at the event.

After we were dressed, Meg and I studied each other. We had each chosen a fashionable dress of white lawn with empire waist, low square neckline, and small puff sleeves.

For trim, I had chosen blue ribbon, while Meg had selected yellow embroidery. Under our skirts, we wore flesh-toned pantaloons edged to match our dresses. We gave each other high praise on our appearance, and when I saw Meg smile at herself in the mirror, I suspected that for the first time, she knew what it was like to feel pretty.

This was my first formal outing with Mr. Boran, and I must admit, though I was excited by a new experience, I wished myself in Meg's position. I knew from the moment Mr. Boran arrived with his carriage that the evening would provide a challenge. On the ride over, he would not take his eyes from me, and to my embarrassment, he would not stop staring at the low cut of my gown. He repeatedly remarked at my beauty until Meg asked him to please find another topic. He fell silent, and I was relieved when we reached our destination. The Maddens were already there and came to greet us.

Mr. Boran did not wait but took me immediately to the dance floor. He moved with dexterity, but I was not put at ease when, with each pass, his eyes covered me in such a way that I feared how the evening might end. Clearly, he considered me his prize, and as this was our first public outing, I did not doubt that gossip circled the room. He did not want to leave the dance floor, so when I spied Meg off to the side, chatting with Henry, I insisted I needed a rest. But even then, to my frustration, Mr. Boran remained my shadow. I wanted to speak privately with Meg, to ensure that she would return home with us, but it wasn't until I had the inspiration to request some refreshment that Mr. Boran reluctantly left my side. Of course, this was the moment when Meg agreed to dance with Henry, and knowing this was a triumph for him, I did not hold them back.

From the dance floor, Miss Sarah beamed her approval, first at Meg, then at me. To my relief, I saw Marshall making his way toward me. My first thought was one of safety, and I eagerly watched his approach. Marshall looked striking in a dark green velvet coat, matching vest, and white muslin cravat. He glanced but once at my form, bowed politely, then stood to my side looking out at the dance floor.

"You've never looked more beautiful," he said.

"Marshall . . ." I began, but did not know how to proceed.

"What is it, Lavinia?" He leaned down to better hear.

"I'm afraid," I said.

"Afraid? Of what?" He looked directly at me, and at once I saw his concern.

"Marshall! It's good to see you watching out for Lavinia." Mr. Boran approached us with a newfound confidence. "I will see to her now," he added, offering me the drink. Marshall said not a word, and my heart plummeted when he bowed abruptly, then walked away.

"My dear," said Mr. Boran, "I have a favor to ask."

"Yes?"

"I promised Molly that I would bring you by the house tonight so she might see how beautiful you are."

"But what about —"

"I've already spoken to the Maddens. I told them we would return once we've satisfied Molly."

I looked across the dance floor and saw the Maddens laughing with another couple while Meg danced by with Henry. "Let me say good-bye," I said.

"No." He grasped my elbow. "We'll return. Come now, the carriage is ready."

"But I don't wish to go."

"You would disappoint Molly?" he asked.

I hesitated and looked around, trying to think of a way out.

"Well, I won't have her disappointed," he

said, and pressing his fingers into my arm, he steered me through the packed room and out the door.

I was silent on the ride to his home, and I felt some relief when he ordered the carriage to wait in the front. He took me into a parlor, but as I feared, Molly was not home. When I realized that his housemaid was also away, I became truly frightened. "Mr. Boran —"

He did not wait. 'You will be my wife in a few short months," he said, as though offering an excuse for the attack he began. I fought as though my life depended on my virtue, and I might have lost had he not tripped on his breeches when I made my escape. I ran from the house, leaving behind my wrap, not caring that I was half undressed. When I reached the carriage, I grabbed at the door handle and sobbed directions to the driver. I screamed when I felt hands clutch me from behind. The horses jerked forward, but I would not release my hold on the carriage door and was dragged along until I lost my grip.

"Lavinia! It's me! It's me!"

It was only when I fell away from the carriage that I realized the man holding me was Marshall.

■ ■ ■ ■

Marshall covered me with his jacket, then took me home. Once there, he intended to leave me while he went for the Maddens, but, certain that Mr. Boran would reappear, I pleaded for him to stay. To my relief, Marshall waited while I went upstairs to change, and he promised to do so until the Maddens' return. When I came downstairs, I couldn't stop shaking until he poured me a large measure of brandy and had me drink it down. The liquid bit into me but helped settle me, and after a short while, since I was unaccustomed to liquor, it loosened my tongue. I told Marshall of the liberties Mr. Boran had taken, and I spoke openly of my revulsion at the thought of marrying him. Suddenly, I had a terrible thought. "Must I still marry him?" I asked.

"No, Lavinia. You are quite through with him," Marshall assured me.

"But I agreed to it," I said.

"And I never understood why," he answered.

"I thought it the only solution. The Maddens have been so good to me. I can't expect them to provide for me much longer."

"Vinny! Vinny!" Meg flew in with the Maddens close behind. She rushed to my side, then stopped and stepped back to look at me. "You've been drinking!" she said. "You smell of it."

"I gave her some brandy," Marshall said.

"Marshall!" Miss Sarah scolded.

"She had need of it," he said.

Meg began the questions. "Whatever happened, Vinny? Mr. Boran came to find Father. He was white in the face. He said some terrible things about you."

I turned to Marshall for help, but he was already leading Mr. Madden from the room. Miss Sarah took a chair opposite me and demanded to know the story. After I told her everything, Meg put her arms around my shoulders. That was when I began to weep.

The engagement was ended, but I hated to have humiliated the Maddens with my failure. I felt especially guilty knowing that Mr. Madden had been a friend of Mr. Boran's; I knew how closely their work was related. I could only guess at the questions and the gossip that Miss Sarah was subjected to, and I could not think of a word to say to her as apology. No one told me the story the vile man circulated, but the little I did hear was evil enough to have half the town question the integrity of my character. How I regretted putting this family in such a position. I realized more than ever that I must soon make my own way.

I determined to wait until my seventeenth birthday before I appealed once again to Mrs. Ames. I was hopeful that she might see my need more clearly and be willing to take some steps to help me secure a position as governess. With that in mind, I concentrated more than ever on my studies. Marshall never referred to that night, but embarrassed to think of what he had witnessed, not the least being my near state of undress, I was more reserved with him. He continued to teach the Saturday class and once again joined the family for Saturday dinners.

Meg stood by me, as always. On a day not long after the ball, Mr. Degat, in a snide manner, questioned my part in the failed engagement. Meg cut him short by asking him about a particularly ugly piece of gossip that paired him with Mr. Alessi.

During that fall and winter, I welcomed my twice-weekly visits to Miss Martha. Her needs were such that mine paled next to hers, and each time I saw her eyes light up at my appearance, it let me know that I had something to offer.

Miss Martha was finally responding to treatment. The doctors had discovered that when laudanum was given four times a day, rather than just at bedtime, her outbursts all but disappeared. With this improvement, all other treatments were discontinued, and gradually, her behavior stabilized. There were times when I spoke to her of my daily affairs and she showed interest, appearing to comprehend my words. I did not include my concerns but told lighthearted stories based on village gossip. She listened intently and, during the telling, often took my hand and stroked it with what I took to be affection.

One day when she reached for my hand, I felt such warmth toward her that I wondered if that feeling was akin to what I might feel toward a mother. She noted my mood, and when my eyes welled up, she touched my hand to her face for the first time ever. Following that, my affection for her deepened, and I resolved to continue to see her no matter where my future might take me.

May arrived, and with its sweet greening, I tried to convince myself that my future was not as bleak as I had imagined. I still had not written to Belle, for I held a deep hurt that she had not seen fit to tell me the reason for Will's visit — that of securing her for himself. But in truth, it was not the only reason I did not write. I knew there was no chance of returning to the family I loved, and the thought of further contact had become too heart-wrenching.

I arranged to meet with Mrs. Ames the day following my seventeenth birthday. I decided that if she was unable to help me, I would prevail upon the Maddens one last time, to assist me in finding a family in need of a governess.

Meg was sixteen, the age when a girl's schooling was considered complete. It was expected that a young woman of that age fill her time with social obligations, but this being Meg, no one questioned when she announced that she would continue her study as before. Although we did not speak of it, Meg assumed I would go on with her, but I had already been given a year's grace. It was time for me to find employment.

About a week before my birthday, the mood in the household changed. For no reason that I could understand, the Maddens were more lighthearted in their approach to me; even Meg, normally oblivious to her parents, noted the difference. I guessed it had to do with their gratitude for my visiting Miss Martha. Indeed, Miss Sarah remarked often how well her sister was doing and said she was certain it was I who had made all the difference.

Over the winter Marshall had begun to visit on Wednesday evenings to play cards with Meg and me. I remained most grateful for his rescue of me, and because of it, I found myself in frequent romantic daydreams that included him. They embarrassed me, and afraid of giving myself away, I was often more reserved with him than I meant to be.

When Henry asked to join our midweek card party, I became more my old self. Henry initiated a cautious flirtation with Meg, and I began an easy banter with Marshall.

I was melancholy when I returned from the hospital the afternoon of my birthday. The day before, Miss Sarah had asked if there was anything special that I might like to mark the celebration. Nostalgic for the times the twins and I had shared an outdoor meal, I asked if I might take a simple afternoon dinner to share with Miss Martha. Miss Sarah seemed pleased with my request, and after she obtained permission from the hospital, she had Bess prepare a basket.

When I arrived, the hospital staff had set up a small table beside a bench in the shade of the mad yard, and I was told that Miss Martha and I had exclusive use of the yard for one hour. She was more alert than ever, and she watched closely as I covered the table with a white cotton cloth and set out blue and white china plates and silver cutlery. I had her sit beside me on the bench, then covered our laps with large linen napkins before we began our small feast of pickled asparagus, baked ham, fresh bread, and apple tarts topped with thick sweet cream. She waited until I began to eat, then delicately picked up her cutlery and began to sample the food.

While we ate, I spoke of the meals I had enjoyed in the outdoors at Tall Oaks. From the corner of my eye, I saw that she listened, so I indulged myself and spoke to her as though she understood everything. I immersed myself in memory and lived again the joy as the twins and I, sated from a basket feast, lay back onto soft pine needles. When I came back to present day, I told my silent dinner companion that this day was my birthday. I was seventeen, a grown woman. Miss Martha looked at me, dabbed her mouth with her napkin, and for the first time since her hospitalization, spoke a full sentence.

"When the captain arrives, Isabelle, we will leave for home," she said.

I stared at her. I waited for more, but it was as though the effort to formulate the thought had drained her. She looked about as if lost. Her napkin dropped to the ground when she rose from the table, and she did not retrieve it before she walked off. Later, when I said good-bye, she was still far away.

I meant to go straight to my room to finish what I had been working on. I was preparing a list of my qualifications for the prospective employer whom I hoped Mrs. Ames would help me to find. When I disembarked from my carriage, I was surprised to find Marshall there to greet me. He took my basket from my arm and set it down. "Walk with me?" he asked.

"Is Meg coming?" I looked for her.

"No, not today."

"But Miss Sarah —"

"I have her permission."

I might have been apprehensive had he not such a pleasant look. He took my hand and linked it to his arm, then confidently set the two of us out on a path into the golden afternoon. In silence, we walked to the park, where Marshall seated me on a bench under a blooming dogwood tree. I glanced up at him uncertainly.

"Lavinia," he said, facing me, "I understand that you have once again demonstrated your kindness."

I did not understand his meaning and said so.

"I have only recently learned of your visits to the hospital."

"Oh."

"What kindness, Lavinia. How extraordinary your loyalty."

"It isn't really so extraordinary, Marshall," I said. "Miss Martha gives me comfort. She reminds me of home — that is, of Tall Oaks."

"And do you consider Tall Oaks your home?"

"It is the only home I remember."

"And it is your birthday today?"

I laughed, wondering where this conversation was going. "Yes, I'm seventeen," I admitted.

"You are aware, then, that today you are a free woman?"

I looked at him in surprise. Although I knew I was indentured, I no longer thought of myself in bondage.

"I will have papers drawn up if you like."

"Will they be necessary?" I asked.

"No." He smiled. "Not if you agree to my plan."

I questioned him with a look.

He took a deep breath. "Lavinia. I have a proposal for you."

At once I was filled with enthusiasm; I realized what he was about to suggest. He wanted me as a companion for his mother! He would take the two of us back with him! I fought to control my growing excitement.

"This fall I will inherit Father's estate. By then I'll have completed my studies, but I won't stay here to practice law. I plan to go back to Tall Oaks to run the plantation myself." He took a seat beside me. "You must know I care for you. I want you to come with me, Lavinia. I want to marry you."

I was speechless with astonishment.

He took my hand. "I've already discussed this with Aunt and Uncle, and both think this a fine match."

Still I was unable to speak.

"Lavinia," he said, "you must know how very dear you are to me." Taking my stunned silence as a negative, he continued, "Please consider my proposal."

"Well . . . yes. I would be honored," I

managed to say. In response, he kissed my gloved hand and smiled at me. I reached up to tenderly loose one of his sandy blond curls, caught under his crisp white shirt collar.

"We will be happy," he said, and he drew me toward him in a warm embrace.

I immediately sought Miss Sarah's counsel. What did she think of a marriage between Marshall and me?

"You are both young," she said, "yet I see your influence on him. He is a happy man when he is with you, Lavinia. I do believe that you bring out the best in him."

I was flattered to hear this.

"I know how you long to return to Tall Oaks," she continued, "and I'm sure that you are aware of the social advantages this marriage will bring to you." She stopped, studied her hands, and then looked at me again. "Do you care for Marshall?"

"Yes," I replied honestly, "I do."

"Then," she said, "Mr. Madden and I are happy to give our blessing."

That same night I broke my silence and wrote to tell Belle of my good fortune. I was elated! I was coming home! I wrote how happy I was and how grateful I felt to Marshall for his saving me from an unknown future.

How I played over my homecoming! Married to Marshall, I would be in a position to cast favor on my waiting family, and I spent many hours daydreaming of how we might improve on their homes and find ways to ease their workload. I took the fantasy so far that I even believed it possible Marshall would give them their freedom one day, as I had been given mine.

I did have some concerns about him, but I kept them to myself. He clearly trusted me as he trusted no other, and because of it, I saw his vulnerability — something he hid well from others. He was considerate of me, but if I gave opposition, offering an opinion that differed from his, he took it as a personal offense and would isolate himself in a dark mood. As a consequence, I learned quickly to stand with him on any subject. Fortunately, making myself amenable was not foreign to me, as I had lived this way for much of my life.

A lesser worry, yet one that I noted, was Marshall's lack of physical affection. Our social outings were few, though he escorted me twice to theater events. He clearly took pride in having me on his arm, but we did not stay after to socialize. In fact, we came home immediately after, and once I was safely deposited, Marshall soon made an excuse to leave. As his time at university was ending, his need for study time had increased, so our Saturday classes were dropped. He came for evenings of card playing, where Henry and Meg were always at the ready, but he never stayed late, nor did he request to see me alone. In truth, after Mr. Boran's display, I was relieved, yet I wondered why Marshall did not at least attempt a kiss. In many ways, his treatment of me reminded me of the way I had behaved toward the doll that Mama Mae had given me as a child. I favored it so that I had refused myself the joy of playing with it, daring to love it only with my eyes. But in doing so, I had denied myself its very purpose.

Though Meg and I remained steady companions, she was curiously silent about my relationship with Marshall. Sensing her reluctance to discuss the topic, I did not bring up any of my own concerns.

In the last week of August, when I was being fitted for three new dresses — a gift for my upcoming marriage compliments of the Maddens — the dressmaker came with the stunning news that Mr. Boran was dead.

The town hummed with gossip. The unfortunate man had been found in the woods, close to a wayside tavern some miles out of town. This tavern, it was rumored, sheltered women who, as Miss Sarah put it, "saw to the needs of a certain type of man." What made it curious was that it was well known Mr. Boran did not drink. However, it appeared that he had imbibed so heavily the evening of his death that he had fallen from his horse and fatally struck his head on a rock.

My first concern was for his daughter, Molly, until I remembered that she had an aunt who loved her well. I could not say that I regretted to hear the news, as I still had fear of the man. Though I had not told the Maddens, I had confided in Marshall that on more than one occasion I was certain I had seen him at night on the street outside my window.

Miss Sarah, Meg, and I gossiped wildly, but at dinner that day we were subdued. Mr. Madden, we did not forget, had been a friend to Mr. Boran. I offered my sympathies to him, and though he thanked me, his look was troubled.

I wanted desperately to discuss the news with Marshall, so I was disappointed when he sent his regrets and did not visit that week. When I next saw him and raised the subject of Mr. Boran, his comment was dismissive. He was bored with the topic of that miserable man's death, he said, and I knew from his behavior to let the matter rest.

Through that summer I continued to visit Miss Martha. She and I did not have conversations as others might know them, but she always appeared interested in what I had to say. If she was particularly drawn to a subject, she often repeated one or two of my words. I knew then to embellish, to give further details.

I had not spoken to her of Marshall, nor of our relationship, but as our wedding date approached, I knew the time had come. The day I chose to tell her, we sat outside in the shade of the mad yard. It was late afternoon, and the hot August sun had no mercy for those in the enclosure, but the outdoors provided us the most privacy.

"I am going to marry Marshall," I said bluntly.

She did not respond.

"Miss Martha," I said, for some reason wanting to cry, "do you understand? I am to marry Marshall, your son."

She began to pick at the sleeve of my

dress. "Marry Marshall," she said in a singsong voice, "marry Marshall."

I interrupted her as I had learned to do. "Yes," I said. "In September we will marry, and we'll go back to Tall Oaks."

"Tall Oaks," she whispered, "Tall Oaks." She lifted her head and stared off as though seeing beyond the wall.

"What do you think?" I asked.

She turned back to me and smiled, something I had not seen her do in the past five years. It touched me so that I began to cry.

It was Miss Martha's smile that gave me the courage to plead her case with Marshall. From what I knew, he had not seen her since that unfortunate visit years before with Miss Sarah. I did not tell him that I had knowledge of that time, but instead asked him if he would accompany me on my next visit to his mother.

"I cannot do it!"

I heard the pain in his statement and pressed him no further. But I asked him if it was not possible to take her home with us. I promised to be responsible for her care.

His initial response was no, but I noted a small hesitation, and the next time I felt the mood right, I remarked on the benefits that Miss Martha would have in her own home:

how Mama Mae and the twins might care for her and how good food might stimulate her appetite. I was optimistic and said that I thought it possible she might fully recover. I used to my advantage his eagerness to satisfy me, and a few short weeks before our marriage, I won him over.

Our wedding ceremony took place in the late afternoon on the sixth of October, 1801. We had meant to have it in the parlor, but the day was so beautiful, the garden still so pretty, and our wedding party so small that we decided at the last minute to change plans. Meg and Henry stood with us as we took our vows amid the sound of birdsong and the scent of late-blooming honeysuckle. I wore an ivory satin gown, very high-waisted, with elbow-length sleeves, and on my feet I had the prettiest pointed slippers ever made. Meg pinned up my hair and nestled in it pearl clips and small rosettes of ivory satin ribbon.

About a month before the wedding, in a rare moment of privacy, Marshall had informed me that an account had been set up in my name. Mr. Madden was in charge of it, but I was to use it for the sole purpose of seeing to my needs. When Marshall told me the sum, I was astounded and said I had no need of that amount. He laughed. "You will require all of that and more! I want you to have a new wardrobe."

"But I don't need —"

"This is not about need, Lavinia. You will be my wife, and I want to see you well dressed. Remember, if this is not a sufficient amount, you have but to ask."

"Might I use some of this for gifts?"

Again he laughed. "You may use it for whatever you like, but promise me I will see a new wardrobe. And don't forget your wedding gown."

On our wedding day, as Mr. Madden led me down the brick walk toward my intended, I looked up to see Marshall's approving smile and was flooded with gratitude. Because of him, my future was secured, and I was going home. After the short ceremony, drinks were made available, and our guests — among them Mr. Degat, Mr. Alessi, and Mrs. Ames — joined to offer us a toast for a long and happy marriage. Then began a round of individual toasts that ended with everyone very gay indeed. After the sun set, we went into the front parlor, which had been cleared of furniture. Mr. Alessi, with a group of musicians, played music that no one could resist, and soon we were all dancing joyfully. I was pleased to see that Marshall handled the drink as well as any of us. As a matter of fact, it relaxed him as it did me, and the two of us laughed and teased each other as though we were children.

Later, Miss Sarah called us all into the dining room, where we enjoyed a feast that Nancy and Bess had prepared over the last few days. By eleven o'clock that evening, everyone had left. Marshall and I stayed that night with the Maddens, and we all soon retired, each to our separate rooms. Marshall and I slept apart; he had suggested we get a good rest before the start of our journey the following morning.

In bed that night, when I reflected back to the joy of the day, I could not sleep. Added to that was the excitement of going home.

We left early the next morning, our coach piled high. Meg and I clung to each other until Marshall teased that he would leave without me. Meg ran into the house when I climbed into the carriage, and I didn't look back to wave at the Maddens for fear of my own tears beginning. When we drew up to the public hospital, another coach waited, with Miss Martha already settled in. Two hospital attendants were with her for the journey; after we reached Tall Oaks and their patient was settled, they would return to Williamsburg.

Words could not express what I felt that morning. The other carriage led the way, and as it left, our ready horses bolted. Distracted, I flew off the seat. Marshall's quick embrace caught me or I would have been thrown. I turned in his arms and met his eyes, then surprised us both when I kissed his mouth. I sat back and blushed while he chuckled quietly. We were on our way! We were going home! A profound gladness overtook me. Tears of joy filled my eyes, and I looked out the window through prisms of color as Williamsburg faded away.

CHAPTER THIRTY-SIX

Belle

We don't hear from Lavinia for a long time, until she writes that now she's gonna marry Marshall. I don't write back. What do I say? What happened to the other man? How do you get with Marshall? What are you thinking to marry Marshall?

I say to Mama maybe this'll turn out good, but Mama don't like it. "Nothin' good gonna come from this," she says. "That boy got trouble comin' his way, and I don't like to think that Lavinia gonna be part of it."

I start to worrying about Marshall getting at me again, but Will Stephens says that I'm his now, and Marshall got no say over me. Will says he's got one more year to run this place, then we're going to his farm down a mile from the quarters, other side of the creek. I know his farm's gonna work out good, 'cause since Will's here, Ben and Papa say this place is doing the best it ever do.

One day after we get Lavinia's letter, the Maddens send a wagonload of crates from Williamsburg. Will Stephens takes them up to the big house, and we're all there while he opens them up. We stand back, nobody saying nothing, when he pulls out the red and white paper to put up on the walls. Papa helps him unwrap two new red chairs and then bolts of cloth that looks like the color of top cream and feels soft like my own skin. When they're done, Will reads us the letter from Mrs. Madden that tells us to put all of this in a bedroom for Lavinia.

Fanny's wondering if this is why Lavinia's gonna marry Marshall, that she's wanting all these pretty things. "If that's why she's marrying him," I say, "she sure is changed. The only time I ever see Lavinia wanting something for herself was the time she took Beattie's baby doll. And then she was just looking for something to love."

Will says he got orders for us to move Marshall's bedroom down to the good parlor. We don't ask no questions, we just work hard to get everything done like the letter says. The big house looks as good as when Miss Martha leaves, and we're all wondering if she's coming back. Her room's ready for her if she do.

Everybody knows a big change is coming. Fanny, Beattie, Sukey, they're all watching for the carriage every day. Me too. But Ben says if Marshall ever touches me again, he's a dead man.

I never did see Mama this quiet before.

CHAPTER THIRTY-SEVEN

Lavinia

It was a long journey home. In spite of the experienced attendants, I was required to travel in Miss Martha's coach for extended periods of time. I learned quickly that Marshall had little patience for his mother, though I noted he had planned ahead to meet her needs. At every tavern stop along the way, she was immediately taken to her room, where her attendants cared for her until the following morning. At great cost, I was provided with my own room. I did wonder why Marshall did not join me; I knew he often spent the nights in a communal room with other travelers.

Each day became more difficult for Miss Martha. On our last day of travel, I knew it would be easiest for her if I spent the full day in her carriage, so that morning I urged Marshall to saddle his own horse and ride ahead. I could see his relief at my suggestion, and he did not wait to do exactly that.

In the late afternoon, with Miss Martha finally sleeping, we drove up the long drive that led to Tall Oaks. The green boxwood on either side of the winding road had grown tall, and when the grand house came into view, it glistened with a fresh coat of whitewash. As we pulled up, I saw smoke rise from the kitchen house, and I could scarcely keep from leaping out. I felt certain everyone would be at the big house waiting to greet me and was disappointed to see only Papa George out front. When he opened the coach door and helped me down, I reached to embrace him, but he deftly stepped back. He must have recognized my hurt, for he held tight my gloved hand and gave me a small formal bow. He pretended to look into the carriage before he asked, "Did you see Miss Abinia? They say she comin' home."

"Oh, Papa." I laughed. "You know this is me."

"My, my." He looked at me and shook his head. "Miss Abinia come back to us, and now she a lady."

"I'm the same as ever, Papa." I looked around. "Where is everyone?"

Before he could answer, Mama Mae came through the front door. I forgot all about

Miss Sarah's proper decorum and called out Mama's name as I raced up the steps to greet her. I threw my arms around her, and though she did not discourage my embrace, she did not prolong it. I would have worried at this had I not seen another's sparkling eyes over Mama Mae's shoulder.

I doubt I would have recognized Fanny if it hadn't been for her familiar eyes. At seventeen, with a broad forehead and prominent teeth, she remained as plain as ever.

She had grown tall and was very thin, but what so changed her appearance was the head rag she wore. I was used to seeing her black hair, usually in braids, framing her face. The wrap of dark navy did nothing to flatter her deep brown color. "Fanny!" I called out as I crossed the threshold and went toward her. From the corner of my eye, I saw Mama give Fanny a nod.

Fanny stepped back to execute an odd attempt at a curtsy. "Miss Abinia, it sure good to have you back home with us."

I thought her formality a joke and would have laughed had the exhausted attendants not then appeared with Miss Martha. Their patient was confused and upset, and to my disappointment, she did not recognize home. Mama, Fanny, and I took Miss Martha to her room. I measured out her next laudanum dose, and as it took effect, Mama and Fanny readied her for bed. While she settled, I looked around and saw how everything shone. I complimented Mama and Fanny on how well the house had been cared for.

Mama smiled. "You gonna be the fine young mistress," she said.

"Oh, Mama," I said, "don't call me that!"

"That who you be now," she said. "When he come home this mornin', Masta Marshall make it clear that we to call you the mistress."

Embarrassed, I didn't know how to respond. My face burned.

"Abinia," Mama said softly to me, "that name don't mean nothin'. Everybody here know who you are to them, don't you worry about that." Fanny nodded her agreement.

When Miss Martha slept, Mama told me to go downstairs, where Marshall waited for me in the dining room. I had little hunger, though by now it was suppertime. When I got to the dining room, Marshall was already seated. I saw Uncle Jacob waiting by the table.

"Uncle!" I rushed in joyously until I caught Marshall's eye. His look cooled me, and I slowed to a walk. Once seated, I turned to Uncle. "How are you, Uncle

Jacob?" I asked.

"I just fine, Miss Abinia," he said. His eyes did not meet mine, and I was reminded of the coolness of the servants in Miss Sarah's home. Before I could attempt further conversation, Marshall broke in with talk of the plantation and his ideas for the future. At the end of the meal, Beattie came to clear the table. Although she, too, was wearing a head rag, hers was a pretty yellow, and I would have known her anywhere. She was shorter than Fanny, but her body was more curvaceous. Her gentle brown eyes shone, and when she smiled, she was as beautiful as I remembered. I rose to go to her, but Marshall caught my hand and frowned. Reluctantly, I reseated myself. "Beattie!" I said. "How are you?"

"I just fine, Abinia." She glanced at Marshall, then corrected herself. "Miss Abinia."

Marshall asked Uncle for more wine, and Beattie took that moment of distraction to give me another smile. My eyes followed her when she left the dining room, and as the door swung open, I caught a glimpse of another young girl peeking through. This time I could not stop myself. I pushed my chair back from the table, ran to the door, and flung it open. The child's hair was braided, and she was without a head rag.

She had a full pink mouth, a round face, and large, serious eyes. She fingered the embroidered pink edging on the collar of her brown homespun shift, no doubt some of Beattie's handiwork. I went through the door and let it close behind me. "Sukey?" I asked, unmindful that I knelt on my best traveling dress. "Is this Sukey?"

She nodded shyly.

"Don't you remember me?"

"You my Binny," she said, and the world stopped when she came into my arms.

Marshall flung open the door with such force that, startled, we pulled apart. He looked at me strangely, then nodded at Sukey. "Who is that?" he asked.

"This is Sukey." I stood and put my arm around her shoulders. "I've known her since she was a baby."

"Lavinia," said Marshall, "I've had enough. It has been a long trip. Could we finish our meal without further histrionics?"

I obediently released Sukey but whispered in her ear, "I'll see you later," before I followed Marshall into the dining room. There, my new husband and I finished our first meal at home in awkward silence.

I did not need Marshall's encouragement to retire early. I was told that I would have the room opposite the nursery, what had been the tutor's room. I remembered it as dark and fearsome, and though Mama knew my trepidation, she led me to it nonetheless. When she opened the door, I gasped in amazement at the change I saw before me.

A red and ivory toile covered the walls, while the two tall windows and the four-poster bed were curtained in ivory damask. Two small wingback chairs were upholstered in red silk and set invitingly in front of the fireplace. A small fire burned, and across the room, on a small writing desk, an oil lamp flickered, illuminating two of Meg's botanical prints.

Mama looked at me hopefully. "It's beautiful, Mama," I said, determined to show my appreciation. But everything felt wrong. Since my arrival, I had felt an uneasiness taking over, and somehow, this room epitomized that disquiet. This did not feel like my home. True, it was lovely, but it did not feel like the home I remembered, the one I had envisioned. My homecoming was nothing I had hoped for.

Mama smiled at me as if to ease her next words. "You don't call me Mama no more. You best call me Mae. Masta Marshall say that what he want." I frowned. Mama spoke softly. "This all gonna take some gettin' used to, but you know we all standin' by you."

Fanny came to the door to ask for Mama's help with Miss Martha. I wanted to go with them, but Mama told me no. "Tonight we take care of her," she said. "You stay here."

Fanny peeked in before she left. "Abinia, how you like your room? We all work to get it right for you."

"Oh, it's beautiful, Fanny," I said as sincerely as I was able.

After she closed the door, I wandered the room, then settled on the edge of the bed. I stayed there for a long time until, overcome with loneliness, I crossed over to the window. My room was adjacent to Miss Martha's rooms, and when I looked out on the familiar backyard, there was enough moonlight to see the kitchen house and the path that led to Mama and Papa's cabin. I could make out the barns, and when I thought I saw smoke rising from a chimney down at the quarters, I breathed in deeply. "I'm home," I whispered, hugging myself. "I'm home."

Later that night, after I was already in bed, Marshall came to my room. He had been drinking since supper, and it was easy to see that he had overindulged. He came into my room carrying a beaker half filled with brandy, and on his way to me, he stumbled and spilled a good portion of it on one of the red silk chairs. I would have rushed to clean it, but something told me it was better left alone.

I was tense, for we had not yet been intimate. I wondered if he was as virginal as I, but when he discarded his clothes and pulled me to him, I did not wonder further. The act was quick and rough, and he showed no tenderness, but after, when I pulled my gown down, he laid his head on my stomach and drunkenly pleaded for my forgiveness. I fingered his curls and stroked his head, soothing him until he slept. I wanted desperately to ease away, to run down to the kitchen house to see Belle, but I did not. True, I feared to wake my husband, but there was another reason, one that had haunted me throughout this past year. I could not bear to see Will Stephens sharing Belle's home.

I sat awake and watched the light from the fireplace die down. Engulfed in darkness, I admitted to myself that perhaps, in thinking this marriage would return me to my family, I had made a dreadful mistake.

When I awoke late the next morning, I saw

that Marshall had left a note saying he and Will Stephens had gone out to survey the farm. He would be back to join me for a two o'clock dinner.

I dressed quickly and went directly to Miss Martha's room. Mama met me in the blue room and fussed over me, telling me to go down to eat, or did I want a tray upstairs?

"Please stop, Mama," I said. "Please don't trouble yourself with me. You know I can take care of myself."

"You call me Mae," she said firmly.

I didn't answer. "How is Miss Martha?" I asked.

"Come see for yourself," Mama said.

Miss Martha was already seated in a chair with Sukey combing her hair. A breakfast tray was pushed to the side, and from all appearances, the patient had eaten a good breakfast.

"Isabelle," Miss Martha said when she saw me, and I was delighted to see how alert and happy she appeared.

I went to her and gave her a hug. Then I put my arm around Sukey's shoulders. "Hello, baby," I said, and we laughed as we hugged. "Mama," I asked, "can you spare us if we go down to the kitchen house for a while?"

Mama didn't answer.

411

"Mama?" I asked again.

"Miss Abinia," Mama said, "you call me Mae."

I stood my ground. "No, Mama," I said, "I won't." I had never defied her, and we both looked at each other in surprise.

Mama turned and walked out to the blue room; I followed, leaving Sukey and Miss Martha in the bedroom. "You call me Mae," she said.

"No," I said.

"Chil', I raise you up, and I sayin' that you gonna call me Mae!"

"No, Mama," I pleaded.

Mama sat down on a wooden chair and waited awhile before she looked up at me. "Why you do this to me, chil'?" she asked.

"Because you are Mama." I began to cry, the stress of the previous day and night fueling my tears. Mama stood, and I went to her open arms. "Nothing's the same, Mama!" I cried. "Nothing's the same!"

She pulled a rough handkerchief from her pocket and wiped my face. "This all gonna work out," she said. "This need time, that's all. You go on now. You take Sukey down to the kitchen, and I stay here. Somebody down there waitin' on you."

Belle, coming up from the orchard, balanced a large basket of apples on her shoulder. A young boy of four or five circled her, tossing an apple in the air. I hesitated, then increased my pace. When Belle caught sight of me, she placed the basket on the ground, called my name, and ran to greet me. We embraced until Belle held me away to see how I had grown. Sukey brought the little boy to me.

"You knows Jamie?" she asked, pulling him forward.

"Why, yes, I certainly do." I had known him only as a babe, but when I crouched down, I could scarcely believe what I saw. His sandy-colored hair had a soft curl, and his blue eyes looked out from a face that might have been Campbell's. However, I immediately noted that his left eye was clouded over, and from the way he held his head to look at me, it was clear that his vision was impaired.

"Hello, Jamie." I took his hand. "The last time I saw you, you were just a wee one."

He pulled away from me and ran to Belle. She patted his head. "He never sees no lady before." She sent him on ahead with Sukey, then put her arm through mine as we made our way toward the kitchen. There, Beattie was preparing dinner. She continued her work when we came in, but when I offered to help, she invited me to sit. Soon Fanny came from the big house, where Mama had relieved her of her duties so she could join our reunion. Sukey sat next to me, and I put my arm around her shoulder as she put hers around my waist. I felt a tenderness toward her that I might have felt toward my own child.

It wasn't long before we all began to talk at once, and soon the kitchen rocked with our laughter. So there, in the kitchen house, I finally felt some of what I had been longing for. But it was short-lived.

Mama was short of breath when she appeared at the door. "Come." She waved to us, looking back toward the barns. "They back, and Masta Marshall comin' up soon."

We could not miss the anxiety in her voice, and we all responded at once. Beattie and Belle went back to their work in the kitchen, while Fanny, Sukey, and I quickly followed Mama up to the big house.

CHAPTER THIRTY-EIGHT

Belle

When Lavinia was a child, every time you turn around, she's sick. Somebody looks at her the wrong way, her food comes up. Most of the time, Mama and me don't think she's gonna live to grow up. How this girl comes back looking good as she do, I don't know. Now she's taller than me. She stands straight up, and when she walks, she moves almost like her feet off the ground. Her bones still look like they'd break easy, but she's filled out enough to look like a woman. Her hair's dark, but it's still red — no question about that. She talks like before, soft and quiet, but now she's got a way of saying things that let you know she's a lady. Mama says it's hard to believe, but if you see her standing next to Miss Martha, except for the eyes, she looks just like her.

The first time I see Marshall, he's going down to the barns, and I jump back so he don't see me. Sukey and Jamie are playing outside, and Marshall walks right up to them. He don't say nothing, just keeps looking at Jamie like he don't believe what he sees. I know it's like he's looking back at hisself. I go out and call to Jamie to come to the kitchen house. Marshall looks up and watches Jamie run to me. My hands are shaking so bad they hardly work to close the door. Then I got to sit down. That's how much that man scares me.

I know I'm going to Will's farm, but until I get there, I sleep with one eye open and the kitchen knife under my bed. I know that Mama and Papa are wanting me and Ben to get out of here before something happens. Ben don't think like Papa. Papa says Ben got to know his place, but Ben says he knows his place all right, and it ain't under no white man that don't do right.

Marshall's home for only a few days, but already he's got everybody feeling skittery. It's like you know a storm's coming, and lighting's bound to strike.

Chapter Thirty-Nine

Lavinia

At dinner on our second day, I was alarmed at my husband's bad temper. As Uncle quietly served the delicious meal that Belle and Beattie had prepared, I tried to eat. Finally, my stomach churning, I set down my cutlery and began to nervously smooth the heavy linen napkin that covered my lap as I listened with growing apprehension to the railings of my young husband. Will Stephens, he said, had made a mess of the plantation. Oh, Stephens was good enough with words, and he had fooled Uncle Madden in Williamsburg, but one only had to look for oneself to see how poorly the place had been run. Marshall interrupted himself only once. "Jacob," he instructed, "bring us another bottle of wine."

I saw a momentary look of surprise on Uncle Jacob's face. I reached for Marshall's hand. "Might that wait until tonight's supper?" I asked, but when Marshall hastily withdrew his hand, I realized my mistake.

When Uncle left for the cellar, Marshall turned to me, his face set. "Don't you ever speak over me again, Lavinia," he said.

"Marshall, I didn't mean —"

"I don't care what you meant," he interrupted, "you are my wife. You do not question me!"

I searched his furious face and found no opening for reason. When Uncle Jacob returned and began to pour the wine, Marshall insisted my glass be filled as well. He drank two glasses of wine in quick succession, then sat back and observed me after he had Uncle fill his glass a third time. Too anxious to introduce a new topic of discussion, I made an effort to resume eating. When my cutlery accidentally scratched against the china, I glanced up in apology and was surprised to see that my husband's mood had changed. He gave me a pleasant smile, raised his glass, and nodded for me to join him. "Let us drink a toast, Lavinia," he said.

I forced myself to smile when I held my glass up to his.

"To us, Lavinia," he said. "May we always be this happy."

■ ■ ■ ■

Marshall did not come to my room that night, but he did the next, and again he was inebriated. He was not gentle, and the act was not pleasant for me. However, I knew my responsibility and did not think to deny him.

In fact, I had hoped that our coming together might be a way to establish a closer bond. Soon, though, I realized that for Marshall, it was not an act of intimacy. Rather, it was a function to be done when intoxicated. In the weeks that followed, when he did visit, he did not stay the night but left soon after he finished. Alone then, I lay awake, wondering what had happened to the Marshall I had known back in Williamsburg.

Morning was Marshall's best time. He rose early, eager and ambitious to begin the day, but at dinner he began to drink, and his mood usually turned sour. Seldom was his frustration with me, for I anticipated his needs and always acquiesced if necessary. However, as the days passed, his anger escalated toward Will Stephens.

I began to dread our daily afternoon meal,

when his tirades against Will began. I took comfort in having the security of Uncle Jacob's constant presence in the dining room, and in Beattie, who came to serve the food. Often when she lifted or set a plate, she brushed my hand or caught my eye, and I was reminded that I was not alone.

A few weeks after our homecoming, Beattie wore the gold locket I had brought back for her as a gift from Williamsburg. Marshall noted it and, after a few glasses of wine, asked in a friendly manner who had given it to her.

"Miss Lavinia," she said proudly.

"Miss Lavinia?" he said as he turned toward me. "And where did your mistress get the funds for such a fine gift?"

"From you, Marshall." I smiled at him. "From the money you gave me in Williamsburg. You said I could buy gifts if I chose."

His face turned hard. "Naturally, I assumed you meant Uncle, Aunt, or Meg."

"But you said —"

"And who else in this household benefited from my generosity?"

"Marshall, please, you are embarrassing me."

"Who else?" he shouted.

I shook my head, refusing to answer.

"Give it to me," he directed Beattie, who removed her gift with trembling fingers. He slipped it into his waistcoat pocket and stood to deliver a final dictate to me. "You are never to buy gifts for the servants without my approval. They are your servants! For God's sake, Lavinia. Try to elevate yourself to your new station!"

After he left the room, Beattie and I looked at each other, both of us shaken.

"I'm sorry," I said to Beattie.

"It all right, Miss Abinia," she said as she cleared the dishes, then left the room. As I sat at the table alone, I was reminded of the day Miss Martha first played her harpsichord for me. She spoke of loneliness, and this day I understood her position as never before. But with that memory, I became determined to establish a better relationship with Marshall and to find again the friendship that we had shared in Williamsburg. Then would I appeal to him for the needs for my family.

Mama Mae tried to guide me into the role of mistress. It was her idea that we set aside time to inventory the house, to go through each room and empty cupboards and chests, drawers and linen presses, and to make a complete list of the household's belongings.

Mama suggested I tell Marshall of this undertaking, to let him know how I was spending my time. I did so, and when I saw his approval, I knew that Mama understood my role, and perhaps my husband, better than I. Soon a good part of my day was taken up with sorting through the house.

I helped care for Miss Martha, and in the afternoons I took pleasure in reading to her. Some mornings after I was sure Marshall had left the yard, I ran down for a quick visit to the kitchen house. I knew that those times made Mama uneasy, but I went nonetheless, always hoping to see Belle on her own. She was the one I thought might answer the intimate questions I had about my marriage, but the few times I saw her, others were always with us, plying me with questions about my life in Williamsburg.

We had been home no more than a month, and a routine of dinner drinking had already been established. Without my knowledge, Marshall must have observed me on a morning visit to the kitchen house. At dinner that afternoon my husband nodded for Uncle to refill his glass, then he took my hand. "So, Lavinia," he said not unpleasantly, "what have you been doing today?"

"Mama and I are doing an inventory of the nursery," I said quickly.

Marshall squeezed my hand, and I realized too late the trap.

"But you were down in the kitchen house. I don't want you down there. Do you understand?"

I tried to pull my hand away, but he continued to press with force. His eyes gleamed at my discomfort.

"But Mama and —" I whispered, glancing back at Uncle Jacob.

"Mama." He spat out the word. "You are my wife. She is Mae to you!"

"Marshall! You're hurting me —"

He continued to squeeze, and I gasped from pain as I tried to free my hand.

"I said you call her Mae! Did you hear me?"

"Yes," I moaned.

When Uncle Jacob slipped from the room, I wanted to call out for him not to leave but dared not. Fortunately, Marshall had released me by the time Uncle returned. I sat stunned, my hand throbbing, while my husband resumed eating.

Suddenly, Mama burst into the room. " 'Scuse me, Masta Marshall! Miss Abinia, I need you for helpin' with Miss Martha!"

When she dashed from the room, I rose, alarmed. "I must go," I said, and followed quickly. I rushed up the stairs behind

Mama, and when we reached the blue room, she hastily shut the door behind us, then sent me into the bedroom while she stayed behind. Miss Martha, seated in her chair, smiled contentedly at me. Fanny stood by her but studied me anxiously. The three of us jumped when we heard loud bangs from the blue room. Fanny and I rushed out to find Mama banging a wooden chair against the floor.

"Mama!" I couldn't imagine what she was doing.

She put her fingers to her lips, then whispered for Fanny and me to run back into the bedroom. "Like this," she said, stomping both of her feet. "Go, go." She waved us away.

Fanny ran heavily, and I wondered if they had both gone mad. Uncle Jacob knocked on the door. "Masta Marshall wantin' to know if he got to send for the doctor."

"No," Mama said, "you tell him that we just need a lil time, that's all." When she came to me, she raised my arm to inspect my swollen hand, and I finally understood. "We gonna have to soak this," she said.

"How did you know?" I whispered.

"He ring that," Mama said. She pointed to the bell and tapestry panel hanging beside Miss Martha's bed. I knew there was a system interconnected throughout the house, but in my experience, it had never been used. "If this ring more than one time, we know that Uncle Jacob callin' for us. We always here to help." Mama's firm look held my eyes. "You understand this?" she asked.

I nodded.

She smoothed my hand. "Why he do this?"

"I'm not to go down to the kitchen house." I fought back tears. "And I must call you Mae."

Mama gave me a long look, and unshed tears burned my throat. "It just a name," Mama said, "but when you calls me Mama, it sayin' too much. You call me Mae, and I come fast as when you call me Mama. The same thing with Papa — you call him George. He Papa to you, that we know, but Masta Marshall don' see it like that."

When I could speak, I gave Mama my word that I would do as she asked.

Life became increasingly uneasy as winter approached. Marshall continued with too much drink at dinner, and I no longer dared go to the kitchen house to see Belle.

Almost always, once he was inebriated, Marshall's focus turned to Will Stephens. The final break between Marshall and Will took place on a hog-killing day in early December. It seemed that Will had promised everyone a feast of fresh pork and a drink of brandy when they finished. Marshall took strong objection, seeing it as an extravagance, though Will argued that the workers not only anticipated it but deserved it. Marshall cited this as an example of Will's excess and mismanagement of the farm. When Marshall came for dinner that day, he drank much and ate little. I tried to soothe him, but my comments only seemed to feed his agitation. Why was I standing up for Will Stephens and going against my own husband? he demanded. Was it Will Stephens I was more concerned about?

My face flushed at the suggestion, and with that I gave Marshall new fuel. "So! You have an interest in Will Stephens, is that it?" he shouted. I remained silent, but I could not control the burning of my face. I had seen Will Stephens only twice since my arrival, both times when he was still employed by Marshall. The first time was of an early morning scarcely a week into my return. I was brushing out Miss Martha's hair, and Fanny was changing the linens on the bed. I had turned to draw the blinds up to let in the full measure of daylight when I caught a glimpse of Will as he came out of the horse barn. He was with Ben, and they were laughing. Fury such as I had seldom felt before flooded me, and when I turned back to Miss Martha, I could scarcely control my anger. How dare he be so happy! Fanny took note and came to look out the window for herself. "That's Will Stephens walkin' with Ben," she said plainly, as though wondering what had so affected me.

"For heaven's sake, Fanny! Anyone can see that."

"You remembers what you say when you lil?"

I was silent, remembering all too well.

"You always say you gonna marry that boy." Fanny laughed.

"I was a foolish child!"

Fanny stopped laughing. "Maybe not so foolish. Will Stephens a good man."

"Oh, for pity's sake! Must we discuss that man all day?"

Fanny, not given to holding in her words, looked me over but said nothing further.

The second time I saw Will Stevens was a few weeks later. It was dusk. Again I was at the window, this time studying the purple, pink, and blue of the sky, when Will walked into my vision. I went weak at the sight of him. With his strong shoulders back, he strode with the gait of a man sure of himself. He was on his way to the kitchen house, where I guessed Belle and his son waited for him. I spent the night hating him but comforted myself after settling on a plan of revenge. I vowed that when I finally came face-to-face with Will Stephens, I would hold my head high and look through him as though he did not exist.

However, I did not have that opportunity, for this day, he and Marshall had an altercation that ended with Will leaving for his own farm.

I knew trouble lay ahead when Marshall left to vent his anger on Will, who was working in the kitchen yard alongside the people from the quarters. As the argument escalated and then climaxed, Marshall struck Will and knocked him to the ground.

It was Papa George who stepped in and somehow convinced Marshall that the day's work could finish without him. And it was Papa who led him back to the house and settled him by the fire in the study with a bottle of brandy for company.

Early the next morning, Papa George came to the big house with startling news. During the night Will Stephens had packed up and left for his neighboring farm, taking with him Belle and Jamie, as well as Ben and Lucy and their two children.

Incensed, Marshall rode into town. Mama and I were at the bedroom window when he returned later in the day. The sheriff rode with him, but what alarmed me was seeing another rider alongside my husband. It was none other than his old friend Rankin. I was about to turn from the window when Mama gasped. I looked again and this time saw a little boy seated on a horse in front of the sheriff. It was Jamie, Belle's son. I took Mama's advice and stayed with Miss Martha as Mama ran from the house to take the crying child from the horseman.

I was required to share my afternoon dinner with these men. As Beattie and Uncle served us, we three listened to the men recount how they had taken the child from his frantic mother. Marshall claimed that Will had broken his contract, and furthermore, Jamie, at the least, was his property. Seeing Marshall's delight, I wondered if this was what he had been planning all along.

When I could take no more, I declared a headache and excused myself. Once out of the dining room, I slipped out the back door and ran to the kitchen house. Mama frowned when I appeared. Sukey was sitting on a bench holding Jamie in her lap. The little boy was asleep with his thumb in his mouth, so exhausted by his ordeal that he did not disturb himself with his own loud hiccups.

"What can I do?" I asked Mama.

"You best go back," she said.

"Surely there is something I can do."

Mama didn't have an answer, but to my relief, she said she had sent word to Belle that Jamie was safe. I told Mama of my suspicion that Marshall had maneuvered all of this, that he knew the law.

"Will is bound to do something soon," I said to reassure the both of us. "Surely he won't let Marshall keep his son."

Mama looked at me sharply. "What you say?"

"Will Stephens. If I know him at all, he'll fight for his boy."

Mama's eyes narrowed. "What you mean?" She frowned and looked at me disbelievingly. "You mean you thinkin' . . ." She stopped short when Marshall appeared at the door. He wasted no time but came directly over to me and grasped my arm.

"Well," he said, "I see you've recovered." He glanced at Sukey and the still-sleeping Jamie, then glared at Mama. "What foolishness were you talking about with my wife?"

Mama dropped her head, but not before I saw her fear. "Masta Marshall," she said, "I don't know nothin' 'bout foolish talk."

Marshall twisted my arm painfully as he drew me from the kitchen. He turned back to Mama. "I'll sell anybody who brings talk like that up to the big house."

My arm burned. "Marshall! You're hurting me," I said, trying to pull free. I looked to Mama for help, but her eyes were down, and I saw for the first time the true extent of her helplessness.

We were but a few months into our marriage, and already I knew how troubled it was. Desperate to right things, I doubled my efforts to gain Marshall's goodwill. When I was with my husband, I gave the appearance of being unmindful to anyone but him. I no longer spoke openly to anyone but waited for stolen moments to catch up with the latest news or to hear of a small need that I might be able to satisfy. It was Beattie I felt closest to; she best understood my dilemma, as she witnessed it daily in the dining room. Fanny mostly saw to the care of Miss Martha, and though I knew she cared, she remained distant from me.

Jamie stayed down in the kitchen house, and my beloved Sukey was often needed there to care for him. I dared not go down to see for myself, but soon I heard of everyone's concern. Beattie confided that Jamie had always been uncommonly attached to Belle. Now, she said, without her, he was becoming increasingly withdrawn.

I feigned indifference when I learned from my husband that Will Stephens had filed papers in court in an attempt to take the child back. Privately, I feared that Marshall's knowledge of the law would enable him to win the battle. I could only imagine Belle's despair. I longed to ease it, to send her words of relief, but I knew how tenuous the situation was, and I certainly knew that I was not in a position to make a bid for the release of her child.

I was not surprised when Rankin was again brought on as overseer. His attitude toward me while in Marshall's presence was just short of simpering. Away from my husband, however, he let me know that he considered me of little consequence.

I encouraged Marshall to speak to me of the farm, to tell me his plans for the future. One day he informed me that he and Rankin had decided to move away from the diversification of crops, a method Will Stephens had incorporated, and go back to growing only tobacco. In my eagerness to show my interest, I made a mistake and asked if he was not concerned that continued growth of the same crop might not deplete the soil. Marshall instantly became outraged and accused me of defending Will Stephens and his way of doing things. That was not the first time I saw Marshall's jealousy, and I began to wonder if, back in Williamsburg, he had guessed my feelings for Will. I reassured Marshall of my loyalty to him, but he ended the conversation by telling me to mind the household and leave the business to him. Knowing I had reached an impasse, I agreed. Following that, I kept my conversations with Marshall light and superficial.

With her scheduled doses of laudanum, Miss Martha's days were now routine. What for me was tedious provided structure and balance for her. Mama encouraged her to walk, and though she tired easily, in time she became steadier on her feet.

Mama, Fanny, and Sukey shared in her care, and I fell into a daily habit of coming to see her first thing in the morning and again in the late afternoon. I continued to read to her and at other times sat at her bedside doing my needlework. Miss Martha now spoke, sometimes even using full sentences, though her mind only hovered in reality. I remained Isabelle to her, and it was I who most easily calmed her when she grew agitated.

We had been home a few months when the doctor made a routine visit to see Miss Martha. I remembered Dr. Mense well from my earlier years; he was the same doctor who had treated both the captain during his illness and Miss Martha before she left for Williamsburg. Since I had last seen him, his hair had gone a snowy white. If he remembered me, or if he had misgivings about my new position, he did not show it. After his examination, "Continue on with what you are doing" was his instruction to me, although Mama Mae and Fanny were both present.

Since dinner was about to be served, I invited Dr. Mense to stay, and he readily accepted. When Marshall joined us, although he looked surprised to see our guest, he did not appear unhappy. As we dined, Dr. Mense reported his findings to Marshall. Though Marshall had not paid a visit to his mother since our arrival, he gave the impression that he was involved and up to date on Miss Martha's condition. He thanked the doctor and made it clear that he gave all the credit to me for his mother's improved state. When he spoke of his appreciation, his eyes rested on me, but I was no longer certain of his sincerity.

CHAPTER FORTY

Belle

Marshall knows what he's doing when he takes my boy. You take a baby from a mama, there's nothing more you can do to her.

Will Stephens says he'll do everything he can to get Jamie back. He says, "Whatever you do, Belle, don't go back there. He's waiting for you. If you are on Marshall's property, I can't protect you the same way I can if you are here."

My mind don't move. It just sits there. All I can see is my Jamie screaming. Two days, two nights, I don't cry, I don't talk.

When Ben comes, he says, "Belle, don't worry. You know Mama takin' good care of Jamie."

I just look at Ben. I don't say nothing, because if I do, I say, "What do you know? You still got your two boys! Maybe you give one of your boys to Marshall so I can get my Jamie back?" But I don't say nothing. I just tell him to go away.

Then Lucy comes. First time she's here in my kitchen house. "Belle," she says, "I know you and me, we each got a side of Ben, pullin' on him. But here, at Will Stephens's place, you and me got to work to get along. I know what Jamie is to you. You take my boys, same as takin' my life. I come here to let you know I stand alongside you now."

Lucy's big like Mama, and when she puts her arms around me, I start to cry. I cry for Jamie. Then I cry for Mama and for Papa, too. I cry for my kitchen house, I even cry for the cap'n. "Everything's gone," I say. "Everything's gone."

"No," Lucy says, "Jamie still here. So is Mama and Papa. They just livin' on the other side of the trees. You got to stand up, Belle. For sure your boy comin' back, and when he do, he needin' you strong."

At dark, Ben comes to see me again. He says Lucy sends him to me. She tells him that I need him. Maybe all this time I got Lucy wrong.

That same night Papa comes, following the creek. He comes fast, puffing and having to sit before he can talk.

Ben says, "Papa, next time there's news, maybe you oughta send Ida's boy, Eddy. He know the way, and he get caught, he know how to keep his mouth shut."

Papa says, "Son, you say I'm gettin' too old to get over here?"

Ben says, "Papa, I'm sayin' . . . well, yup, I guess I'm sayin' you gettin' old."

They laugh like old friends. Papa says, "Belle, Jamie doin' just fine. Everybody watchin' over him. Marshall don't have nothin' to do with him. Beattie now livin' in the kitchen house, and she keep Sukey and Jamie with her. Everybody watchin' out for Jamie." Papa look down, fool with his hands, then say, "But Rankin back. Down at the quarters, they all tryin' to stay one step ahead of that debil. And Abinia got her own trouble up at the big house. Marshall drinkin' real hard."

After Papa tells me that Jamie's doing all right, I settle some. I'm gonna wait to see how things go. For sure, though, if Jamie don't come back, I'll go get him myself, then I'll take him and run.

Next day I get back to work and get this kitchen house set up. Ben and Lucy got their own cabin, and they're both gonna work the fields. Will Stephens is building a big house. Maybe when he's done, I'll ask Will if Lucy can work the big house with me.

I work hard, then after a week, I can't take

no more and go to see my boy. I follow the water up, go past the quarters, and stay down in the trees. Sure enough, there's my four-year-old boy, sitting out by the kitchen house, looking around like he's wanting his mama. I bite my own hand so I don't call, "Jamie, Jamie, I'm here," but right then Sukey comes out to give him something to drink. She's playing with him when I see Marshall over at the horse barn. Sukey sees him, too, and real quick she takes Jamie into the kitchen house and closes the door.

Going home, I can hardly walk for crying. But then I remember something. I know where Papa keeps the gun down in the barn, and I know where he keeps the key. That settles me. Marshall does anything to my boy, BAM! he's good as dead.

CHAPTER FORTY-ONE

Lavinia

I take full responsibility for the relationship that developed between Miss Martha and Belle's son, Jamie. I gave my permission the day Sukey asked if she might bring Jamie with her to the big house. She suggested he play in the blue room while she assisted me in caring for the mistress.

It was August 1802. I had not yet been married a full year, but both Mama and I suspected I was already with child. While the others did the harvesting of the garden that autumn, I stayed in the big house and took on more responsibility in caring for Miss Martha. I requested to have Sukey there to help me. Since my arrival, she had been the one I depended on. She was the one who loved me as before. Try as I might, I could not get back the friendship with Fanny or Beattie that I once had. I continued to make friendly overtures, but the twins kept a distance. I tried in every way I knew how to show I had not changed, that I considered them my equals, but it was obvious since my return that they saw me in a different light. I was terribly lonely and was so grateful for Sukey's friendship that I did everything I could to accommodate her. She rewarded me with unfailing loyalty.

"Miss Abinia, he so sad," Sukey said about Jamie. Her large dark eyes were sorrowful. "He just sittin' there when I up here."

"Bring him along, then," I told Sukey. "We'll take some play-things from the nursery to keep him occupied in the blue room."

It had been almost nine months since his capture, and both Beattie and Mama had expressed their concern about Jamie's deepening retreat into himself. He spoke little, and what distressed them most was that he refused any comfort from the family. "He blamin' us, thinkin' that we keepin' him from his mama," Beattie said.

Will Stephens had been unsuccessful in his legal fight to reunite Belle with her son, and Marshall was jubilant the day he won possession. I made one attempt to discuss Jamie's release with Marshall. The vehement anger that he expressed at my request made obvious that any intercession on my part was not only hopeless but, if continued, might draw attention to the boy, who Marshall, on the whole, disregarded.

By now I fully understood the position I was in as Marshall's wife. I had discovered what my family had known all along: Pretense of ignorance could serve me well. I learned to not react, nor to give my opinion but, with a smile or a nod, suggest agreement with all of Marshall's plans. I became guarded and no longer spoke about my true feelings.

When I allowed Jamie in the big house, I gave little thought to Marshall learning of this. He never visited his mother, and the only times he ventured upstairs were on the increasingly infrequent nights when he came to my room.

On the very first day, Miss Martha sensed Jamie's presence in her outer room. In the weeks before, Mama and I had decided to lessen her laudanum dosage. As a result, though there was an emerging clarity and our patient had become physically stronger, she also was more restless and more easily agitated. That morning, before either Sukey or I could anticipate her move, Miss Martha rose from her chair and walked to the blue room. She stopped when she saw Jamie, then approached him slowly. She stared down at the child, who looked as though he might have been one of her own, then bent to his level.

"I want my mama," he pleaded.

"Yes," she said, and he went into her open arms.

Over the next few days, as Miss Martha spent hours distracting the boy, it was remarkable how her agitation eased. We brought many of the old nursery toys down from the attic, and while she rested on her bed, my mother-in-law encouraged Jamie to bring the toy soldiers and play alongside her. As she had with Sukey, Miss Martha read to him, and it did not upset him that she often repeated the same lines over and over. Clearly, he felt safe with her, and through mutual need, they clung to each other. By the late fall, the two had become so close that Miss Martha had a small bed brought from the nursery, and Jamie began to spend his nights in the blue room.

Mama was uncomfortable with the relationship but relieved that Jamie had begun to eat and sleep once again. He no longer begged to see his mother and appeared to accept Miss Martha as a substitute; perhaps she quieted the anguish of what he perceived as Belle's abandonment. As well, Miss Martha was more coherent and content than ever.

Sukey and I understood their attachment easier than did the others. I cared for Sukey as deeply as I might my own child, and I knew that she reciprocated my feelings.

I was resting on my bed the day Marshall made an unexpected visit to his mother's room. To this day I do not know why he came. Perhaps he was on his way to see me and saw something that drew him toward his mother's bedroom. I heard his voice and quickly made my way to Miss Martha's room. I met a frightened Sukey in the blue room and sent her to the kitchen house for Mama.

"What is this new madness?" Marshall stared at Jamie asleep on the bed next to his mother.

"Shh," Miss Martha said.

Marshall stepped forward as though to take the child from her. Jamie woke and grasped Miss Martha.

"Sir!" she said. "Leave us!"

"Mother," Marshall shouted, "that's a ni-gra's boy."

"He is mine!" she said.

I rushed to Marshall's side and touched his arm. "Let her be, Marshall, please don't

444

upset her."

He swung toward me, his arm raised, and I pulled back in fear. "Marshall!" I cried.

He stopped and looked around as though disbelieving of the scene. When he rushed from the room, I followed him, but he refused to answer my call. That night he did not come back to the house for supper.

I was a few months along and now certain that I was to have a child. Marshall was still upset at dinner the next day, but before he could begin a tirade, I informed him of my pregnancy. His reaction was immediate. At once he became tender toward me. Was there something I needed? Could he send to Williamsburg for anything? I had not anticipated this response, and to my great relief, we finished the meal peacefully, discussing plans for the child. How grateful I was that with the news of my pregnancy, Marshall appeared to have forgotten about Jamie and Miss Martha.

Following my announcement — and I must admit to no regret on my part — Marshall no longer came to my room for marital intimacy.

Then came a shift within the household. The very air was charged. Something had happened that I did not understand. All of my family had become more reserved, more withdrawn. Mama Mae was the most changed. She was distracted and easily upset. She didn't speak her mind as openly as she once had, though she did say that she felt Jamie should be immediately taken from Miss Martha. Foolishly, I did not listen to her but insisted that the two be allowed the comfort they found in each other. Mama gave in, and I tried to please her in other ways.

Beattie stopped coming up from the kitchen. When I asked for her, Mama made the repeated excuse that she was too busy. Sukey alone remained unchanged, and I clung to her. I used my pregnancy as an excuse to have her with me, and soon had the other nursery bed moved into a corner of my bedroom for her. Fanny was more distant than ever, so when I heard she wanted permission to jump the broom with Eddy, Ida's son from the quarters, I was anxious to help. To please me, Marshall agreed to Fanny's wedding and a celebration. The ceremony was scheduled for Christmas Day, and I took great pleasure in planning the event.

As my girth grew, so did Marshall's tenderness. To my relief, he did not mention

Jamie to me again; nor did he make another visit to see his mother. Although he continued with heavy drink, his bad behavior around me lessened, and our afternoon meals were taken in a more peaceful atmosphere. I grew hopeful that perhaps all was not lost, and I began to wonder if our baby might be the salve for our ailing marriage.

But I was wrong. Insulated as I was, I was spared from learning what I would have been helpless to stop.

As I said, the air crackled of it, but I did not understand.

The day before Christmas, lonely and wanting to see Beattie, I decided that I could justify a visit down to the kitchen. If questioned, I would tell Marshall the truth: I needed to know if Beattie required extra help with food preparation for Fanny's wedding feast.

Papa was at the back of the kitchen house chopping wood, and I was so happy to see him that I dared stop for a minute to tease. The stack of wood was so high that I asked him what he planned to do with all that fuel. He brought down the ax and shattered the log, then brushed the back of his hand over his eyes before he looked at me. I could not mistake the fact that he had been crying.

"Papa," I said, "what is it?"

"Nothin', chil'." He set up another log. "I workin' hard and the water come in my eyes."

Unsure what to say, I reached out to touch his arm. "Papa?"

"Abinia," he said, looking around, "you best get back up to the big house."

Hurt but determined to have my way, I continued on to the door of the kitchen house. The pleasant aroma of pies and spices belied the heavy atmosphere in the warm room. I walked in to hear Beattie in conversation with Mama.

"Don't cry, Mama." Beattie stood with her arm around her mother's shoulder. "I don't fight no more, so he stop hittin' on me. It not so bad. Come on, Mama, stop this cryin'."

"Who is hitting you?" I spoke louder than I had intended, startling both women. Mama dried her eyes while Beattie turned to the fireplace.

"Nobody," Beattie answered, her back to me. "Nobody hittin' on me."

"But I heard you say —"

Mama interrupted me. "Miss Abinia, like Beattie say, everythin' all right. Besides, what you doin' down here?"

"I came to offer my help," I said defensively.

"You know that Masta Marshall don't want you in this house," Mama said. "Now, you best get back up there."

Her words stung me so that I left for the big house, passing Papa, who continued to pound his ax into the wood.

I went straight to Miss Martha's room, where Uncle had a strong fire going and where Sukey and Jamie asked me to join their game of cards. I thanked them, declined, and sat back to watch. But my thoughts were not with them. Was it possible that Rankin could be hurting Beattie; worse, if he was, what could I do about it? I thought to appeal to Marshall, but something warned me not to go in that direction.

Fanny's wedding was a big event. In the early evening, a bonfire was built in the kitchen yard, and a feast was set out on long wooden tables. As I was in the last month of confinement, it was not considered appropriate that I show myself, so I was not there when Marshall conducted the short ceremony. Later, though, I decided that I had had enough seclusion, and I took it upon myself to go down and watch the festivities from a sheltered spot in the trees.

I had not expected to see Ben and Lucy up for the evening from Will's farm. When they caught sight of me, they came over.

"When you gonna have that baby?" Lucy asked shyly.

"One more month," I said.

"Lil Birdie, havin' a baby." Ben shook his head as though disbelieving.

I felt warm when he used my pet name. "Not so little." I patted my stomach, and Ben looked embarrassed. "How is Belle?" I asked, to ease Ben's discomfort.

"She missin' her boy," Ben said, "and I know she missin' the family, but Masta Will, he good to her."

"Belle have her own fine house just like this one," Lucy said, pointing. When we all looked to the kitchen house, we saw Beattie rushing about and Lucy decided to go offer her help. Ben remained at my side.

"Isn't Will's big house finished yet?" I asked.

"It done enough that he livin' in it," Ben said.

In spite of myself, my voice turned cold. "Isn't Belle living up there with him yet?"

Ben's eyes opened wide. "Abinia. What you sayin'?"

My head felt light with anger. "Well, they might as well live in the same house. Everyone knows they have their son . . ."

Ben looked around uneasily. "Will Stephens not the daddy of that boy, Abinia," he said quietly. "Sure you knows that." I must have swayed; Ben sat me on a large rock. "I get Mama for you," he said.

"No, Ben, don't go," I protested, but he rushed off, and soon Mama hurried over.

"Come, chil', you best come up to the big house with me. Masta Marshall thinkin' that you up there."

But I grew stubborn. "No one can see me," I assured Mama, and told her that I would soon go back up to rest. First, I said, I wanted to watch some dancing; I needed to see some fun.

"Masta Marshall not like this."

"He doesn't need to know," I said.

Mama looked uncertainly back toward the kitchen house. "I gonna help Beattie with the food, but I come back to get you," she said before she hurried away.

As the music played and I watched everyone dance, my mind kept returning to Ben's words. Nothing made sense. Was it possible that Will was not Jamie's father? If so, then who was?

Ida came into the shadows where I sat, and I knew that Mama had sent her. "Ida!" I said with happy surprise. I had not seen her since before my years in Williamsburg.

She smiled warmly. "They sayin' that you the one that get this weddin' for Fanny and my boy, Eddy."

I made room for her to sit beside me on the large flat rock. I was shocked at how she had aged since I had last seen her. Her hair was now white, and her shoulders were stooped. When she reached over to pat my protruding stomach, I caught her twisted brown hand in mine.

"Ida," I whispered, "you must tell me something."

She looked at me with concern.

"Ida. Who is the father of Belle's child? Who is Jamie's father?"

When Ida looked away, I saw that she was checking the proximity of others, and I knew that she would tell the truth. She spoke low, close to my ear. "It Masta Marshall. I know this 'cause at that time Rankin still usin' me to make babies and he tell me. But you don't say nothin'. They kill me, they find out I say somethin'."

Ida said nothing further. We sat without words while I tried to absorb this sickening news. Marshall with Belle! How could that be? I had thought that he hated Belle. Then it struck me how alike Jamie was to Marshall in appearance. How could I have missed something so obvious?

Our attention was drawn back to the bonfire by the loud shouts and clapping as Mama Mae and Papa George were singled out for a dance. Off to the side, Rankin slumped against a tree, a bottle of brandy in his hand. My eyes traveled, and as I took in the kitchen house, I saw Beattie emerge and wipe her forehead with her apron. Seeing her, I was reminded of our friendship and of the trust I had in her. I needed to speak to someone of this bitter news and knew that I could take Beattie into my confidence. I was about to turn back to Ida to ask if she might bring Beattie to me when I saw Marshall emerge from the shadows of the kitchen house. He came to the kitchen door, and in disbelief, I watched him greet Beattie. Her smile was hesitant, but she quickly gave him her hand as they went into the kitchen together and Marshall closed the door behind them. I could not miss the meaning.

Ida saw what I saw, but we did not exchange words. When I struggled to my feet, Ida rose, too. She walked alongside me as I made my way up the hill to the big house; she came up the stairs with me and helped me into my nightclothes, then assisted me into bed. I was grateful that she, having

lived through her own unspeakable trag-
edies, knew that words were unnecessary.

CHAPTER FORTY-TWO

Belle

When Papa comes to tell me that Jamie's staying up with Miss Martha at the big house, I start carrying on so bad that Ben goes for Lucy. Every day I'm thinking that I'll get my boy back. Now I just know I'll never see him again.

Papa says, "Belle, Belle, Jamie doin' real good up there. He eatin' again, and he have all the nice toys to play with. Miss Martha treat him real good."

"No! No!" I start breathing hard, then I can't get no air. All I can think is Jamie's up in the big house and Marshall's gonna get at him.

When Lucy comes, she takes me outside, away from Papa. "Come on," she says, making me walk. "You got to take in the air."

"No! No!" I say. "I don't want him in the big house! Miss Martha's crazy, and she'll make my boy crazy."

"You got to breathe," Lucy says. "Stop talkin' and take in some air."

"Lucy! They have him up in the big house," I say.

"Keep walkin'," Lucy says.

"I'll go for the gun," I say. "I'll go get my boy." I try to pull away, but Lucy won't let go.

"Belle! You got to settle down. Papa in there waitin' on you. He got to go back up. You know if Rankin find him, Papa in big trouble."

"But they have Jamie in the big house!"

"Belle! Carryin' on like this won't help. Papa don't leave 'less he know you doin' all right. You got to think of Papa . . . the chance he take to come here and tell you how your boy doin'."

I know Lucy's right, so I try to slow myself down. I look up for the moon. I pull air in and push it out again. I do this until I settle some.

"You all right now?" Lucy ask.

I nod. When we go back in, Papa's sitting there, not looking me in the face.

"I'm all right now, Papa," I say. "I get so scared about my boy."

"Your Jamie doin' fine, Belle."

"I don't want him up at the big house, Papa. What if Miss Martha don't ever let

456

him go? What if Marshall — ?" I see Papa's face go tight. "What, Papa?" I say. "What else you come to say?"

"It Beattie," he says.

"What?" I ask.

"Marshall usin' Beattie," he says. Just like that, Papa drops his own head and starts to cry. I never, never before, see Papa cry. Ben, me, Lucy, we all look at the other, waiting for somebody to say something. Ben stands up and starts to walk back and forth. I go to Papa and put my arm 'round him. He takes out the rag that Mama makes him carry and blows his nose. "There nothin' I can do for my own girl," he says.

" 'Course not, Papa," I say.

"When this start to happen?" Ben ask. He don't sound like hisself.

"A while now," Papa says. " 'Round the time Abinia tell him she havin' a baby. First it go real hard on Beattie, but she say things eased up. You know that girl, she don't complain 'bout nothin'. She even tellin' Mama and me that she gonna make this work for everybody. Marshall gets with her almost every night, and he talkin' to her. Beattie say, least this way she find out what happenin' on the place."

"Maybe he'll leave her alone when Lavinia has her baby?" I say.

Nobody says nothing to that.

Next day I talk to Will Stephens, tell him Jamie's up in the big house. Will says that he'll go back to court and try again to get Jamie back here with me. "You just hold on, Belle," he says.

"Will."

"Yes?"

"There's something else for you to know," I say.

"What is it?"

"Ben was talking with Lavinia at Fanny's wedding. He finds out that she's thinking all along that you're the daddy of Jamie."

"What!"

"All along, Lavinia never knows that Marshall's the one. I never did tell her about that night when Marshall got me. When she's living in Williamsburg, Marshall tells her that you're the daddy."

"Good God!"

"Mama says in some ways, Lavinia thinks like a child. She don't always get what's going on. She comes back here, wanting everything to be the same. It's like she don't know that when she marries Marshall, she's gonna take on his world. Mama's trying to help her see it right, but like Mama say, sometimes we got to live it out before we learn."

I'm talking away, but when I look at Will Stephens, he looks like he don't hear a word I'm saying. When he goes, I stand at the door. I watch him walk real slow up to his new house and think how big it looks for one man living there all by hisself.

CHAPTER FORTY-THREE

Lavinia

I stayed in my bed for two days, feverish and without appetite. Marshall came with questions of concern, and when he reached for my hand, I pulled it away, sick with disgust. Mama nursed me silently, but on the third morning, after I refused yet another breakfast, she secured my bedroom door before she pulled a chair to my bedside.

"Ida say you know some things," Mama said, positioning herself to face me.

I turned my head away.

"Ida say . . ." She spoke quietly. "Ida say you see Marshall go with Beattie."

I heard the struggle in her voice, and still I faced the wall.

"Ida say you know 'bout Jamie?" she whispered.

I swung my head to look at her. "Ida's saying a lot," I snapped.

Mama's head dropped.

"I'm sorry, Mama."

"Times, this life not easy, Abinia," Mama said.

"But how . . . When was he . . . with Belle?"

Mama shushed me and looked toward the door. "We don't talk about this no more. It happen, now you got to forget about it. He find out you know 'bout this, he don't stop until he find out who talkin' to you, and then there no tellin' what he do."

"But Beattie, Mama! How could Beattie go with — ?"

"You think this what Beattie want?" Mama whispered. "You think she want get with him?"

"I saw them at the kitchen house!" I said. "She didn't even make an attempt to refuse him."

"Abinia! You lookin' through your eyes, you not even tryin' to look through Beattie's. You know that girl don't have the right to say no! After Masta Marshall leave for the day, I bring Beattie to you. You see for yourself what happen when that girl say no." Mama's chin trembled as she fought tears. She rose and went to look out the tall window.

I was quiet for a long while before I dared

461

to speak. "I'm sorry, Mama," I said, "you don't have to bring her. I know you're right."

"This a hard thing," Mama said, wiping tears from her face. "This a hard thing."

I looked out the window past Mama and saw that it had begun to snow. I looked at the fire blazing in the fireplace and thought of Papa George chopping wood behind the kitchen house. Now I understood what had driven him that day.

"Mama," I whispered. "Is there something I can do?"

Mama came back to sit in the chair beside me. She blew her nose before she took my hand. "There times all we can do is pray to the Lawd," she said. "We say, 'Lawd, we don't know, but we sure do need some help.' " She rested her hand on my large stomach. "And we don't forget to say thanks for the blessin's, Lawd." Mama spoke to me tenderly again. "Come, chil', it time for you to eat, then get up and move. All this fussin' not good for the baby."

A month later, at the end of January, Mama was there with Fanny to deliver my daughter, Eleanor.

We called her Elly from the start, and everyone loved her. Marshall expressed great delight that he was the father of our infant girl, and in the heady joy of motherhood, I tried desperately to set aside my grievances with him.

Sukey would not leave Elly's side; during the night, she kept the cradle next to her bed. When I nursed Elly, Sukey sat alongside to watch that I positioned the baby's head correctly. Mama came often to hold Elly and to sing to her until she slept. And then there was Fanny! One might have thought that Elly was her very own. In every spare moment, Fanny peeked in, requesting to hold her. Uncle Jacob, too, stopped by often on the pretext of tending the fire. Even Papa George came up to see the baby late one afternoon after Marshall had left the farm. Papa held her, and my heart soared when he said, "She look just like our lil Abinia." Finally, when Beattie had not yet come, I asked to see her.

I was nursing the baby when Mama brought her up. "Come in, Bea," I said, seeing her hesitate in the doorway, "come see her." Beattie refused to meet my eyes when I offered my baby for inspection. "Isn't she perfect?" I asked, full of new motherhood.

"She look just like you," Beattie said with a shy smile.

She was right. My daughter had the same

elfin ears, the same oval face, and the same vibrant hair color. Everyone noted the likeness. And it seemed everyone considered it a triumph.

In the early autumn of Elly's first year, we spent some time in the shade of the great oak tree. The scene was idyllic. Often in the late afternoon, Uncle Jacob set up our quilting frame and we brought out our chairs. Fanny and I stitched while Sukey sat on a blanket with Elly. If Mama had time, she joined us, though Beattie always begged off, saying that she had work to do in the kitchen.

Miss Martha was content to rest in her room with Jamie playing quietly at her side. Her doses of laudanum were at a minimum, and her condition had changed dramatically. Though she had limitations, she often appeared quite lucid, and we accepted it when she referred to Jamie as "my son." Jamie never mentioned Belle, and his attachment to Miss Martha was so strong that one wondered if he remembered his life before. I was content with this, though Mama Mae was not. She did not speak of her disapproval outright, but often I saw her watch the two of them interact, and her frown told me more than words might have.

Miss Martha's response to my baby was curious. A few days after I gave birth, I brought Elly to visit her grandmother. For the first time, I saw my mother-in-law accept a child into her arms and then release it, aware that the child was not her own. When I told her the baby's name, she repeated it a few times and did not forget it, though she continued to refer to me as Isabelle.

On the whole, my time was consumed with caring for my newborn, but when I saw Marshall, he was drinking less and appeared more content than he had been since our arrival. He remained solicitous of me and continually asked if I had want or need of anything. I assumed it was the birth of Elly that had brought Marshall some peace, and for the sake of our child, I attempted to set aside the horrible truth of which I was now aware. But my success was short-lived.

In the months after Elly's birth, though Marshall had not visited me at night, I had hoped that his relationship with Beattie had ended. However, in late fall, I was horror-struck when it became clear that Beattie was with child. She continued to serve our meals in the dining room with Uncle's assistance; daily, the situation grew more awkward.

Marshall did not know that I was aware of their relationship; nor was he aware that I watched as his eyes followed her.

I grew more resentful with each passing day. I did not want my husband to resume his marital rights, but I was horrified to think that his relationship with Beattie continued. There were moments in the dining room of intense strain, moments when I caught an approving look or a smile given to Beattie that felt like an insult to me. I felt unable to direct my anger toward Marshall, and in an effort to rid myself of it, I looked instead toward Beattie, a safer target.

I spoke to no one of this, and my unhappiness festered. My reasoning became diseased, and as my anger grew, so, too, did my resentments. I began to wonder why Marshall made the choice to stay with Beattie. I did not want him near me — in fact, the idea of our intimacy repulsed me — yet why would he chose her over me? What did I lack as a woman? Where had I failed? In spite of myself, in spite of knowing how their relationship had come about, I began to blame Beattie. I couldn't rid myself of the belief that Beattie had encouraged Marshall in this wrongdoing.

I dared not confront Marshall, so I struck out at Beattie. I often spoke sharply to her and did not seek for her the privileges I sought for the others of my family. I made unkind comments about her appearance while I watched Marshall attempt to show indifference. But it was his failure to do so that had me question a deeper possibility: Did he care for her? Did he love her?

Finally, I could stand it no longer and went to Mama. I used Beattie's growing size and her cumbersome efforts to serve us as my complaint. To my great relief, Mama agreed and sent Fanny to replace Beattie in the dining room. This, however, had its own repercussions.

Fanny, while serving, of course overheard the dinner conversation. As was her nature, she found it impossible to maintain a uninterested stance, and when she heard something that did not sit well with her, she was quick to purse her lips or roll her eyes. Marshall frequently called her on this. "Do you have something to say?" he often asked, and I was always surprised at how forthcoming were Fanny's comments. There were times when her opinions angered my husband and he would dismiss her from the room, but more likely, he would laugh heartily. I greeted those times with a mixture of relief and envy. Why, I wondered, couldn't I be more like Fanny — more unafraid?

During this period, I began a correspondence with Meg in Williamsburg. I sought to renew my interest in botany, and I wrote of it to Meg, with apologies for my lack of earlier communication. She held no blame and said that she knew how busy I must be, caring for my daughter. She had not yet married, and her letters were quick to point out that she was not in a great hurry to do so. Along with her correspondence, Meg sent books, and I, in turn, gifted her with those I thought she might enjoy. I clung to my connection to Meg, though I told her nothing of the problems within my marriage.

About a month after Fanny began to serve us in the dining room, Marshall and I received a letter from Will Stephens. In it, he offered a great deal of money for Jamie. He said that Belle, in her grief over the loss of her son, had become ill. Will feared for her life and asked for Marshall to exercise compassion in the matter.

"Compassion for a whore!" Marshall tore up the letter.

Still too frightened to speak up for Belle, but feeling guilty for my failure, I decided to take other action. That night I wrote to her. In an attempt to give Belle relief, I told her that I watched over Jamie as I might my own son and that he was safe in my care. I told her, too, of my concern for her and her health. I asked her to be patient and concluded that one day soon, she would be reunited with her son.

I do not know how Rankin got hold of the letter. I had passed it to Fanny, and she had given it to her husband, Eddy. Marshall was furious when Rankin brought the letter to him, and at dinner the next day, my husband informed me that Eddy would be punished for my foolishness. Fanny stood at the sideboard, shocked into silence.

"No, Marshall," I said. "Please, no. I alone am responsible."

"You work against me, you undermine me, someone must be held accountable for your disobedience," he said.

"Be angry with me, Marshall," I said. "I meant no harm."

"You correspond with a whore?" he said. "You write that her child is like your own. You sound as mad as my mother!"

Armed with the knowledge of Jamie's paternity, my anger rose. "I was at his birth," I said, "of course I care for him. Belle was like a mother to me."

"Belle!" He slammed the table with his fist. "My father's whore!"

I rose quickly, giving Uncle Jacob no time

to assist with my chair. I rested my hands on the table to steady myself. "As Beattie is a whore to you?" I asked, my voice slow and deliberate, and I saw in his face his shock at my knowledge of his unholy union.

Behind me, Fanny gasped. When Marshall reached for his wineglass, I noted a tremor in his hand, and seeing his momentary weakness, I struck. "I trust that I can count on you not to punish Eddy for my indiscretion."

As I left, Marshall called after me, but I did not turn back.

In the middle of January, Beattie lost her child. I was not there for the birth, but Fanny reported on the difficult labor. She told me that Ida and Mama had feared for Beattie's life. Inwardly, I was relieved that the baby died.

A week later, we celebrated my darling Elly's first birthday. That day, when I held my precious child to me, I felt a wave of compassion for Beattie and was guilt-stricken that I had not sent word to her about her loss. I decided to go to the kitchen house to apologize and to see if she had need of anything.

It was late afternoon when I slipped out the back door. Fanny was busy tending to

Miss Martha, and Mama was cleaning in the library, so I left Elly in the care of Sukey. I knew Beattie was likely beginning the preparations for supper, so I planned only a short visit. As I made my way to the kitchen house, my thoughts of Bea were warm, and I felt certain that she and I could be friends once more. Surely Marshall was done with her. I would have walked directly through the open kitchen door had I not heard Beattie speaking to someone. "This so pretty," she said. "I never have somethin' like this before."

I froze in place when I heard Marshall's voice. "I thought you might like it," he said.

I willed myself to quietly back away. Turning, I saw Papa come around the chicken coop. He waved at me in greeting. My fierce desire to run to him for comfort was overruled by my feelings of shock, then shame. Did he know my husband was back in the kitchen house with Beattie? Did they blame me for not keeping my husband away from her and at my side? I turned my back on Papa and went up to the big house.

I wonder what depths of despair I might have reached had Meg's letter not been waiting.

CHAPTER FORTY-FOUR

Belle

Will Stephens gets two more men and sends Lucy up from the fields. We work together good, cleaning the big house and putting food away, but Lucy's getting big with another baby, and seeing her like that makes me think of my own boy. Will Stephens does everything he can to get my Jamie back, but nothing works. When winter comes and I still don't have him, the life just goes out of me. Without my Jamie, I don't care about nothing no more.

When Ben's holding me one night, he says, "You sure quiet, and you gettin' skinny."

I don't say nothing, because there's nothing to say.

"Belle," he says, "is somethin' wrong?"

"No," I say.

Next day Lucy says, "Belle, you know you not actin' like yourself. Somethin' wrong?

You hear somethin' more 'bout Jamie?"

"No," I say, "I don't hear nothing."

She looks at me hard, but she stays quiet.

A few weeks go by, and I keep working, but I'm real tired. All I want to do is sleep. Papa comes with the news that Lavinia's baby is doing fine, got hair like fire, just like her mama. He tells me that Jamie's doing real good but Marshall still don't want to let him go.

That night any fight I got left goes right out of me.

Ben and Lucy tell Will Stephens that I stop eating, so he comes down to ask me if I'm sick.

"I'm fine," I say, "I'm feeling tired, that's all." He's wanting to get the doctor, but I say, "Thank you. I'll feel better soon."

One cold night, Lucy starts to have the baby. Ben comes running for me, banging on the door. "Lucy wantin' you! Lucy wantin' you!" He's yelling so loud, I know he's scared. I run. She's in trouble, all right. Ben gets a pass and rides out for the doctor, leaving me alone with Lucy.

I try to remember what Mama tells me. "Lucy," I say, "this gonna hurt." Then I get to work. That baby's head needs some help coming out, so Lucy pushes and I pull, and

473

when we finally get him out, I don't know who's more tired, Lucy or me. But when we see the baby, we start to laugh. That boy looks just like Ben. How a fat little baby looks like a big old man, we don't know, but he do.

"You get him out, you got to take care a him," Lucy says. "What you gonna call him?"

"How about George?" I say. "Like Papa."

"George?" she says. "That a name for a growed man."

"Well," I say, "look at this boy. He's almost as big as Papa."

We start to laugh again, till the last of her pains clean the rest of her out.

When Ben comes with the doctor, Lucy's sleeping, and I'm sitting by the fire, holding George. I don't know how it happens, but somehow, this child feels like he's my own.

Food is looking good, and I'm starting to eat again. I'm thinking that I got to stay around, make sure somebody takes care of this sweet boy.

CHAPTER FORTY-FIVE

Lavinia

"Come and open them! Come and open them!" Sukey met me at the door and pulled me in, dancing with excitement. While I had been down at the kitchen house, overhearing the conversation between Marshall and Beattie, parcels and a letter had arrived from Meg.

Sukey led me to my room, pressed me onto a chair, and placed the packages in my lap. She begged me to open them before I read the letter. To satisfy her, I unwrapped the first. It was a large picture book of trees.

"What does it say?" Sukey asked. She lightly traced the copper-plated illustration with her fingertips and repeated after me, "Quercus, Quercus," in her eagerness to learn.

Sukey then opened the larger package, and amid excited exclamations, she pulled from it a vasculum. The tin box was painted green and adorned with my initials in gold leaf. I remembered how Meg, with such pride, had shown me her own.

Her gifts were always generous, but Meg's correspondence that day was my salvation. She began by referencing my letters of last autumn in which I had described the sewing parties held under our oak. She wrote how this homey picture gave her and her mother much discussion over the past winter season. Now they wondered if they might visit this fall to be part of that very scene. My heart leaped at her request. Meg was as committed to her studies as ever, and she had become particularly interested in oak trees. Did we have a variety in our area? she wondered. Would I collect some leaves and bark, catalog my finds, and hold them for her visit? Then she ended the letter with another question: Was I as happy as she envisioned?

I set her letter aside. I gazed over at Sukey studying the book, and then at Elly asleep in her cradle. But my thoughts did not settle on them. I could not remove the image of Marshall watching Beattie as she opened her treasure, and I heard over and over her words of pleasure. I longed to speak to someone of my outrage, my sorrow, and my confusion. Dared I write to Meg? Might I confide in her? But even as I asked myself these questions, I knew that I would not. How could I tell her of this evil twist in my marriage?

When Jamie came to the door, Sukey glanced up. She held her finger to her mouth and pointed to Elly, who lay fast asleep. Jamie nodded his understanding and tiptoed over to Sukey to have a look at the book she held. He had grown little this past year and was small for a seven-year-old. Miss Martha insisted we allow his sandy curls to grow to shoulder length, and but for his bad eye, he was a pretty child. He was exceptionally precocious, and perhaps because of it, there was something disconcerting about the boy. He had already learned to use his disability to his advantage. When he was particularly determined, he fixed his eyes on you. One could not ignore the unseeing white eye, while the blue intensity of the other bore through.

This day he looked at me over Sukey's head, then came to slip his hand in mine. "Are you sad, Miss Abby?" he asked, using the name the children had given me.

I cupped his serious small face and kissed it twice. His presence reminded me again of Belle, and in that instant I decided where I would turn. Why hadn't I thought of this sooner?

Fully aware that Marshall would never give me permission to see Belle, I began to plot my visit.

"I want to learn to ride," I told Marshall the next day at dinner. "And it would please me a great deal if Sukey could be my companion." I gave no hint of my unhappiness, instead acting light and gay. I told him of Meg's letter and, presenting her latest gifts, informed him of her request that I gather certain leaf species. I needed a horse, I explained, to travel out a bit. Did he not think this a good pastime for me?

Yes, Marshall agreed, this was excellent diversion — provided, of course, that I use caution. George, he said, had taught Miss Martha to ride, and he would have George teach me to ride as well. There was a fine sidesaddle in the stables that his father had provided for his mother; would that suit me? He would choose the horse, an older, quiet one, one that would not get away from me. Happily, he was also in agreement that Sukey should act as my attendant.

I thanked him for his generosity, then read aloud Meg's letter. Though Marshall did not voice an opinion, I noted that he was not entirely pleased when I read to him of Meg and her family's upcoming visit.

Sukey did not need a riding lesson. She approached her pony confidently, took hold of his reins, patted his nose, and led him to the mounting block. There, she slid easily onto his back. She clicked her tongue and walked her small horse around me while she and Papa George laughed at my surprise. Sukey explained that Papa had taught her to ride when she was "just a lil chil'."

"Oh," I said to Sukey, winking at Papa, "I suppose that now, at the age of eleven, you consider yourself a grown woman?"

"Well," she said soberly, "I'm not as old as you!"

At that, Papa laughed, and I gently poked his arm in reprimand.

"Miss Abby, how old are you?" Sukey asked.

Papa pointed to the hills in the distance. "You see those hills, Sukey gal?"

"I do, Papa," she said.

"Why, our Miss Abinia, she old as those hills." He laughed.

I made a face at Papa. "I'll be twenty years old this May," I told Sukey.

"Ohhh." Sukey was impressed, and both Papa and I laughed at her reaction.

"I wonder if Miss Abinia too old to learn to ride," Papa teased, leading a small horse from the barn. "This Barney," he said to me.

Barney was a small bay gelding, just the right size for me. I pulled back when he nudged me with his soft nose, but I relaxed when Papa George explained that the horse was only seeking a treat. Tentatively, I stroked Barney's head and remarked on the white blaze that was almost covered by his long dark forelock. When the horse stomped his foot and shook his long mane, Papa explained that he was eager to begin our lesson. Once we did so, Barney proved a patient horse, and I was smitten with him before my first lesson was complete.

Marshall was pleased by my enthusiasm for riding. He insisted that I order for myself the latest riding clothes, and I agreed, requesting that Sukey be outfitted as well. To my surprise, Marshall did not object.

Measurements for our riding habits were sent off, and when the packages arrived from Williamsburg, Sukey was almost overcome with excitement. She had chosen a fine blue petticoat and a matching jacket trimmed with a black velvet collar. The jacket had double rows of gilt buttons, and Mama Mae, Fanny, and I watched them sparkle when she twirled. She wore a black hat with a gold chain around the brim, topped with a high blue feather set to the front. Her riding habit was complete after she tied the half boots of black leather and pulled on leather gloves.

My new clothes were very similar in fashion, although they were green. I had a second plume added to my hat, and around my neck, I tied a white silk cravat. I must say, the two of us did look smart our first morning in mid-May when Papa gave us permission to ride out alone together.

From that day forward, with Elly safely in Fanny's care, we went out almost every day. We each sported a vasculum; I had ordered one for Sukey, justifying it as necessary equipment for our botanical excursions. Inside hers, Sukey proudly tucked a leather-bound sketchbook. She was becoming an accomplished artist, able to draw a true likeness of people, and I hoped she might have the same success while sketching trees and capturing their specific properties for Meg's use. On our return from these excursions, we brought our bounty back to the library, researched and cataloged the specimens, and added them to our growing collection.

As spring unfolded, I began to have a renewed interest in life. I loved nothing more than to ride out, but I never lost sight of my true goal. I waited patiently for the right opportunity when I might safely visit Belle. Finally, at the end of May, Marshall left the farm for a day. He was off to a town some two hours away, and when I learned that he planned to take the wagon, I knew he would not be back before nightfall.

Papa alone knew of my plan. Sukey had the sniffles, and I used this as an excuse for her not to ride with me that day. Mama met me in the blue room. It was early, before breakfast, and Jamie was still asleep. He did not wake when I clipped a lock of his hair. Out in the hallway, Mama watched as I curled it inside a locket and dropped that into my jacket pocket. She peered at me. "Where you goin', chil'?"

I would not lie to her, yet I would not involve her. I hugged her. "I'm going riding, Mama," I said.

"Masta Marshall say you not go out on that horse by yourself," she scolded.

"Mama," I said, "I'm going."

"You be careful, chil'," Mama whispered, "stay in those trees."

Papa was waiting. I was frustrated when I saw he had saddled Barney. "Oh, Papa," I said, "I need a faster horse."

"This horse know you. He get you there,

and he get you back, and you stay in one piece," Papa said, and I knew there was no use arguing. "You follow that stream, like I say. Stay in the trees and take it slow. Ben watchin' for you." He handed me a riding crop. "Use this if you needs to," he said, "and the Lawd ride with you."

I set off at a trot, intoxicated by my freedom. My little horse moved quickly, and his surefootedness enabled me to look around as I rode. Nature was at its most lush, and for the first time in a long while, I felt hopeful.

I had been riding for what seemed a short time when, up ahead, I heard the sound of a horse and rider. My heart thudded until a voice called out, "It jus' me, Abinia," and I recognized Ben's voice.

"Ben!" I called, and we laughed aloud as we rode toward each other. Our horses danced as we greeted, and we soon broke through the trees into a large clearing. To the front of it, I scarcely noted the large house still under construction. Neither did I give attention to the large finished barn standing farther down in the clearing. What had my interest was the small clapboard kitchen house and the familiar figure standing next to it.

As Ben led the way, Belle ran toward us.

Our reunion was bittersweet, for I did not have her son. Instead, I presented a drawing, a close likeness of Jamie, which Sukey had done recently. Then I gave Belle my gold locket that held her son's hair, and I told her how I had cut it but an hour previous. I put my arms around her when she fingered this treasure, and as she cried, I felt her suffering. Only later, when we talked, after no detail of Jamie had been left unanswered, did I ask her about herself.

She missed all of us so, she said.

Was Lucy, Ben's wife, not a favorable companion? I asked.

Belle said yes, but though they were close, Lucy was not Mama.

"And Ben?" I asked. "Do you see much of Ben?"

Curiously, she evaded the answer.

"Does Will Stephens have help other than Ben?" I asked, trying to remember if I had seen quarters.

"Yes," she said, "he got four new men. He's wanting a big farm, and the way he works, he's gonna have it."

"Is he good to you?" I asked.

"He's a good man, but I'm his property."

I did not know how to respond, acutely aware that through my husband, I owned people as well. Belle continued, "Will brings me here, but I'm not a free woman."

I took a deep breath. "Belle, I thought you loved Will. I . . . I thought he was Jamie's father."

"Ben told me what you was thinking."

I was embarrassed and looked at the floor.

"Will always helped me, Lavinia, nothing more. He never came at me like that."

Then I asked for the truth about Jamie. Belle hesitated. "Marshall's his daddy. That all I'm gonna say. You're married to the man now, so you got to let this go."

"But now he's after Beattie!" There! It was said. What I had come here to confide. I burst into tears. Belle reached for me and let me cry, but once released, my tears wouldn't stop. When I could speak, I told her about the misery of my marriage, of Marshall's drinking and his deceit, and of my resentment toward Beattie. When Belle spoke on Beattie's behalf, she angered me.

"So you think she does not encourage him, that she does not enjoy his gifts?" I asked.

Belle was firm with me. Did I forget that Beattie had no choice? Marshall owned her.

"But he owns me as well!" I said.

"Yes, but you picked that," she said. "Beattie don't get to pick nothing except to figure out how she's best gonna handle this." I stared ahead, not meeting her eyes, fighting the truth. Belle spoke softly. "You know what I'm thinking, Lavinia? I'm thinking that you're mad with Beattie 'cause you can't get mad with Marshall." She paused and took a deep breath. "I know this 'cause I got something here that's almost the same thing."

I looked at her.

"When you was away in Williamsburg, Ben and me got together. I'm not saying it's wrong or right, it's just the way it happens. For a long time, I don't like Lucy. She's this, she's that, and I'm saying all this to myself so I don't have to see that she's hurting, too. Turns out she's a better woman than me. She set aside her bad feelings when they took my Jamie."

I was shocked. I had always guessed that Ben and Belle cared for each other, but that they acted on it . . . "Do you still . . ." I stopped, astonished that I should ask such a personal question.

"Yes," Belle answered frankly. "Lucy and me, we work it out. She loves Ben, same as me. She gives him three boys. They're all good boys, too."

"But what about —" Again I hesitated, and again Belle guessed at what I referenced.

"First, Ida gives me something so I don't get caught with no baby. Then, after Jamie's gone and I'm wanting a baby of Ben's, nothing happens. Now, Lucy's little George, he's like my own. Most nights he sleeps here." She nodded at a wooden cradle in the corner where, draped over the side, was a small patchwork quilt made of red and blue squares. We talked further as Belle set out some food. "Come, child," she said, "come, eat something."

I was surprised at my enormous appetite until I realized that I felt a burden had been lifted: Belle's strange circumstances somehow made me feel less alone in mine. We were finishing when Ben came to the door to remind me that it was soon time to leave. The horses were ready, and he would travel part of the way back with me. He left to give us a few minutes alone, and soon after, there was another short rap on the door. Thinking it was Ben, Belle called for him to enter. When the door opened, Will Stephens stood framed in the sunlight. I had not spoken to him since his visit to Williamsburg, and my pounding heart told me that my feelings toward him had only grown. Belle invited him in, and he removed his hat as he strode toward me. Flustered by his smile, I forced myself to meet his eyes.

"Miss Lavinia," he said, nodding at me, "we meet again."

"Mr. Stephens," I answered, returning his nod.

"You are well?" he asked.

I reached for Belle's hand. "Yes, I am."

"I understand you are leaving. Must you go so soon?" he said.

To my embarrassment, I burst into tears and quickly turned my face.

"I'll bring her out soon as she's ready," Belle said to Will. After he left, she used a handkerchief to dry my eyes.

"I can't go back!" I cried, clinging to her. "I can't bear to go back to him."

"You know you got to go," she said. "Elly's needing you. And you got to watch out for Jamie."

Reality sobered me, and I gathered myself again. Outside, I was surprised to see Will Stephens sitting astride Ben's horse. "I thought I might ride out with you," he said.

I hugged Belle good-bye. Ben smiled when he helped me up on Barney. "You ride real good," he said. "Papa say you good with the horse."

"I love to ride," I said, patting Barney's neck, then turning him toward home. I waved a final good-bye, but as we rode off, to my own astonishment, I began to cry again. It felt a wall had come down; exposed and vulnerable, I did not want to leave this safe place. Will took my horse's reins from me and led us forward.

"I'm sorry, but I can't seem to stop crying," I said when I could speak.

"Then you go ahead and cry," Will said.

That ended my weeping. Had he asked me not to cry, I would not have been able to stop, but his permission somehow quit my tears. In a short while, I asked for the reins.

Will spoke first. "You are not happy, then?"

I shook my head.

He pulled in front of me and reined in his horse. "Lavinia . . ." he began, then stopped himself.

Unable to speak, I took in his every feature.

"Belle told me that you thought she and I . . . that Jamie . . ." he said.

"Yes," I answered, "I did believe that."

"Lavinia," he asked, "how could you ever think that?"

"I was young," I said by way of explanation.

He surprised me with a hearty laugh. "And now, at nineteen, you consider yourself old?"

"I'm already twenty," I informed him.

"Well" — he laughed again — "that certainly makes the difference."

"Will Stephens! Are you suggesting that you still think of me as a child?"

He disarmed me with gentle words. "I think of you as a beautiful young woman who has the heart of a child."

Well! What does one reply to that? I said nothing, but with his tenderness, my tears began once again. Will dismounted, then reached up for me. "Lavinia," he said, his arms inviting me down. I slipped into his embrace, and he kissed me then, as I did him. We continued until I was awakened to a passion that I had never before experienced. I wanted only to continue, to give myself up, so when he stopped, I pleaded for more. Yet he held me away.

"No, Lavinia." He stepped back. "This is too dangerous, and it can lead nowhere." I began to sob. He looked at me helplessly. "You are married, Lavinia!"

I turned from him. He was a coward! If he loved me, he would declare himself and offer a solution to the madness of my marriage. In fury and despair, I managed to mount my horse, and before Will could object, I slapped Barney's rump with my

crop until he leaped away.
Will did not follow.

CHAPTER FORTY-SIX

Belle

That little George is the light of my life.
He's got the face of Benny, and he's got the
dimples of Beattie. Lucy and me, we never
hear him cry. Oh, there's times he fusses to
eat, but he don't care who's holding him,
Lucy or me. He looks for me the same way
he looks for Lucy. Lucy don't care, she's
only too happy to hand him over. In some
ways, I got to say, I love this child as much
as I love my boy Jamie. I don't know how
this happens, but just when I'm needing
something, this little fat baby shows up. I
can't get enough of holding and kissing him.
Lucy and Ben laugh and say, "What got
over you? You don't pay no mind to the
other boys?" They're right. I just fall in love
with this one, and that be that.

After Lavinia comes and brings a picture
of Jamie and a locket with a curl of his hair,
I put it on my neck and don't take it off,

even at night when I go to sleep. Lavinia says Jamie's doing real good, that he learning to read and write. The best thing is, Marshall don't ever see the boy. Lavinia says Marshall's not around much in the big house, he only comes in sometimes to eat. At night she don't know where he is, but she knows for sure he never comes upstairs.

Lavinia says she looking out for Jamie, but I don't know. She don't look so good. She's too jumpy . . . crying too easy.

I see, too, she's got feelings for Will Stephens. The day she was here, when I see the two of them together, I know right away that they're same as Ben and me — they got the same fire. When Will Stephens gets up on his horse to ride her home I'm thinking, Oh Lawd! After they set out, Ben, Lucy, me, we're all watching. Ben says, "Will Stephens a church-goin' man, he don't do nothin' with a married woman."

Lucy says, "Well, Ben, you a church-goin' man. What happen with you?"

First time ever, I see Ben with nothing to say to Lucy. The way Ben looks at her makes Lucy laugh, then I got to laugh, too. Ben gets out of there real quick. First, though, he looks back at Lucy and me laughing. Then he shakes his head, but we both know he's feeling good that Lucy and me is a team.

Ben's thinking nothing happened in the woods with Will and Lavinia, but Lucy and me is not so sure.

CHAPTER FORTY-SEVEN

Lavinia

At night I could not stop my mind from racing. I did not care that my thoughts were irrational; I needed to see Will again. But for Sukey, I would have been lost. Because she shared my room, she was often wakened by my restless sleep. Then she came to me, and with her nestled close, I had some comfort.

During the day, we were busy preparing for Meg's visit, but we faced a growing problem with Miss Martha. Although she appeared lucid in most matters, Miss Martha's concern for Jamie had become so obsessive that she wouldn't allow him out of her sight. Fanny reminded us that this had been Miss Martha's way with Miss Sally until she had finally loosened her grasp, only to have Sally die.

There was no doubt that Miss Martha considered Jamie her own. She had children's clothes brought down from the attic and, from these, outfitted Jamie. The two took their meals together in the blue room, where Miss Martha had Jamie sit with her at the table while Fanny served them. Even I was growing concerned at their deep attachment, and I at last agreed with Mama Mae that it was time to put some distance between the two of them.

The problem facing us was that he could not go back into the kitchen house, as apparently, Marshall spent some time there. Mama said that Uncle Jacob was willing to take Jamie into his small cabin. Mama further suggested that once that transition took place, Papa could begin to teach Jamie the work required down at the barn. It was a good plan, but we knew the upheaval this change would create, so we decided to wait and begin the separation after the Maddens' visit.

Since Belle's confirmation of Jamie's paternity, I could scarcely maintain civility with my husband. Yet I knew that I could not mention it, for I dared not think of the repercussions. As the visit from the Maddens grew closer, Marshall began to drink more heavily.

On an early September morning a few weeks before the Maddens were due to arrive, I made a quick decision to visit Will's farm one more time. My excuse was that I wanted Belle to know about Jamie's upcoming move to Uncle Jacob's cabin, but the truth was that deep in my foolish young heart, I believed Will Stephens held the solution for my happiness. I had waited too long for some contact from him, some word that he thought of me. But it had not come. I could wait no longer.

The morning I went, Marshall was already down in the fields with Rankin. I knew I had at least four hours before dinner, when I was expected to join my husband. I told no one of my plans. Down at the barns, Papa was nowhere in sight, and I quickly saddled Barney of my own accord. I was up and away faster than I had thought possible, and as I rode out into the trees, exhilaration rose in me and I began to sing.

I was almost to the clearing when I heard a shout from behind. I could not mistake Rankin's voice. I realized that he must have been trailing me. Terrified but furious, I slowed Barney's pace, though I continued to ride. It did not take long for Rankin to catch up to me.

"Mrs. Pyke!" he said, as though surprised to see me. "I don't know, but I think your husband's gonna want to know about this."

497

"About what?" I asked.

"Why, that you are out here riding alone, off to Will Stephens's farm."

My face burned with fury. Trapped, I did not care what I said. "You miserable man!" I shouted, and turned my horse back for home.

Rankin laughed as he circled around and positioned his horse behind mine. " 'Course, a fiery little thing like you might have a way of convincing me not to do the telling."

With that, I clipped Barney with the whip. I bit my tongue to hold back the tears, and by the time I reached home, I was swallowing blood. Papa was at the barn, and after I dismounted, I handed the reins to him. We were both only too aware of Rankin seated on his horse, scrutinizing our every move. I kept my voice as steady as I could.

"Good morning, George. I didn't want to trouble you earlier, so as you can see, I saddled my own horse."

Papa nodded. "I see, Miss Abinia, but next time you let me know when you go ridin' so I can saddle up for you."

"Thank you, George," I said, and wasted no more time before I headed up to the house. I knew Marshall would soon learn of this, and I had little time to prepare my defense.

At dinnertime, I stalled as long as I dared. As luck would have it, Fanny was ill that day, and Beattie was serving the meal. When I entered the dining room, Marshall was already seated. I had seldom seen him look so dark. I knew then that Rankin had spoken to him. Marshall did not rise when Uncle Jacob seated me. When I met Uncle's eyes, I saw in them his deep concern and went cold with fear. I forced myself to lift the spoon and began to eat the soup. I ate in silence as Marshall drank wine. My stomach rebelled, but I continued to force down the hot liquid while bracing for the tirade. When Beattie left the room, in shock I saw that she was again with child. Without warning, all of my fear transformed to rage. The insanity of it all! How dare he! Who was this man to so control my life? Each day I was forced to bear my husband's intolerable behavior, and with Beattie I was forced once again to see the results of it. I was as enslaved as all the others. I could not fight back the anger that coursed through me.

"This has got to stop!" I slammed both of my fists on the table.

"What?" Marshall asked, taken unaware.

"This! This! With Beattie!" I said.

Marshall's face flushed, and he gave a drunken smirk. I saw Uncle Jacob turn for the door. I didn't want him to go for help. I would end this on my own.

"Don't leave, Uncle!" I shouted. "You know what's going on. Everyone does!"

I pushed back from the table and swung toward Uncle Jacob. I don't know why I was addressing him; I suppose I didn't have the courage to face Marshall. Uncle did not speak but gave me a look of warning that I did not heed.

"You know what he does with Beattie — how he takes her by force! And now," I spat, "she's going to have another child!"

I heard Marshall rise and come toward me, but I was beyond caring.

"He uses her, Uncle!" I cried. "Can you imagine! He takes her like an animal!"

I stopped when I felt the grip of Marshall's hand in my hair. His fingers twisted as he pulled me from the room. I cried out in pain, and Uncle tried to help. Marshall, in a rage, shoved Uncle back against the sideboard; the force sent a platter of meat crashing to the floor. I was pushed past Beattie, who was entering the door. She half reached for me, dropping the china cups she was carrying, but Marshall shoved me on. Beattie's eyes were wide with fright as she watched Marshall pull me out and into his bedroom. I could not move from fear when he slammed the door behind us.

He did not shout but began to strike me. His face had gone a dull red, and I no longer recognized him. He was full of drink, but I will not blame the wine. Nor will I place the responsibility on my earlier words. The act of violence that followed was so abhorrent that I will not speak of it.

When it was over, after he rushed from the room, I went to his washbasin and cleaned myself, not caring that I left my blood on his towels. Then I began to vomit and could not stop. Exhausted, I leaned on the edge of the bed until I decided I must have dreamed this nightmare.

When Mama came for me, I smiled. "Mama," I said, "Beattie is having a baby."

Mama nodded. "Come, chil'," she said, "you come with Mama."

I went with her to my bedroom, where she put me to bed and stroked my head for a long time. Often she looked out the window. Neither of us, it seemed, had words to suit the occasion.

Three weeks later, in the first week of October 1804, amid the splendor of the autumn leaves, Meg and her parents arrived, laden with gifts for Elly. The first few days, I was so determined to have them enjoy their stay that I felt ill. Marshall drank heavily and, to their surprise, excused himself for most of the daylight hours. On the evening of the fourth day, Meg came to my room and asked if she might speak privately with me.

She closed the door, and I offered her a seat on one of the red chairs in front of the fire. Meg was now nineteen, and although she had matured in these past two years, she remained much as I remembered. The study of botany remained her first passion, and she confided to me that her relationship with Henry continued, but at a slow pace, which suited them both.

Meg rearranged herself, and though she did not complain, I saw that her affected hip was giving her discomfort. I knew from the past that she did not want me to reference this, so I chose another topic. What did she think of the leaf collection that Sukey and I had put together for her? I began.

It was wonderful, she said, but that was not the reason for this evening's visit. "Lavinia," she said, "are you not well?"

"I'm fine," I reassured her.

"Are you having difficulty sleeping?" she asked.

"No, Meg," I lied, "why do you ask?"

"You aren't yourself," she said, "and you are so . . . so full of nerves. And Mother and I both think you are too thin. Much too thin."

"Oh. Well, yes. It is the excitement. You don't know how I have looked forward to your visit."

"Lavinia. What is wrong with Marshall? We hardly recognize him. I can scarcely believe how he has removed himself from my parents."

"Oh, Meg," I said, "I'm sure he wants their approval and fears that he will fall short."

"And you are certain that you are all right?" she asked again.

"I'm fine," I lied. What could I say? I was afraid to speak of anything, afraid that if I began, I would tell all. And I could not do that. How could I tell her about my feelings toward Will? How could I speak to Meg of Beattie's pregnancy, of Marshall's relationship with her? And as for the terrible event that had so recently taken place with Marshall, I could barely acknowledge it to myself, never mind telling her of it.

Meg, sensitive to my uneasiness, looked

about the room and deliberately changed the subject. "How warm this room is," she said, "how pretty."

"Oh, yes," I said, relieved that she had abandoned the idea of uncovering my problems. "How can I ever thank you and your mother for having done this for me."

We spoke of my room and of the house and its many treasures. After she left that evening, I fell into bed, wondering how I could ever manage to finish out their stay. A few short weeks before, I had longed for our guests' arrival. Now, afraid they might discover our shameful secrets, I couldn't wait for them to leave.

Miss Sarah was pleased with her sister's recovery but was gravely concerned with Miss Martha's attachment to Jamie. When alone, she questioned me. Who was he? What did I know of the child's background? "I know he's from the quarters," she said, "but with his coloring, one would question that."

"He is Belle's child," I said.

"Belle's child! Wasn't she . . ." She stopped herself, but not before I heard the disgust in her voice. I knew then that she, too, had been misinformed about Belle's relationship to the captain, but I did not know where to begin nor end with the truth, so I said nothing.

Following our conversation, she launched a campaign to have Jamie taken from Miss Martha and, in the process, all but destroyed the slow progress her sister had made. After Miss Sarah insisted that Jamie be removed from the house, Miss Martha became so agitated that large doses of laudanum couldn't settle her. After two days, witness to the extreme distress of her sister, Miss Sarah conceded and had Jamie brought back. But by that time, my mother-in-law was back on heavy doses of laudanum, and Jamie's dependence on Miss Martha was as marked as her need was for him.

The Maddens' visit passed more slowly than I would have thought possible. Although I spent a great deal of time with Miss Sarah and with Meg, I cannot recall a conversation of merit. I simply did not know what to do or what to say to explain our sorry circumstances. Each night I fought for sleep, but it eluded me as I worried about the days to come. I ate little as I presided over awkward meals, with Marshall either absent or drinking heavily. It was almost too painful to bear.

The day before our guests were to leave, I was alarmed to hear loud shouts from the library. I rushed down the stairs, but Mama stopped me from going into the room.

"It Mr. Madden, he talkin' to Masta Marshall," she said. "You best stay outta there." Mama stood next to me as we listened outside the door.

"But you know better! You knew how hard tobacco was on the soil!" Mr. Madden said.

"Rankin says that —" Marshall began.

"Rankin is nothing but a drunkard! What does he know about diversification?" There was silence until Mr. Madden continued. "Marshall. Your people look half starved. How do you expect them to work if they are hungry and sick?" Again there was silence. Then Mr. Madden spoke more quietly. "What has happened here, son? You must know that you will lose this place if you continue on in this way."

Marshall erupted. "This place is no longer your business! Leave me be!"

Mama and I jumped back when Marshall threw open the door, but I don't believe he saw us when he rushed past and out of the house. Mr. Madden saw me and motioned me in, cutting off Mama when he closed the door behind us. "May I speak frankly, my dear?"

I nodded, frozen in place.

"I'm afraid that Miss Sarah and I are

deeply concerned," he said. When I did not reply, he continued, "Since our arrival, we have observed the sad state of this household."

I sank onto the settee.

"This does not reflect on you, Lavinia," he said, reading me. "No, I'm afraid the responsibility rests with your husband."

Hearing his kindness, I had a sudden hopeful thought. "Mr. Madden —"

"Please call me Uncle," he interrupted.

"Yes. Yes. Uncle. Thank you. May I ask something of you?"

"Anything, my dear."

"Would it . . . Might it be possible for Elly and me to accompany you back to Williamsburg?" I held my breath for his response.

"In what capacity were you hoping to come back with us? For a visit, perhaps?"

"No." My voice sounded thin even to me. "I thought we might come to live —"

Mr. Madden sat beside me and spoke quietly. "I do not think that Marshall would allow you to leave for an undetermined amount of time. And if he were to release you, I am certain he would not give permission for his daughter to travel with you. Do you have doubt that I am correct in this assumption?"

"No. No. Of course you are right."

"Would you come without your daughter?" he asked.

Leaving Elly was not a consideration, and I told him so. He understood my position, he said, and he wanted to impress upon me that should I ever need his assistance, I had but to write. He would do all in his power to help. I thanked him for his generosity, careful to keep my tone free of despair.

It was only after their carriage had pulled away and I stood alone and waving the next morning, that I allowed myself to feel the utter desolation of being left behind. Long after they had gone, when I could no longer see dust from the carriage wheels, Uncle Jacob came with a wrap. Placing it around my shoulders, he urged me to come inside. I searched his kind old face for an answer.

"Uncle?" I asked.

"Come, chil'," he said, and offered his arm to walk me up the stairs.

I sat motionless for most of that day; I had lost all hope. When Sukey came, I sent her away. As darkness approached and I began again to see the futility of my dilemma, I became anxious, sure I could not endure the torture of my reflections for another night. I was pacing when the thought came.

I crossed to Miss Martha's room, where

Mama was settling her for the night. I went directly for the laudanum bottle and added a dose to a glass of water. Mama watched as I swirled the mixture, and before she could protest, I drank it down. Minutes later, as the drug's heady effect transported me, I knew I had found an escape.

CHAPTER FORTY-EIGHT

Belle

Lavinia tries to get here one more time, but Rankin catches her. After that, Papa don't come for two weeks. Ben goes over to see what's happening, but Papa sends him back, says to stay away, that Rankin's watching everybody real close.

Fanny and Eddy come here in the middle of the night to tell Ben, Lucy, and me about everything that's going on.

Fanny and Eddy look funny, walking together. He's real short, and Fanny, she's real tall but skinny as Eddy.

Eddy is Ida's boy, and he's a good man, even though Rankin is his daddy. Ida don't have nothing to say about Rankin getting her with babies over and over. Out of all Ida's babies, only one was not Rankin's. That was Dory's man, Jimmy, but Rankin did him in, beat him till he was gone. Eddy was just a child, but he watched when

Jimmy died. It's no secret in the quarters that Eddy, small as he is, is wanting to kill his own daddy.

Eddy's real quiet, and Fanny does all the talking, but after she says something, he says, "Yup, that's right. Fanny right. Yup, she right." Like he's got to put a blessing on everything she says.

Fanny tells us what Marshall does to Lavinia when Rankin catches her coming over here. "She still not acting like herself," she says.

"Yup," Eddy says.

"Somebody got to hurt that man!" Ben says.

"Don't talk stupid!" Fanny says. "All you do is get yourself killed."

"She right," Eddy says.

Ben don't say nothing. Fanny sees she hurts Ben's feelings. "Ben, remember how you always call Abinia a lil bird. That what she look like now. Like a scared bird sittin' on the ground. Take more than wind to get her up flyin' again. Course, she actin' just like a white woman, just give up, sittin' in her room. Beattie got the same trouble, but she figure out a way to make it work for her. Don't know why Abinia don't do the same. It make me mad!"

"Yup. She sure do make her —"

"Hold on, Fanny!" I say, cuttin' right through Eddy. "Sounds to me like she tries to fight back, but Marshall's too much for her. Don't you forget, Fanny, I know what Marshall's like. I don't talk about it because you was too little back then, but when he turns ugly, there's no fighting back."

"I don't mean to say nothin' 'bout you, Belle," Fanny says.

"Just remember that Lavinia's like my own, Fanny."

"Belle, you know times I say too much. Right now, up there, we all worked up. Mama and Papa don't know what to do. And now Mama sayin' that Abinia startin' to take the drops like Miss Martha."

Eddy don't say nothing, but you can see he don't like it when words are flying between Fanny and me.

"No getting around it that she's a white woman, Fanny, but the way I see it, she's part of this family. And she got no way out, same as us," I say.

"But why don't she go away?" Lucy asks. "She free, not like us."

"Mama say Abinia ask Mr. Madden 'bout goin' back to Williamsburg," Fanny says, "but he say she got to leave Elly with Marshall. We all know she never do that."

We all get quiet, thinking about it.

"How's my Jamie doing?" I ask, even though I'm scared to know.

Fanny looks away. "He doin' real good," she say, "but we gonna take him outta the big house soon as we can."

"Why?"

"Uncle Jacob wantin' him in his house, and Papa say he needin' to learn the barns." I can see that Fanny's holding back.

Before I have the chance to ask her more, they get up, saying that they got to leave. There's times I feel sick, worrying about Jamie, wondering how to get him back with me. If I didn't have my baby George here, I don't know what I'd do.

These days Lucy and me get along real good, but when I see she's getting big again, I get mad at Ben.

"When're you doing all this with Lucy?" I say.

"What you mean?" he says.

"You think my eyes don't see?" I ask.

That night when he comes knocking on my door, I tell him no, go see Lucy. After a while, though, I start thinking that without him being with Lucy, I don't have my George. I got to say that Lucy counts on me to take care of that baby. All she does is feed him, then hands him over to me, saying, "Go to your mama Belle." Those words are sweet as honey to me.

It don't take long, and Ben's back with me again.

CHAPTER FORTY-NINE

Lavinia

I discovered the six full bottles of laudanum the same day I found Belle's missing papers. After Meg's visit, I could not find a sense of purpose, and frequently, I found myself wandering through the house. Winter was encroaching, but that was not the reason I no longer went out to ride. Too afraid of the consequences, I dared not visit Belle, and without that, I had no destination. Irrationally, I could not understand that Will had not attempted to see me. Reading had lost its appeal, and in an effort to quiet my nerves, I sought other ways to keep myself occupied. Mama and I had done an inventory of the house the previous year, but for various reasons at the time, we had stopped short of Miss Martha's suite.

After Miss Sarah's visit, Miss Martha once again required constant vigilance. We each took our turn, Mama, Fanny, and I, and it was during my scheduled time, while the children and Miss Martha slept, that I took note of the tall linen press set in the blue room. I remembered that we had not inventoried its contents. It was a task I did not relish, but I could no longer bear to sit idle for endless empty hours, and I decided to do the job.

I used a wooden chair to reach the top shelves. Removing the stacks of linens and hatboxes from them was tiresome, so I was relieved to bring down the last remaining box. Curious at the sound of clinking glass, I opened it to find six full bottles of laudanum. Had Miss Martha hidden them years before? She must have; there was no other explanation. Was this then a hiding place for her? Were other secrets hidden up there? While standing on the chair, I could not see to the back of the shelf, so I reached in as far as I was able. My fingers almost missed the package, but once I felt it, I managed to maneuver it into my grasp. It was an envelope addressed to Belle. I recognized it immediately as the package Miss Martha had intercepted that Christmas so many years before. I knew it contained Belle's freedom papers. The envelope frightened me. What would the papers mean to her now? Could Marshall somehow use them against her?

Before Fanny came to relieve me, I took the sealed envelope and the bottles of laudanum to my room. I did not speak to anyone of my findings, and I had full intention to smuggle the papers to Belle at the earliest possible opportunity.

That night I used the laudanum to quiet myself before sleep. It worked so well that the next day I decided to mix a few drops with sherry a half hour before the afternoon meal. The combination was magical. It eased me in Marshall's presence and diminished my anxiety so that I was able to eat without feeling sick. Over the course of that dinner hour, I noted with great relief that even Beattie, in her pregnancy, did not disturb me as before. Marshall seemed pleased with my new relaxed attitude, and crediting our dinner wine, he encouraged me to drink more with our meal. I did not argue.

I continued to use the drug, and when the results were consistent over the following weeks, it was not long before I began to rely on it daily to lift my spirits.

I wrote to Meg telling her of the help I had found for myself, but when she wrote back warning me of the dangers of opium, I became so angry that she would wish to deprive me of this small comfort that I ceased correspondence with her.

Christmas night of that year, Fanny woke me from a deep sleep. "Mama needin' you," she said. "Beattie havin' the baby."

"Where's Ida?" I asked, trying to wake myself.

"She sick," Fanny said.

"You go," I said. "I'll stay with Miss Martha."

"Mama say she want you," Fanny said, "she say this a hard baby comin'."

I dressed reluctantly. Papa George met me at the back door and gave me his arm, then led our way with a lantern. From the kitchen house, I heard Beattie call out. Still holding on to my resentment, and angry that this task had fallen to me, I would have walked slower had Papa not pulled me along.

My cold attitude did not remain for long. Mama had Beattie up and walking, and when I saw Beattie's distress, I threw off my wrap and went to give her my assistance.

"Hold her up and help her walk," Mama said.

"Lean on me, Bea," I said. I took her arm securely, and with her face contorted in pain, she looked at me. "I so sorry for this, Miss Abinia," she said.

"Hush, Bea," I said, but another contraction pulled her back into such pain that I wasn't sure she heard me.

In the early morning, when the baby came, all three of us were exhausted but jubilant at our success. I felt nothing but deep relief when Mama handed the little brown boy to Beattie.

The new mother slept while Mama Mae and I prepared a morning meal. When Mama took it up to the big house, I stayed, holding the baby, stroking its soft face until Beattie awoke. I placed the babe in her outstretched arms, and we laughed when he scrunched up his tiny face. She spoke while looking down at him. "I so sorry for makin' this trouble for you," she said.

I shushed her. She reached for my hand and kissed it. In return, I kissed hers. I did not tell this childhood friend that while she was giving birth, I had seen for myself the marks on her body. I needed no further convincing that she was the hapless victim of my husband, and I felt deep sorrow that I had added to her troubles.

I stayed while she fed her baby, then I sat with them while they slept. Sitting there in the warmth of my childhood home, I became determined to set things right.

■ ■ ■ ■

My heart pounded, but my voice was calm when I spoke with Marshall at dinner the following afternoon. "Beattie had a very difficult time of it," I said.

He flushed but did not look at me.

"She needs time to recover," I said. He rose, and I stiffened, fully prepared for an outburst, but he left the room without comment.

When the weather took a warm turn in the middle of January, Marshall unexpectedly left on business for the day. With courage derived from opium, and fueled by a desire to see Will, I decided to take this opportunity to deliver the freedom papers to Belle. I took Sukey into my confidence, as I knew she would not allow me to leave without explanation. "I need you to stay back, but I must go to see Belle," I said.

"Why?" she asked. "Why do you have to see Belle?"

"I found papers," I whispered.

"What kind of papers?" she whispered back.

"I'll tell you when I get back," I said, "but you must promise to keep this a secret."

"I will." She nodded. I trusted her as I did no other.

Papa and I argued when I insisted that he saddle Barney. He guessed immediately where I was going. The weather wasn't stable, he said, and we had no idea when Marshall would return. Besides, he told me, Rankin was more likely to come down to the barn during the winter season. I dared not tell Papa of Belle's papers, nor of my need to see Will. I stubbornly held my ground. In spite of the grim look on his face, I insisted that he do as I asked, then I rode off at a gallop. I did not turn back to wave; instead, my hand felt for the package that Sukey and I had bound against my breast.

I was almost halfway there before I dared to slow my horse to a walk. It was then, from behind me, that I heard the neigh of another horse. I reined Barney in and turned to face the oncoming rider. Of course it was Rankin.

"Well, Mrs. Pyke," he said, "I was hoping that I might catch up to you. I was wondering where you were going at such a speed, but now that we are near his house, I'm not wondering no more." He smiled. "Will Stephens is quite a friend of yours, isn't he?" When I did not answer, he reached for the reins of my horse and turned us toward home. "You know your husband don't want you out here."

I cracked my whip smartly across his wrist. Barney, responding to the crop, jumped ahead, and I gave him his rein when he headed for home.

I was ready for my husband when he came to my room that evening. At my request, Fanny had taken Elly to the nursery for the night. Sukey refused to leave my side, so she and I sat playing cards. When I heard Marshall's footsteps on the stairs, my hands began to tremble. Sukey whispered, "Don't worry, Miss Abby, I'm staying here with you."

"Please go, stay with Mama," I whispered, but she shook her head. When Marshall entered, Sukey rose, as was the order. Marshall strode over to me and slapped my face. Sukey gasped.

"Where were you going?" he asked.

I kept my eyes down. "I went out for a ride."

This time the force of his slap threw me from the chair. He came at me again, and before I could prevent it, Sukey charged him. She bit deep into his arm, and Marshall yelled a profanity as he threw her from him.

To my great surprise and relief, he abruptly left the room. Sukey and I were comforting each other when Marshall returned with Papa George.

"Take her," Marshall said, waving toward Sukey. "Get rid of her!"

"No," I pleaded, holding Sukey to me. "Please, Marshall, she did nothing wrong."

"You let your nigra bite me, and you say she did nothing wrong!" he shouted.

"She was only trying to stop you."

"Stop me? Stop me!" He turned to Papa, who was standing back at the door. "George, I said get in here and take her out!" he said. Sukey's arms were locked around me, but Marshall ripped her away and tossed her at Papa George. "Get her out of here!"

Papa's eyes flamed, and his body shook, and for one terrible moment I thought that he might refuse Marshall's command. Yet he contained himself, and with an uncommon gentleness, he convinced Sukey to come with him.

I fell to my knees after they left. "Marshall! Please! Please! Don't harm her. Where will you send her?"

"She will go to the quarters, where she belongs."

"But what about Elly?" I pleaded, trying

523

another approach. "She is so attached to her."

"Elly has others to care for her," he said.

"But Sukey's never lived down there, it will be too hard on her!"

"This is all your doing, Lavinia," he said. "You dare to embarrass me! You go to meet another man!"

Still on my kness, I begged him. "Please, Marshall. Punish me, not Sukey. Don't take her from me. She's like my own child."

He kicked at me. "Get up! You disgust me! The titles you give these nigras. You say she's like your child. You call them Papa and Mama like they're kin to you! More of this and I will rid you of them all."

After he left the room, I ran to the window. Blackness loomed up and prevented me from seeing out. The house was quiet; no one dared stir. I locked my door before I went to my tall linen press. Shaking, I unwrapped Belle's papers from my bodice. When I hid them on the top shelf, I placed them behind the hatbox that held the laudanum bottles. After little deliberation, I poured a generous amount of the black liquid into my sherry glass, drank it, and waited for it to quiet me.

In the morning, Mama whispered to me

that Sukey had been taken to Ida's cabin and forbidden to bring any of her belongings. Everyone was warned that if they helped me contact her, they would be sold immediately. I remembered well the warning Marshall had given me. If he would take Sukey away from me, I did not doubt he would remove any of the others. After that, I dared not question anyone about Sukey.

Desperate, I wrote to Mr. Madden, then remembered that Marshall was sure to intercept all of my correspondence, so I burned the letter later that night.

Over the next weeks, I went to Marshall on two separate occasions to plead my case. On my first approach, Marshall warned me to let the subject go. The second time, I again implored him to change his mind. He laughed bitterly at my attachment to Sukey, calling her my long-lost child. Who was her daddy? he asked. Reckless in my desperation, I slapped him. I demanded that I be allowed to see her. He looked at me through eyes that I did not recognize. The next afternoon he sent Mama to tell me that Sukey had been sold. Mama's eyes were swollen and her face contorted when she gave me the news.

"I supposed to tell you that Sukey gone."

"Gone where?" I wailed.

"She been sold."

"No, Mama! No! Not Sukey, Mama! Not Sukey!" I cried. But Mama was as grief-stricken as I, and she looked at me helplessly while tears streamed down her face. I ran to the window. Surely there was still time.

"They took her durin' the night. She gone," Mama said.

I stared at Mama, not willing to believe her.

She came close to whisper in my ear. "Miss Abinia, I got to go downstairs. Masta Marshall waitin' on me."

"For what, Mama?" I asked.

"He say he don't want me babyin' you no more. He say if I do, he gonna sell me next." Her frightened face told me that she did not see this as an idle threat. I stared after her as she left the room. A wooden chair that stood against the wall felt weightless when I picked it up. I smashed it against the bed with such force that both the bed-post and the chair shattered. Still I continued to batter away. When nothing was left in my hands, I sank to the floor and gave way to my grief.

Following the sale of Sukey, I refused to go to the dining room for my meals, and

Marshall did not send for me. We did not see each other, as I stayed upstairs when I knew he was about.

Marshall had driven home his point. Everyone was afraid. After the sale of Sukey, no one felt safe. I felt that my whole family blamed me for her exile, and why would they not? I was responsible. Furthermore, I was terrified that Marshall would misinterpret any exchange I had with them, so I kept any conversation brief. I grieved for Sukey as I had no other, and ashamed of my part in the matter, I closed myself off from any consolation my family might have offered.

In complete despair, I relied heavily on the laudanum; soon I depended on it to function. I had already discovered that the drug was not difficult to obtain; it was easily ordered by mail. Every morning, dissolved in a glass of water, a few drops dulled my reality. Hours later, when exhaustion overtook me, another dose with wine gave me a boost to help me finish out the day. In the evening, alone in my room, I schemed. I would leave, find Sukey, and help her to escape. Late into the night, I drew maps of the woods as I remembered them, planning our route, only to burn them for fear of Marshall's discovery. When sleep eluded me, a heavier dose of opium carried me into sleep. I continued this way, believing the opiate my friend, while its ever tightening arms wrapped around me.

During that time Marshall continued on with Beattie, though he found other diversions as well: He began to bet on the horses, and he developed a passion for cardplaying.

Fanny let me know that he sold people from the quarters to pay off debts. Meg wrote, and I ignored her pleas for communication. As my need for laudanum took over, I felt more helpless than ever, and with each passing year, I burrowed deeper into oblivion. I scarcely wept when Mama told me that Will Stephens had married.

CHAPTER FIFTY

1810
Belle

It's five years that Sukey's gone.

In that time, Beattie gets two more boys from Marshall. She got him figured out, and now he spends more time in the kitchen house than he does in the big house. Mama says if Marshall cares about anybody, it's Beattie. Beattie says he don't hardly even get on her no more. He just comes to sleep. Sometimes, she says, he even plays with the babies. Most times, though, he's too drunk to know where he's at.

Will Stephens tell us that Marshall's losing the whole place from playing cards and betting the horses. He's getting rid of more and more land, and he's even selling off people from the quarters. I get worried that he'll sell my Jamie, but Will Stephens says that's never gonna happen. Marshall knows Will Stephens is watching out to buy Jamie if that day ever comes.

They tell me my Jamie's real smart. He reads all the time. Mama says he talks real good and sounds like he comes from the big house. They say he has no trouble passing for white. The times I miss him, I tell myself, Maybe this is the way he'll get free. Maybe one day he'll go off and live like a white boy.

They're saying Lavinia uses drops the same as Miss Martha. Lavinia's still up and moving around, but Mama says there's nothing coming from her eyes no more. The only thing she still cares about is her Elly.

That little Elly, Mama says, sure is something. She looks like Lavinia, but she got more sass and spark in her than Lavinia ever have. Most of the time, she's out running and playing with Moses, Beattie's oldest boy, but she gets along good with my Jamie, too.

A couple of times I hide up in the trees, thinking to see Jamie when he goes down to the barns, but this last time Papa says, "Don't come here no more. Rankin's got a nose for trouble."

Ben says after Sukey got sent off, Papa's scared of everything. Papa 'specially don't like it when he hears that Ben's helping people run. Ben fixed a place to hide them in his house, but we don't talk about that to nobody. We think maybe Will Stephens knows, but he don't say nothing. Lucy don't like it one bit. She's afraid for her little ones.

This place here is growing. Will Stephens finally got married. We all know he was waiting to see what's happening with Lavinia. One time Will goes over there to see how she's doing. He goes to the front door, like a gentleman, and asks to see Lavinia. Marshall comes to the door, puts a gun to Will, and tells him he'll shoot the next time he sees him.

When Will sees for himself that he can't do nothing, he don't go back. Last year he marries a girl at church, and we all like her good enough. For sure, she nothing smart to look at. She's real white with yellow hair, and she looks like she don't have no eyelashes. She don't laugh too much, and she sure does talk about the good Lawd even more than Mama Mae ever done. Don't you know, her name's Martha, so here I go, calling another woman Miss Martha.

Lucy works up at the big house. I stay down here doing the cooking and looking out for the babies. Lucy's happy. She says never in her whole life did she think that she'd get to work in a big house. I say I never did think that I'd be working in a kitchen and looking out for babies that some woman have with my man. We laugh, 'cause it's the sorry truth.

Ben means everything to Lucy and me, but some days Lucy comes and says, "Belle, you take that man, I don't ever want to see him again!" Other times I say, "Lucy, he's all yours! Keep him away from me." So that's the way it works out for us, both with the same man. 'Course, there's times I think Ben wants a place for himself to get away from two women who each got their own way.

My George is gonna be six years old this Christmas. He writes his name already, and my name, too. He call me Mama Belles, and the way he says it, those two words I can never hear enough. He lives with me from the time before he can walk, and Lucy don't never say she don't want me taking over this child.

Ben asks, "What you gonna do when it time for him to work the fields?"

I say, "I'm getting George ready for the big house. He's not going down to those fields."

Ben and Lucy think that George takes the place of my Jamie, but they don't see it right. Each boy got half my heart.

CHAPTER FIFTY-ONE

1810
Lavinia

Much of the land was sold by the spring of 1810. I kept myself dosed with laudanum as everything fell away. Marshall was seldom present on the farm, and the few times when I did see him, our meetings were cold and brief. I made sure that Elly was taken to her father when he asked to see her, but those times were infrequent. Fanny, who accompanied Elly on these visits, told me that Marshall appeared ill at ease with his daughter.

"He don't know what to say, 'cause the older that lil girl get, the more she look like you," Fanny explained.

My daughter was the light of Fanny's world. To Fanny's sorrow, she and Eddy did not have children, so she treated Elly as her own. Every morning after Fanny fed and dressed Elly for the day, they had their own small ritual. "And who is Fanny to her little darlin'?" Fanny would ask. Elly's arms would go around her neck for their morning hug, and her words always made Fanny laugh out loud. Elly would draw out the words and mimick her perfectly: "Fanny, you know you just my bes' blessin'!"

Fanny was also Miss Martha's nurse. On the whole, my mother-in-law's mental health had stabilized. There were days, though, when the sharp cry of an animal from the outdoors might cause her extreme alarm. She would call for me then — "Isabelle! Isabelle!" — and if I did not come running, the only other who could settle her was Jamie. She was as obsessed with Jamie as ever, and though I knew its eccentricity, in that unusual household, it no longer seemed that peculiar.

Jamie was thirteen years old that summer. The previous spring he had grown very tall; he had a thin build and, but for his one eye, a beautiful face with finely carved features. Fanny best described him to Mama: "He too pretty for a boy," she said.

Jamie was unusually fastidious. He insisted that his clothes fit perfectly, and he always kept his softly curled hair carefully tied back with a black satin ribbon. I tried to love him as I did Elly, but there was something about him that would not let me close. He was never disagreeable with Miss Martha, nor was he to me, but if anyone else crossed him, he would call up an air of superiority that caused Mama to remark more than once that he was "thinkin' too high on hisself."

Through the years Papa tried to interest Jamie in outdoor activities. He taught Jamie to ride, and when Marshall was away, he even taught him to hunt with the shotgun that was kept locked in the barn. But Jamie's time with Papa was limited, and for the most part, Jamie remained indoors. His passion was books, and he spent hours at a desk in the blue room, where he read, wrote, and studied poetry. His other fascination was with birds; in this he often reminded me of Meg. Jamie's most prized possession was a book about North American birds that I had given to him. After days spent poring over the book, he announced that one day he would go to Philadelphia to meet the ornithologist who had published it. His determination left no doubt that he would make it happen.

The blue room held stacks of other books, and it became routine in the evenings to gather in Miss Martha's room and listen as Jamie read aloud. Miss Martha had coached him, and his elocution was superb. In many ways, those evenings saved me. Uncle Jacob always came to my room to fetch me. If I argued lethargy, if I told him that I was not feeling well, one look from his old brown eyes was enough to remind me of my duty to the household. I was often in a stupor when I took his arm and he led me to Miss Martha's rooms. After he would seat me, he'd pull a wooden chair from the blue room and sit quietly behind me. The evening almost always ended with Elly dozing on Uncle Jacob's lap.

Beattie and Marshall's oldest child, Moses, was six years old that summer, a year younger than Elly. They were constant playmates.

In the first years, Beattie tried to keep Moses from the big house, but after a time Mama Mae must have told her that I did not care if he came to play with Elly. In truth, Moses, with his easygoing manner and his deeply dimpled face, so reminded me of Beattie as a child that I welcomed his happy presence.

I no longer concerned myself on Beattie's behalf. I knew that she had found her own way of coping. I was happy to learn that she invited Elly into the kitchen house and treated her there with kindness. Beattie and I saw little of each other, as I no longer went down to the kitchen house; I never knew when Marshall was about.

In the last months of the summer of 1810, Marshall was seldom home. His drinking and gambling had worsened, and I could only guess how close we were to complete disaster. That summer many of our workers had already been sold, and the few people left in the quarters were so worn out that I do not know how they survived.

I saw no way out. Tormented by my inability to act, I paced in an opium haze during the night when everyone slept. Where was the solution? Marshall was aware of all my expenditures, so how could I finance an escape? And overcoming that, whom would I take with me?

There were Elly and, of course, her beloved Fanny. But what of Miss Martha? I felt extremely protective toward her. And Mama Mae! How could I leave her? She was my foundation, and I could not envision life without her. In these later years I had only two disagreements with Mama. One was about Jamie. The other had to do with my laudanum use.

All along I knew of Mama's objection to Jamie's presence in the house and the resulting dependency between Miss Martha and Jamie. Whenever Mama suggested that we separate the two, I always pleaded for more time. I could not forget Miss Sarah's visit and the disastrous results when Jamie was removed for those few days. Besides, Jamie was as attached to Miss Martha as she was to him. They spent long hours in each other's company, though Miss Martha often slept while Jamie wrote or studied. Jamie was always respectful toward me, but there were times — after his thirteenth birthday in particular — when he was particularly insolent with Fanny. I corrected him, but he continued until Fanny finally complained to Mama Mae.

On an early morning that May, at Mama's request, I went downstairs to help her open the house to the spring air. We pushed open the dining room windows; the room was seldom used these days, and as I looked it over, I noted its grandeur was beginning to fade. Mama stood quiet as I looked around; as I made to leave, she asked if we could speak. I pulled a chair out for Mama and then seated myself. "What is it, Mae?" I asked.

"We got to get Jamie outta this house," she said urgently.

I shifted in discomfort. I had managed to

evade this discussion many times, but hearing Mama's tone, I doubted I could do so now. I brushed my finger to and fro along the edge of the polished dining table until Mama interrupted me.

"Miss Abinia?"

"But why now?" I heard the whine in my voice.

" 'Cause trouble just waitin' on this. I can feel it."

"Well, what can we do? Where would he go? We can't send him back to the kitchen house. Marshall goes there all the time."

"Jacob say he take him in his house, and George say he take him to work out in the barn. He say Jamie good with the horses."

"But you know Jamie won't want to work in the barns."

"That why he need to go. He growin' up fast. He need to know his place."

"But what is his place? I doubt he even remembers Belle."

"Last time Jamie down at the barns, Papa talk to him about Belle bein' his real mama. Jamie get mad, say Papa don't know what he talkin' bout. Jamie say he a white boy. Papa say, 'No, you a nigra, just like me.' Jamie go runnin' off, and now he don't go down to the barns no more. He gettin' too old for this, Abinia. And his mouth gettin' too smart. It time he know he a nigra; he got to learn to work like one."

"I know you are right, Mae. I've heard him with Fanny. But you know that Miss Martha thinks of him as her son. It's no wonder that he feels he belongs up here in the big house."

"It got to end. These days he thinkin' too much on hisself. There gonna be a big comedown for that boy," Mama said.

"Maybe we could send him off. He looks white. You would never guess —"

"His mama, Belle. That make him a nigra! 'Sides, he got no freedom papers."

"Do you think he knows who his father is?"

"All that boy got to do is see his own face. If he don't look like Masta Marshall, then I don't know who do. All along that why Miss Martha thinkin' he one of hers."

"I know we've got to do this, but I'm so afraid of how Miss Martha . . ."

"Jamie still come up to see her," Mama reassured me.

"Can we wait a few weeks? Summer will be here in a month, and in the heat, she sleeps most of the day. She might not miss him as much."

Mama was silent.

"I promise that if you agree to wait until

June, I will speak to Jamie then."

"I countin' on you for this," she said.

I gave her my word.

We did not know that Jamie, on his way out of the house, had listened to our conversation.

Following that morning, Jamie became moody and sullen. Often he left the house in the early morning and stayed away all day. On his return, he stubbornly refused to tell anyone his whereabouts. I wondered if he had somehow gained knowledge of the impending change; I wondered, too, exactly what he knew of his parentage.

On the first of June, I knew I must uphold my promise to Mama. That morning Jamie was alone with Miss Martha. Knowing that the others were down in the kitchen house, I bolstered my courage with a dose of laudanum, then went in to see him. Miss Martha had been upset by his absence in the past few weeks, and this morning she was clearly overjoyed to have him at her side. When I asked Jamie if, on Fanny's return, I might have a word with him, his face paled, and I felt my resolve weaken.

I went back to my room to await Fanny's return and decided to give myself yet more courage. I found that the small brown bottle at my bedside was empty. Quickly, I pulled up a chair to get another from the back of the linen press, where I kept a supply. I was already unsteady on my feet, and the chair wobbled under me as I reached for a bottle. My fingers felt the envelope that contained Belle's papers. Suddenly inspired, I pulled them out, thinking they might somehow help Jamie understand something of his true mother.

Jamie startled me when he unexpectedly opened the door. I swung around, clutching the air as the chair wobbled, then I tumbled over. Before I crashed, Belle's envelope flew out of my hands. When my head cracked against the hardwood floor, I lost consciousness.

As Marshall was not at home, Mama took it upon herself to send for the doctor. After the examination, Mama was instructed to observe me closely and not, under any circumstances, to give me laudanum.

A day later, I woke with a terrible headache. My body trembled at the slightest sound, and I ached in every bone. I pleaded with Mama for laudanum. She was firm in her refusal, and for the next week, I was too ill to argue.

When Marshall came home at the end of the week, he was informed of my accident but did not feel the need to see me. Now, though, I began to plead in earnest with Mama for laudanum. Tired of my begging, she stood at my bedside. "You don't get the drops from me no more," she said, "and that be that!"

I had no choice but to acquiesce to her dictate, and each day following I began to feel somewhat better. One day I had a visit from Fanny, and after one of her candid observations, I laughed aloud. After she left, I heard her say to Mama, "Maybe that bump on her head do her some good. She soundin' again like the girl I grow up with."

"You right," Mama said. "I just hate to think when that doctor come and say she can get those drops again."

It was weeks before the dizziness passed enough that I could be seated in a chair. For the first few minutes, the room whirled but eventually steadied itself. That day, on Elly's insistence, Mama brought her to me. I heard Mama instruct my daughter before entering the room, "Now, you don't go up-settin' her, else she wantin' the drops again."

The words struck me like a blow. I had no idea that Elly knew I used laudanum. As my daughter cautiously approached me, my heart ached at her fear for me, and I smiled to reassure her.

"Are you finished being sick?" she asked.

"I am almost well, sweetheart." I reached for her small hand. "Mae said that tomorrow I'm going for a walk."

"Will you be all better then?"

"I believe I will," I reassured her.

"Will you take the drops again?" Her voice shook.

"The drops? Why do you ask, darling?"

"I don't like it when you take drops," she said.

I forced myself to ask the question: "Why don't you like it, Elly?"

I saw that it took all of her courage to tell me. "Then you sleep all day, or else you cry and tell me to go away." Her eyes filled with tears, and her chin quivered.

"Come here." I opened my arms to her. As I held her, she sobbed without restraint. Her tears opened me to a painful truth. In my selfish escape, I had abandoned my own child.

"Do you know, darling," I said, "Mae and I were just talking about those drops today. I do believe that I will not take them any longer. Truly, I am feeling so much better." I took her face in mine and smiled. "Can you imagine? Your mother needed a good bump on her head to make her feel better." I reassured her that she was not to worry, that Mama Mae was taking excellent care of me and that I would soon be back on my feet.

I was drained after Elly left, but as Mama helped me back into bed, I made her promise to keep the drops away from me. Mama looked unconvinced. I asked her to bring Fanny to my room, and after she did, I asked the two of them to give their word that should I ask, they would refuse me the drops. They exchanged a skeptical look but gave me their promise. As a gesture of good faith, I told Fanny where I kept the extra bottles and asked her to retrieve them. When she was up on the chair, reaching to the back of the shelf, I had a momentary recall of Belle's papers. I quickly decided that if Fanny brought them down, I would show them to Mama; I had forgotten that they had flown out of my hand with my fall, and I did not know that they were already in Jamie's possession. When Fanny pulled out only the laudanum, I was so caught up in getting rid of the drug that I decided to tell Mama later about Belle's papers.

And I would have done so had the withdrawal from the drug been less difficult. Though I was determined to follow through on my promise to Elly, I couldn't have known that as my physical strength returned, so, too, would my obsession to take the drug. In the weeks that followed, in my darkest hours, I pleaded for release from my promise. But Mama refused me. At night she slept on Sukey's cot, and during the day she would not leave me alone. After a time Mama began to insist that I walk outdoors with her. I was reluctant to go, afraid of seeing Marshall, but she assured me that he was seldom home.

When I relented and ventured forth into the healing sun, I realized how much of a recluse I had become. Then came the day when we walked to the barn to see Papa George. He greeted me so warmly that I wondered why I hadn't come to see him sooner. I was surprised at the gray in his hair and told him so.

"Yup," he said, smiling and brushing his worn hand over the top of his head, "time passin'." He looked into my eyes, then nodded his approval. "It sure good to see our Abinia again," he said, and I knew that the use of my childhood name was intended. I wanted to hug him, but I knew that such a gesture could place us both in jeopardy. I spoke instead of the hot weather and of how the dry brown grass was in such need of rain that it crackled underfoot. I remarked that the sound reminded me of walking on dry leaves. Mama and Papa agreed, and I recalled the first dance that I had attended with them down in the quarters. I had a fond memory of watching the two of them dance together. That set us to remembering other good times, and as we did so, I was reminded of the many years they had cared for me.

"Mama, Papa," I blurted out, "I'm so sorry about Sukey."

They looked at each other, then Papa spoke. "We all sorry 'bout Sukey, but we know you don't mean her no harm. We know you do the best you can when it come to Sukey. Now we askin' the Lawd to make you strong again. We here all needin' that."

"Thank you, Papa," I said. That day, with Papa's words of forgiveness, my obsession for the drug began to recede.

CHAPTER FIFTY-TWO

Belle

Early morning, beginning of August, I'm working in the garden. It's so hot and dry this year, all I seem to do is carry water. I look over and got to smile at George playing the fool with the babies, splashing water on them, keeping them happy. All the time, though, I got this feeling somebody's watching. I stop, look around. Nothing there, but I feel it strong.

When it's time to eat, I bring out the food, and we all sit outside by the kitchen house. Today I don't need to cook for the big house, just send up soup from yesterday and some biscuits from this morning. Lucy comes down from the big house to eat with us and to feed her last baby. I fix her some butter and ham on a thick cut of bread and give it to her to eat while she's feeding. I know she's hungry, 'cause nobody likes food the way Lucy do.

"Ain't we havin' those pickled cowcumbers today?" she asks.

"Sure," I say, "I'll get them." I go in, take down a jar, and cut up a few, then bring them out. This time, for sure, I know somebody's watching. Again I look around, but I see only Lucy eying the pickles. Then I start to laugh. "Oh no!" I say, looking hard at her. "You getting big again, Lucy? Last time you wanted those pickles morning and night!"

Lucy rolls her eyes and says, "Up at the big house, Miss Martha calls it a blessin'. I calls it more work."

I laugh again, but truth is, I feel sorry for her. Her last one's still nursing. "You know you got me to help," I say.

"If you not here, Belle, I don't know what I do. You like a sista to me." Lucy's eyes fill up. This happens easy when she's getting big. Her tongue gets sharp, too. Ben comes to me some days, says he don't know what's going on with her. I say, "You try walking around big as a privy in the Virginia sun, and we'll see how much singing you do."

"How's Will's Martha doing?" I ask Lucy.

"She doin' better, but the more her stomach grow, the more her legs get big. Her head hurtin', too. That stuff the doctor give don't do her no good. Maybe make it worse."

I say, "Next time Fanny comes, I'll ask her if Ida got something for that. Maybe she'd try it?"

"Maybe she do. I know she scared. Her own mama die like this when she have her last one," Lucy say.

"I sure do hope that this baby comes easy," I say. "You know it's gonna be on us to help her out."

"Maybe we get Mama Mae over?"

I shake my head. "It's too hard for her to get here. Last time Eddy's here, he says there's so much trouble going on over there that everybody's scared to walk out. Marshall already sells most everybody from the fields."

Lucy asks, real quiet, "You worried 'bout your Jamie?"

I nod 'cause sometimes just saying his name hurts too much. "I can't sleep some nights thinking about him," I say. "But Will Stephens promised me that if Marshall ever sells Jamie, he'll find him and get him for me."

Lucy hands the baby to me. "I got to get back up there," she says.

I head into the kitchen house, turn back to tell George to watch the little ones, and out the corner of my eye, back in the trees, I see a boy. Just for a minute, mind you. He sees me looking and he's gone. I got to sit, my heart's pounding so hard. It's my Jamie! I know it's my Jamie!

Next morning I go to the garden and tell George to stay back in the house with the little ones. He don't like it, but I say, "You do this, and later, I'll make those sugar cakes you like." He's still not happy, but he'd do almost anything for my sugar cakes. That way he's just like Lucy.

I pick up my hoe, and facing the trees, I chop away at the weeds. Sure enough, there he is. I keep my head down, look at the dirt, and start to talk real loud. "If that's Jamie Pyke in those trees," I say, "he don't have to be scared. I'm gonna keep weeding my garden, but I sure do wish Jamie Pyke would come over here and show me what he looks like now that he's a growed boy."

I don't look up, just keep working my hoe, but I hear him coming out the woods and walking toward me. I don't know why he's scared of me, but when he gets closer, I start feeling scared of him. What's he doing here, anyway? What's he want?

"Are you Belle?" he asks.

I look up real slow, afraid he's gonna run. I hang on tight to my hoe, my head spinning, my mouth dried up. Standing there in front of me is a white man. My Jamie. Thirteen years old. Not a boy, not a man.

"I is," I say.

Quick, he holds out some paper. "Then this is yours," he says. "I believe these are your emancipation papers."

I stand, just looking at my boy's face. I don't hear what he's saying. I got to take him in.

"Here," he says, "take them. You're free."

I take the paper. My hand's shaking. "Jamie?" I ask.

"Yes?" he says.

"Do you know who I am to you?"

"Yes. You're my mother."

I nod.

"I don't remember you, though."

"That's all right," I say. "You was little when he took you."

"All of these years . . . Papa George told me . . . I thought I was Miss Martha's son."

I look good at him then. He's white as Marshall, but Jamie got the same face of the captain's mama. Seeing his face, in some way, is like seeing my white grandma here again. I can't stop looking, but I know I got to say something.

"She don't know no better, Jamie, but Miss Martha your grandma. Mama Mae says she's real good to you and —"

"So it's true that Marshall is my father?"

"Yes," I say. "He used me."

Lucy comes 'round the corner of the kitchen house, calling out, saying she needs George to come help out in the big house. Jamie don't wait. He turns, and before I get a chance to say, "It's all right, it's just Lucy," Jamie's gone.

My whole body starts shaking. Lucy sees Jamie run off. "Who that? Who that?" she calls out when she comes huffing over.

"Lucy! Shush!" I say.

"Who that?" she whispers real loud when she gets to me.

I hand her the papers. She opens them, looks real close, then gives them back. "You know I can't read," she says. "What's a white man doin' here, talkin' to you for?"

"He gives me my free papers," I say. I look off, hoping Jamie's still in the trees, but my heart tells me he's gone. "That's my Jamie." I sit right down in the dirt and start to cry.

I go to see Will Stephens that night. He looks over my papers and says, "Well, Belle, this means that you are a free woman."

"But you give a lot of money for me," I say.

"And every penny was worth it," he says.

"If I stay and work real hard for you, can

you give me money to buy Jamie?"

"I don't think that Marshall will sell him, but in a court of law these papers just might be enough to set him free."

"He'd kill my boy before he'd give him papers! Marshall needs money real bad and I'm thinking if I pay him enough for two people, he'll let Jamie go."

Will shakes his head. "It would take you a lifetime to pay off that kind of debt."

"I got no place to go. The thing is, you want me, I'm asking to stay here anyway," I say.

Will Stephens push his hands through his hair the way he does when he thinking. "I'll tell you what. I'm sure Lucy has told you that the doctor said I have got to take Martha to the mountains for a few weeks. He thinks the cooler air will make it easier for her. I'm leaving Ben in charge and I need to count on you to support him. As soon as I get back, we'll deal with this. Then, if you choose not to go through the court I will find you the money. When you decide the action you want to take, we will send a solicitor with your proposal."

I keep myself from saying more. I know Will Stephens is good as his word. If he says he'll find me the money, then he'll find me the money. But I know for sure that his law man will do no good. We tried that over and over. No. I know Marshall got to see me. He got to see me on my knees.

The morning Will and Miss Martha drive out, it's so hot and dry, the wheels on the wagon sound like they're going over cracklin'. We all know Will don't want to leave this place, but he's the kind of man who do right by his wife.

Almost two weeks go by. I know Will Stephens is coming back any day. Every morning I look out for Jamie, but he don't come back. After seeing my boy, I can't think of nothing else. I know I got to help him, get him out of there, away from Marshall. I keep waiting for Jamie to show up so I can tell him about the money that Will's giving me so I can get him free.

When Jamie don't come, I think, I got to get over there before Will gets back. I got it in my head that just maybe, if I talk to Marshall, he'll see my way. I'll show Marshall my papers, maybe even tell him the cap'n's my daddy.

I wait until suppertime, when Ben and Lucy's eating, then I send George over to them, say my head's hurting and I'm gonna have a lay-down. Then I head out. I walk fast and don't think about nothing, so I don't get too scared to keep going. When I get there, I head right to the kitchen house. I count my steps to keep myself from turning back. One, two, three. One, two, three. I don't look around, I just watch my feet heading to the kitchen house. One, two, three. One, two, three.

Sure enough, there he is with Beattie.

He don't say nothing, just stares at me. Scared as I am, I stare back. It's five years, maybe, since I see Marshall. I know he's got no more than thirty years on him, but he looks almost as old as the cap'n before he dies. Most of his hair is gone from the top of his head, and his color's more yellow than white. I know he's drinking because I can smell it coming off him. I walk over and hold open my papers for him to see. I say, "I'm a free woman, Marshall. Your daddy, he gives me the free papers a long time ago. Now I'm wanting to buy my Jamie from you. I'll give you the money for two strong men."

Marshall's slow to stand, but when he does, his face gets all red. "Have you lost your mind?" he says. "What is she doing here?" He look around like there's somebody who's gonna give him the answer.

I keep talking. "I'm hoping it'll be all right with you," I say, "if I send Jamie to Philadelphia. He can live there like a white boy."

"Live like a . . . He's a nigra, you fool! He's a nigra!"

"But he's white as you. You're his daddy," I say. "It's time you stand behind that."

"Get out of here!"

"Marshall," I say, "Jamie's your boy —"

Beattie's standing behind Marshall, shaking her head at me to stop talking, but it's too late. I'm gonna say what I got to say.

"He's your boy, Marshall! What're you gonna do? Are you just gonna sell him like you're selling everybody else?"

Marshall moves so fast that I don't see his fist coming. It hits so hard, everything spins.

"Where's my gun?" he starts hollering. Beattie's yelling and crying and holding him back. "Run, Belle, run!"

So I do.

CHAPTER FIFTY-THREE

Lavinia

The air shimmered from the heat. One unbearably hot afternoon toward the end of August, I insisted that Elly stay indoors, away from the intense rays of the sun. Fanny sat with her, the two of them dressing Elly's baby doll. Miss Martha was restless, and I tried to soothe her by reading aloud. Jamie, who had been out since early morning, had returned only a short while before. He sat slouched in a chair watching me. His attitude toward the new me, the person minus the laudanum, was wary. In return, I was watchful of him. I had searched my room for Belle's papers and realized they were missing. I guessed by process of elimination that Jamie had them in his possession, and though I wanted to query him, I was not in a hurry to confront this sullen boy.

Jamie's disagreeable attitude baffled Miss Martha, and though he was still kind to her, he said not a friendly word to the rest of us. A few days before, I had gone to Mama Mae and brought up the subject of Jamie's presence in the house. I had told her that even I could see it was time for a change and I was ready to carry through on the promise I had made.

Still protective of my recovery, Mama suggested that I wait for another week to have my discussion with Jamie. She thought I should gain more strength to cope with not only Jamie's response but Miss Martha's reaction as well. I was relieved, for I dreaded the outcome.

My mother-in-law reached out her hand to stop my reading, then asked Fanny to readjust the window blinds to let in more of a breeze. As Fanny carried out the request, she peeked through the wooden slats. At her sudden cry, Jamie jumped up and ran to join her. His startled gasp had me put down my book. I went to the window as well.

Rankin was down at the big barn alongside a rough-looking stranger. They had Eddy, Fanny's husband, tied between them, and while the stranger pulled, Rankin prodded the captive from behind. The blinds clanked as Fanny dropped the cord and at once was outdoors, sprinting across the yard to her husband. She catapulted herself into the middle of the three men and threw her arms around Eddy to hold him back. Rankin yanked her away and shoved her to the ground as they pulled Eddy on toward the quarters.

When Marshall came out of the barn, he was carrying a horsewhip. Fanny, who had fallen to her knees, begged his help, but he ignored her and strode on down the hill, following the men to the quarters. Fanny did not get up but knelt in the hot sun, staring after them until Beattie ran to her from the kitchen house. Within minutes, the two of them were with us in the bedroom. Fanny was frantic.

"They gonna sell him." She shook my arm. "They gonna sell my Eddy. Please, please, Miss Abinia, don't let that happen. He a good man, you know this, please do somethin', please do somethin', Abinia."

Miss Martha's voice was high and thin, but she spoke with authority. "Get the captain," she said. "I'm certain there's been a mistake."

"No! No!" Fanny bolted to Miss Martha's side. "They takin' him, there no mistake, they takin' him. Beattie say the nigga trader here, he sendin' him off."

Mama Mae and Uncle Jacob, doing inventory down in the basement storage rooms, had heard the commotion and joined us. Mama's breathing was heavy, and she dropped onto the nearest chair. Fanny ran to her while Elly, frightened at Fanny's distress, went to Uncle Jacob.

"They got Eddy," Fanny sobbed, "that nigga trader here for Eddy. I think they takin' others from the quarters, too."

Beattie spoke for the first time. She whispered. "They take most everybody from the quarters. They all tied up. They leavin' tomorrow." Unable to look at us, she covered her face with her hands and spoke through them. "I hear them talkin'. They talk 'bout takin' Mama and Jamie, too."

Her muffled words were all too clear. I turned to Mama Mae. "That's impossible!" I said.

Mama Mae looked at me but didn't answer.

"Somebody got to do somethin'! They takin' my Eddy!" Fanny cried again.

"For God's sake!" I said helplessly, then turned to Beattie. "Do you know anything more? What else, Beattie?"

"All I know is they gettin' most everybody from down the quarters ready to go in the mornin'. And they talk 'bout sellin' Mama and Jamie."

"That can't be! You're mistaken!" I shouted, and stomped my foot.

Beattie shook her head. She whispered, "No, Abinia, I knows this. Masta Marshall say if I tell about Mama and Jamie, he sell my boys."

"And the others? Papa George? Is Marshall planning to sell him, too?" I asked.

"No," Beattie said, "he say that he needin' him."

"He can't do this!" I clutched her arm and willed myself not to panic.

Beattie spoke in a rush. "He say he needin' the money, that he got to sell. He say Mama gettin' old, but she still bring a good price. Fanny and Uncle here take care of the house. Masta Marshall say he gonna sell Jamie after Belle come and tell him that she have her free papers and that she wantin' to buy her Jamie. Masta Marshall say he gonna sell her boy to make sure she don't get him."

Mama Mae's face had turned ashen, and she looked as though she might topple off the chair. I rushed to her side. "Are you all right, Mama?" I asked. When she didn't answer, I grabbed the glass of water from Miss Martha's bedside stand and gave it to her. While she drank, I ran to look out the window. "Beattie," I said, "go back to the kitchen. He mustn't know that you were

562

here. Go now, while it's clear. Hurry! And say nothing."

"But Mama —" Beattie began.

Mama Mae finally spoke. "Go, chil'. Go now, quick."

I pushed Beattie through the open door, then closed it behind her. "Jamie," I said, "you must go to Belle — tonight."

Miss Martha sat up and swung her legs over the side of the bed. She reached out toward Jamie, and he went to her side.

"We'll hide you until dark," I said. "Mama, you'll have to go with him."

"That not gonna work." Mama shook her head. "That the first place Masta Marshall look for me. I stay here. Jamie get to Belle, they get away."

"Mama, please," I pleaded. "You must go with them."

"I stayin' here, Abinia. I talk to Masta Marshall. That the best way for me. I don't leave George. Masta Marshall know this."

"Mama, please!"

"No, Abinia, I stay here," Mama Mae said, "and that be that." She leaned back heavily in her chair.

Jamie knelt beside Miss Martha but looked at me. "Should I go now?"

"No. We'll hide you until tonight." My mind frantically sought out a hiding place:

the attic, the basement, the smokehouse? Suddenly, there were loud voices, then footsteps on the stairs, and the bedroom door flew open before I could reach it. Rankin stood beside Marshall, his drunken smirk directed toward me.

"Marshall! What in heaven's name?" I asked.

"Get her out of here," he said, nodding toward Elly. Uncle Jacob, who had taken the child onto his lap, began to rise, but I motioned for him to sit down again.

"No, Marshall," I said, "I want Elly here with me."

"Very well," Marshall said, "suit yourself. Let her see the mess you've created." His words were slurred, and even from a distance, he stank of liquor. He strode over to Jamie and yanked him to his feet. "Boy," he said, "you're coming with us."

Jamie was too frightened to react. Miss Martha straightened herself. "Sir," she said in a formidable tone, "send for the captain. He'll settle this."

"Mother, I've had enough!" Marshall turned on her. "This is a nigra's boy! Look at him! He's a nigra!" He grabbed Jamie's neck and shoved his face toward her as Jamie cried out in pain.

"Isabelle!" Miss Martha screamed for me

to intervene.

"Marshall, don't do this." I stepped forward and forced myself to speak calmly. "Jamie means everything to her."

Marshall tossed Jamie to the side and came toward me. "You! You've created this insanity. But it will stop. The boy is sold," he said.

My terror drove me to speak. "But Marshall! He is yours! You'd sell your own son?"

There was an awful silence before I felt the crack of his hand across my face. My ears rang, and it took a moment to balance myself. With all the fury from the years I had held back, I swung at him. My resounding slap surprised him, but Rankin's drunken guffaw enraged Marshall further.

Before his hands could reach my neck, Mama Mae stepped between the two of us. "Masta Marshall, you stop this," she said.

Marshall did stop, but his voice took on a deadly tone when he addressed me. "You are as insane as my mother. Prepare yourself. You'll be leaving in the morning. Both of you are going to the hospital in Williamsburg. I'll see to it that you'll never leave."

"You wouldn't do that!" I said, knowing full well he had the authority to do so. "What of Elly?"

"Fanny stays," he said.

Before I could respond, Marshall motioned Rankin toward Jamie. As Rankin pulled Jamie from her side, Miss Martha began a shrill scream. Jamie jerked away and went back to her. He dropped down and clasped her hands. Everyone watched, unable to look away. "Shhh, Grandmother," he said, "it will be all right." She quieted, and he continued, "I'll come back for you, Grandmother. I'll come back." Then he stood of his own accord and fixed his one good eye on Marshall.

"Get that nigra out of here!" Marshall shouted to Rankin.

After they had gone, Mama Mae was the first to speak. "Abinia," she said, "you gonna have to take Elly and get to Will Stephens before it too late."

Miss Martha's wails had reached a familiar pitch, and I knew what to do. I mixed a heavy dose of the drops and water. The very smell offered the escape that I ached for, and though my hands shook with desire for the drug, I gave the drink to the woman who needed it and did not take any for myself.

It was dark when I woke Elly. As I dressed her, I explained that she must be very quiet, that she must not speak. "We are going on an adventure," I said.

"Will Fanny come?" she asked as I fastened the buttons on her shoes. I put my finger to my lips and nodded. Mama Mae and Fanny came to the door. I could see their fear.

"Hurry," Mama said, "George say to come now."

"Here!" Fanny thrust a small sack into my hands, eager to relieve herself of it.

"Was she sleeping soundly?" I asked, biting my lip to keep from crying.

Fanny nodded.

"Did you empty the whole box?" I asked.

Fanny nodded again.

"Did you remember the pearls?" I asked. Fanny, speechless from fear, motioned that they were in the bag.

Mama Mae hurried us on; Papa George was waiting downstairs. He had seen the signal from the kitchen house, which meant that Beattie's work was done. Uncle Jacob was with Papa George at the front door.

"Please, Uncle, reconsider?" I said to him.

"No, I stay," Uncle Jacob said, "I too old for runnin'. 'Sides, I look after Beattie and Miss Martha."

Papa went over our last-minute instructions before we left the house. He would lead us into the woods and up past the cemetery to bypass the quarters. If the plan worked, if Beattie could get to Jamie and Eddy to cut their ropes, they would be free to meet us in the woods. But, Papa warned, we must all leave without them, and no carrying on if they weren't waiting for us. He looked at Fanny as he spoke, and we all knew what was in the balance for her. Eddy was her life.

"Go on, now," Uncle Jacob said, quietly opening the door, "Allah go with you."

I grasped one of Elly's hands, and Fanny took the other. Elly was warned again not to speak, and I prayed that I could count on her silence.

As our eyes adjusted to the dark night, we were more easily able to follow Papa. When we saw Eddy standing in the trees, Fanny gasped and let go of Elly's hand to run to him. In the far pasture, one of the horses neighed, and Elly, forgetting her promise, asked Papa which horse had called out. As one, all the adults shushed her.

Eddy spoke quickly. Beattie had come to them after successfully using the drops. She assured Eddy that Marshall was in a drugged sleep in the kitchen house and that Rankin was passed out down at the quarters.

"Where's Jamie?" someone asked.

"He go straight to Belle," Eddy said. "I

tell him wait, but that boy don't listen."

Our plan was that once we reached Belle's house, Elly and I would stay behind. I planned to appeal to Will Stephens to shelter me, then assist me with passage to Williamsburg. I felt hopeful, given the present circumstances, that Meg's parents would be willing to help Elly and me. The rest of the party would set out on foot to find their way north. That journey seemed their only hope.

"Let's go," Papa said, leading us deep into the woods. "Ben say he get us goin' the right way."

We walked quickly, and though Elly did her best to keep up, she began to complain as she grew tired. After Eddy picked her up and carried her, the pace increased so that I soon found it a challenge to maintain the speed. Ahead, I heard Mama breathing heavily. We were almost at the clearing when she fell. Papa helped her up and Mama leaned heavily when he walked her over to sit on a fallen log. She was angry with herself and spoke sharply to Papa when he said that we would stop for a short rest. He put his arm around her shoulders, and un- like herself, Mama Mae burst into tears.

"Everythin' gon' be all right, Mazzie." Papa used an endearment I had not heard before, and the tenderness of it burned my throat.

"But what gonna happen to Beattie and her boys?"

"Mae, you know this the only way. How she gonna run with those lil ones? And you know she not gonna leave them behind."

"How we gonna live? Where we gonna go, George? We got nothin'."

Mama's words reminded me of the sack Fanny had filled for me back at the house. I opened the bag containing all of my mother-in-law's jewelry. The stones sparkled when I removed a handful. "Take off your head rag, Mama," I said, "and put these under it."

Mama Mae blew her nose and shook her head. "No, those for you and Elly. You gonna need that."

"Take them, Mama," I said, forcing the jewels into her hands, "they're yours as much as they are mine." I did not wait for a further response but untied Mama's familiar red head wrap, nestled the jewelry in her gray hair, and retied the scarf. When Papa announced that it was time to leave, I saw how slowly Mama rose, and I wondered if I should have given the jewels to Fanny. But there was no time.

"Come on. Come on," Eddy said urgently, and we were off once more.

Ben and Belle were waiting at the clearing by the edge of the trees. "Where's Jamie?" Belle asked anxiously.

"He not here?" Eddy asked. "He go ahead. He say he comin' to you."

"Eddy, he don't come," she said.

"He got free, I knows that," Eddy said. "Soon's that nigga trader pass out, Beattie cut the rope."

Belle's voice shook. "Well, there's no time to wait," she said, "you all got to go."

Ben nodded. "She right, Papa."

Everyone fell silent, uncertain. Belle pushed them away. "You go on," she said, "when Jamie gets here, I'll send him after you. You go now."

Mama held back. She embraced Belle, then pulled me close. "Abinia," she whispered, "I always your mama."

I kissed her but dared not say a tender word. "Mama," I said, "don't worry about Beattie and her boys. When I'm settled, I'll send for them."

Papa reached for Mama Mae's hand. Ben led the way. Belle and I watched as they disappeared into the dark, and after a final look back at the woods for Jamie, Belle hurried Elly and me into her house. I hesitated at the doorway. "I think we ought to go directly to Will Stephens," I said.

571

Belle pulled me in. "Lavinia, Will Stephens not back yet. He's up at the springs with Miss Martha."

"What! What do you mean? He isn't here?"

"They're coming back any day now. Miss Martha's going to have a baby. It's too hot for her here. Will took her up to the mountains, to Salt Springs."

I went cold from fear. "Belle! I never would have come had I known. We can't stay here. There is too much danger in that."

"It's gonna work, Lavinia. You'll hide with Ben and Lucy," Belle said.

"No. No! We can't take that chance," I said. "He'll kill Ben if he finds me with him."

"Ben say he'll hide you until Will Stephens comes home."

"Dear God, he'll kill us all." In my panic, I began to pace. "I have to go back, Belle. I have to go back!"

Belle caught my arm and turned me toward her. "Lavinia. What you going back to? There's nothing left. Marshall's not right in his head no more. You know this."

"What should I do?" I pleaded.

Elly began to cry. "What's wrong, Mama? Where's Fanny, Mama? I want Fanny."

I forced myself to calm down, to reassure

my child. I took her to a pallet in the corner and soothed her until she fell asleep. Then I paced as Belle and I waited.

Late in the night, when Ben returned, he was wet with perspiration. "They get a good start," he said. He wasted no time. He went to my sleeping daughter and scooped her up. I looked again at the purple line from his jaw to his neck and to his missing ear. What gave him this courage? I wondered.

"Ben, are you certain about doing this?" I asked.

He looked at me as he had when I was a child. "Come, Abinia," he said, leading the way.

That night we slept off and on until the heat of the day pounding through the shingled roof made our hiding space almost unbearable. I doubt we could have survived in the enclosure if trees hadn't shaded the cabin. When Ben opened the small trapdoor, Elly and I hung our heads out to breathe in the blessed cool air. Lucy, Ben's wife, handed up water, but the door was soon closed again. The small crawl space we lay in was directly under the roof of a small lean-to attached to the back of Ben and Lucy's cabin. On our arrival, I thought we should hide under the floorboards, in the pit where their root vegetables were stored. But Ben said no, that was the first place someone would check.

Ben's cabin was unusual in that it had this small unknown space. I do not know why it existed, but I suspect we were not the first to be hidden there.

I explained our situation as best I could to Elly. Initially, her cooperation surprised me, but I soon realized that she had long been aware of the terrible tension in our home. Her one concern was for Fanny. I did my best to reassure her and tried to pass the time with whispered stories of my childhood, stories that included Fanny and Beattie. I tried to keep Elly cool by wetting her clothing with water; fortunately, in her exhaustion, she often dozed.

To our great relief, Lucy opened the trapdoor late in the afternoon to hand up some corn bread and milk. I guessed from her cool manner that Lucy resented and feared having us, and I did not blame her. To add to this, though Lucy was a stout woman, it was easy to see that she was carrying a child. I attempted a whispered acknowledgment of gratitude, but she only nodded.

We had dropped our heads out to gulp at the cool air when Lucy hissed for us to get back up. She did not wait to slam the trapdoor shut, once again enclosing Elly and me in the smothering dark. Soon after, we heard horses, and then, to my horror, I heard Marshall's voice. I placed my hand on Elly's mouth to remind her of her promise not to respond should her father call out her name. But he did not. Instead, I heard him tell Lucy that he had been up to Will Stephens's house, and finding him not home, he had gone through it in a hunt for me. He had gone next to the kitchen house and, finding that empty as well, had searched it. Marshall did not get off his horse but said only, "I don't suppose you'd be stupid enough to hide anyone?"

"Oh no, Masta Marshall," Lucy said, "I know not to hide nobody."

"Where's Ben?"

"He workin' the niggas down the field."

"And Belle?" he asked. "Where is she?"

"I don't see that girl, Masta Marshall," Lucy said. "That Belle never here doin' her job! She run off all over the place! That Masta Will, he neva get work outta her. She good for noth—"

Marshall gave an ugly laugh. "Don't you worry. I'll keep a lookout for her, and if I find her, I can tell you, she won't give him any more trouble." He began to ride away, then turned back. "Lucy," he said, as though this were an afterthought, "you tell Ben that his whole family will hang if I find out he has helped any of my runaways."

"No, sir, Masta Marshall, Ben neva do that," Lucy said.

For a long while after he left, Lucy did not open the door to give us air. I waited until I thought that we might be in danger of suffocation before I tapped on the boards. When Lucy responded, her face was still slack with fear.

"Where is Ben?" I asked.

She shrugged.

"Belle?"

She shook her head.

During the next long night, Lucy opened the door twice. Elly slept fitfully, and I slept not at all. Over and over I played out various conclusions to this nightmare. None of them ended happily, and by morning, convinced that my surrender was the only solution, I was near desperate to act. Yet I knew I could not go forward without Ben's direction.

The wait felt interminable.

CHAPTER FIFTY-FOUR

Belle

After Ben take Lavinia and Elly to his house, I sit up all night in case Jamie shows up. I think of Beattie and how scared she's got to be, waiting for morning. I think of Uncle Jacob, left in the big house with Miss Martha, and how he got to carry on by himself. I wonder how far they got, how Mama's holding up. And where's my Jamie?

In the morning of that first day when Lavinia's hiding under the roof, Ben says he got to get out and work the fields. He knows that Marshall is likely coming over here, and he says we got to make this look like any other day. He tells Lucy and me to keep working and when Marshall comes, we're to say, "Yessir." Nothing else, just "Yessir."

Late afternoon, Marshall does ride up. I'm taking milk down to the springhouse, but I hear him ride up and stay back so he don't see me.

I wait all day, but after it gets dark again, I tell Ben I can't take no more. I got to find Jamie. Maybe he's laying somewhere needing my help, or maybe he just hiding in the trees. Worse yet, maybe he goes back up to Miss Martha. I know Marshall and Rankin are out far, looking for everybody, so I'm sure they're gone for the night.

First Ben says no, we got to stay here, we got to wait for Will Stephens. I say I'm going anyway. Ben don't want me going alone, so he says he's coming with me.

There's half a moon up when we head out, taking the back way 'round past the cemetery, then into the basement of the big house. We walk real quiet, like when we was little and playing at making no noise. Heel, toe, heel, toe. I listen good before I open the door, the one leading to the hall. Everything's dark, nobody's around, so we get upstairs fast and go straight to Miss Martha's rooms, where I know Uncle got to be. There's one lamp burning, and sure enough, Uncle's sitting beside the bed next to Miss Martha, who's sleeping like a baby. Ben stays standing back at the door. I don't know that he's ever been up in Miss Martha's room before.

"Uncle!" I whisper real quiet. He don't hear me, so I say it again. This time he looks at me, but he just sits there, so I go on over. Then I stop. Something's wrong. I stand there, looking 'round, until I make out that Miss Martha don't look right. She's too quiet, and when I get close, I see her eyes open, her mouth open, but she's not breathing no more.

"She carry on somethin' awful," Uncle says. "I give her drops, but she still screamin' for her Jamie, so I give her more. I never dose her before, so I keep puttin' drops in the water and give it to her till she get quiet."

"She gone," I say.

Uncle Jacob just keep looking at her like his eyes are gonna wake her up.

"Uncle!" I shake his arm. When he looks at me, I say, "You go get Beattie. Tell her to get up here." Uncle Jacob nods, but he don't move. "You got to go fast, Uncle." I kiss the top of his old white head, then pull him up and send him out the door. He walks past Ben like he don't see him. "Go on," I say, "go down and get Beattie. Send her up here." He don't say nothing, but he heads on down the stairs. I go back to check out Miss Martha.

"For sure she's gone," I say to Ben. I peek out the window, see that Uncle Jacob's almost at the kitchen house.

"Come on, Belle! Let's get outta here," Ben says.

"Wait," I say. Sure enough, I see Beattie come running out of the kitchen house, heading up to the big house. "Beattie's coming," I say to Ben. We head down the stairs and wait for Beattie at the back door. She comes in crying, she's so happy to see us.

"You see Jamie?" I ask.

She nod. "I think maybe I see him one time," she say, "other side of the barn. After everybody go, I go out lookin' for him, but I don't see him again."

"You find him, you tell him to come to me," I say.

"Belle! We got to go!" Ben says.

Beattie look up the stairs. "I goin' up to see Miss Martha."

"She's gone," I say.

"That's what Uncle say. I go see for myself," say Beattie.

Ben and me head out, same way we come. We go up and 'round the big-house cemetery, then down past the apple and peach trees, until we head past the quarters. It's plenty dark, but we both know this land so good, we know just where to go. Ben's the first to hear the horses, then we both hear the talk. We get down low.

"Uhhh!" Ben says.

"Shh," I whisper, but I raise up to look at what he sees.

There they is, all tied together, Rankin and two men sitting up on horses, pushing everybody on. Everbody. Mama, Papa . . . then I see Jamie! He's tied up, too. They're heading them all to the quarters.

"You see Marshall?" I ask Ben.

"No. He's prob'ly still out lookin' for Abinia."

"What're we gonna do?"

"We got to go back to the big house, catch Beattie," Ben says.

"What's she gonna do?" I ask.

"I don't know, but we got to think of somethin'," Ben says, and grabs my arm.

By the time we get into the house, Beattie's coming down the steps, carrying the lamp from Miss Martha's room. She almost drops it when she sees us. "What you two doin', scarin' me like that?" she says.

"Shh," Ben says, "put out that light. Rankin back, and they got everybody."

"Papa, Mama —" I say.

"No!" Beattie says. Then she sit right down on the steps and starts to cry. "Marshall says he catch 'em, he sell 'em all, even Papa."

Ben says, "Beattie, there no time for cryin'."

"But they all gonna get sold!" She cryin' hard. "Mama, Papa —"

"Stop cryin' and put out that light!" Ben says. "We got to think of somethin' to do."

Beattie tries to work the lamp, but she's shaking so bad Ben grabs it from her. Between them both, they drop the light. The fire catches the tablecloth, and we all got to stomp on it to put it out. Then Ben gets the idea.

"Beattie," he says, "tonight you gonna get a house fire goin' up here." Beattie and me look at Ben like he's gone in the head. But he keeps talking. "When everybody up here puttin' out the fire, I cut everybody loose. This time they cross over the river by the smokehouse and head up that way. It hard, but it give 'em a better chance, 'cause Papa know the way."

"How I s'posed to get a fire burnin'?" Beattie ask.

"It burn easy," Ben say. "Belle and me get it set up for you. Then we go down other side of the quarters and we watch from the trees. All you got to do is wait till everythin' is settled, then if anybody around, you say you got to check on Miss Martha, get up here, and start the fire. Get it goin' real good and get out. When they see the fire, Rankin and the men get up here to put it out. When they doin' that, we cut everybody loose. You get your boys and run with everybody."

"Oh, Ben! You sure 'bout this?" Beattie say.

"What else we gonna do?" Ben say.

"Belle?" Beattie ask.

"We got to do something," I say.

It seems all night that Ben and me is waiting in the trees, watching. Ben starts breathing hard when we see the fire going up at the big house. Beattie get it going real good, but the trouble is, Marshall's still out looking for Lavinia, and Rankin don't see nothing because he's off getting drunk. The fire's coming out the windows by the time Rankin gets there, and he's so drunk his thinking ain't good. First he runs up to see for himself, then he starts calling for his men to carry up water. Ben and me, we don't wait no more. Ben goes to the quarters to cut the ropes, and I go to help Beattie with her boys. But Beattie's standing outside her kitchen door, crying. She's saying she don't know where Uncle got to. The fire's whooshin' and howlin', and I grab Beattie, tell her to get her boys and come on, there's no time, everybody's waiting on her. But she just keeps crying, worrying that Uncle's

583

in the big house. The fire's turning everything bright as day, and all I'm thinking is, We got to get out of here, so I hit Beattie and tell her to get her boys now!

When we get down to the quarters, Ben got everybody loose, and they're getting ready to go, but Mama's making a fuss. She says she won't go. She says everybody gets caught the first time because she can't run good, so she's staying, and that be that. Then Papa says if Mama stays, he stays, too, but Mama gets mad and says he got to go.

Ben says, "Papa, you got to take them out, show them the way. They needin' you for that."

So Papa says he'll get them on the way, then he's coming back for Mama.

Mama say, "George. You go, stay, help Beattie and her boys. I gonna be fine here." But we all know that Papa's bound to come back.

The big house fire is wild, and it looks like my Jamie is thinking of going up. I go to him quick. "Jamie. Miss Martha, she's gone," I say.

"What do you mean she's gone? How do you know?"

"I see her. She's dead," I say. "She takes too many drops. She's dead before the fire gets going. She's gone, Jamie."

"Marshall did this! He killed her! It's all because of him!"

"Come," I say, pushing him off. "You go with the others. After you get away, you write me. I'll send you money; you get your free papers."

"Come on!" Ben say. "We got to go!"

Fanny's crying, Beattie's crying, Papa's crying.

Ben says, "Each a you! Stop cryin'! Take the lil ones up and get goin'!"

Fanny takes up one of Beattie's boys, Eddy takes up another. Jamie looks at me like he asking me what to do. He's tall as me, but the way he looks at me now, he's still my baby boy. "You go," I say. "Quick, with the others. You write to me, I'll send you money."

Ben says, "Come on!" He pulls at Papa, and once he gets Papa going, everybody takes off running.

After they're gone, Mama just sits. The sky is red, and the roaring coming from the big house sounds like a storm. I tell Mama to come with me back to Will Stephens's, but she says she going up to her own place to wait for Marshall there. She's looking too sick to get there by herself, so I take her, but she don't even make it to the kitchen house before she got to sit down again. She says that her chest's heavy on her, and I see that her breathing ain't right. She keeps telling me to get out of here, that she's gonna be fine.

"We'll just sit here, Mama, here in the grass, until you feel better." We sit, and she don't say nothing. I put my arms around her and hold her up while she closes her eyes. When I get her going again, she only makes it as far as the kitchen house. By then the big house fire's shooting up all over the place, and the roof is going in.

"You think it come down here, burn this kitchen house?" I ask Mama.

"No," she says, "this place built far enough away so a fire start down here, it don't set fire to the big house."

I get Mama sitting down, and she tells me again that I got to leave. I know she's right. I give her a hug, say to hold on until I come with Will Stephens to get her. I'm heading out the door when Mama calls me back. She's taking off her head rag and pulling out pearls from her hair. I know them from the big house. They're Miss Martha's! Mama wraps them tight in her head rag and pushes it in my pocket. "You get this to the others," she says.

I go to leave, but I hear Mama talking to herself. "My head feel cold," she says, patting at her ears and looking lost as a little girl.

I take off my own dirty green head scarf and wrap it around her head, then I kiss her and say, "You stay right here, Mama. I'm coming back for you."

I know I got to go. At the back of my neck, I can feel that something bad's gonna happen. I turn to the kitchen door standing open, and there I see him. His face is so black from the fire, I don't hardly know who he is, but when he says my name, everything in me goes soft and my mind stops working. Next thing I know, Rankin's pulling me up the hill, where Marshall's waiting, rope in his hand, saying I'm gonna hang for setting fire to his house.

They're about to tie my hands when up the hill comes Mama. She's yelling at Marshall that he better stop, and he better stop right now! She's talking to Marshall like he's a child, and sure enough, he stops and listens to what Mama's saying. She's puffing real hard by the time she gets to us, but she knows what Marshall's got in mind, and she comes right on over to pull me away.

"Marshall! What you think you doin'?" Mama says. "You don't think you do enough already?"

587

Marshall comes to grab at me. I jump behind Mama. He's got the rope in his hands, but Mama stays standing there, looking straight at him.

"Masta Marshall," she says, "you gonna hurt the mama that takes care of you when you a lil boy?"

Marshall grabs for me again, but Mama gets in his way.

"Marshall," she says, "you stop this now! What you doin'! The debil have you? Ever since that time lil Sally die, I see how that temper of yours hurtin' people. You got to stop yourself! All this time you usin' my girls like they some animals down at the barn. You make all those babies, they white, they cullad, but you don't pay no mind. Your Elly, she a sister to Jamie, to Moses, to Beattie's boys — they all her brothers! Yes, they is! But they all gone. They all run from you. Abinia gone, lil Elly gone, even my Beattie go with her babies, runnin' from you. What you gonna do now?"

One more time Marshall reaches for me, and one more time Mama steps in the way.

"Marshall!" Mama say. "I say this enough! Now you wanna kill Belle? She your sista! You leave her alone! It time you know that she your sista. First you have the chil' with her, now you gonna kill her! You the debil

588

himself, you kill your own sista!"

Marshall stands real quiet. He looks at me funny. I can see this is the first time he hears that I'm his sister.

But Mama don't stop. "That's right, Marshall!" she say. "Belle your sista. Your daddy love this girl, but not the way you and Miss Martha think. I there when she born, and I know that Belle your daddy's chil'."

Now Marshall is fixed on Mama. She keeps talking.

"That's right, Marshall! You come at me! I the one who burn this house down. I the one hidin' Abinia. I the one who tell Beattie to go, I even know where they run to, but I don't tell you nothin'."

Marshall is yelling when he grabs at Mama. I try to pull her away when he starts putting the rope on her, but Rankin hits me from the back and I go down.

CHAPTER FIFTY-FIVE

Lavinia

We in Lucy's cabin knew nothing of what happened during that long night. Near dawn, Ben rushed in. His distressed words filtered through the ceiling boards. He was going for Will Stephens, he said. Lucy pleaded with him to stay, afraid for him to leave the property without a pass. He had to go, he argued. Marshall and Rankin had Belle. They were certain that she had knowledge of my whereabouts, and they were going to hang her if she was not forthcoming.

On hearing this, I could no longer hold back. I knew Belle would die before putting all of us in danger, and I knew Marshall would not hesitate to kill her. I became wild and pounded on the trapdoor until Ben opened it. He tried to quiet me, but I no longer could be reasoned with.

"Let me down!" I insisted. "Let me down!" I would have leaped to the floor had

Ben not reached for me, and once on my feet, I began to run.

But Elly was not to be left behind. She, too, jumped into Ben's arms, following my lead. I shouted for her to go back, to stay with Ben, but she refused. I couldn't think of what to do, so I grabbed her hand and began to run again, staying to the path that ran along the wide stream. It seemed we had been running forever when I heard the whinny of horses ahead. I grabbed Elly and pulled her with me into the shrubs, where I signaled her silence. I heard horses approach and then a man's voice.

"Rankin," I breathed, then pushed both of us into the underbrush. We stayed down while they passed a distance from us but close enough for me to see them and learn from their conversation that they were again looking for runaways.

Where's Marshall? I wondered. Where's Belle? We were up and running again as soon as I thought it safe. I pulled Elly along, frustrated at her pace. Finally, she could go on no longer and began to resist me. She pulled back, and her hand slipped from mine. I might have stopped to reason with her, but as we grew closer to home, a strong smell of smoke began to permeate the air, and new fear fueled me. I raced ahead of her, oblivious to my child. My legs were numb, unused to this speed, and my lungs threatened to refuse their purpose. I forbade myself to think that I was too late and focused all my strength on moving toward home. Then I misjudged. Meaning to take a shortcut over the stream, I left the path and tried to dash through the trees, where, to my horror, I found myself trapped. I ripped and pulled to free my long skirts from the thorns of the blackberry brambles that snared me. As I tore my way out, Elly caught up to me again. She clung to my arm, sobbing and trying to hold me back. But a seven-year-old is no match for a grown woman, and in my frenzy, I pushed her onto the ground. She stared at me with unbelieving eyes.

"Stay there," I pleaded. I turned and ran again down the path until I reached the stream. I meant to cross over by stepping on the rocks in the shallow water, but it was a mistake to not remove my shoes. Halfway over, I slipped on the river stones and fell into the water with a splash. The cold water shocked me, and for a moment I sat stunned, water bubbling by, until I looked up and recognized our springhouse on the other side of the stream. The gray building reminded me of how close I was to home. I rose, my skirts soaked and heavy, and scrambled across the water by clinging to the jutting rocks.

At the base of our hill, I leaned forward to breathe, gasping for air. Somehow Elly had reached my side again, and this time she clung like a kitten to my wet skirts. I was terrified of what she might see ahead, but it was too late now, so I grasped her hand, and together we crested the hill. I froze. With a whimper, Elly dropped my hand as she sank to the ground. I moved forward slowly, as though in a dream.

Our massive old oak tree stood near the top of the hill, its lush green leaves shading the thick branch that bore the weight of a hanging body. My eyes refused to look up, but I had already recognized the handmade shoes pointing down. My chest ached. I leaned forward, salivating, retching. I must get to the house, I thought, stumbling ahead. I'll get a knife, I thought, I'll cut her down. She'll breathe again; she'll be all right.

But there was no house to enter. I stared in disbelief. Our home had dissolved; rubble and smoke marked its base. I fought to make sense.

I heard a shout. Words sizzled through the August heat. It was Jamie's voice. "You killed her! You killed her!"

I dared to look again at the tree. Marshall stood beside it. Jamie walked toward him with long purposeful strides, a young man stepping as an adult. He carried a shotgun. Flies buzzed and a dog whined.

Marshall looked my way. "Lavinia." He waved and called as though pleased to see me.

Jamie aimed the gun at Marshall. "Father!" He shouted the word. "Father!"

Marshall turned to face him. The gun blasted, and Marshall flew back, bits of him scattering like seeds from a dandelion head. I couldn't control my screams as I rushed forward. I pulled the gun from Jamie. "Run," I cried, "run."

I waited and stared but could not approach the tree. Wails of anguish signaled that others were coming up the hill. I turned to face them, pleading for someone to get the wagon, for someone to get Mama down. Then I sank onto the hot dry grass.

The wagon came clanking over the rocks. Lodo, our mule, balked at the scent of death, but the sharp smack of Eddy's whip pushed him forward. Finally, the mule stood under the oak, shivering and shining in the heat, the cart behind him.

"Be careful," I begged, not daring to

watch, but before I heard the thud, I looked up to see the bright green of Belle's head rag fall into the wagon. As Lodo began his descent, Papa's anguished cries pierced the very soul of our hill.

I was taken to jail when I insisted that I shot Marshall. The first day, filled with anguish, all I could do was pace. I could not get the terrible image of Mama out of my mind. I refused to see anyone until the second day, when I was told that Will Stephens had come on a matter that concerned my daughter.

It had been years since I had last seen Will. Now his worried eyes betrayed his calm manner. He sat opposite me.

"I thought you would want to know that Elly is taken care of," he said. "She is with Fanny in Belle's house. I had her taken to my house, but she carried on so that I took her down to Belle, thinking that might give her some comfort. Belle, though, is not herself, and Ben suggested that we bring Fanny in. That helped. Elly has settled."

I nodded.

"Lavinia," he said, his voice low. "You must speak up for yourself. We both know the truth."

"It was all my fault! It was all my fault!" I

said. Will attempted to reason with me, but I began to rant. Even to myself, I made little sense.

"I have sent for Mr. Madden," Will said before he left.

Will returned with Belle the following day, and he left as we fell into each other's arms. In her awful despair Belle needed to talk. I listened as she choked out her story.

Belle, in Rankin's grip, was made a witness to Mama Mae's murder. When Belle was released, she stumbled down to the kitchen house. Perhaps even Marshall was sated by her despair, for he did not pursue her. No one knew why Marshall stayed back on the hill when Rankin rode out to pursue Papa George and the others.

A few hours into the escape, the fugitives began to have doubts. Papa did not want to go on without Mama, and no one wanted to go on without Papa. Jamie was the first to turn back. Earlier in the week, telling no one, he had taken a gun from the house and hidden it under the smokehouse. Now he went to get it. The others had almost reached home when they heard the shotgun blast.

"And Jamie? Where is he now?" I asked.

She assured me that he was on his way to safety.

How I dreaded the next question. "Miss Martha? Uncle Jacob?"

I was relieved to know that Miss Martha had died before the fire. Uncle Jacob's body had not been found, though it was thought that he had gone back into the house and perished there.

"What became of Rankin?" I questioned.

No one knew, but Will had armed Ben and Papa, who were caring for what was left of Tall Oaks.

When Belle finished, I held her close to me for a long while. Before she left, I asked that she instruct everyone from my home to stay away. I was afraid of what they might say within hearing distance of the wrong ears.

When I was led to the bar, I pleaded guilty. It was the opinion of the court that I be prosecuted, and I remained in jail through September to await the trial. I was not unhappy to sit in the small cell, to eat the meager rations, nor to sleep on a pallet in the damp. In this manner I punished myself, not just for the death of Mama but also for the loss of Miss Martha and Uncle Jacob. Surely, I might have done something to save their lives. I gave little thought to

Marshall's end; in truth, I was relieved to be free of him.

As Will predicted, Mr. Madden came to my aid. Immediately, he, as my lawyer, insisted that I plead not guilty. In private quarters, he assured me that he knew I had not murdered Marshall. I would not admit to Mr. Madden what had taken place, knowing that if Jamie were tried as a Negro for the murder of a white man, it meant certain death. Instead, I argued that I was the guilty party, and in an effort to convince him, I unburdened myself of my past behavior, of the years of self-obliteration, of self-absorbency.

He peered over his spectacles as he listened carefully. After a long silence, he spoke. "My dear," he said in his gentlest voice, "it is possible for me to believe that you have been guilty of selfish deeds, for are you not now still acting in a selfish way?"

"Whatever do you mean?"

"You say that during your years of laudanum use, you were not a good mother, is that true?"

"Yes, I was in a haze. I left Elly's care to Fanny."

"And you would once again deprive your daughter of a mother?" he asked.

"But she has Fanny . . ." I began, then

stopped myself, for I saw his point. He needed no further words to convince me to allow him to defend me in the best way he saw fit.

On the opening day of the trial, Mr. Madden, together with another lawyer, argued that I had not shot Marshall but had been in shock when I confessed to the deed. Into the next day, they argued that Uncle Jacob had not only set the house afire but lain in wait for Marshall's return. He alone had access to a shotgun, which, they said, only could have come from the big house. They suggested that Uncle had made his escape, and they went so far as to say he had been seen as he made his way north. I am not certain the jury was completely convinced of Mr. Madden's argument, but I suspect that Marshall's reputation had an influence on their willingness to have me acquitted.

On the afternoon of my release, I was taken by carriage to Will's home. I exited at Belle's kitchen house, where I had a tear-filled reunion with Elly, Belle, and Fanny. It wasn't long before they had me in a water tub. I was not shy when all three insisted on helping me to scrub off the past month of grime, and I would have soaked there forever were I not expected up at Will's home for a celebratory supper. While I was in the tub, Belle washed my hair, and after she combed it dry, she piled it on top of my head. I dressed in Belle's clothes, which fit me surprisingly well, then kissed everyone before I set off.

Will's home was large, and when I entered, I felt a sense of familiarity. It was made of clapboard, and its layout was not unlike that of Tall Oaks. It was not as grand in size, and it lacked fine furniture and treasures, but the detailed woodwork and the fireplaces showed quality and skilled workmanship. The plastered walls were painted white, and the pine floors shone, though they did not have the luxury of carpets.

Lucy met me at the door, and I embraced her. "I will never forget your kindness," I said, and when I loosed her, she smiled.

Will appeared at the door of the parlor. "I thought I heard you," he said, then came to escort me into the room. He led me to his wife, who was seated on a blue-and-green upholstered chair next to the fire. Mr. Madden rose from the chair opposite her when I entered, but I waved him back into his seat.

Will's wife was a plain woman, but immediately, I sensed her kindness. I did not know what she knew of me, but her greeting was without judgment. She was pale and large with child, and I saw from her drawn look that she was not well. I did not take note of her dress, for my attention was drawn to the oversize slippers needed to accommodate her swollen feet. Soon after our introduction, Martha asked me to excuse her. She explained that her doctor had recommended she spend the majority of her time in bed until, as she worded it, her "blessing came." Lucy helped her from the room, and their receding silhouette stabbed me as I was reminded of Miss Martha and Mama Mae. I was saved from myself when Will suggested that we go in to dine.

Lucy was back to serve us, and though I had little appetite, it was wonderful to once again sample Belle's cooking. When Will offered a toast, I chose to drink from the water goblet rather than from the glass of red wine. I no longer had a taste for the liquid that had so negatively affected my life.

After dessert, the talk turned to my future. Will rose and offered to give me privacy with Mr. Madden. I asked him to stay, saying that I would welcome his input. I admitted that I was afraid to learn what my future held.

What did I want to do? Mr. Madden asked. Would I consider returning with him to Williamsburg, bringing Elly with me, of course? He assured me that his family would welcome the two of us. As a matter of fact, he said with a laugh, Meg — who was still unmarried — had elicited a promise that he would not return without me.

I thanked him with true sincerity for all he had done, and I said that he must not leave without a letter from me. I wished to express my gratitude to Meg and to Aunt Sarah for their kind offer. "But," I said, "I want to remain here. I will do whatever needs to be done to have that happen."

Mr. Madden was not surprised at my resolve to stay. Earlier, on his arrival, I had requested that he review my situation and act on my behalf. Now he told me of the results. He had been able to salvage one hundred acres, including what was left of Tall Oaks and its outbuildings. Will Stevens had agreed to buy the few remaining Negroes from the quarters. As I had requested, the emancipation papers for Papa, Eddy and Fanny, and Beattie and her three boys had been drawn up; I planned to ask them to stay on for the food and shelter I could provide. In time I would give them wages. Mr. Madden suggested that with ingenuity and hard work, we could make a success of a small farm. Then he made an offer that overwhelmed me. He would give me a loan, he said, to finance a new house. I was to repay this sum by sending a letter once a month to his family, telling them of my progress so they could all be partners in my achievements.

Mr. Madden received my tears of relief and gratitude with some embarrassment, while Will excused himself to check on his wife.

On Will's return, he extended his wife's offer for my use of their guest room. When I thanked my host and said that I was happy to retire to Belle's home, I did not need to explain myself further.

Later, when Will walked me back to the cabin, my relief was such that I could scarcely contain myself. Stimulated by the elixir of hope, I breathed deeply the crisp air of freedom. Elly and I could remain at Tall Oaks with our family, and we had the resources to begin again.

It was October. The orange moon was so large that Will and I both remarked at its beauty. When we reached the cabin, he took my ungloved hand in his. A shock of desire ran through me, and with it I knew how surely I still loved this man. Before I could throw myself into his arms, I quickly withdrew my hand, then offered my help if his wife should need it. I dared not linger and hastily said good night.

Back in Belle's cabin, I shared my news, and together we rejoiced. After Elly slept, I asked Belle of Jamie. He was, she told me, safe in Philadelphia. I told Belle that I would have Jamie's papers drawn up and sent to him. Belle thanked me, then told me of the day Jamie had brought her own papers.

"Do you want to join Jamie in Philadelphia?" I asked. "I could see to it."

Belle declined. Will had already extended the offer and given her permission to leave at any time, she said. Belle was silent as she studied her hands. When she looked up again, her eyes were moist. Could she ask for something else?

"Anything," I said.

Could she come back with me to live at Tall Oaks?

I went on my knees and gathered her hands in mine. "Of course you can come home," I said.

Early the following morning Ben arrived on horseback, trailing a horse for me. I had not seen him since I was taken to jail. This day he and I alone set out to what was left of Tall Oaks. As my horse led the way along the very path that Elly and I had so recently taken, I searched for words. Finally, I plunged in. "How can I ever thank you, Ben, for helping me the way you did?"

"You my family, Abinia," he replied.

My throat was so tight I could scarcely respond. "As you are mine," I said.

Papa George waited at the barn. Where once his hair was gray, it was now white. I hesitated until I saw his smile. Then I leaped off my horse and ran, free to embrace him after all of these years.

When I gave Papa his papers, he took them and turned away. "Papa." I touched his shoulder. "You are free to go, but more than anything, I want you to stay. This wouldn't be home without you. I can't pay you yet, but . . ."

Papa turned back to me. "Where I gonna go, Abinia? This place my home. I don't belong no place 'cept here."

In my relief, I wanted only to cry, but I could no longer indulge myself. Instead, I began to speak of our future. I told Papa of Mr. Madden's offer to finance a new house. We studied the property together, and I knew when Papa George suggested that we walk up to the old home site how very much the thought disturbed him.

"No, Papa," I said, "we won't build there. That hill is sacred. We must find another place."

We both stared silently up the hill and at the oak that still stood, but we were saved when Moses, Beattie's oldest son, joined us. Following behind, Beattie and her two other sons hurried to greet me. Our embrace was as true as our childhood friendship.

Together we discussed the possibilities of a new home site. Papa led us toward a spot through the orchard and across the way from the kitchen house. We all thought his choice ideal. Mr. Madden and Will came later that afternoon and gave the location their approval. Within the week, construction began.

The barns were in good condition, and fortunately, a few good horses were left. It was agreed that we could build from them, and in the following years, we prospered after we established our name as providers of reliable horse stock.

Belle did come to live at Tall Oaks, and together we faced our future. When she died many years later, she was laid to rest in the big-house cemetery alongside her father. Her headstone was engraved:

BELLE PYKE
DAUGHTER OF JAMES PYKE

AUTHOR'S NOTE

A few years ago, my husband and I restored an old plantation tavern in Virginia. While researching its past, I found an old map on which, near our home, was a notation: Negro Hill. Unable to determine the story of its origin, local historians suggested that it most likely suggested a tragedy.

For months it played on my mind. Each morning I walked across our land to go down to the stream where I would meditate. On my return trip, I faced the direction of Negro Hill and, to myself, wondered aloud what had happened there.

Finally, one morning when I returned from that walk, I sat down to do my daily journaling. What happened next left me baffled. In my mind's eye, I saw a scene play out as clear as a movie. I began to write, and the words flew onto the paper. I followed in the footsteps of a terrified little white girl, running up the hill behind her frantic mother. When they reached the top, through their eyes, I saw a black woman hanging from the limb of a large oak tree. I set my pencil down, appalled at the story line. I had written the prologue to *The Kitchen House.* Although fascinated by antebellum history, I abhorred the thought of slavery and had always shied away from the subject. Quickly, I slipped the writing in my desk drawer, determined to forget about it.

Some weeks later, during a conversation with my father, I learned that an acquaintance of his had traced his ancestry back to Ireland. Around the turn of the nineteenth century, this man's Irish ancestors had come over on a ship, and on that journey, both of the parents had died. Two brothers had survived, along with their little sister. The family was able to track what had happened to the boys but couldn't find any trace of the little girl. As my father related the story, a deep chill ran through me. In my deepest core, I knew immediately what had happened to her. She had been brought home to the captain's plantation as an indentured servant in Virginia, and put to work in the kitchen house with the kitchen slaves. She awaited me in my desk drawer.

I began to do the research. I visited the

many plantations in this area, particularly Prestwould. I studied slave narratives from the time period and interviewed African-American people whose ancestors had been slaves. I spent hours in local libraries, the Black History Museum, the Virginia Historical Society, and Poplar Forest. I visited Colonial Williamsburg many times over. Finally, I began to write. Each day more of the story unfolded, and when I finished, often emotionally spent, I was left to wonder what the following day would bring. The only time the work came to a standstill was when the characters took me to an event or to a place where I had not yet done my research.

I tried on a number of occasions to change some of the events (those that I found profoundly disturbing), but the story would stop when I did that, so I forged ahead to write what was revealed.

I am forever grateful to the souls who gifted me with their sharing. I can only hope I have served them well.

ACKNOWLEDGMENTS

I have many to thank, but foremost, Mrs. Bessie Lowe, who so generously shared her family history with me, and Quincy Billingsley, who patiently schooled me to look through brown eyes as well as through blue.

Invaluable resources for me while writing this book include: the Prestwould Plantation, the Black History Museum in Richmond, the Legacy Museum in Lynchburg, the Virginia Historical Society, Poplar Forest, Colonial Williamsburg, the public libraries of Appomattox, Charlotte Court House, Farmville, and the libraries at Longwood University and the University of Virginia.

I am grateful to the Farmville Writers' Group: Reggie, Melvin, and Linda, who started me off, and to the Piedmont Literary Society, who guided me on.

How do you thank your dearest friends? From the beginning, Diane Eckert believed in my ability to write. Carlene Baime lifted me when I faltered. I could not have written this book without the leadership and support of Eleanor Dolan, nor completed it without the insight and tireless help of Suzanne Guglielmi.

Thank you to my agent and my champion, Rebecca Gradinger, and to Trish Todd, my gentle editor. I extend gratitude to my brave copyeditor, Beth Thomas.

I am deeply grateful for the support of my daughters, Erin Plewes and Hilary Cummings, and my son-in-law, Kyle Cummings, who created the music for my book trailer.

My husband carried the camera, took notes in the libraries, and was at my side for countless weekend visits to plantations, museums, and historical sites too numerous to mention. Thank you, Charles, for your unfailing belief in me and in this work.

TOUCHSTONE READING GROUP GUIDE
THE KITCHEN HOUSE

FOR DISCUSSION

1. Why do you think the author chose to tell the story through two narrators? How are Lavinia's observations and judgments different from Belle's? Does this story belong to one more than the other? If you could choose another character to narrate the novel, who would it be?

2. One of the novel's themes is history repeating itself. Another theme is isolation. Select scenes from *The Kitchen House* that depict each theme and discuss. Are there scenes in which the two themes intersect?

3. "Mae knows that her eldest daughter consorts with my husband. . . . Almost from the beginning, I suspected their secrets" (page 181). Why does the captain keep Belle's true identity a secret from his

wife and children? Do you think the truth would have been a relief to his family or torn them further apart? At what point does keeping this secret turn tragic?

4. Discuss the significance of birds and bird nests in the novel. What or who do they symbolize? What other symbols support the novel?

5. "When I saw their hunger I was struck with a deep familiarity and turned away, my mind anxious to keep at bay memories it was not yet ready to recall" (page 45). Consider Lavinia's history. Do you think the captain saved her life by bringing her to America as an indentured servant? Or do you think it was a fate worse than the one she would have faced in Ireland? Discuss the difference between slavery and indentured servitude.

6. Marshall is a complicated character. At times, he is kind and protective; other times, he is a violent monster. What is the secret that Marshall is forced to keep? Is he to blame for what happened to Sally? Why do you think Marshall was loyal to

Rankin, who was a conspirator with Mr. Waters?

7. "I grew convinced that if she saw me, she would become well again" (pages 313–314). Why does Lavinia feel that her presence would help Miss Martha? Describe their relationship. If Lavinia is nurtured by Mama and Belle, why does she need Miss Martha's attention? Is the relationship one-sided, or does Miss Martha care for Lavinia in return?

8. "Fortunately, making myself amenable was not foreign to me, as I had lived this way for much of my life" (page 390). Do you think this attribute of Lavinia saves or endangers her life? Give examples for both.

9. Describe the relationship between Ben's wife, Lucy, and Belle. How does it evolve throughout the novel? Is it difficult for you to understand their friendship? Why or why not?

10. "I was as enslaved as all the others" (page 499). Do you think this statement by Lavinia is fair? Is her position equivalent to those of the slaves? What freedom

does she have that the slaves do not? What
burdens does her race put upon her?

A CONVERSATION WITH KATHLEEN GRISSOM

What information surprised you while doing research on white indentured servants?

When I first began my research I was astonished to discover the great numbers of Irish that were brought over as indentured servants. Then, when I saw advertisements for runaway Irish indentured servants, I realized that some of them, too, must have suffered under intolerable conditions.

At times in the novel, you can almost smell the hearty foods being prepared by Mama and others. In your research, did you find any specific notes or recipes from kitchen houses that you can share with your readers?

In 1737, William Byrd, founder of Richmond, wrote of the many types of fruits and vegetables available in Virginia. Watermelons, pumpkins, squashes, cucumbers, artichokes, asparagus, green beans, and cauliflower were all being cultivated. I discovered that many of these were preserved by pickling. For those interested in how this was done and for recipes from that time, an excellent resource is Martha Washington's *Booke of Cookery and Booke of Sweetmeats,* transcribed by Karen Hess.

While in Williamsburg, I watched reenactors roast beef over a spit in a kitchen fireplace. Small potatoes in a pan beneath the meat were browning in the drippings, and I cannot tell you how I longed for a taste. That was my inspiration for the Christmas meal. For basics, such as the chicken soup, I built a recipe around what I knew would have been available for use in the kitchen house at that time.

Whenever Belle baked a molasses cake, I craved a taste. I did try several old recipes that I found, but I was unsatisfied with the results. So, using the old recipes as a baseline, my daughter, Erin, and I created our own version of a simple yet moist and tasty molasses cake. I am happy to share it with the readers.

1/2 cup butter
1/3 cup packed brown sugar

1 egg
1/2 cup milk
1 cup molasses
2 cups flour
1 teaspoon baking soda
1 teaspoon ground ginger
1 teaspoon cinnamon
2 dashes ground cloves
1/4 teaspoon salt

Preheat the oven to 350 degrees. Grease an 8-inch-square baking pan.

In a large bowl, cream the butter and sugar. Beat in the egg. In a separate bowl, combine the milk and the molasses. In another bowl, combine the flour, baking soda, ginger, cinnamon, cloves, and salt. Add each of these alternately to the butter mixture, beating well between additions. Spoon batter into the prepared pan.

Bake for approximately 45 minutes, or until a toothpick comes out clean.

Why did you chose not to go into detail about some of the most dramatic plot points in the novel, for example, the death of Waters or the abuse of young Marshall?

For the most part, Lavinia and Belle dictated the story to me. From the beginning, it became quite clear that if I tried to embellish or change their story, their narration would stop. When I withdrew, the story would continue. Their voices were quite distinct. Belle, who always felt grounded to me, certainly did not hold back with description, particularly of the rape. Lavinia, on the other hand, felt less stable, less able to cope; and at times it felt as though she was scarcely able to relate her horror.

It is interesting that your novel has two narrators — Lavinia and Belle. Do you have any plans to continue the story into the next generation — perhaps from the perspectives of Jaime and Elly?

In 1830, Jamie is a well-respected ornithologist in Philadelphia and Sukey is enslaved by the Cherokee Indians in North Carolina. Theirs are the two voices I hear. In time I will know if I am meant to tell their story.

Presently I am writing *Crow Mary,* another work of historical fiction. A few years ago I was visiting Fort Walsh in the Cypress Hills of Saskatchewan. As I listened to an interpreter tell of Mary, who, in 1872, at the age of sixteen, was traded in marriage to a well-known fur trader, a familiar deep chill went thorough me. I knew then that I would return to write about this Crow woman. Some of her complex life is documented, and what fascinates me are her acts of bravery, equal, in my estimation, to those of Mama Mae.

This is your first novel after diverse careers in retail, agriculture, and the arts. How have each of these experiences contributed to your writing style?

I don't know that any endeavor specifically contributed to my writing style, but I do know that every phase of my life helped prepare me to write this book.

The dialogue of the slaves in this novel is very believable. It must have been a difficult thing to achieve. How did you go about creating authentic voices from two hundred years ago?

At the very beginning of my research I read two books of slave narratives: *Bullwhip Days: The Slaves Remember* and *Weevils in the Wheat: Interviews with Virginia Ex-Slaves*. Soon after, the voices from *The Kitchen House* began to come to me. My original draft included such heavy dialect that it made the story very difficult to read. In time

I modified the style so the story could be more easily read.

You said you wrote the prologue in one sitting after being inspired by a map you found while renovating an old plantation tavern. Since this is your first novel, do you think you were "guided" by residents of the past?

Not only do I feel I was guided but also that I was gifted with their trust. However, I am not alone in this. In Alice Walker's book *The Color Purple,* she writes: "I thank everybody in this book for coming. A.W., author and medium."

Unless I misread that, I'd say, in this experience, I'm in good company.

Your book has been described as "*Gone with the Wind* turned upside down." Are you a fan of Margaret Mitchell's novel? Which writers have inspired you through the years?

I have only recently read *Gone with the Wind.* Although I did enjoy it, a few of the writers that have truly inspired me are Robert Morgan, Alice Randall, Susan Fromberg Schaeffer, Edward P. Jones, Nuala O'Faolain, Alexandra Fuller, Susan Howatch, Rick Bragg, Breena Clarke, Beryl Markham, Alice Walker, Joan Didion . . . this list could go on forever. I love to read.

There are many characters in this novel. How did you go about choosing their names?

They were all taken from different lists of slaves that I found in my research.

What advice do you have for writers working on their first novels?

If you feel called to write a book, consider it a gift. Look around you. What assistance is the universe offering you as support? I was given an amazing mentor, a poet, Eleanor Drewry Dolan, who taught me the importance of every word. To my utter amazement, there were times she found it necessary to consult three dictionaries to evaluate one word!

Take the time you need to learn the craft. Then sit down and write. When you hand over your completed manuscript to a trusted reader, keep an open mind. Edit, edit, and edit again. After you have written a great query letter, go to AgentQuery.com. This site is an invaluable resource that lists agents in your genre.

Submit, accept rejection as part of the process, and submit again.

And, of course, never give up!

The employees of Thorndike Press hope you have enjoyed this Large Print book. All our Thorndike, Wheeler, and Kennebec Large Print titles are designed for easy reading, and all our books are made to last. Other Thorndike Press Large Print books are available at your library, through selected bookstores, or directly from us.

For information about titles, please call:
(800) 223-1244

or visit our Web site at:
http://gale.cengage.com/thorndike

To share your comments, please write:
Publisher
Thorndike Press
10 Water St., Suite 310
Waterville, ME 04901

626